NEITHERIUM

Prose & Poetry from the Neither

K.A. Schultz

K.A. Schultz

NEITHERIUM
POETRY & PROSE FROM THE NEITHER
by K.A. Schultz

Dakeha Taunus LLC, publisher

Inquiries should be addressed to kimannschultz@gmail.com

Cover art by Roberto Diaz, used with permission of the artist,
entitled, *Do You Love the Flowers?*
@roberto_diaz_arte_del_caos

https://linktr.ee/K.A.Schultz

Ingram edition:
ISBN 979-8-9867569-4-3

Also available at Amazon
Library of Congress Control Number: 2022914777

Also by K.A.Schultz

Khrystmass
Holiday Horror Collection

Göthique
Ravenscraft Anthology of Horror III
Romantically dark short stories & poems

Jacob – A Denouement in One Act
For anyone who may have asked, "What about poor, old Jacob Marley?"
First edition illustrated hardback at eBay
Second edition for Kindle or Print on Demand at Amazon
www.jacobmarleystory.com

Rugs on Puddles Coats Over Oceans
Collected poems & lyric poetry
Available for Kindle at Amazon

Milia Verboru*

Anathelogium *

Blind Justice illustration by K.A. Schultz

**no longer in print; newly edited content absorbed into Neitherium*

www.butterflybroth.com
www.jacobmarleystory.com
www.shewhowas.com

@kaschultz_writer
@butterflybroth
@lilahravenscraft

"...younger Trav'lers discovered they too could ever increasingly remain in the abstracted hold of the Neither – and they liked it there. In no time flat, Trav'lers were choosing to spend time in the Neither as a destination, not only as an interim point on a path to some other lineal time or place, past or future. This phase of discovery was a cultural explosion for all Trav'lers, for it quickly morphed from renegade teen practice to an aspirational *place* of being for all Trav'ler citizens."

From, "A Brief History of Trav'lers"

- 6 -

Graphic, possibly offensive & triggering content
Reader discretion is advised

TABLE OF CONTENTS

I.	The Perigean Turn	13
II.	The Drowning Man Game	25
III.	Coronet	55
IV.	The Monstrance & the Relic	61
V.	The Coppe-Snippen	83
VI.	Indulgences	93
VII.	Soft Warm Good	105
VIII.	The Happiest Hour	111
IX.	The Last Hour	137
X.	Gamma Gaia	149
XI.	Butterflybroth	167
XII.	Romeo & Juliet Enthroned	183
XIII.	A Brief History of Trav'lers	197
XIV.	Storia dell'arte dei Vampiri	215
XV.	Paradise	225
XVI.	The Rest	243
XVII.	Ravenscrafted	259
XVIII.	D R A F T M I T E	291

continued

XIX.	Consummation	311
XX.	Lil Bebee	321
XXI.	My Gigi	337
XXII.	Throne d'eau	351
XXIII.	Joined with the Seas	359
XXIV.	Christmas Punch	365
XXV.	Dance of the Sugarplums	367
XXVI.	Santa Domnia	369
XXVII.	Flash Fiction	373

Meddie

Sub Marine

Tender Moment

Metamorphosis

XXVIII. Poems   379

Horror, Haunted

Crucified

Underworld

Maniacal

So Beautiful

Tenebrian Lament

Eau de Mama

Beautiful Bed

Talisman, Mine

Corruptible

Cottage Crypt

To My Beloved, in her Cemeterial Abode

The Portraitist's Lament

Exhibition-ist

Mam'sette

Solstice's Eve

Shipwrecked

Genesis 1:6 v.2

Hurricaned Beast

XXIX. Lyrics   393

From RUGS ON PUDDLES COATS OVER OCEANS, 2013

Art

Gun Metal Ghost

The Haunting

Words

XXX. Final Memo   399

For a comprehensive content guide
visit www.butterflybroth.com

To my Muses
Dark, Light, Past, Present, Yet to Come

"Justice Blinded" by K.A. Schultz

THE PERIGEAN TURN

Jonah-Blue was born blue, and Jonah-Blue was also more often blue than he was not – at least, that's the way our Oma put it. I was regular and pink, and our Mama said I cried right on cue. Jonah-Blue, on the other hand, had all his insides squooshed up, way up inside of him when he was born, which was just a few minutes after me, so he didn't cry or fuss or hardly even move. Mama said they rushed him to the NICU, where they operated on him and moved all his insides back to their rightful places. Then they stitched up his chest. My little-by-a-few-minutes brother eventually turned a decent enough shade of pink that the doctors and nurses let him go home. We were both about a month old by then.

If being born blue wasn't enough, Jonah-Blue spent most of his years with me feeling sort of blue, too. I wore lots of colors because I usually felt bright-colored sorts of feelings. I guess you could say I was on the inside as I looked on the outside. Oma called my little brother a melancholy sort of bean. That's what cinched his name for me. Blue from day one and Blue 'til day last. My brother didn't even seem to mind the name I gave him. Before too long, everyone was calling him that.

I still wonder if that was the right thing to do, like I almost suggested *It*.

My bright-colored feelings gave me lots of energy that last spring. I couldn't wait to get up and out of bed each morning. Mama would tell me she wished if only for once just once I would sleep in like all the other kids. I think she just wanted her first cup of coffee without having to say anything to anyone. I also think she wanted to pretend, at least for a few minutes early in the day, she was a lady of leisure. My getting up so early got in the way of her daydreams, I guess. I loved my mother, so I at least had enough sense to stay out of her way and fix my own breakfasts. For years, all I ever had was cereal, generally dry, and right out of the box, because we were always out of milk. Jonah-Blue, on the other hand, would sleep all morning long but then lay awake all night, staring up at his bedroom ceiling, his inside-clock turned around up like all the rest of him had been. Oma said Jonah-Blue was a nocturnal bean. Both Jonah-Blue and I liked the way she used such big words on us, even when we didn't always understand what she meant. I could at least *feel* what it was she was talking about. As we were sort-of twins, Jonah-Blue and I didn't have to use many words at all. I knew what he was thinking, and Jonah-Blue pretty much always understood me.

My bright-colored feelings pulled me outdoors from morning 'til night. I'd strap on my metal roller skates the moment it was light outside and make up skate dances and pretend I was an Olympic skater competing for gold medals. I'd make Jonah-Blue do the medal ceremony with me. We would sing our versions of the National Anthem and I would fake cry. I'd even try to squeeze out real tears, for the sake of what Oma called mellow drama. Jonah-Blue would get bored though, especially if I'd ask him to watch my skate dances. He'd roll his eyes in that big, sighing way of his. By the way, my eyes were brown. I wished my eyes could have been the color of his – Jonah Blue's were the color of sea glass.

What Jonah-Blue liked best to do was to sit out on the beach or the back porch and read or draw. Jonah-Blue's blue feelings gave him a different kind of energy. Oma called it Storm and Dung, whatever that was. When Jonah-Blue wasn't in the water – where he wasn't supposed to go alone but did anyway – Jonah-Blue would stay outside and read book after book after book. Or he'd draw in his notebook, which he kept hidden from me. I never got to see what he drew 'til he was gone. When I finally did get hold of his notebook, I wished I hadn't, but it helped me understand, sort of, a little better. I did throw that notebook into the public trash bin at the end of the beach access path after I looked through it. Neither Mama nor Oma or anyone else needed to see what Jonah-Blue had drawn into those pages.

Mama worked all the time, so she didn't do much with us, but she would take us to the library once a week. When we got home, Jonah-Blue would sometimes stay in the car and read and not even come out until his first book was finished. Mama would be all mad at Jonah-Blue and tell him to take himself out into the fresh air this instant young man. Jonah-Blue would then just take his book and walk off with it and start reading again where she couldn't see him.

When Jonah-Blue was at the house but not reading or drawing, he was playing with his one toy, which was an old glass terrarium he had found in a twenty-five- cent box at an estate sale we had gone to with our Oma. Jonah-Blue once kept miniature toads in his terrarium. He fed them tiny red ants, but our cat knocked the terrarium over and set the toads free. They jumped their itty-bitty hearts out to everlasting freedom. We sure couldn't blame them for doing that. That summer, after the toads had escaped, Jonah-Blue turned his terrarium into an enchanted lagoon. He would fill the terrarium with water and add a smidge of blue food coloring and one drop of green. That, he said, was to create a barrier wreath effect. Jonah-Blue would then sift a handful of sand into the bowl, which would settle at the bottom. That became the sea floor. Next, he would draw mermaids, two of them, one a boy, and one a girl. He would cut them out like paper dolls. Jonah-Blue never let real grown-ups see his paper dolls, though. When we were alone at the house, Jonah-Blue would set everything up and then he would drop his paper figures into the pale-colored water of the terrarium. He then would take the eraser end of one of his school pencils and push the mermaids around in the water, making them dance and bend and bob about until the ink dissolved and their paper shapes turned to mulch and floated to the top, just like dirty sea foam on the beach after a storm. The whole, pulpy mess he'd then dump into the toilet and the weird game would be over.

There were two reasons why Jonah-Blue played this paper game when our mother was out: First, Mama had once told him mermaids were for girls. We suspect Mama was just thinking of that stupid cartoon movie mermaid with her big wad of red hair, but we both knew better than that. Jonah-Blue had told me all about Neverland's mean and nasty mermaids, and he also taught me about selkies and sirens – not the wailing things up-top of ambulances, but women who sang to sailors, who bewitched them, causing their ships to crash on the rocks and leaving the sailors to drown. Jonah-Blue showed me a picture in this book he had, from a set of books called, "Legends & Lore from A to Z." It was a super old illustration of a very ugly, dog-faced mermaid with saggy boobs, in the chapter called, "On Ancient Sea Creatures & Monsters of the Deep." No, I agreed with my brother, these mermaids were definitely not girly-girl things – they weren't even meant for kids. When Jonah-Blue played his paper mermaid game, it felt a little naughty, and that made us feel a kind of grown up, which made it way more fun than a whole lot of other stuff we could've been up to.

The main reason why Jonah-Blue kept his paper mermaids a secret was because he drew them naked, sometimes with their private parts showing. Jonah-Blue didn't cover his mer-figures up with dopey scallop shells or bikini tops or long, blobs of hair. That, he'd say, was lame and small-minded. But Jonah-Blue's mermaids were like mysteries to us too, because neither one of us were too sure what naked grown-ups, let alone mermaids, looked like. We'd caught glimpses here and there, and of course I knew my body and Jonah-Blue knew his. We both could still remember playing in the sprinkler without any bathing suits on when we were little. But, as we were only eleven that summer, there wasn't a whole heck of a lot else for us to see or know – not yet anyway, as far as either one of us could tell. So, Jonah-Blue's mermaid bodies wound up being part stolen-glance fantasy, part science, and part wondering. But Jonah-Blue sure liked to draw that stuff. And, sure, I liked to watch. I'd giggle – lots. I thought it was funny and liked it best when their bodies turned to mush. That's where we were different; for me, it was mostly about silly, melting characters. For Jonah-Blue, it wasn't silly. It was something else – I just didn't know what that was.

Jonah-Blue could do one other thing really well, and that was swim. He said he wanted to be a marine biologist someday, doing research or something like that, just so long it was connected to the ocean. Jonah-Blue would often have me time him holding his breath – he said if he didn't feel like going to college, he could become a professional free-diver. That freaked me out. Why ever would someone want to go way, way down into the ocean, holding on to dear life with one single breath sucked into their lungs?

Being that we lived on the beach, Rule Number One was to never, ever go into the ocean without adult supervision. So, we went into the ocean by ourselves all the time. As I loved to swim and could hold my own against the waves, I had no problem breaking Rule Number One alongside my brother. We swam in the ocean when it was too cold, we swam in the ocean when it was too choppy, we swam in the ocean when the jellyfish swarmed and warning signs with pictures of jellies with red slash marks over them were stuck in the sand all over the place. We loved best to swim in the ocean, the "salty beach," as Jonah-Blue called it when he was little, when most other humans didn't want to be there.

Sometimes hurricanes, hundreds of miles out, would churn up the ocean floors, and the tides would throw up all kinds of new shells from the ocean bottom and toss them onto our sands. Those were our best times at the beach, when we could gather seashells like Easter eggs, as if they had been left there just for us. Naturally, we had baskets and baskets full of seashells. On rainy days, I would sort them into collections and pretend to sell them to my dolls. When the hurricanes brewed and the beaches were empty, the world belonged to us. The shore felt endless because there were no fences, not even in our grassy, sandy back yard. The big empty ocean was, I thought, ours too. Just because.

When we snuck out to the beach, Jonah would cut through the breaking waves and go far out beyond shore, farther than I'd ever dare to. He'd swim out so far, his head would look like a brown apple seed on the waves, bobbing up and down, sometimes disappearing altogether. Since I was only a few minutes older than him, it wasn't my place to scold him and tell him to stay closer to shore. If he wanted to swim around like some daredevil, that was his business. It was kind of cool, anyways, to have a sort-of-twin who was so unafraid. Sometimes – I'm not sure though – it would look like another apple seed would appear, even farther out than Jonah-Blue's. It would look like another swimmer was way, way out there with him. I always figured it was a stray buoy or my eyes playing tricks on me. Jonah-Blue never said anything about that other apple seed in the water. He never said he saw anyone out there; but then, he didn't usually have all that much to say about anything.

As I already told you, Jonah-Blue could hold his breath for a super long time, much longer than anyone I have ever known. He would dive under the waves and appear super far from where he had started, never minding the salt in his eyes or nose. Jonah-Blue once told me he could see underwater, that his retinas worked like camera lenses. I almost believed him, because he'd tell me what he saw on the ocean floor, including when it was way deeper than where either one of us could stand in the water. Jonah-Blue's long eyelashes, when they were wet, even looked to me like the spines of black sea urchins – so much about him was about the ocean. I might have been the blond haired, brown-eyed sister with the bright-colored energy, but my brother had been the blue baby, with blue feelings and blue-green-colored eyes from the get-go. We were each matched up to our true selves. I was a garden, and Jonah- Blue was the sea.

After he was gone, I would sometimes wonder what my brother had been doing on land all those years.

†††

It was a Thursday, about a week after the last hurricane had come through, which had almost but not quite made landfall. We had seen some great shells on the beach the last couple of days, and Jonah-Blue and I had been busy gathering up the best ones and throwing them into our buckets. Jonah-Blue had then decided we ought to make a tidal pool behind the boulders. He had read, the sea was our last resource and wanted to see how it would work, to have an ocean-garden to take care of, much as our Oma had her garden.

A tidal pool near the boulders seemed like the perfect way to set about our project. It was an out of the way spot and hard to get to, in a place pretty much left alone by all those pesky, pussy-footed tourists. Jonah-Blue decided on a small, natural trough behind some boulders that formed a pretty solid berm near the shore, which you could only get to by climbing up and over them. This craggled row of sharp rocks we had always called our jungle gym. Once we got there, we dug and dug and dug, hands and shovels both. When we were done digging, we lined the hole solid with all the best shells we had gathered. We worked for a long time, arranging and re-arranging the seashells, adding rocks as we needed to. When our pool was done, it was really more like a grotto – so pretty – it was practically fit for a Mer-King. Or a Mary, Mary, quite contrary, how does your garden grow sort of grand bath, all silver bells and cockle shells and pretty maids all in a row....

The next morning, this thing called the Perigean Spring Tide was supposed to have come in and filled our tide pool garden. This extra little-bit-higher tide only happened ever so often. Jonah-Blue seemed to know when to expect it. He said it had to do with the moon lining up with other stuff, also being only when the moon was full, which it had been. I know that much for sure, because the moon had been extra bright that last night; it had even woken me up from my sleep. I remember looking out my window and seeing Jonah-Blue, awake as usual, standing at the edge of our yard where the grass met up with the dunes, just staring out over the ocean, into the face of the biggest moon I'd ever seen. He sure did look blue that night, out there in all that blue light.

Thursday started up as an especially blustery day. I guess the Spring Tides whip the air around with them, too. Jonah-Blue said we needed to hurry, so right after breakfast we ducked out. Mom had left for work and our Oma was only expecting us at lunch time, so we had the morning to ourselves. Jonah-Blue dashed off the back porch with his pail and I followed, carrying mine.

The wind caught my hair up hard and tangled it across my forehead so I could hardly see where I was going. It also caught in my mouth, so I could hardly say a thing. I was having trouble keeping pace with Jonah-Blue, who in his blue-energy was all about that ocean garden, and way ahead of me. My bucket was heavy, full of these awesome shells we had found, big and colorful as the teacups Oma collected. I couldn't keep up with Jonah-Blue and fell behind, he was going so fast. I almost felt left out. When I called his name, wanting to ask him to slow down, the breezes took the words right out of my mouth and threw them in the opposite direction. He never heard me.

When I finally came around the first boulder, the biggest one of all, I could see my brother again.

Jonah-Blue was standing as still as a statue, his eyes as wide as I'd ever seen them, and they weren't blinking, either. His mouth was open too, frozen, not in an "*Oh*," but an "*Ah*." I followed his eyes to where they were looking, and I took a few steps closer. I really needed to see what the heck had made him freeze up like that.

That was when I first saw her. Or it. No, it was a Her. Definitely a Her.

There was the tide pool. Our beautiful shell-lined ocean garden, as long as I was tall, about half as wide, and pretty deep. We'd dug long and hard, so the shallow trough we'd found by the boulders was now about the size of a big bathtub. The water from the surge had sure enough filled our pool to the brim, and it was as clear as the water in Jonah-Blue's terrarium. The prettiest shells we had used to line the top edge of the pool, so our fancy ocean bed was all framed up with our best scallops and cockles. Dark seaweed had washed in and floated upon the smooth-as-glass surface. It looked like a soggy patch of black lace slapped onto a windowpane. We could even see ourselves in the mirror our pool made. Everything looked like it ought to, like what I would have expected, but for this thing – this person, a girl, who was lying on the bottom of our pool, under the water, facing up. *Our* pool.

The girl was resting on her back, on our bed of shells, looking straight up at Jonah-Blue. I could see her blink – blinking at Jonah-Blue? – just like anyone would normally blink. She did it again, still staring at my brother. Then again. This girl, just sprawled across the bottom of our pool, our ocean-garden, under about two feet of water, was as still as the water itself, but for her blinking eyes. The seaweed, slinking about on the top, had shaped itself into a sort of slimy wreath over her face. It touched the curls of her long hair, which had floated up too, making a weird sort of crown. Lying where she did, her waist was at about where the floor of our pool started to curve up towards the edge, where my brother and I were standing. But along the inside of the pool, it wasn't a pair of legs resting on the slope, nope. Instead of legs, there was a huge, blue-gray tail. The tail was draped up and over the pool's edge, where it curled around like a question mark. It did not bend like our legs would. There was nothing there that would make anyone think a pair of knees were inside.

Up, over the edge of our pool and onto the sand trailed the rest of this girl. Her smooth – *body?* – tapered off and ended in what looked to be a big set of fins. They fanned out as wide as my arms could reach, end to end, and were shaped like a pair of harps, set facing away from each other. The fins were frosty-clear. Skinny spines shone through, flashing all the colors of an abalone shell, all the colors you could ever wish to see. Silver, blue, green, gold, pink. Wow, was she creepy. Creepy but awesome. Creepy but gorgeous.

This – this *omigosh could she be a real, live mermaid* – just lay there, super still beneath the water but for this tap, tap thing she did with her tail on the sand, just as any kid might tap their fingernails on a desktop at school. Her crazy, amazing fins hitting the ground, showing off their colors, keeping time with something I guess only she could hear. And each time her tail hit the wet sand, it jingled, because, you see, dozens and dozens of earrings were pierced through the fins' edges. The earrings – and not a single one of them matched the other – twinkled in the sun. They made the sound of tiny bells, chiming every time her tail hit the ground. Me, being a girl who also liked jewelry, knew right away what this was: It was a collection of lost-n-found earrings belonging to swimmers and boaters that this girl had gathered up in just the same way Jonah-Blue and I collected our seashells. She saw me staring at her tail and all those earrings, and she smiled. She understood about loving pretty things.

The girl then looked back over again at Jonah-Blue, and I swear I saw her face change. Her eyes, almond-shaped, with long, white eyelashes, blinked at him again, and the smile she gave my brother was this melting kind that you only give to someone you care a whole heck of a lot about. What a bunch of baloney, I thought when I caught myself thinking that. Oh boy, I sure had watched too many old romance movies with my Oma. Here I was, turning a freaky-amazing discovery into what my grandmother would surely call yet another mellow drama.

Jonah-Blue's pail fell to the ground. It landed on its side and the shells spilled out. He didn't notice. He just stood there, like some spell-bound Prince who had just discovered his Sleeping Beauty or his Snow White. I wanted to gag. Sure, the girl was pretty, even if she was so darn pale, even if her lips were purplish, and even if she did have a tail that looked like a dolphin's – a pierced-up, punked-out fish tail, a tail so long and skinny, it trailed like the wet root of a swamp tree all over everything, sleek and shiny and freaky. Sure, she had one of those cute, heart-shaped faces as people called them, but she had no legs or feet, which was kind of gross if you thought about it. And what hair of hers wasn't floating in curly- Qs around her face was braided into a long, fat ponytail, which she had wound around her neck like a winter scarf. The human-girl thing, about loving pretty things, was obvious there, too. I saw it in the coral beads she had strung through her hair. Like strands of Christmas tree cranberries, they were twisted in and out through her braids. I hated how pretty she – every darn thing about her – was.

The girl started to play with her ponytail, her eyes moving back and forth between me and Jonah. She was studying us, comparing us, trying to figure out who we were to each other. She looked to be about our age, not much older than either Jonah-Blue or me. I mean, well, maybe she was a year or two older than us, at least in human years, because she already had little, round boobs which sat on top of her skinny ribcage, while I was still as flat as a board. Yep, she had ribs and a bellybutton and arms and hands just like me, but that was it. There was one thing I noticed right away about her body though, which was totally different from mine: her chest was totally – and I mean completely – motionless. Her ribs and her belly didn't move like ours do when we breathe – in, out, in, out, up and down. That's because she wasn't breathing. Only land people, like me and my almost-twin brother, did that.

The girl, who seemed to be reading me, my eyes, and my mind, then turned her face away from me and lifted her ponytail. Behind her pointy ear I could see three bright red slits, feather-edged in the same blue as her tail was. Gills.

A mermaid. A real, honest to God mermaid. *Our* mermaid. The mermaid saw, I finally got it. She smiled. I thought I knew, at that very moment, we would all be best of friends – forever. *The* best.

The mermaid in our beach garden turned her eyes back to Jonah-Blue, who had now gotten to his knees at the edge of the pool. There. I saw it again, her whole face changing when she looked at my brother. Everything about her went soft. My tummy tickled; my heart skipped a beat. All of a sudden, I felt left out. And afraid. I would not have been able to tell you why at that moment, though later I could have.

My brother leaned forward – way forward. His ocean eyes stayed on the mermaid's eyes. They were both frozen, kind of hypnotized. A boy on the sand and a girl under a couple feet of water, staring at each other, sending something – thoughts, feelings, magic, who knows – between them. Stuff I couldn't read. Stuff I wasn't meant to. I wasn't a part of *it*. The energy, what was happening between them, whatever it was I could sense, was strong. So strong, it separated me from them, without me budging one single inch. It was like they had known each other for a long time but had never had a chance to actually say *Hi*.

They were already holding hands with their eyes.

†††

In the next fraction of a second, like a hooked marlin breaking up and out of an ocean wave, the sea maiden leapt out of the water, sending salted droplets flying, blinding the sister's eyes with the force of their briny sting. In a supernatural maneuver, the mermaid hovered momentarily in the air, bolt upright, her slender arms wrapping themselves around the boy, who remained motionless, transfixed. With the lethargic, lightning speed of a boa constrictor striking its prey, she pulled him into her embrace.

But this was no mere embrace; this was a capture, and the boy was her willing hostage.

As they hung suspended for that infinitesimal slice of time, the boy melted even farther, deeper into the circle of the mermaid's strong arms. The sister gasped audibly, too stunned to produce any additional sound. Her voice was gone, her lungs refusing to release the air onto which they held with reflexive, survivalist desperation. The sister remained there, helplessly rooted to the ground, the only firmament she and her brother had known as theirs until that day, her white knuckled hands still clenching the handle of her bucket. She was holding on for dear life.

The mermaid then leaned in and kissed the boy. In that instant, he was no longer a child, an almost-twin brother, the son of an overworked, single mother. And he, no longer a child or a brother or a son, kissed the mermaid-girl back, with a passion so innocent, so devoid of showmanship and masculine bravado, that what he returned to her was, by all standards of seduction and promise and hunger, a perfect kiss.

The mermaid then raised her right arm. With her index finger outstretched, she brought her hand down and across in an arc with such speed, the action was but a blur. In that blur, the mermaid's fingernail, a razor-sharp, serrated talon, met with the boy's neck, just below his right ear, and cut a gash deep into his flesh.

Before the boy's sister could even *think* to muster a scream, the mermaid repeated her attack, slicing crossways to cut another gash into the other side of the boy's neck, right below his left ear. Blood, after the body's momentary shock, streamed from the wounds, ribbons of red winding their way down, ever brighter against his fading skin. The boy opened his mouth to cry out, but he was quickly stilled with a second, deeper kiss from his captor. As the mermaid held her mouth to his, she pressed her bony hands against his neck to stop the flow of blood. A dark pool had already formed in the sand beneath his feet, her tail.

The mermaid soon enough pulled free from their kiss, the water-bound vampire coming up for some air. And the boy, he exhaled – long, long, long. Deeply, and with finality.

The mermaid turned her head just enough to look around and meet once more the eyes of the boy's hapless, paralyzed sister, who still stood offsides. The mermaid's pale eyes said:

Thank you, and I know you understand, because you will soon feel about someone like I do about him, though right now, you don't feel any of this. The mermaid's eyes then also said: *But you weren't supposed to. This is about him; it always was. And I don't care what you think, because I have been waiting for this longer than you will ever know.*

So, I guess I'm sorry if I scared you, but your broken heart isn't going to change anything. You don't get to get to keep this one. He is mine now.

The mermaid looked back to the boy, tenderly assessing her victim's condition. She pressed him to her. The blood flowing from the wounds in the boy's neck had slowed to a trickle, oozing only occasional droplets. The boy still clung to his willowy succubus in a fully drowning state of – something. He looked bewildered, but not frightened. His expression was full of feeling, but what he conveyed was not anything even remotely associated with pain; at least, not any more. Shock, bewilderment, and momentary pain had melded and progressed into something far deeper.

The mermaid stroked the hair out of the boy's eyes, pleased to see the last whispers of mortal breath fully eradicated from within her companion.

One second, one epoch after that, the mermaid sprang to action. With a single, powerful thrust of her tail, she catapulted herself and the boy high into the air in a graceful arc, which, as it turned out, was perfectly timed to coincide with the overhead explosion of a rogue wave which burst over their heads and came crashing down, raining wet diamond droplets all over the three of them, all over the sand. The wave engulfed the mermaid and her captive and hurled them deep into the rush of its massive crest. As it did so, the almost-twin sister was thrown aside, knocked hard onto the ground.

In a grand splash two were gone, and the girl sat alone.

The big sister, the almost-twin, sunk boneless onto the sand and sobbed silently, beyond tears, beyond crying out.

When a fairytale unfolds before your very eyes, it is not necessarily a pretty thing. It can, in fact, be a rather grim, even gruesome event.

Andersen be damned.

Efectus

THE DROWNING MAN GAME

Do not try this at home.

It had been about forty years since the abduction. Some people would call it the "disappearance" of *that* boy. They would call it weird, mysterious, un-solved, but the word 'abduction' was rarely, if ever, uttered. Most people, having little to no idea of the circumstances, would simply start out by saying, "There once was this boy...." There were even a few Grimmatically inclined traditionalists, who would venture to begin with a "Once upon a time...."

Beyond that, the details of the abduction, or disappearance – depending on if you were the one woman, the boy's sister, who *did* know, or if you were any other person at all who would never know – morphed and grew in time to become the stuff of modern maritime lore.

Spreading over miles and years, the story metastasized to the rank of urban legend, for it was easily injected with morbid conjecture which grew the fish, so to speak, of the boy's disappearance, thanks to embellishment-prone posting, tagging, and sharing of what was *thought* to have happened.

The anniversary of *that* boy's disappearance was best charted by the tides, with their organic fealty to the rules of the lunar pull and its tangentially whipped up winds, whose clocks kept cadence with the universe, not those blocked-shaped pieces of time humans called days, weeks, months, or years. The sister, cognizant and thankful the exact day could not, at least without somewhat complex calculations, be easily earmarked for any single, solitary day of mourning, was content to acknowledge the anniversaries over the years as she *sensed* them, when the Spring Tides were hitting their highest marks. She would muse on the tragic event by looking out over the ocean to where the moonlight on the waves met the moonlight in the sky, and glass in hand, toast the horizon. Then, she'd go back inside to fill her glass again.

Forty years is plenty of time for the dissipation of a life-changing, imprinting event. But, as news is wont to become a story, and stories can sometimes grow to become legends, so too can legends circle back to their simplest renderings, to lend themselves by name, narrative or interpretive, knee-jerk activity to the songs and games of children. And fools.

†††

Remember, do not try this at home.

"Dark, deep
Dark, deep
Breathe out out out
Go to sleep!

Dark, deep
Dark, deep
Breathe out out out
Go to sleep!"

They chanted in unison, voices low and rhythmic, matching cadence with the gentle pulse of the ebb tide. The cold water, almost at chest height, had soaked their clothing, none of them having planned on a midnight dip in the ocean. Its dense salinity held the body of the young woman aloft, just under its surface, with only her face exposed. She looked straight into the clear night sky, which was as fluid as the water around them. As her pupils dilated, the Milky Way took on the clarity of a diamond-studded swath of fabric. As her oxygen levels depleted, the fabric began to sway, an undulating shadow writhing far above.

The girl breathed in and out with rapid, sharp exhalations, expelling air from the deepest recesses of her lungs. Her eyes, wide open, glazed over. The group repeated the chant as they held her. Her face grew paler by the second. At first, the effect was of a restful radiance. Soon, it was the look of one dead.

"Dark, deep
Dark, deep
Breathe out out out

Go to sleep!"

Their chanting shifted. Though the voices remained hushed, the urgency elevated. It could be felt and heard, the building up, the insistence, luring her, luring them:

"Dark deep
Dark deep
Breathe out out out
Go to sleep!"

The young man who held the girl's head shouted, "Now!"

He pinched her nose, and with his other hand covered her mouth. The girl's glassy stare slackened into a slit-lidded half-sleep, lashes lowering onto cheeks drained of all color. Her face had transformed from a young woman to that of an old wax doll, left too long on a sun-lit shelf.

He submerged her in time to her fainting, willing It to work.

She was under water only a few seconds. The game required that the recipient, the "victim," once completely deprived of their last breath, needed only to be exposed to the act of submersion at their last moment of consciousness. It was not about anyone being kept underwater for any measurable length of time; rather, the game's objective was to achieve a pernicious intoxication through hyperventilation amidst submersion, the cold caress of water pairing with the vocalized, rhythmic instruction of the chanting, to bring about – if it was going to work at all – the trance of one drowned, purportedly a dream-like undersea experience of life suspended, just like what *that* boy was said to have experienced, when that record-breaking, rogue Spring Tide had washed up, over the breakers onto the beach and grabbed him and taken him back into the sea, never to be seen again. Elder locals had described it as a wave having come alive and literally swallowing the boy in one gulp, like a Jonah and his whale. *That* boy, they would say, shaking their heads, had never even time to scream.

The only witness, the boy's sister, had never said much about the incident, though her trauma manifested itself in shock, which had required hospitalization, later counseling, way too many prescription drugs, and, after that, rivers of wine.

What no one really knew about the incident and the sister's traumatization, was that it was not what she had witnessed that had shipwrecked her psyche; it was that the sister, for all the talking she had been made to do, *had never been able to tell anyone what had really happened.* No one. Not only that, her single, overriding emotional takeaway of the incident, that of *having been left behind,* was the one bit of "damage" everyone had relentlessly tried to purge from her. What sorrow-filled longing the sister knew, to her more real than anything else, was what others sought to erase; it was as if her most profound awareness was an invalid aspect of her identity, a splinter lodged inside her core mandating extraction.

The sister grew up and moved way. After going off to college and journeying in and out of a career and a dead-ended marriage (no children), she had recently moved back into the very house she and her brother had lived in as children. She had come back to write, having carved a solid niche for herself as a crafter of dark fictions – part fantasy, mostly horror. The creative enfilade of haunted rooms in the sister's head, wherein she loitered to her heart's content, had evolved into both a place of catharsis and a wellspring of morbid inspiration. But a real roof over her head was also needed. So, to help provide alongside a literary income stream that never quite equaled in cash what her cult following should have netted her, the sister decided to reclaim the ocean-front house she had inherited from their late mother. She would live in it full-time and serve as proprietor over its latest incarnation, as a quaint, oceanside vacation rental.

The legend of the boy taken by the Spring Tides, having survived the decades well, translated into fiscally advantageous interest in the house. Given its lost-at-sea associations, the sister's oceanfront rental was booked solid for the next two years, April through October. With a waitlist. Home became the place where the reclusively inclined writer could busy herself attending guests' needs, where she could hobnob with them when it suited her, where she could still feed her incessant need to write. The sister was not happy there, but then, she was not happy anywhere. Ever. This was alright by her, for joyless resignation was a familiar mindset. When the sister's feelings were at even keel, like the plain of the ocean on a wind still day, that was good enough for her.

†††

The girl did not breathe, but only for a few, interminable seconds. She was held in place by four others, and by the young man who had submerged her, who had brought her face back up above the surface almost immediately. The one at the helm of this escapade was her boyfriend, a devil-may-care musician type who had charmed his girlfriend with precisely that which now afforded him the audacity to tinker with her life. He for some reason thought it essential to initiate his girlfriend into an ill-refuted and wildly dangerous, consciousness-altering game as part of a spring break experience he further thought would be made all the more memorable for it, maybe open a door to other experimentation with her....

This game, sprung from the incentives of risk takers and reckless partiers, had in and of itself already gained urban legend status by way of having been ruled official cause of death for at least six other people in three different countries. It remained untold what other damage the game had wrought on others who had "played" it. It was called the Drowning Man Game.

"Maryn!" he shouted, slapping her cheek. "Maryn!" he shouted again.

The girl awoke and gasped, her arms lifting reflexively then dropping, splashing water into her friends' pensive faces. Most of them were sympathetically holding their breaths in fear and anticipation of her resuscitation. The salt in their eyes went unnoticed. As the girl resumed breathing, so did they. Relief.

Wonder. Whoa, cool.

Would someone want to go next?

"Conner. Jesus," was all she whispered.

Maryn looked past her boyfriend's face, back to the Milky Way above her, which she remembered as the last thing that had come down towards her before her vision had gone dark and turned inward. Everything had been so clear. She remembered discerning the Proterozoic forms of the galaxies, distinct from the smaller flecks of neighboring stars and planets. The cloud of the Milky Way had even grown dimensional, the arm in which the Earth resided all a-sparkle, chock-full of life. Engulfing black hole entities, whose pull she believed she had felt, lurked far enough offsides to allow for a serene comfort amidst the infinity with which she had just been confronted. All would remain as it should, for the time, Being.

Oh, my God, she had thought.

Maryn's coming-to reverie was stopped short when her friends abruptly pulled their hands out from under her in shocked fright, when their attention was ripped from the enveloping draw of the moment to an outsider intrusion, a blinding light and harsh voice that called to them from the beach.

"Hey!" a woman yelled, "What's going on out there? Are you alright?"

Maryn flailed and righted herself. Connor straightened up. Shielding his eyes from the halogen glare of the flashlight, he yelled back, "Yeah, yeah. We're fine!"

"What's going on, kids?" the woman started in again, not satisfied, worried. "The beach is closed at night and you're all kind of my responsibility, as my guests. Maryn, are you ok?"

Maryn called back, "Hey Edith. Yep, I…I'm fine. I'm ok." Her voice rang hollow, there was an absence of presence in her tone. Edith was unconvinced.

"Come on, kids. Come inside. I'll make tea." Late April, the nights remained decidedly chilly, not suited for moonlight dips in the ocean. "Let's get you re-situated indoors."

The spring breakers did not appreciate the motherly ways of their beach house proprietress. The more she lorded over them like some house mother, the less mischief they could incorporate into their days – and especially nights – while they were there.

The five reluctantly trudged ashore, wet feet grown numb, unnoticed until that moment.

"Here, come on. You're freezing. Girls, let's go," Edith said, putting her arm around Maryn, whose teeth were chattering, her breathing shallow. Maryn refused to make eye contact with her host or her friends. Their faces were the last things she wanted to see as the half-life of her trance – or had it been a dream? – lingered, leaving her to wonder what she had witnessed in those few seconds. Her journey had been something beyond place or time.

Edith queried the girls, "What on earth were you all doing out there? Maryn, you look like you've seen a ghost. Anna, what were you kids up to in the water? And you're still dressed in your day clothes. You'll have to peel all that off in the vestibule. I'll throw it in the wash for you."

Anna, figuring some version of the truth would make the odd interruption more plausible, thereby perhaps more easily dismissed, replied, "Oh, it was just this thing, this game we were playing. You know, silly truth or dare kind of stuff. It was nothing."

"Sure didn't look like nothing, from what I could see. You should've seen yourselves out there. I know fear when I see it."

Damn people readers, these writers, Kai thought as he sent a sidelong glance to Connor. Connor responded with a roll of his eyes. The eyeroll acknowledged the risk, that a few more questions tossed their way by this weird woman, and the girls might spill all. They had three days left in their rental, and it had been an expensive vacation to book, being at the house of *that* boy, who had disappeared way back when, in some infamous Spring Tide, blah, blah, blah. Damned if they'd get themselves kicked out, Connor thought, but damned if they'd fully comply in order to be able to stay on. Some whiskey added to the tea would help balance this rescue out, he decided smugly. Both Connor and Kai had wanted to book a hotel, but no, Maryn had insisted on the Segel rental, dark-lit-fanatic that she was.

Connor changed the subject, Kai followed suit. The group made their way to the house, eager to doff wet clothes, change into sweats, settle in, thaw their limbs, and raise a cup.

†††

The "kids," as Edith called them, wrapped in afghans and seated in a semicircle near the fireplace, were jovial and appreciative enough. It almost felt like a slumber party, she thought, amused, nostalgic. The tea had been made and poured, dashed down, then made again. So good, the kids had said. Such tea drinkers, Edith though, amused, nostalgic.

"A penny for your thoughts, Maryn. Are you sure you're ok?" Edith asked as she curled up with her glass of wine, her third that night but the first one the kids had seen her with.

Maryn sighed, drawing breath, still unsure why that essential action didn't produce greater calm. "I'm fine, really. I kind of was, um, in a trance, you could say. Or a dream. I'm not sure."

"I still don't think you guys should be doing stuff like that," Edith countered, shaking her head, "It's dangerous any way you slice it."

Kai and Connor, knowing the girls might overshare, could only maintain a dismissive attitude about their underwater experiment. They diminished it by denigrating The Game, telling how they – such dorks – just couldn't quite yet leave behind such foolish, vestigial holdovers of their childish ways.

"Aw, Edith, you know we're just being stupid kids on spring break," admonished Connor.

"There's about a thousand other things we could be doing that would be way worse *and* more dangerous," Mop chided, also thinking some self-deprecation would help ease the situation.

"Ha, and you know me. I was always trouble with a capital T!" Connor added.

"You can say that again," Anna chimed in, tugging on a corner of the blanket. She didn't trust Connor any farther than she could have thrown him, but she had complied, been a follower, which bothered her.

The young men, downplaying their game, had already agreed to not disclose Connor had already tested "The Game" on his buddy the first night they had been at the ocean. It just had to be tried out. They would not share that Connor had had to beat on Kai's chest while Mop had administered mouth-to-mouth to resuscitate him. Thank goodness two of them were trained in CPR. Thank goodness Kai, who had no active memory of his own unconscious interval, had no problem adhering to their code of silence.

Edith prodded, "Maryn, what kind of a dream do you think you had?"

"Oh, wow," Maryn said, "The main thing about this was how long it felt I was 'under.' I mean, when I came to…"

"Woke up," Mop interjected.

"…when I came to," Maryn insisted, not playing along with the downplay, "I felt weirdly refreshed, as if I had slept for hours. Floating in the water morphed into this sensation of lying on a cool bed, though not on anything solid, but it was intensely comfortable. And I could feel the warmth of your hands on me. The heat – this was so awesome – came through your fingertips like, um, threads of warmth. It travelled the way blood moves through our veins. And I could *see* the warmth, like yellow streamers, winding around me. They wrapped around me and became a barrier between me and the water.

"But the dream? Yeah, I was underwater at first. I could see the surface of the water from below, a rippling mirror above me. And I could see the moon off to one side. It just sat there, as big as a grapefruit, textured skin and everything. But then, I remember the grapefruit pulled back, grew small, until it was just a spot of white. Then, when I started to drift away from it, it followed me."

"Man, listen to my pretty, little poet," Connor smirked, "you can thank me later."

Maryn groaned audibly. His needs were unrelenting, and his cliché-ridden entreaties were wearing thin. She mustered a chuckle, dismissing his quip. There were three days left in their week-long vacation, and Maryn wanted it to be a fun time for all of them. Once back at State and busy with classes, it would be a much better time for the weaning and breaking off of their fast-fading relationship.

"I forget what happened next. Sorry." Maryn lied.

"It does paint an interesting picture," Edith replied, intrigued. "I can totally imagine what you've described…"

Maryn was not going to tell their host what she had seen next in her dream. Maybe, when the time was right, she would let her friend Anna in on the rest of the story. Meantime, Maryn already knew that what she had felt, or seen, or whatever, would make for a great bit of writing. She couldn't wait until Connor was asleep so she could sneak out her laptop and enter a few lines, try to lay down the memories before they would fade away in the ordinary face of the daylight. While Maryn sensed a kindred sensibility in her host, who was indeed one of her favorite authors, Edith had yet to be told this spring break getaway was also a fan-girl pilgrimage. Edith, whose books Maryn had read, annotated, and collected, held a special place for Maryn, right up there, alongside Shirley Jackson, and Ann Rice. And as Maryn well knew, it was said that Edith was also the real-life sister of the boy who had disappeared all those years ago, with that crazy tide.

That boy, Maryn believed, was who she had seen in her underwater dream.

†††

It was nearly three a.m. when Maryn put her laptop away. The notes she thought to quickly jot down had grown into a 3000-word draft she was loathe to close, so engrossing was the journey back through the previous hours for her. The universe Maryn had touched on was in no way merely something housed inside of her – it had connected her to infinitely distant places and times in the space of a few seconds. And, relative to relativity, what were a billion moments of sublime hyper-awareness for their ability to move one to a serene self-awareness, to carve into one's core, a crystalline understanding as to how short and futile mortal existence otherwise truly was? Was this a rhapsodically suicidal knowledge? No, it wasn't a callout for a forced ending. It was a nascent awareness of a vastness the living were not intended – in their collectively pithy, evolutionarily centric condition – to fathom. But that glimpse of comprehension had captivated Maryn.

Stiff from her writing session, Maryn eased herself out from under the covers. Connor, his naked form splayed across most of the bed, moved immediately to take up the entirety of the space as she exited it. Maryn pulled the comforter over him. Typical - what a bed hog. Maryn padded out of the room and made her way to the kitchen. She was thirsty. The cheap whiskey Connor had poured into her tea had tasted like shit, and though it had calmed her, it had left her somewhat parched.

Maryn filled a glass of water, then a second. Even in her re-normalized, calmed state of mind, she started when the floorboard creaked to announce the materialization of a berobed form in the doorway. It was Edith, something of an apparition in her white hostess gown, still holding onto her glass of wine. She swayed a little as she stood there, and immediately sought to support herself against the doorframe.

"Alright." Edith gestured to the porch swing, "Now you can tell me the rest of your 'dream.' I'm all ears." Though her words were slightly slurred, her intent, to mine past Maryn's partial revelation, lent a hard, cold, and sobering tone to her voice. Maryn knew, Edith knew.

"Tell me," Edith repeated, "*who* did you see?"

The women sat in the sunroom and talked until sunlight broke free of the barrier islands' shores to the north. Edith listened, fiercely rapt, her eyes bright with unshed tears.

Maryn, when it was her turn to listen, cried when she learned what had really happened to Edith and her brother. She cried less over Edith's revelations on the abduction of her brother, and who – or what – had taken him; she cried more in response to the loss and loneliness Edith laid bare for her, overwhelming in its descriptive eloquence, in its raw factuality. The tragedy of her brother's abduction was starkly illustrative. Why had Edith never written *this* story? Clearly, to circle around this life changing – ending? – event had been the creative fountainhead for this author, who, unlike the proverbial, steadfast soldier, refused to this day to spill her guts in their entirety.

Maryn was convinced her host, curled up in the swing next to her, was among the most remarkable of survivors to have never had *her* story told. How, *just how*, had Edith managed to channel such internal tempest into the darkly beautiful narratives of her novels? The books Maryn had collected of E.V. Segel, as Edith Victoria was professionally known, were proof of the coping powers of the creative realm. What accursed gifts *Sturm* and *Drang* would at times bestow upon its most generously punished recipients…

Maryn resolved, she would stick with her English lit major despite the pragmatically driven suggestions of others. If poets remained the paupers, so be it.

The rising sun pushed against a bank of heretofore colorless clouds, sending them out to sea. Coral-lined clouds cast their shadows onto the endless table of the Atlantic as the first pelicans skimmed the shore on their morning trek. The women retired to the kitchen to make breakfast – hours of storytelling and soul baring had fed, among other things, their appetites.

As for Edith, her hunger had been more than that of one merely curious. Hers was a long-held, obsessed need to know, now somewhat fulfilled. And her instincts had been right about the girl; the story she had hoped to hear, she had heard. And more. The writers saw this is a metaphysical opportunity. The young woman saw this as a crossroads. The left behind sister saw it as the past rushing at long last forward, towards her, finally coming back to overtake her present.

Maryn, her heart overflowing, worried about what portals she had opened in her host. The women were now bonded by their experiences, though they remained two islands, with two disparate perspectives joined by bridges forged of mutual inclination amidst divergent desires. One was glad to be back, one had never left.

†††

Soon enough, it was the final evening of their vacation. The spring breakers had depleted their funds, and so, having been offered a meal at the house, had accepted Edith's offer of a farewell dinner "at home," together with her.

Edith set about in the kitchen, a fat pour in one of her omnipresent, schooner-sized wine glasses, ready to serve. The reclusive literary maven was enjoying a rare feeling of being in the moment alongside these kids of hers, as she had come to regard them. Plus, the alcohol was beginning to take its customary effect. At least this daily fix was legal and, so long as she didn't fall or knock something over when in its throes, it remained a more elegant poison than a whole lot of other, mind-numbing options. Edith took another decisive swig, and with her cleaver split a head of cabbage in two with such force, one-half bounced clean off the table, making everyone jump. When the blade remained stuck in the wooden counter, they kids exchanged glances as they laughed along with their host.

†††

The clock in the hall chimed eleven. Dinner was long over, but the group still lounged at the table. Host and guests were now, by both standard and superficial definition, friends. Empty wine bottles stood at table center, plates had been pushed back from their places, and the conversation had grown more fun and familiar, even bordering on the ribald. It was a good time for all, but, as a couple of them knew, it was only a matter of time until one of them would bring up *that* topic again.

†††

"Tell us once more your story of your underwater dream, Mar'!" It was Connor who resurrected the subject. That his near-lethal misadventure with Kai could be viewed as a fluke, still begged a reaffirmation with him.

"Yeah, Maryn, you never finished your story," Anna added.

Edith and Maryn exchanged glances.

Edith nodded, but deflected, "Go ahead. If you can't quite remember, make it up as you go. More fun that way."

Maryn shrugged, "Sure, why not? If it's a story you all want, why not embellish a bit? Up to you, what you choose to believe. Up to me, what I choose to say."

Anna leaned in, glass in hand, "Go for it. Spook us."

"Well," Maryn began, "I was lying in the water, and I could hear you guys saying whatever it was you were chanting…"

"…dark, deep, dark, deep…"

"That's it. As you were saying it over and over again, although I heard the words, it *felt* like they were circling inside my head. I felt the water around me lose its coolness. I don't know how to say it any other way. I started to feel as if I couldn't tell where my body, my skin, left off and where the water began…"

"…like being suspended…"

"…and that warmth you mentioned…"

"…yes, like being suspended in nothingness, hovering, but comforted. I'm pretty sure I was still breathing. Your chanting was like a metronome I had to keep up with. I suppose that's part of the function of a chant, right? Anyway, the 'out out out' you spoke I would hear, and it seemed to pull the air right out of me. And the more 'out out out' I did, the farther I felt I was sinking – and the brighter the sky grew above me.

Your faces literally disappeared. It was only sky I saw then. It came alive. It was like fabric, sparkling with sequins, or diamonds. I have never seen anything so beautiful. I have never seen the Milky Way like that. I mean, it was like looking through a telescope and being so close to it, I could've reached out and grabbed a handful of stars.

And that's another thing I felt – wanted to – was to leave the me hovering in the water behind. And I didn't care. I've thought about that since then. Lots. How we all die and leave behind our bodies, and for the most part, how it's not something ever fought against. It's positively Thanatopsian."

"Thana…?"

"A Poem about dying – and living – so one doesn't fight it when it's time. I mean, God willing, Fates willing, powers willing, we get to be here, do this life thing for what to us *seems* like a long time. But if we don't know for sure what it is we are headed to, or when, how is it we aren't fighting, kicking, screaming in utter dread against it? My grandpa passed last year. I was with him. He was okay with it. He fell asleep, right there with all of us standing around his bed, and that was it. It was sad, but it wasn't a horrible thing to witness. How is it we seem to accept this total snuffing out?

But now, seeing what I saw and feeling what I felt, I gotta wonder. That there just might be *this thing* that makes the moment of exit acceptable, like a launch of some sort as opposed to a shutting down. All I know is that I felt no fear, despite knowing at any second, Connor, you were going to finish me off, make me stop breathing. And *I knew* it was risky. I *knew* it was stupid, but just like *you* guys were willing to do It to me, *I* was willing to do it to myself. A moment's passing brush with something we are all destined to go through. And why? That, I can't answer."

"So, go on. Tell us about the sinking…"

"Yep. I began to fall slowly, I sunk down and away from the water's surface. The only thing I can connect to this is, that the sensation of you all easing me down, under the water and Connor's holding my nose and mouth closed as he pushed my face below the surface, made for a split-second imprinting of a new sensation I took with me into my unconsciousness. And the moon – oh boy, the moon – it took on this hyper-clarity and size, totally 3-d and fully on me, like some orb I could carry to light my way, wherever it was I thought I was going.

I fell and fell. Slowly. I was comfortable, cradled. And like I said, I felt no fear. I was eager – yes, eager – to go farther."

"…and that's where you left off!"

"I know, I know. I'm getting there…"

Maryn glanced at Edith, who said nothing. Edith's eyes were fixed on the far away, beyond the windows, on the blackened tableau of ocean and sky. While she was right there with them, caught up in this re-telling, Edith was leagues away. With Maryn's story playing out in her mind, Edith, the most rapt audience member in the room, waited with such a need to hear the retelling, *she* was almost forgetting to breathe. Maryn felt the trepidation again, as she had felt it on the night she and Edith had talked until dawn, that some window in the psyche of her new friend was being opened, which held something of great questionability.

"Maryn. Go on. Go on." Edith whispered, putting down her empty glass, "Don't stop now!"

Maryn resumed her story.

"So, I'm deep, down now. It's dark but not cold. It feels good, even. The water then seemed to thicken, turn to black, becoming as dark as the sky had been, but just as soon as the black *felt* complete, it began to change. It was like the lights were being turned up in a theater; not all the way, just enough to shine a path into the distance. The moon grew smaller. But it wasn't like the moon was shrinking; rather, it was travelling – fast – going off into the distance, in the direction of the ocean's horizon, away from shore to where the shelf falls off, where the deep-water chasms exist, where we humans still can't manage to go, for all our scientific know-how. That deep, which exists beyond our capabilities, is where I sensed I was headed…."

"…yeah, honestly, how can we tackle Mars if we can't even walk our ocean floors?"

"Exactly. That's one of the other takeaways of this thing I experienced. It's like I have this understanding of the overwhelming immensity of what I – we – don't know. An understanding that we aren't even supposed to know all of what's out there. Like, it's not meant for us. Yet."

"But we are nearly totally made of water!"

"Yes, we are of it, we need it. We love it, too. Heck, we create spaces in our hearts for bodies of water, as if they were living, sentient entities."

"Yeah, that outlast a whole lot of human-based ones."

"Isn't that the truth!"

"And how ironic – we love, need and are made of an element that is the single most destructive force of all. The seas literally seek to erase us. Daily."

"Twice a day."

"The tides…"

Yes, the tides. Over and over, the ocean tides seek to eradicate everything we have ever built and been. And yet we celebrate them, we personify them, want to be by them, any chance we get."

"Even so…" Edith sighed.

"Edith – you okay?" Anna asked, touching Edith's arm.

Edith flinched, rousing from her reverie. But her look had no gratefulness for the care just shown her. It was tinged with hostility, as if the interruption was an afront.

"I'm fine, I'm fine!" Edith snapped, sitting up. "Come on, Maryn, your friends are waiting. Tell them!" Edith's impatience was obvious; matronly inclinations had been cast fully aside. Damned if the kids were going to interrupt her again.

"Okay, okay; it's alright, Edith," said Maryn, concerned, seeking to reassure her friend.

"…that orb," Maryn resumed, "what had started out to be the moon morphed into this glowing ball beneath the water, going far off to where I felt the space became, um, infinite. It travelled in an arc and slowed down. As it did, and the deep water lit up around it, the light fell upon a shadow, a human form. Though far away and small, I knew this was a person. The glowing moon-ball slowed to a stop and, like, floated into this being's hand. Now I could see it was a male; a slender, dark-haired man. Somehow, I knew he was not old. He was broad shouldered, slender, elegant."

Maryn's friends gasped audibly. Conner's brow contracted with a jealous spark. Illogical as this was, he did not like what had taken an instantaneous turn to become a competitive narrative.

"Jesus," Conner said, "No wonder you've held off on that part."

"Oh Conner, lighten up," Kai retorted, eager to hear more. "It's a dream. You can't hold that against her."

"Yeah, there's no way Maryn could help it." Anna added. "And look, you're the one who talked us all into doing the Drowning Man Game. You're the one who said…"

"Okay, okay, fine. Got it, Miss Mama Anna."

"Oh, shut up, Connor," she retorted.

"I'll shut up when I want to shut up!" Connor growled.

"Jesus, Con', calm down. Let Maryn finish her story so we can all go to bed. I'm too stuffed and too tired for this," Kai interjected.

"Fuck you!" Connor, cornered, snapped.

"Dude!" Mop replied.

"Yeah, what?"

Anna and Maryn yelled in unison, "Connor, stop it!"

Before Connor could counter, Edith jumped up from her chair, hitting the table so hard with her fists, the crystal candle holders lurched, nearly tipping over. Plates and silverware rattled.

"For the love of everything, would you kids shut the hell up and let Maryn finish her story?" Edith wailed.

Edith's eyes shone with tears. There was no way these stupid kids would highjack the story a second time with their stupid attitudes and arguments.

Edith hissed, "Shut the hell up. Grow up and shut up. You have no idea. No idea!"

Maryn turned to Edith, concern transforming her expression, "Edith, maybe it's time we all…"

"NO!" Edith cried. A tear rolled down her cheek. *"Finish the fucking story!"*

This response to Maryn's warmly intended words shocked her. The window she had worried about was flung open wide, and their host was stepping off its ledge.

"Edith, dear," Maryn began again, "I can…"

"No!" Edith stopped her, lifting one hand to block the words, to blockade any entreaty for her to calm down, *"I* want to hear this to the end. Do you get this? *I* need to hear this to the end! This fucking story is what I have been waiting for, for forty fucking years!"

The group sat, frozen.

"No, no, no!" Edith continued, "Why couldn't it have been me to be the one to come up with a story like this, when it's been *my* story all along?

"You come along – you and you *friends,*" she sneered, "with more money than sense, and sure, fine, you pay to stay a few days at this house with me before you go off again. And I know you know full well who all lived here and who I am, and that's fine. But don't you fucking play with me, with my heart, by leaving me out in the cold again with this!

"If I'm going to be left behind at this house – again – and if I'm going to be the one who has to stay back to slug it out again with all this stupid life shit, then at least you can oblige me with the rest of your goddamn story so I can be clued in to what the fuck happened to my goddamn brother and what the fuck I have missed out on!"

Edith's drunken rage fed itself as long-held hurts finally found their fissures and erupted, reducing rationalizations that had postured as circumspection and wisdom down to nothing. The almost-twin, the little girl left behind, had been resurrected.

"Yeah, and so what if I drink too much? Hey, my mother showed me the way! While she muddled the fuck about with her stupid life, I got to muddle about with mine. And I was just a kid!" Edith sobbed, "I had no one who would listen to me, who would *hear* me! Do you think I could dare tell someone what *really* happened if no one even cared for the watered-down versions I gave them?"

Connor ventured, "Edith, what are you talking about?"

Maryn interjected, "Connor, let it go, please. Edith is exhausted. She's triggered by my story, but if you give me a chance I can…"

"Triggered, my foot! Maryn, I feel more fucking alive right now than I have in I don't know how long!"

"Edith…"

"No! I do! Why fight the pain? Why fight the rejection? Shit, it's my legacy. First my mother, then my grandmother, the only grandmother I ever knew, who keeled over on my fucking birthday – my fourteenth birthday! God, what a nightmare that was – and before all that, my twin brother fucking taken by some fucking beast of a mermaid, leaving me here, all by myself, this little kid, to contend with a mother who actually fucking blamed *me* – me! – for his disappearance and a grandmother who never knew what to say to me after that. After *he* was gone. Shit!

"So, go on, Maryn. *Tell me about that fucking boy*!"

Maryn's eyes welled up. Edith's words stung her, but this was about Edith needing to hear about *him*, again.

A breeze started up amidst the momentary shocked silence, bringing to life the candle flames, the crystal pendants and the curtains. The humans sat still, as if in suspended animation, in the weighted, dead pause Edith's outburst had wrought.

Maryn, her voice shaking, began to speak, again.

"He was holding the orb, and it lit his face."

There was no way Maryn would repeat to the full group what she had told Edith the other night, how this man in the distance, his face and his form, were so bewitchingly beautiful, how she had been drawn to this shadowy being. To utter that assessment would likely cause Connor to jump out of his seat and come at her. No one could know she had dreamt of *him* every night since then.

But Edith remembered Maryn's words from their late-night talk. She sighed, and added, "And he was beautiful."

Maryn ignored her.

"Wai…wait a minute," said Mop. "Backtrack here. A *mermaid* took your brother?"

Edith shushed him with a wild look and a slashing gesture across her throat.

Maryn ignored them both. For the good of what was left of the evening, she knew she needed to keep going and get her story over with.

"He began to move closer. It's like he was miles away, but in no time, he was at my side, and I could see his eyes…"

"…and they were the color of sea glass…" Edith interjected.

The romantic add-on was too much for Connor. But rather than simply react on jealous inclination, he decided to take the reins and take over the conversation. The old lady was losing it, and so he would orchestrate a distraction. He assumed this was doing Maryn a favor, hoping it would impress her. Evidently, he had competition. If it would serve to calm down their host, who was falling down some personal rabbit hole, all the better for him.

"Edith – I know what to do!" Connor stood up. "I know what needs to happen!"

"What?" Edith started, caught off guard.

"This is all about the Drowning Man Game, isn't it? It's about you wanting to see for yourself. I get it! So, why not we have *you* do it?"

"Are you fucking kidding me, Con'?" Kai asked.

"Sure! Why not?"

"Oh Connor, I don't know," Anna ventured, "How about we just let Maryn finish her story and…."

"Wait! Stop!" Edith held up both hands. "Yes! The Game. Yes, I want to do The Game too! Do me, Connor, do me!"

"No, no, Edith! None of us should've done it to begin with…we don't want to take any more chances…" Mop chimed in.

"You never know how it could go wrong…"

"All kinds of risk…"

"No! I mean yes!" Edith cut short their entreaties. "I want to do this. Let me try it! You kids can't patronize me by going on and on about all this and then just saying 'No' to me like that!"

"Edith…"

"If you kids refuse me, I'll go alone with Connor right now! I don't need the lot of you for this…"

"Edith…"

"Maryn, why? Why can't I try something I want to? Why am I being left out again?"

The past had fully caught up with Edith and dissolved her disposition, doing away with all learning, logic, and rationale she had worked so hard to live by. Her petulant sorrow permeated the room; they could all feel the drag. The pressure was measurable. They were all under water.

Edith began to sob.

"For the love of God, just do this for me," she heaved, "Do it with me, don't leave me out, let me have a chance to know what you know. Let me see, let me see…"

Maryn's empathy got the best of her. She crept out of her chair, and hoping Edith would not lash out, put her arms around her friend, a woman who was imploding with the force of an unrequited desire for inclusion.

Edith would not be assuaged. She started in again, "You've got to let me participate for once. I don't care – I really don't – what happens after this. But don't any of you leave this place, this time with me, and think you can walk off to your own lives and let me sit here and wonder now, what it was *you* did, what *you* would deny *me*!

"You want me to beg? Is that what you need, to get it? Be convinced that what I might want could be so much more than anything any of you may have ever thought you wanted? You're willing to just go off like that and leave me out in *this* cold? You want to kill off a person over this?"

The wedge had been driven in; the guilt had been forced.

Connor saw it as his cue to "give in."

He delivered in his most conciliatory tone: "Shush now, Edith, no one is leaving you behind. We're here and with you. And yes, we can do this. I mean," He turned to his friends, messaging persuasion with his eyes, "What've we got to lose? Maryn is proof The Game works, and if you ask me, the one way to wrap this whole thing up is to go out there, right now, and do this. With Edith. For Edith. It's the least we can do, let our host make this call."

Anna looked down at her lap and said, "Never thought I'd go along with you, or this, again, but okay; I'm in."

Mop scanned their faces, his reluctance evident. "I'm in."

"Oh, Edith, please…" Maryn implored.

"Maryn, Maryn, don't. You of all people. If you abandon me on this, we are done. I'm done and, yeah, it's a threat. It's my life, my wish."

Anna sighed, "C'mon, Maryn, let's do this. Let's get it over with."

Kai touched Maryn on the shoulder and nodded, a wordless negotiation. Maryn's expression changed. As she rose from her chair, Maryn said to Edith, "Alright. Let's go." Then to Conner, "But you better…"

Connor interrupted her, "I will be."

Kai and Connor moved to help Edith up from her chair, but she shrugged them off. Gathering herself up, she drew a fresh breath, pulled her shoulders back, and lifted her chin.

"This way, kids."

Edith sprung the latches of the French doors and threw them wide. The doorway framed an endlessly vast nighttime expanse. The rush of the unseen surf was rhythmic and gentle. Being the time of year when sea turtles returned to land to lay their eggs, the mandatory shoreline blackouts had left the beach devoid of illumination but for what little the moon and stars could spare. In that moment, the lunar entity was still in hiding, but the winds, having picked up, were coaxing its cloud cover inland, away from the shore.

Edith took a candle from the hurricane glass on the credenza and lighted it with one of the tapers on the table. The remaining candles, she blew out. She crossed the threshold and stepped onto the deck, the kids following her. Edith held her candle close, a middle-aged vestal leading the way to her own sacrifice. Her face reflected a mix of serenity and determination. She was being included. She was in. She was, in fact, at dead, damn center.

The farewell dinner having degenerated into a turbulent exchange, had next managed to instantly morph into a solemn ceremonial procession. These were no longer college friends making their way over a sand dune, but a council of practitioners towed in the wake of their Andromeda, her linen caftan at full sail in the breezes, which in one moment pushed against the group, and in the next, pulled them forward towards the water.

Without any measurable pause, the group followed the beach to the shoreline and walked into the black water. They were bare footed but fully dressed. The candle cut a small path of light, Edith lifting it higher as the water reached her waist. The flame's reflection broke into a thousand pieces of gold and danced upon the gelatinous ocean surface.

†††

"We call forth the energies of the deep and dark…"

Connor made it up as he spoke.

Edith lay perfectly still, obedient. Her hands held the candle upright at the level of her heart. Her caftan billowed about her, the fabric disappearing into the watery shadows at its hemlines. The ghostly effect of Edith suspended in a sea of ink was not lost on anyone. She was their captive specimen, an anesthetized manta ray.

Two friends were stationed at Edith's shoulders, two were at her hips. Guilty glances were exchanged as Connor commenced with his ad-libbed version of the recitation. The ruse, dangerous to begin with, was now a mockery of a stunt gone way deep and way dark, for the very spirit of a fragile woman now lay in their hands. The physical risk to her person was only one aspect of what had descended into a multi-level charade, and even Connor could understand, he had to find a way to keep at bay the most obvious of worst possible outcomes.

The other four were progressively repulsed by their complacency in the face of the charismatic lug's repeated attempts at leadership.

Connor, feeling none of the remorse of his friends', only focused on what the hell he would be saying next.

"We call forth the energies of the deep and the…"

It was Edith who cut into Connor's thread. "For Christ's sake, Connor, say it like you mean it!"

Connor, nonplussed, lowered his voice, slowed his words, and kept on. He focused on Edith's breathing and timed the cadence of his words to it. No one had instructed Edith to begin any sort of rapid-fire exhalations. They were deathly afraid she might remember that part from Maryn's narrative.

"Breathing slow and out, your mind like the sea, drifting, adrift…"

Connor glanced at Kai, who blinked once to indicate his approval.

"Out and out, in and in, feel the drifting off…
We call forth the energies of the deep
We call forth the energies of the dark
Sleep, drawing close, soft and…"

Edith was far too drunk to remember details of The Game and how it was "played." Connor was grateful for the wine's effects. He and Kai were even more glad they had resolved to keep their mouths shut about that other time.

Connor commenced with his randomized incantation:

"Sleep with the dark
Sleep with the deep
Numb of body and of soul
Sleep, sleep…"

Maryn longed for Edith to drift off. A brief period of ordinary slumber for the "victim" had become their defacto objective. The five of them could hold Edith in place, let a couple minutes pass, then awaken her, and that would be it. There was no reason this should not work.

Kai, Mop and Anna got it, too. They stood motionless, quietly on call for any cues from Connor or Maryn. They also stood still so to avoid catching the attention of any scavenging, nocturnal ocean creatures.

"You are relaxing
you feel the ocean now a bed
A bed for your body

and for your head…"

The corny words caused Maryn to shoot a look at Connor. He pretended not to notice. He was on a roll; he could see Edith's face relaxing. The lines in her face had disappeared.

This was going to work. It *had* to work.

"Dark and deep
Dark and deep
The oceans now call you
Tell you to sleep…
Dark and deep
Dark and deep

The oceans now call you
Tell you to sleep…
Dark and deep
Dark and deep
The oceans…"

A single, ripping snore burst from Edith's mouth.

Edith's body lurched and her eyes popped open in surprise. They flicked back and forth, scanning the sky, then the faces closest to hers. Realization set in.

"Nothing!" she sputtered, furious. "Fucking nothing!"

Oh, shit, they all thought.

"Edith," Connor said, his mind racing, seeking to salvage, "Sure, sure. You've got to let the trance take hold of you. It can take a few minutes before you see something…"

"Yeah, the moon's still behind the clouds. You had no, um, object to focus on," Maryn stammered.

"Well, damn it." Edith cursed. Her voice became child-like, so badly did she want to trust what these kids were doing. "You think that's it?" Her eyes filled with fresh tears.

Edith still held the candle upright. But the splash of water that occurred when Edith had so abruptly come to had extinguished the flame.

"My candle's out," she said, and began to cry.

"Shh, there, there now," Maryn consoled Edith, hoping to distract her and keep her calm, "It's no big deal. And look! Here comes the moon. The clouds are splitting in two, right above us. That's gotta be a sign."

"Definitely a sign…" Anna whispered.

"Now, it'll work…" Mop chimed in.

"Connor, do it…" Maryn urged.

"Okay, okay…" Connor shifted in the water, his feet burrowing into the sand. "But guys, this time say it with me. Let's just say the thing the way…"

"…we all know it?"

"Yeah."

"But…"

"No 'Buts'. Let's do it. Right."

"Connor…"

"Don't 'Connor' me! Fall in or I'm outta here…"

Edith shot daggers at the group. Turning glassy, red eyes to Connor, she cut them all short and commanded, "Do. It. Go."

As one, the five began the Drowning Man Game chant. They knew it well. Four simple lines. Repeat.

Edith lay in repose upon the hammock of hands, her caftan, freshly unsettled, billowed about her. The wet candle aimed for the stars. She closed her eyes once more.

The friends implicitly knew they would keep at the chant until Edith was asleep, come hell or high water.

Slowly, slowly, with a quelling singsong, the five began to recite:

"Dark

Deep
Dark
Deep
Breathe
Out
Out
Out
Go to sleep…"

They lost count of the repetitions. Edith's face relaxed; it glowed, reflecting the cool light of the moon, which had emerged, right on cue, from behind a curtain of clouds. The edges of Edith's caftan moved gently, to the ebb and the flow of the watery blanket that surrounded and held them all.

As Connor chanted, Maryn ventured a look around. Everything was awash in shades of blue. Azure to indigo to darkest midnight, all was blue. Beyond the shush of the waves, the breeze, the lull of their voices, there was nothing. Nothing but *this*. And *this* felt familiar. She looked over her shoulder, towards the horizon, scanning for signs of something.

"Dark, deep
Dark, deep
Breathe out out out
Go to sleep…

Dark, deep
Dark, deep
Breathe out out out
Go to sleep…"

They willed The Thing along with every syllable. Gently, persuasively. Connor was fully immersed in the words – where the force of his determination left off, the rune's hypnotic effect had picked up.

Anna felt herself grow sleepy; her eyelids begged to close.

Mop too felt himself sway, ever so slightly, to the rhythm of the words.

Suddenly, the blackened tip of the candlewick sparked. A bright orange pinprick appeared, catching Anna off guard. She felt her stomach twist. The next words caught in her throat as she watched the tip of the wick smolder.

It was coming back to life.

When the glowing wick fired to a flame, Anna inhaled sharply, which drew Mop's attention, then Kai's, who stood across from them. The two followed Anna's gaze to the candle, where the tiny flame danced, taunted.

Edith, eyes closed, was oblivious to the kids, the cold water, the abrupt change in their chant, and to the flame newly resurrected upon her breast. She was once more on the cusp of another water-borne nap, sinking into a netherworld where, at the very least, perhaps a dream awaited.

Connor, so focused on his role, was likewise unaware. Maryn, distracted, with her face turned to the horizon, did not realize what had just happened. Anna, Mop and Kai croaked along as best as their dry mouths and constricted throats would allow. Heaven forbid any one of them take responsibility for screwing this second and, pray, final attempt at lulling Edith into some level of unconsciousness.

What next reeled Maryn's attention back to the group, to Edith, and to the burning candle upon her breast, was a sensation she suddenly felt, the softest of swipes as it brushed against her calves. By the time she registered the feeling, it was over.

Then Kai felt something, though no soft, sweeping touch was to be his. A row of sharp tines, or teeth, punched into his right heel. Intensely painful, by the time Kai could think to yelp, it was over.

Kai's high-pitched cry did, however, stop them all short. The four looked at each other, silent panic in their faces. Edith did not appear to register anything. She remained motionless, committed to her somnambulic dive.

The candle shone like a beacon. Only Connor still chanted.

The four friends all saw the fingertips emerge from the water, each where they stood. Four sets of humanoid fingers slithered up, out of the water's mirrored surface, delicate as sea serpents, reaching skyward. Hands, wrists and then arms appeared, bending around to embrace the billowing form of their hostess, grabbing surely at the fabric of her caftan and at her bared flesh. Closing in with their grips, the hands clenched, and arms held fast. The water-borne limbs were a dark, bluish-gray color, the hands sporting long, black talons, more claw-like than humanoid. Mop, Maryn, Anna and Kai recoiled in shock and horror as the serrated claws dug like fishhooks into Edith. This unplanned handover had the menacing grace of a practiced military maneuver.

The four looked over at Connor, who had finally noticed the burning candle. He had yet to notice the silence of his friends, uniformly debilitated, frozen with fear, their arms hanging limp and lifeless at their sides. He had yet to see the shark-skinned hands that held Edith.

"Dark deep…" Connor stopped short. "Jesus Christ… How'd that candle light itself up?"

"Connor," Kai whispered, "that's not all."

"What do you…" was as far as Connor got. Something had wrapped itself around his left thigh and was pulling him back.

"What the…" Connor cried out, when all of a sudden, he was tossed aside in a move oddly reminiscent of violent horseplay. Connor fell beneath the water.

Inexplicably, especially considering her outburst from minutes before, Edith remained in her suspended state, her calm expression unchanged. But when Connor was yanked from her, and his hands were ripped from her head, she came to. This time, however, Edith did not stir. She made no sound. Only her eyes registered wakefulness. They were open, wide. Awake now but *utterly and completely* still, Edith lay there, afloat.

Desperation and hope demanded she do *nothing*.

Edith was not about to scare off whatever was starting to happen. To her.

It was happening.

Something, someone, grabbed her hair.

Edith gasped.

Connor struggled to aright himself. He swam a few strokes to find ground and regain his footing a short distance from the circle. He, like his friends, was helpless; they were out of their league. All they could do was stand down. And watch. The wine, the chant, the moment, the blue light, the night, had infected them with a ridiculous capacity for acceptance and rendered them devoid of any desire to resist. They understood. This was what Edith *wanted*.

Muscular, slender arms now encircled Edith's body, clearly coordinated in their effort. Edith was held solidly aloft, her body, legs and feet barely breaking the water's surface. The fabric of her caftan undulated, the manta ray re-animated. Dark and slick, the marine beings' limbs shone in stark contrast to their captive's swathed form. They held fast, so much so, their talons had cut through the fabric and broken the skin beneath her robe. Edith's caftan was soon infused with a marbled bloom of pink, her blood mixing in the salted dyebath. The pain was excruciating, but Edith remained stock still, believing any reaction whatsoever would break the spell.

What she felt, past the fear and all that pain, was pure joy.

The glowing pillar Edith had so stoically held aloft began to sink into her breast. Whether the candle was burning itself out or slowly impaling her heart was impossible to tell. Molten wax pooled and hardened, forming a scabbard, molded upon her chest. The corporeal parcel which had housed her soul for over fifty long years was sealed, stamped, ready for delivery…

Edith began to slide along the water's surface, away from the group and towards the open ocean, held securely by this cadre of unseen sons and daughters of the sea.

Still. Absolutely still. When Edith looked down upon herself, she beheld a Viking funerary passenger setting final sail. She clasped her reliquary tighter and gave thanks. Edith's eyes turned back to the skies. There, she found the moon, then the planets, then the Milky Way, and when she looked through and beyond even that, she saw Heaven.

The five spring breakers watched in silence from the shallows, humbled, frightened, relieved. They watched the bier that had been their host – this kind but disturbed and oh, so lonely woman – move away from them, her candle's flame marking a stealthy path towards the horizon.

In minutes, the flame was a pinprick of light. Then, it was gone.

Edith would presently forget to even draw breath; such was the agony of her anticipation. The dregs of her threadbare soul welcomed it. And so, this was how she left the firmament of life, and how she let herself be taken towards the edge of something, she knew or cared not, where the light of the moon and its answering reflections met and became one.

Efectus

CORONET

Forget the pithy pouch Elizabeth Hamilton strung about her neck, which held the scrap of some love poem Alexander wrote to her. Forget the silk-wrapped heart of her beloved's, which Mary Shelley kept with her until the end of her days. And all Victoria could think to do was dress in black? Shit. Forget dances with corpses, ash-filled vessels, carved stone tablets, satin-lined boxes. Forget statues, flowers, lighted candles, plastic wreaths. And forget those weird, little halogen lanterns that keep nominal vigil at forgotten gravesites, where only listless spirits drift about, wondering where everybody went.

Those are nothing. They are ordinary, customary, and don't begin to reflect what's inside The Losing, what lies at the foundation of the penance I seek, long to pay. Sorry or sorrow, what funny, companion ills of the soul! Mine – both of them – are positively afloat, blended into the blackest of ash-muddled depths. We positively drown where we are put, and, for my part, I am glad of it.

I loved him so much.
No, I *love* him so much.
I love him still. Forever. Amen.

I thank the dark angels who offered me this, where for thousands of eyes I become the main attraction, where, when the Jeweler is finished with me, I will have perhaps, with luck and some version of artistry, earned elevation to the innermost circle of this Place, in which I know I must reside for whatever it is that counts as an eternity. I earned my entrée to this realm, dammit, and here I am.

Let the show begin. I seat myself on the dais. I am ready to entertain.

He was with me twenty short years. Fates and Furies willing, he will be with me twice that times twenty, and more, going forward. His memory shines like a halo over me; I hold it aloft, false supplicant that I am. Soon, very soon, he will be seen *with* me, in me, a true participant in profile and countenance, a framework for this sinner's devotionals, a crowning tribute to whom was my best friend, my partner in crime, my lover, my other.

Fourteen performances, it was determined. Fourteen sessions for the process and the imprinting of a fresh pain that would, perhaps, serve *to begin* to encompass what I felt, feel, possess, and hold dear, intend to keep fresh, alive, upfront and have so fucking well earned.

No, the experience will never be dulled. My screams will bounce off the vast, damp walls that encase us. The fabricator, his model, the audience, in fellowship, we have been consigned to everlasting u-call-it. Every lamentation ripped from my lungs as scalpel and drill do their work will speak in tribute to the songs the carved and peeling cherubs can no longer sing, who like I are imprisoned upon their pedestals and altar bases; our plasticized kindred – mottled, fading, ever more decrepit. Aimless echoes are absorbed like cheap drink for those who observe, enrapt, who thirst (as we all thirst), parched upon their rock-hard perches, upon the bird shit slathered bleachers which line the cavernous rooms of this underworld. They encircle us, where I am to remain seated for the entirety of the crafting. The crowds are ready to cheer us on with chants so ancient, it makes the "virtuous" gals from Salem look like 7th grade cheerleaders.

Worm tossed soil and deeper strewn rubble of the earth hold fast the cellars which dot the netherworlds in which we subsist, mired in our legacies of infernal compliance. 'tis a fine web we weave, in this three-ring circus spectacular of pain and dismemberment.

As for me? There will be no compassionate human to receive my cries, no rescuing me from the train tracks to which I willingly bind myself in a gesture as pure and profound as what landed me here. There will be no help when the unbearableness descends to the extreme, *as is my wish*. This is the penultimate, perfect inversion of joy. And the season pass holders? They will eat it up.

Let my enthronement commence!

The Jeweler forges on. I sit for him, stone still, obedient, meditative, from a place of displaced calm only the dead can attain.

The Jeweler glances over and again at his sketch as he works. The diagram, his treasure map, is mapped out in blood and colored by deceit and the agonies of betrayal and revenge. Entrusted to only him, the sheets from which he works are only ever drawn by the hands of souls guided by deepest grief, and regret. He takes from them the outlines which will guide him – a blueprint borne of the saddest of tales over all time, interwoven upon my own skin, trails of finest ink marking the stations where he will cut and pull, set, pin, and sew – and entertain.

The Jeweler is the scribe, and we who seek our shreds of latently blessed benevolence become, by his hand, his illuminated prayerbooks. What, I dare inquire, is in it for him? He throws me a half-smile, which suggests disdain for my even asking. He is just doing his job.

The initials and images my love and I in life designed recorded the best of nights and the best of fights, passionate post-battle reunions, dates, and moments that hover still, legible across the terrain that was once the lifepath of what was I and Me. I held subcutaneous runes and pictures of the west on my body; my love bore the corresponding eastern halves in reverse. When we stood, or lay, together, we became the pages of an open book. In life, we were complete. In life, I sought to make that even more replete. My love surrendered, and was then rendered, completely and profoundly in two. His soul, foolish I, I thought I could inhale, like a well-poured pull of fresh air. But I saw my delusion drift off, a scrap in the winds. And when I saw the mouth of the Earth open wide, and the bone-encrusted stairs descending, beckoning, I took them. I knew the path, knew it was meant for me.

As a sign of mourning, we cut our hair. Elevated to the level of biblical iconographical program, we render ourselves bereft of Samson's wellspring, Godiva's garb, Beauty's tresses, Rapunzel's ropes, so to attire ourselves in shades of hurt. We empower with debilitations, with tragic embrasure, with wounds. As it were, the requirements of my creation mandated there would be a pre-show of a preparatory killing-off of all the follicles on my head. Conventions of loveliness, in tribute, were to be deliberately set aside. Beauty to this beholder was to be fully re-interpreted, inverted.

Moreover, one must provide a clean canvas to the portraitist.

Fourteen sessions with the Jeweler, fourteen performances, it was posted, at the entrance to his tent.

Come One, Come All! Hear Her Scream, See Her Bleed!
There is no cost – You did, after all, pay in the Before.

Numbing potions or medicines are not of this place. If I pass out from the pain, then that will become a part of the experience, the show. Might I, from within a torture-induced unconsciousness, see shadows of my love? Come, my dear; I dare you. Haunt me.

Two are to be featured per show. It will remain as such, two each time. Starting with two molars at center back.

The bleeding is profuse. A symphony of red. The oohs and aahs are genuine, and oh, yes, the pain is profound. My sensorial immersion is a journey to a special corner in Hell from which my return is by design never to be complete. The echo effect of each performance will be imprinted upon me to distract my illimitable non-days and disrupt what token attempts at rest I may ever be permitted. Sleep, what a laughable, chimeric pastime in which the aggrieved indulge! And dreams? Fuck those playthings of the living. My incessant wakefulness should at least be of some purpose, for the enhancement of a burning tenderness to prohibit even the ability to place my bone-weary head into the depths of some mold-stained pillow, which should count for something… May it then require I pay even further penance when forced to sit upright, wedged between rock-hard bolsters, denied even that simplest posture of repose? How better to dredge up in tribute all that I have wrought, all that I have lost?

Two at the second show. Two molars, next to the first. I count down the intervals between performances: Seven days, six, five, four – oh, please come sooner – three, two. I can't wait! One… Go!

Two more molars at session three, two more at session four. More and more, each three-hour dirge, during which I am the song, the words, the melody, I am there to give home to the circular path that is being ever so delicately built upon, within, the top of my naked scalp.

First, come the molars; after that, the pre-molars. Two of these are gold-crowned, no less, shining like Viking's buttons, freshly unearthed from ancient burial mounds. Buried once more, this time, the artifacts are now entombed with the blessing of the bearer, their precious make will surely serve to warm my thoughts.

Real teeth, the Jeweler had told me, were not customarily done. Real teeth, he warned, could turn around and bite their way straight through my brains. Real teeth, he said, could work their way up through my skin and erupt like popcorn out of my head, should my body not accept the teeth and spontaneously seek to expel them. The Jeweler, so accustomed to the bio-aesthetics as he is, whistles idly while he works, his non-descript ditties and nursery tune fragments waft in and around the random, anguished outbursts that escape my lungs, our morbid duet interspersed only with the sporadic, awestruck gasps and silent spells of our audience members.

To serve as a muse and to amuse, what a fine line I cross time and again as the shows accrue and our following grows to standing room only. The work-in-progress is indeed elegantly, repugnantly graphic. But, what else should one expect in a Garden of Miseries? And the Jeweler himself? For my beloved's remains to be implanted into my corporeal depths, for them to become a part of me and walk with me through the course of my un-days, require this craftsman to be and feel in highest, most ego-fed, arrogant form. As such, I willingly play along with him, for him. It is, after all, the only way my tithes can be paid.

The Jeweler is no mere body modification artist; he is my Fabergé.

Performances seven and then eight. Pre-molars, nine; then the canines, and at last come the incisors. Arrayed in careful, ascending order, their pinning requires some drilling into the skull plates to make for a more solid implantation. Their ensured verticality is an especially delicate placement. The Jeweler's smithing of my coronet is quickly becoming the stuff of legend. Why, it almost breathes life into my Beloved's posthumously scattered traces.

Black stitches form their own fretwork. Earlier work is progressively added to as the performances take place and the circlet is built. Subsequent stitches are sewn, embroidery to encase every new tine of my crown; the whole, minute scaffolding creeping forward, towards my brow, with each show, each implantation. The stitches appear like spiders that, having crawled onto my head, dutifully remain outstretched in pursuit of their goal, which is to hold my freshly pulled, grey skin smooth and taut over each talisman. The threads become a lace surround, scarlet dots and blackened hatch marks which outline the handiwork, a veritable signature scrawled across my scalp. The spidery threads are good-byes written in their very own silk, and they do not heal over. Why would they?

The thirteenth, then, almost sadly, the fourteenth shows take place. That I have never grown accustomed to the pain of the incisions, the pinning, the insertions, or the stitching, is part of the subversion of my world. I take comfort in the pain. It has a purpose.

The Jeweler announces to his audience at the last performance: Is this not all about the transforming of our puny repetitiveness into something of *real* expression and *pure* experience? Of living, of dying, of mementos manifested in a tangible physicality? Isn't it? Isn't it?

How they applaud, how they nod in unison at his words! How they cheer when the Jeweler takes his final bow!

But would he please, please, I beg, next insert the splinters of the board I used to split my beloved's skull into a sunburst array at the base of my crown? If he were to refuse, I suppose I could try doing it myself…

The next level of Hell to which I aspire might be a place where one's extra effort is appreciated. No pain, no gain, as they used to say, in sheer, blissful ignorance of what pain really is. What it is in this place. It is the litanies themselves, cries wrought by the smithing of skull-capping coronets, which throw open the damning doors, and wide.

†††

My love for him, and my love himself, were the two best things that ever happened to me. He once called me his little Queen. He had told me, as a motif, next up, would be a new piece that was to be inked over his sternum, which I was to write upon his chest in my own hand. I practiced my capital Q's until they rolled forth in intertwined, scrolling, signature perfection.

We never got around to scheduling that final session. But I at least have this for now: I wear a crown, bear a crown, made of the teeth of my beloved. I hope it will serve me well in this place, as I go forward in glorious subsistence as their freshly anointed bearer.

Love and twenty years' devotion, so fucking awesome. Even his smashed face and that last, wet gasp of his, as he lay there dying, cannot be separators, for *He. Is. Now. Inside. My. Head.*

So, when you peer into your mirror at midnight, I dare you to gaze past the reflection of your own face. Look over your shoulder, to where I and this jagged coronet of mine just might be standing there, smiling at you, from the very darkest of corners of your room – and your mind.

Efectus

THE MONSTRANCE & THE RELIC

The pious, the repentant and the morbidly curious were indiscernible from one another, given the uniformity of their postures and displays of genuflection: hands together, faces downcast, silent, somber. Here and there, furtive gazes swept up and back down, along the winding queue of postulates to assess who else was there, doing this thing.

All were there to look upon Her, perhaps also to pray to those for whom She interceded.

The young woman, a bookish twenty-something dressed in black, took two steps as the line slinked forward, also using that moment to steal a roundabout glance. The anonymous seekers to the front and back of her remained isolated, guarded by their postures of prayerful introversion, further shielded inside their cell-phone user bubbles. Shared hours at arm's length proximity on lovely garden paths of the chapel grounds on a beautiful day apparently meant nothing to any of them.

At this pace of quarter-hour intervals, Sara thought, it would be late afternoon by the time she would make it to the inner chambers, a non-issue, as there was now nowhere else for her to be. Yet another overnight power outage in her building had left her phone barely charged, and with her battery powered noise machine whirring but her vintage radio clock-alarm futilely, silently blinking, in need of a reset, Sara had overslept, again. As her ticket to the chapel was a timed 11:00 am entry, Sara had had no choice but to throw on yesterday's outfit and jump into her car and take off. Being a good two-hour drive to the foothills where the chapel was located, breakfast was a piece of dry bread as she drove. With her phone barely charged, it could not be used to pass time while in line, so her dog-eared copy of Matheson classics would have to suffice for entertainment. The day was definitely not showing any promise of anything good.

Despite clear instructions posted at the front door as to how long any pilgrim was to take in the presence of She Who Was, attendees tended to linger; so, prompts for quick exits ran largely ignored. Sara turned a page and took a few more steps. The loop of piped in music started up again with song number one for the second time that day. A faux boulder on the path emitted the opening strains of "You Light Up My Life." Sara winced, unable to fully tune out the static-edged, saccharin recording.

Tomorrow, Sara had vowed a full dive into a job hunt, but this latest search would have to wait until she had made this pilgrimage to ask for, pray for, some help. Her two previous jobs had ended in disaster, and with Sam now gone and this latest move downtown, no one was there, and little of anything else was left. Life for Sarah had been reduced to a series of days devoid of fun, meaning or substance. The notion of some kind of mystical outreach had suddenly made total sense to her. Sara, anonymous and alone in the bustling city, was merely subsisting. The history of the area was irrelevant to her, and the beauty of the harbor remained unnoticed. What Sara sought, Place could not provide. But bills had to be paid, and the deposit on the studio apartment had left her account dangerously depleted. So, a better, more solid job was a must. Perhaps, with some divine intervention, Sara might be able to turn a corner and stay the course.

When Sara had spied the words "Spirituality and Prayer" on the business card pinned to the board, and when she had further read of an "Innerly Step to Community" if blessed by a visitation with "She Who Was," who otherwise possessed no name, Sara took the chance discovery of the card as a sign.

Open 9 to 5, seven days a week! The card read.

Go to **www.shewhowas.com** *to reserve your slot.*

†††

The 1:00 visitation reservation, preceded by the late morning timed entry, was almost three hours passed by the time Sara finally made it around the last corner of what had seemed a ridiculously long hallway with a series of nonsensical turns. Ridiculous, yes, but no wonder the timed entries had been bookable only up through noon. Everything, everyone crawled in this place. Her last two steps, hours into her having passed through the chapel entry doors themselves, had brought her around one last corner, this time into a much shorter and wider hallway, which appeared to be an anteroom to the pilgrimage's end destination, a dark, inner sanctum lurking just behind a boudoir-invoking, curtained gateway. Beyond the heavily draped, arched doorway, Sara thought she could see a shimmering atmosphere within, most likely candlelight, real or faux, impossible to guess. A musty patchouli hung languidly in the hall, pushing against what was left of breathable air, causing Sarah's head to swim. The windowless vestibule had the residuality of an old attic, feeling more like a portal to some ball-gazing parlor of yore than an entry point to a website-driven, paid attraction.

Two electric sconces, unevenly installed to either side of the wide doorway, held bravely aloft their patches of yellow, which somehow managed to only accentuate the dark. What color the walls, what color the carpet – who knew? The effect was cheaply intoxicating. Be it bona fide worshipper or mere curiosity seeker, once passed through the chapel's many odd turns and infused with its oxygen thinned confines, all who had opted in were left not a little bit unwell and weakened.

That ill effect had long since been mis-interpreted, re-imagined and viralized as part of some mystical experience brought on by the emanations of She Who Was; She who remained, despite all the endless 24/7 billboarding of selves in the online world, oddly left out of the chatter, and of view. For all the anonymous buzz on the chapel, no recordings or photos of Her existed anywhere, even in the Dark Web, though pics of the chapel and its peculiar signage abounded in posts. Did the chapel's visitors heed the "no photos" rules, or was there something more to Her online visual absence? Did She possess some vampiric inability to be captured in a reflected image? Did the weird atmosphere of the place stymie the functionality of recording devices? Happily, for the venue and its anonymous proprietorship, the singular combination of notoriety and secrecy had served well to pay the bills for whomever managed the chapel, who was also assumed to be the caretaker of the Living Monstrance, as She was also known.

It was said, She did not consume food.
It was whispered, She never moved.
It was surmised, She did not sleep.

It was rumored, the Monstrance existed, ensconced in a decorated niche built just for her, that She floated in some sort of suspended animation, on the strength of her own spiritual energies alone, that She embodied some confluence of life and death incarnate, and that to spend time in her presence was as inflictive as was exposure to a radioactive substance.

But as no one ever seemed willing to openly share for which they had paid substantial amounts of coin, or why, vague conjecture was all that existed, beyond of course what little was available at Her official website, or on those business cards posted to random bulletin boards.

†††

Sara's stomach growled. A feeling of nausea was rising in her; the stagnant interior was stomach turning. Surely, it couldn't be long now. She stared at the back of the person in front of her, who was scrolling through something on their phone and swaying slightly, as if they held an infant in arms and were rocking it to sleep. Sara found herself mirroring the rhythmic shifting – it felt like the floor itself was see-sawing, reminding her of the teetering entrance chambers to fun houses. The person behind Sara stood with their back to her, as if they under no circumstances were going to allow for any contact with those in front of them. They had gone so far as to keep their hat and sunglasses on. Fine, Sara thought, she wasn't interested in them, either.

All of a sudden, a heavy-set fellow burst forth from the dark inner chamber, his head floating Oz-like against the curtained backdrop. Sara and the anonymous individuals who stood to the front of and behind her startled in unison, so adrift had they all become in their reveries. As the man spoke, his overgrown mustache bobbed in cadence with his words, his mouth remaining invisible. He reminded Sara of an automaton. She looked for hinges to either side of his cleft chin.

"Welcome, welcome, our dear faithful and subscribers! Welcome to your next path, where going forward you will walk hand in hand with Our Lady of No Name, She Who has no moniker but what your spiritual self and heart anoint her with, which will bind you to her for the remainder of your days, hereupon on this wonderful Earth we all so blessedly share!"

He continued, ushering the three forward with both hands as he scooped the air towards himself, as if he could draw them in on a breeze of his making. "Step right up, now, we are running behind, my friends, but of course, such is the lure of our Mother Without Name."

"You," he commanded to the first of the three, "Go on in. You can light one of the candles and have your time with Our Mother in there."

The supplicant, reeled in by invisible strings, was quickly absorbed into the twilight beyond the curtains, silken fingers of curtain fringe reaching low for a token grab at their shoulders as they passed through. The fringe fell limp as soon as the postulant entered the chamber, and a stillness took over once more. The large gent had also disappeared, about as abruptly as he had appeared. Which exit he had taken was also a mystery. The whole place was awash with a stilted, cabbala-esque vibe, and so it began to seem normal that people would appear and disappear, irrespective of logic or physics.

Aswim in the anomalous potpourri of musty air, dirty carpeting, and chemical refreshers, Sara, felt more ill by the minute. She cast a half-glance over her shoulder at the shadowed stranger behind her. The two finally acknowledged each other with shrugs in silent solidarity of a resigned *Whatever*. They had forked over hard-won coin for the pricey tickets and already spent the better part of a day in this place – one might as well stay with it, see it through, regardless what awaited.

After what could have been a minute or an hour, the mustachioed face materialized once more, this time from around the corner behind the two, to prompt whomever was next in line to yes, please, go ahead and enter in and welcome, and thank you so very much for your belief and support.

Evidently, the previous worshipper must have finished and departed – but how could they have? Where had they gone? No one had emerged from the curtained portal to brush past the two in the hallway. Sara had heard no door open or close. The tiny chapel's exterior, as she had seen it upon arrival, appeared to boast no alternate entry or exit points, so very small was the stone structure, so huddled was it against the rocky walls of the steep hillside into which it had been built. For sheer lack of anything rational to rectify any true structural anomaly, befuddled acceptance was the only option.

And so, amidst this ever-increasing dilution of reality, yet another casual, unanswerable oddity was revealed: How the long line of pilgrims who had bought tickets for that day was even able to file in, through the right-hand side of the double doors and out through the left-hand door, without ever encountering anyone else once inside. Aside from the split hall in the entry, the encroaching solitude defied all explanation. Outside, the long line of ticket holders had snaked its way along the path in an ordinary and organic fashion. A hint of sheepish withdrawal among the postulants, however, kept things distanced and quiet. Amidst this singular isolation, to feel conflicted and curious, crushed and hesitantly hopeful, became the dual mindset of nearly everyone who embarked on this visitation. It was for many a slightly fanciful, embarrassment-laced act of last resort.

Once inside, the halls wound in right, then in left turns, which in any real world would have individuals crossing paths at various points. But such was not the case. Sara had only ever seen a reduction of visitors at every turn of every hallway, which had been inexplicably pared down to the three of them in the foyer, then the two, with only the brief, bobbing apparition of the mustachioed face there to break the monotony as it directed the dwindling loners on to their evermore muddled states and enshrouded end goal, this dubiously anointed "She Who Was."

Sara was up next. The bobble-headed face looked directly at her for the first time and said, "C'mon young lady, with apologies for the huge delays, but there you go. You go on in now, please do and thank you."

The mustache retreated and disappeared.

Sara inhaled and pulled back her shoulders, willing her senses to perk up. She drew from her store of last-resort determination and took the few steps required to bring her abreast with the fringed curtain of the doorway. The corded fingers brushed teasingly against the epaulet of her jacket. Sara felt them drop off, admitting her in. Once through the curtains, the air felt instantly cooler, and the stale odors of the foyer gave way to the scent of hot bees' wax. On the far wall, candelabras bore dozens of tiny votives in various stages of burn-through. The array cast moving patches of light and shadow over the whole space. The room shivered.

Sara's eyes followed the wallpaper, a fretwork of floral striping working like ocular speed bumps, which led her gaze to a tall, arched niche, in which a dark form was barely discernable. It would take a minute for her eyes to adjust to the low light. This allowed for a visual slow-down, rather than a screeching halt, as was intended. The maze of hallways, the ever-darker spaces, the bad air, the curtains, the prolonged hush, were all designed to dull rapid-fire, twenty-first century, at-a-glance, high-tech scanning perspectives. To behold this thing, it, She, required an easing on.

Was this an intentional, compassion inspired softening of impact, or clever marketing, consumerist theater at its tawdry best?

All Sara knew at that point, as her pupils dilated and her brain sought to order the array she now beheld, was that this – it, She – was not what she had expected. What the heck had she expected?

No wonder no one talked, posted, or shared on this.

Sara sunk to her knees, awestruck, queasy, overwhelmed at what – Who – she saw.

†††

Upon an upholstered platform was perched, or hunkered down, a humanoid torso, devoid of arms and legs. The corpulent body was ensconced in a front-laced hourglass housing reminiscent of a corset, which had been fabricated from the same brocade as the curtains which hung at the doorway. The bodice was trimmed with a length of contrasting fabric, draped upwards and over the shoulders to form something that mimicked a portrait neckline, which was fastened at the left shoulder with a massive, stone-studded brooch. From the disembodied form and its fabric-draped clavicles rose the folds of a fleshy neck, upon which was situated a bullish head topped with a massive hive of tightly curled hair. The head sported a glittering diadem into which artificial, flowering vines had been intertwined. The wired vines spiraled riotously outwards and down, winding their way around and alongside the torso in a waterfall cascade of silken – plastic? – flowers, all the way to the pillowy platform of the dais, where they jumbled upon the cushion and obscured – somewhat – what rested upon it.

The face upon the torso was likewise bloated. Jowls hung like water balloons on either side, from which a small nose and puckered mouth barely surfaced. The lips had been painted in the shape of a heart, which appeared almost black in the dim light. The cheeks bore circular strokes of dark blush, with theatrical, clownish effect. Two eyes were set deep under fatty brows, which glimmered like polished onyx. A plump forehead ended where the tight, dark curls began of what had to be a period costume wig. Enormous earlobes sported earrings, big and ornate as regency light fixtures, which had long ago pulled the lobes long and flaccid.

The feminine apparition on its banquette was not what caused Sara to fall to her knees, or her eyes to well up. The armless, legless being on the altar was not what had spurred previous pilgrims to fall – and remain – dead silent up until the point of their leaving the space, the experience. This display was by design such a garish rendering of the overtly feminine as to be a caricature of a human woman in the extreme. It, she, "stood," garishly and opulently impervious to any emotional susceptibility, any sympathetic connectivity by way of its, her, embodying fully all inversions of anything remotely aesthetically palatable.

Was Sara's strike-down borne of shock, sympathy or just plain embarrassment over having been duped into serving as willing, paying witness to not a monstrance but a man-made side-show monstrosity? No. This, thing, this She, was physically, mechanically linked to something more grotesque and intricately fabricated than any faked mermaid or elephant trunked, tusk-bearing human sideshow attraction had ever been. What it, she, was connected to, what sustained it, Her, made a mockery of all the ordinary folk who would have believed themselves to be above "entertainment" of such a base and decrepit nature. The workaday itinerants, on their various, flawed, spiritual, mystical, or other-worldly assistance journeys, were already self-conscious enough about themselves and their predicaments. Whatever it was that might have led them to seek out something like this, what Sarah now gazed upon, had yet to exist in open acknowledged general acceptance.

It was not it, She, which shocked. It was the contraption to which it, She was connected that was the cheap scene, the accidentally clicked on video snippet, the erroneously opened web page that, once beheld, could not be unseen.

It was the industrial fretwork of life sustaining pipes and tubing to which the woman on the dais was connected to that snagged the senses and held her visitors in painful thrall: Tubes hanging down from the ceiling were affixed to either side of Her head, immediately behind the ears. A tube was inserted into the base of Her throat, bolted into place on the surface of a wide collar fabricated of some slightly reflective plastic. Two more tubes, which came up and out from the floor, arched around in front and came together over the sternum, where they were inserted into a plate-like device located at the center of the corset. Two pipes projected from either side of the base of the niche; these were connected to the being at Her abdomen. This was a steam punk visionary's Rube Goldberg contraption, a mechanized artificial life support system having been spliced onto the creative netherworld of a Frankensteinian freakdom.

Sara worked to stay upright, gather her composure, and collect her senses. As the buzzing in her head subsided, she noticed a sound:

Click, click, hiss.

The sound seemed to correspond with each repetition of the torso's chest lifting, and then falling, measured like the tick of a clockwork.

Click, click, hiss.

Once the tears that had involuntarily welled up in Sara's eyes were shed, she was able to see clearly again. Sara felt physical pain for the sorrow this being evoked. It, She, looked positively ancient; her skin, where it was not hooked up to connectors and tubing, resembled the rind of a massive, aged cheese. Sara in her empathic compulsion also grieved for her own sense of loss, for the compromised dignity that had driven her to think, to pay cash to invade the world of someone preternaturally, mechanically undead, a victim of a more grotesque exhibitionism than she could ever have imagined possible, was a sensible way to have spent both her time and her money.

Amidst her mortification, Sara fumbled for her phone. The authorities needed to be called and she needed to get the hell out of there. Sara looked at her phone. Dead as a doornail. Dammit.

At precisely the moment Sara thought to act on a quick exit, the monstrous redux on the dais in front of her croaked from its niche:

"Child, no, no. Child. C'mere girl."

Sara froze. She felt a wave of ice wash over her, fusing her to the floor.

"Child," it, She, repeated.

Sara, unable to muster a word, touched briefly her own sternum, under which her heart raced like a crazed timepiece.

"Girl," it, She, repeated, "You here to pray. Right? Let ush pray." The mouth barely moved, but the words were without question its, Hers.

"You can schtep a bit closher. We will pray togedder."

Another wordless *Whatever* crept into Sara's mind as the only suitable dismissal, the only way she could rationalize staying there in that room, with that thing, that woman, for another moment. Nothing made sense. She had never felt more gullible.

Sara stood up, slowly, agedly. When she finally found her voice, what came out had nothing to do with what she intended to say. What burst forth, unbidden, was:

"Jesus, God. I…I am so, so sorry. So…" Sara gasped, shocked at her utter lack of decorum.

"No, no," it, She, replied, shushing her.

Sara had a flashback, images of the Virgin of the Seven Sorrows she saw as a child. The beautiful, berobed woman in tears, the starburst array of swords impaling her, the carved edifice that seemed to soar three stories high on its altar. She hadn't wanted to look, but even as a frightened child was unable to take her eyes off the gruesome and venerated apparition. How fine that line between beauty and horror, how wavering the boundary of reverential fascination and repulsed fixation…

"No," it, She, said once more. "Let ush pray togedder."

Click, click, hiss.

"Your time will be over in a bit, den you gotta go."

Sara took two more steps, this time to bring herself in proximity to the being, She Who Was, where now from whose bloated countenance she could discern eyes that were indeed as bright and as alive as her own. Her eyes were also adjusting.

Sara put her hands together, open palms pressed together in a prayerful gesture. She had never, ever done this before. But in keeping with the prevalence of ill logic, this seemed like the natural thing to do.

Click, click, hiss, "Shay what I shay, young lady. Repeat after me."

It, She, began to recite:

"Our Fadder, our Modder, you who are…"

Sara echoed, "Our Fadd…Father, our Mother, you who are…"

Click, click, hiss, "Hallowed and beholden…"

"Hallowed and beholden…"

"To none…"

"To none…"

"To all…"

"To all…"

Click, click, hiss, "Deary, let me firsht shay de whole line."

"Deary…oh, I am so sorry! I mean, I apologize…"

Click, click, hiss, "No biggie. To none, to all…"

"To none, to all…"

"Dere you go.

Click, click, hiss, "We call to you, call forth your power…"

"We call to you, call forth your power…"

"To be in ush, of ush, to guide ush…"

"To be in us, of us, to guide us…"

Click, click, hiss, "Ash de dark ish made way, for de light to shine bright…"

"As the dark is made way, for the light to shine bright…"

"In our heart and in our mind…"

"In our heart and in our mind…"

Click, click, hiss, "Forever and for now, in schtep wit de univershe…"

"Forever and for now, in step with the universe…"

Click, click, hiss, "Much ash where de starsh are born…"

"Much as where the stars are born…"

"…ash what light ish dere to shine from our own eye."

"…as what light is there to shine from our own eye."

Click, click, hiss, "Peashe be wit you, my dear. My love will go wit you now."

Sara, fallen lockstep in with the cadence of the simple prayer, discerning the shift in its, Her, voice, knew they were cond. And, that the last line was hers to keep. She responded to the being's final admonishment, as if one who had prayed daily, all her life:

"And alsho…I mean, also…with you."

She Who Was blinked, her tiny eyes glinting. The waxen pucker curled into what might have been construed as a smile.

Click, click, hiss.

The fringe on the curtains began to shiver, heralding a ripple in the air. Sara felt, rather than heard, the disturbance and glanced behind her.

Women had begun to file through the doorway and into the room. Uniformly petite, they were simply groomed, their hair either pinned into topknots or hanging down their backs. The women wore dark, perhaps black, gowns, which swept the floor. The line of women split into two behind Sara. They slid noiselessly past her, around the room's perimeter, towards the dais. Sara watched, bewildered, as the women lined up on either side of the niche and came to a stop, as still as statues. What was going on in that rudimentary sanctum? Was the She Who Was doing this? Was the mustachioed man somehow behind this next display?

Sara remained stock still; her lack of flight or fight confounding her.

The newly arrived women kept their gazes on Sara. Though they flanked the niche, their attention was not directed towards the woman on the dais.

Sara counted; seven stood to either side of the niche. There were fourteen of them.

The women stood, hands clasped and erect of spine, possessed of a schooled and proper posture, but for one uniform anomaly, which was that of the sharp, left-leaning bend of every one of their slender necks. The swan-like turn of their necks was so extreme, it left their heads hanging at right angles to their bodies, heavy as doorstops, their delicate ears nearly pressing against their shoulders. The women's pale visages and starkly shadowed features remained affixed on Sara. Their sentience, perhaps possessed of formed thoughts, remained unreadable, but the projection in their collective energy was a wholly unapologetic baring of something, brought with great intent, into that space and that moment. Whatever it was, it was directed at Sara.

The candle flames danced even more erratically in the currents stirred up by the beings' arrival. With the votive guard putting forth its best, the flickering scene was more reminiscent of a phantasmagoric staging than a true, paranormal fracturing of reality, which left Sara more puzzled and curious than afraid, so acclimated had she already become to the weirdness of the day.

Within the confines of the chamber, the broken-necked women, the entity on Her dais and Sara, together made for a disparate feminine pastiche that was almost a cartoonish, like some crazy projection from a 19th century zoetrope. More aptly, Sara thought wryly, the stuff of a device once called a Devil's Wheel. The women were there with her, but from within what contexts or planes, states, or conditions of unrest, she could not know. There were no words. Perhaps there was no need for them. Perhaps this aberrant assembly was already imbued with all that had been said – and left unsaid – over the course of many hundreds of years, for which each of them, in their own way, had already paid.

The women lifted their arms in Sara's direction, as if reaching for her. In their open palms, upturned to face the ceiling, Sara saw dark pinpricks appear. The pinpricks gathered mass, swelling to pearl-sized droplets. The dark matter filled their hands and began to brim over, spilling, dripping slow and tar-like, to the floor. At their feet, the perverse stigmata formed puddles on the carpet, inky marks soon grown as big as saucers. The chamber floor was now dotted with obsidian pools of supernatural excrement, the centuries-old dregs of random accusations which had spawned a many tentacled death-grab, a piece of an unsanctified past, beholden to insidious deceptions. This was to show how quaint garden paths to Hell could be paved.

As one, the women opened their mouths, and like a choir, they began a tonal "O," which started in low, lifting in pitch and volume as She Who Was continued in her silent meditation, Her mouth forming vague phrases only She could know or hear. Her eyes were now closed, her draped bosom continuing to rise and fall with mechanical precision. She kept time, quite literally, with the hum of the offsides makeshift life support system to which she was effectively welded.

As She Who Was sat in silence, the women continued with their song. Would one rather call it a moan? It continued to build, creeping ever higher, note by note. Its frequency rose, causing Sara's ears to pop in protest.

Sara, startled, realizing the being on Her dais, appearing almost asleep, neither saw nor heard the others. Why were the women doing this? Was it some test, some trick designed to strike even more fear in the visitors who paid to pray with Her? Sara scanned the women, looking for some connection between them and Her, and found none. She Who Was remained lost in her sleepy reverie while the women kept raising their collective voice, who remained unmoving, their hands dripping preternatural ooze onto the floor. Sara, unable to pick up her feet, could only cover her ears. She knew this sound.

The monotone now sat at an unearthly register. With their mouths torn open as far as their jaws would permit, the women's voices crossed over from a note to a scream. The scream built on itself, becoming more shrill, higher, dryer. Parched chords were uttering their spastic last, making the sort of animalistic, fatal cries when by the teeth of beasts, life and limb were torn apart from each other. Tears welled in Sara's eyes, tears of helplessness, tears of pain. The brain-wrenching sound perforated her soul, filled the antechamber.

And just at the point where Sara thought she would pass out, overwhelmed in this intimate theater of sonic pain and entrapment, the women fell silent. Their unblinking gaze remained on Sarah, and Sarah knew, intuitively, in their silent standstill, they were waiting for something from her. For what? A response, an answer, a step towards them? These women had given a face to that which had followed, haunted, Sarah for years, something she had struggled against most of her life. It was that sound, the sound, the unrelenting sound, that lived in her ears, filled her head. Sarah wondered anew, as she sometimes did when sleep evaded her, if the incessant drone was not in actuality *of* her, but *for* her, something received by her rather than generated by her. Bizarre as this was, the notion gave her hope. There was something revelational in this encounter, Sara knew. But why and to what end would she have been thusly targeted?

Sarah's rapidly developing inward reflections were suddenly interrupted by the re-appearance of the mustache and its accompanying face, which poked its head around the curtained door and barked, as it had done all day:

"Young lady! Come on now, your time with Our Dear One is over. We've got a few supplicants left to go before the chapel closes for the day, and we are running late. But is it not a gift, to pray with Our Most Dear One? Now, come on, follow me, kid!" He held back the drapes, his tone messaging emphasis, his broad hand beckoning urgency, his face registering only a perfunctory business-as-usualness.

Sara started. She fell backwards as her feet suddenly regained their ability to lift, find new placement.

"Sir…!" Sarah cried out. She turned to look back into the room, at the women, to point at them, to ask, to accuse, but the room was empty. The antechamber was empty but for herself and She Who Was, who now appeared to have fallen asleep.

Session over?

Only the click, click and the hiss remained, as did the faint rise and fall of Her chest. The carpet was once more a plush field of faint stains and tread marks, the candleflames were still.

What switch had been pulled?

"Sir…" Sara began again.

"Come now, missy, time's up," was all he said.

Had he not seen the women? Was this whole thing some kind of show within a show? What kind of game were they playing with her, and did they do this to everyone who came to this crazy place?

Sara stepped through the doorway, her nerves frayed, sick to her stomach. She reeled with questions, but once back in the small foyer, any chance to insist or inquire on anything was stymied, yet again.

Wait.

Was she the same foyer as before? The ticket holder who had stood in line behind her was nowhere to be seen. There were no other worshippers in sight. Sara was long beyond looking for any semblance of sense or logic, so whittled away was any foundation of familiarity, of normalcy. She didn't care. She turned to speak to the old man, but as he was wont to do, he had disappeared again, as well.

Sara had no choice but to retrace her steps, see her way out. After several odd turns, she found herself back at the entry, which was now devoid of human activity. Sara peered out the sidelights of the entry door. In the distance, she could see traces of dust from departing vehicles still hanging over the gravel road, glinting like a trailing fog in the fractured light of the low sun. How late was it? Sara made her way to her own car, feeling dejected, confused.

✝✝✝

Barely a mile down the road, the right rear tire blew. Tread-worn and unable to withstand the sharp edges of the cheap rubble, the tire burst with a jolt, sending the car into a deep rut at the side of the road. Darn it, of all places; the car would need to be towed. Honestly, Sara thought, how better to wrap up a bizarre day than with a cliché-level road incident? She grabbed for her phone, and while it was now plugged into its charger, a quick glance showed the signal to be so poor as to be useless. Well, damn. Sara groaned; she had no choice but to walk back to the chapel to ask for help. Surely, there would be a phone she could use. The beautiful weather, the balmy dusk worked in her favor, lending a welcome disconnect to the incidents of the day, providing some welcome, late day illumination to guide her back. Sara left her bag and book in the car and began the walk back to the chapel. Her keys she held tight in her fist, at the ready, just in case. Off in the distance, some sort of bird called, or cawed, repeatedly.

†††

When Sara arrived at the chapel doors, the sun had just set, casting all in soft shadow. No exterior lights were lit, no window glowed with any hint of life or welcome. A cardboard square, black with red lettering, had been wedged into the corner of one of the entry door sidelights. It read, "Sorry, We're Closed."

Having no choice, Sara lifted the cast iron knocker on the door and let it fall hard, three times. The strikes sent echoes ringing into the distance, startling the birds to momentary silence. Sara waited a full minute, then rapped at the door again. She heard the echo, heard the answering quiet. No one came.

Having no choice, Sara tried the door. The rusted latch gave reluctantly. The door was unlocked. She entered the chapel for the second time that day.

The wall mounted font was, as before, on the right. The ticket scanner still sat on the table next to it. Sara dipped her fingers into the ostensibly blessed water to wash the rust off her fingertips. Out of habit, she smelled her wet fingertips. She frowned, disappointed. Same as before. Always fresh asphalt. Disgusting. Whatever. Sara wiped her fingers dry on her jeans and proceeded down the hall.

The vestibule offered three doorways, one to the left, one to the right and one straight ahead. Sara, remembering at least this much from her visit earlier in the day, turned left. From that point on, the path of the hallway offered no options. Sara turned left again, then right. Every subsequent hall appeared shorter than the one before. Right and left turns began to feel illogical, same as before. Thankfully, before long, Sara was certain she could make out a sound, somehow familiar to her, coming from deep within the building. She had no choice but to follow the noise to its source. Someone was there, had to be. And if that someone turned out to be that odd, mustachioed fellow, she would ask him for help. She had no choice.

Sara walked for longer than anyone would have expected to walk, given the small size of the chapel building, but like her pilgrimage of that afternoon, she already had developed the capacity to trust in the illogical.

An odd noise presented itself, grew louder. The sound was in crass opposition to the contemplative drone of the day, even more starkly not original to the building. It was broadcast audio, crude and cacophonous. Canned laughter and applause intermingled with the shouting of several voices.

Sara was no longer surprised when she found herself once again in the small foyer.

The curtained, arched doorway to the inner chamber loomed, appearing just as it had before, but the sconces were no longer lit. Instead, a different illumination now came from within, a bright, blueish glow. Sara recognized the sound. It was the blare of a television. Cheers and hoots of some proverbial studio audience broke out and was joined by the loud chortles of a man and the raspy coughs of a woman.

Sara drew breath once more and entered, bracing herself for that second first view of the heart-breaking monstrosity that was She, the Living Monstrance.

But this was after hours.

Seated in a chair in the center of the room, immediately to the front and side of the dais, Sara saw the mustachioed gent. Before him stood a wooden tv tray, upon which a massive aluminum foil pan had been placed. Yes, She of the visitation was still there, situated immediately behind the man, perched on her cushion, in grotesque connectivity at one with the pipes and tubes that projected from her head, neck, chest and abdomen. But what Sara now saw was the two of them, chuckling together over whatever it was they had just seen on an old television, which had been rolled into place directly in front of them. Sara then watched as the man, still smiling, scooped up a heaping spoonful of some baked substance from the foil pan. The food, steamy and trailing strings of melted cheese, he guided up and inserted through the unpainted lips of the Monstrance, Who eagerly held open Her mouth as wide as was possible, which was not very wide at all, in order to receive this next bite of food. It was a messy process, but with a tender patience, the man wiped clean the mouth of the girl he had fallen in love with some four decades ago, the damaged hull to which he had committed, for better and then for worse, much worse, for at least half that.

These were two people having their evening meal together.

The couple finally realized they were no longer alone.

The Monstrance and the Relic froze, their eyes wide with shock. Shades of affront colored their expressions. How dare anyone interrupt their nightly repast at the altar of American sitcom worship? Tonight being Tuesday, it was one of their old favorites, "All In the Family," that was being so rudely disrupted. Who dared do this?

The old man clicked the remote to mute, but it was She Who first spoke:

"What de fuck you doing here, girl?"

Sara sputtered, lost for words. What she had just beheld in this room was such a re-inversion of what she thought she had witnessed just a few hours ago — everything hurled upside down was now being turned inside out. It sent her senses careening, made her want to run somewhere, anywhere. Confusion was confused. Insanity beckoned with luminous lucidity.

She Who Was croaked again, "What de fuck you doing here?"

"I...I..." Sara began.

"Look, young lady," he cut in. "You gotta speak up. I got a gun under my chair, so I got nothing to worry about. But you better state your business."

"I...I'm so sorry," Sara stuttered. "I...I...my car, I got flat...I mean, my tire got a flat. My car is stu...stuck in a ditch and it's nothing I can change...I mean, I don't know how to change tires...but um...I need to get towed. It towed. I need to call for a tow. Plea..."

Click, click, hiss.

"Well, kid, you gotta phone don't you? Why you creepin' in here like dish? She hissed, with the aid of her heavy metal lungs.

"Yes, I do...I mean, I don't... My phone died, and when I was in the car, I had no signal, so either way, I wasn't able to call. I was wondering..."

"You need to use a phone, is that it?" he insisted.

"Yes!" Sara cried, relieved to have made it to the one salient point this most surreal intrusion had demanded.

Calmed, to his wife, the man spoke, "It's ok, dear. I can take her down to the office. She can use the phone there."

To Sara, he asked, "You otherwise okay?"

"Yes, I'm fine," Sara lied.

"You okay with all this?" he gestured to the room in general. Sara knew what he meant.

"Yes, I'm okay with it..."

Click, click, hiss.

"You feeling like you gonna be able to wait for de tow truck, girl?" She Who Was asked. "It gonna take a while. We not in de big shitty, you know."

"I know, I know, um, ma'am," Sara stuttered.

†††

A tow truck was ordered and due to arrive within the hour. Sara had followed the mustache back to the inner chamber, where it was her intent to feign some semblance of normalized civility by bidding the two a good evening. She would then get the fuck out of there and wait outside. It was a pleasant, late summer's evening anyway, and outside was not inside, in there, with them.

Sara crafted as polite a good-bye as she could muster, to which the couple responded, quickly and impatiently. They were dying to get back to their show.

Before she exited, Sara turned back to the Monstrance.

"I wanted to ask."

Click, click, hiss.

"Yesh?"

"About the others."

"Who?"

"The others in the room. Who appeared next you."

"What de fuck you talkin' about, girl?" She Who Was asked, suspicion lowering her voice.

"What are you talking about, kid?" Her husband echoed.

Sara thought it would be a good tactic, to feign a casual inquisitiveness, to try and diminish any defensiveness, and keep any more portals of the absurd and macabre at bay. She was already in the presence of the extreme.

"The others, the women who stood all around us, on either side of you. Were they projections? They looked so real...so, so dimensional. They sounded so...so...I wanted to commend you. The effect was awesome. Pretty darn spooky."

Click, click, hiss.

"Girl, I have no idea what de fuck you talkin' about. Dere wash no one in de room. It wash only me and you."

"But...but, I saw them. I heard them! These other women! They came into the room right after we prayed. They just stood there, singing, or whatever you want to call it. And they were there when I left, but then they...."

"What? That makes no sense. We weren't projecting nothing. It's just my wife in there, same as ever." The mustachioed man's tone grew lower and more defensive with every word. "What are you trying to pull here?"

The Monstrance actually growled.

Click, click, hiss.

"That doesn't make any..." Sara paused. "It's ok. Forget about it."

There was no point.

She hadn't seen them and He had no clue. Whatever had happened, had occurred for Sara and Sara alone.

Just go, Sarah told herself. Get the hell out and get back to real life. Every second in the presence of these two only sought to crack wider some fault line in a hard scrabble, desperately desired sanity. If this was some kind of new awareness, Sara was not yet ready to face, decipher or be a part of it. To understand would be to begin to assimilate, and Sara did not like the prospects any of this hinted at. She felt stupid enough already, to have so willingly wallowed in whatever it was these two charlatans had cooked up.

"I'm sorry. I...I gotta go. Your...this is all safe with me. Godspeed to you both," Sara added, puzzled where the heck that off-hand and dated blessing came from.

Before either of the sideshow reverends, the mad medical-engineer or his wife, the old bitch who had become his life's work, could make any closing admonishments, the girl disappeared.

†††

"Well, my *Taubchen,* that was weird. What an odd bird that one was, eh?" He said, grabbing the remote and taking aim.

Click, click, hiss.

"Kidsh today," She gurgled in response. "You sho funny, you ode modderfokker. Here, you got how many degreesh, and you can't even remember to lock de damn door?"

†††

Sara at long last, arrived at the chapel entrance. She grabbed the handle of the front door. Two more steps and she would be outside. Two more steps and the real world would be there, ready to absorb her back into its welcoming ordinariness. She would exit the chapel and leave whatever the fuck it was in there behind her; and dammit, once out, she would stay there. This visitation had more than done its work. It had transformed prospects of the mundane into the most wonderful of promised lands. It had externalized – could she say exorcized? – pesky inner demons, from which there might now be some surviving.

Sara threw the door open wide. The trees, the grass, the gravel road beckoned. Two more steps, and a few minutes' walk from there, and she'd be in her car and done with this freakishly aberrant place and whatever it was she had been forced to witness.

Sara stopped.

No. *No.*

There it was. Again. That sound. Little more than a hum carried on the breeze. That note. It bent itself, tracing the hillside, sifting through the evergreens, the oaks, and the maples that surrounded her, the chapel, the grounds. The sound – that sound, unstoppable, relentless, insistent – it dove like a small bird of prey, back into the fields of Sara's consciousness, there to resume its resonant burrowing into the crevices of her unyielding, and oh, so weary mind.

That note, what she had grown up assuming was an audial glitch; that sound, for which her hearing had been tested more times than she could count; that noise, which followed her every waking moment, was a torment she had learned to bear. It had remained too much a part of her for too long. It was her silent cross, immensely heavy, but invisible. There had been talk of Meniere's disease, hearing loss, tinnitus and more. That note, which Sarah had always envisioned as some flying insect, digging into her cranium. The evasive thing she had come to accept, as something she would simply have to live with. The sound that would lay with her in bed when she couldn't sleep. And she could never sleep.

Now she knew its source.

It wasn't *her*.

Realization of something else pulled Sara's attention back to the stoop, where she still stood, and to her right hand, which was still held fast to door's handle.

What the hell?

Sticky.

Sara let go of the grip and looked at her palm. It was coated in thick, black goo.

Efectus

*Be sure to visit **http://www.shewhowas.com**
to book your appointment today!*

THE COPPE SNIPPEN

MEMORANDUM

TO: Brythwhyte Board of Trustees

FROM: C. Bunting

DATE: 10 February 2021

RE: Granthe Endowment Progress Report & New Findings

Confidential, press release pending

Esteemed Board:

I am honored to provide with you this report, which includes the first shared transcription of a first-person re-telling of the legend of the Coppe-Snippen, a lesser-known, mythical woodland monster, possessing the head of a man and the body of a furred spider [*Webb's Monstre & Mythos, 1879, p.126*].

This transcription was gleaned from a recently discovered, hand-written pamphlet, excised from beneath the back cover binding leathers of Volume IV of the Tomes of the Brythwhyte Elders, a set of books which had existed, undisturbed and presumed lost until late last year, on the shelves of the hidden library at the Closterium Atticus.

The text's discovery will prove notable for its contribution to Ersachian folk history, and for its significance as linguistic anthropological evidence, as the only known written record of the as-yet unnamed turn-speak of the colonists who settled and maintained the isolated Village Community known as Bløch-Hachen, located in the valley at the eastern end of the Follendet Mountain Range.

Additionally, there is the matter of companion discoveries at the archeological dig near Bløch-Hachen, located approximately one-half kilometer north of the Village center, which warrants disclosure at this time.

At the center of the archeological site lies the so-called Tri-Corneal Mound, whose naming will in due time be changed and accordingly promoted so to better reflect the other, more positive, and commercially viable aspects of the area and its history. It has been popularly surmised, the geometrically shaped, carved oculi of the modern-day Jack-o-Lantern do, in fact, find their very first origins in the traditions of this extinct society; not, as has long and commonly been held, as a legacy of the Irish and later the English, who appropriated the iconography and practices as their own contributions to Halloween/All Hallows Eve/All Saint's Eve traditions and motifs, which in and of itself holds tremendous, potential significance as cultural historical re-write.

The direct correlation of the Ersachsian archeological link to the origins and histories of specifically the cranial detail in question, long universally recognized as the stylized facial features of Jack-o-Lanterns the world over, is what we 1) seek to re-brand and maximize from a pop cultural standpoint and 2) need to further research as to actual origins from an anthropological standpoint. To the one end, the PR firm of Yang, Schminck & Michelsen has been retained to spearhead the promotion of the Tri-Corneal Mounds, set to launch early next year. The goal will be to separate celebratory iconographical connectivity from the potentially macabre nature of its originating manifestations, in context of the Ersachs and their alleged practices, the latter being the focus of the studies for which funding is now being sought.

Kindly note, what follows must be treated as classified information, as the theories drawing on facts gathered to date are at present conjecture and unverified:

What was until now presumed a mass grave for the Village at the site of the Tri-Corneal Dig, has now been confirmed to be a vast subterranean holding facility, containing the skeletons of over seven hundred and fifty humanoid beings, both children and adults. Of question, is the uniformity of the gruesome means by which their skulls were geometrically gouged out just above their eye sockets, near their cranial crests. At team of forensic scientists from the University of Granthe Medical Center and a group of scholars from the Granthe School of Anthropology have been assembled to conduct further excavations, to scientifically test all findings, and to formulate interpretations and theories which will satisfactorily correlate all findings into a congruent history of the lost community of Bløch-

Hachen. It is our hope, the joint committees will be in a position to present their findings sometime late next year.

Growing consensus on what to date has been called a mass grave, is that it did not serve as a conventional burial site, but rather as a ritual repository for some type of transitional undead containment, or confinement, as was chronicled in the Tales of Ancients, which date to the Late Ersachian era. The case for archeological re-classification is further evidenced by the so-called grave's wall construction and in particular the mysterious scratch marks that cover its surfaces, some of which have recently been identified as cyphers, as well as the unconventional design of the barricaded entry (or exit?) portal of the burial chamber.

One additional theory has been put forward, and will be duly researched, addressing the possible existence of the practice of trepanation amongst members of the Bløch-Hachen community, whether done voluntarily – as religious ritual, enlightenment pursuit, status elevator, or membership initiation – or as a form of punishment, carried out with the intent to force upon its victims a painful penance, and to foment control over them via personality transformation (i.e. increased compatibility and/or compliance) if the procedure was survived. It is possible, the legend of the Coppe-Snippen may have been created and perpetuated by citizens of Bløch-Hachen in order to familiarize younger members of their community with the practice, whether as a rite of passage to be eventually faced, or as a warning, to maintain continuity and control over its future citizens.

One panel expert, who at this point shall remain nameless, has gone so far as to suggest trepanation may have produced extreme (and questionable) results among Bløch-Hachen practitioners, namely, a re-animated, post-mortem sentience within its recipients, leading to the necessity of construction of a clandestine containment facility. It is equally possible, extensive practice of trepanation may have been the root cause for the community's ultimate demise, being that primitive, non-sterile medical practices and post-procedural wound care could just as easily have killed off its recipients via infection. A less unpopular, but unfortunately likely post-procedural result, could have been the genocide of Bløch-Hachen's citizens at the hands of their undead, trepanated counterparts. More to come on all of this.

In short, it will be explored, if indeed the carved out the Jack-o-lantern faces as the world knows them today were originally intended to represent the heads, or perhaps fleshless skulls, of trepanated human victims, be they living, dead, or as it were, members of the undead.

All this brings us to the following introduction to the tale of the Coppe-Snippen, which precedes the first-person narrative copied directly from the recently discovered pamphlet at the Closterium Atticus. The introduction is notable in and of itself for its singular phrasing, which possibly suggests descendancy from, or familiarity with, the much older turn-speak of the narrative itself. The author of the introduction, currently unknown and referred to only as the "Anonymous Snippen Scholar," will also be researched separately as to his/her time, place, and origins, pending adjunct funding approval by the University Board of Trustees.

The following transcription is verbatim.

†††

13. Novembre, (?) '47

When the lush fruit of the fields are fresh severed from their twining umbilicant vines, the telling of the Coppe-Snippen must begin again, for, as he had nigh five hundred years hence, he would, thereupon harvesting called, descend from his own sticky coppe-web for to make his rounds, to carve from the melon-scented, ivory-skinned pumpkins best beknownst to yon region, his gawk-smiled, wink-eyed and hook-snooted faces, which, once lit, would set the slumberous village a-glow in candle-lit, Jack-obian communion – but most ever more important, against yon darker deeding other'n, those forest Monstrum, sentientless, ever-ravenous, nether-dwelling creatures of the darkest forest continuum hearkening from longest ageing pasts. These fear breeding lowlies slinkest about, so beneath the Snippen himself in both genus and indeed bereft of their'n drool control, they lurk one and all 'neath ageling trees wide as prayer naves, where no light touch the firmament, where no life but primeval grubbage dost sluggedly subsist, only for to dine fatted pon those villagers they selves.

Children adored this telling, but the oh, so necessary tale-telling delivery served likewise to instruct and instill respectful fear inklings in their recepting but rebellious natures, so they'n not fall victim to the one odiousness the Coppe-Snippen afforded any living being who might dare peer out from within, upon his hideously arachnidial self, he who was shamed to the point of yes killing plumb off any living being who dare venture to behold him, whilst he plied his carving, snippen craft...

Centuries now, the village has homed its inhabitants, far from whence their ancestors took kith and kin in a long-a'gone era of persecutorial strife which mandated stealthy exit, bags lugged and beast laden. Cutaway from the world as time croached forward, where moments and minutes quickestly made for ages and eons, a dialectical turn-speakage grown of its own poetic accord, into a hidden village-founded language only those few thousand who resided deep otherwhere employed, built upon, and tapped as the Village's single-own.

Comes now an elder, having rounded together his young dearest by the crackling warmth of a kitchen hearth fire, for to tell them this:

Draw nigh, dear ye chillen, and heyr me tell, heed me warnen, lest the Coppe-Snippen for sure be a-coming for ye, nigh the seasones turn is accomplished! Listen wit care, for when yon pompions be set pon the stoop to be snip snip snip ye *must* stay a-bed eyes tihtest close neath thy'n covers!

When the mamman and the pappan a-tuck ye all into thy'n bedded cubbies midst darkefall of nacht, maeke ye noted, ye cannot stir from safe confines of yon solid walled safest slaeping roums! For our slaeping roums they'n dost not bear fenestrat'd glass faces, lest anyman o'ye in chancing unitended a-waken to finding self peering pon the leggedy Coppe-Snippen, lest yon Snippen hisself be seeking *thee*!

Spaek on these words longsides me now: Ye cannot peer pon the Coppe-Snippen no matter how curiouser ye might-tiny ones be!

For, to be alit wit yon feuer from thy kitchen hearth be to stand proud and living apart'd from the spirited fools' feuer pon their'n front doorstep. Yon snipp't pompions a-keep all manner Monsturm and myriad beasties at baleful sorrowing bay, for to eat *ye* tasty lil ones be they'n one most desirous deed! The Jack snipp't of yon pompion by the Snippen's good work be standing stolid and stoic to guard our'n selves past sun-fall, when inkest nachts tally and mitternacht sounds pon the clocks in yon halls.

Our grinningest Jacks dost light chasing maeke gone yon puddling-darke traces, othersides dost lend darkest paths to the truest of beasties, aye, most hateful whence held by yon Coppe-Snippen hisself, for they dost yearn swallow him up as welle but could they grab some liken'd chance!

In shushing lull the Coppe creeping dost maeke his travel amidst our hovels, in shushing lull he maeke his craft, in shushing lull we vow to keep our'n selves at slumbering bay and out of his solitary way. Tis but understandment made of hardest lessons pass't o'er the ages. He gettin the darke hour; we gettin the day.

The Coppe-Snippen, when we be a-snooze one and all, from his coppe-web he crawls, aloft pon his four crickling spik'd legs, soon as last light withers from last branches and eaves. The mamman and the pappan tuck their'n cherubs a-bed wit beseeches to big Vaters and deep-down Mutters (for both be heaven and earth warrantin they'n glories), and clasping locks o' the hovels tight afore they alike set their'n selves a-bed. But, me-oh, so eager the Coppe-Snippen he crawleth and scampering come full darke from yon clib'rous web, at full tilt our'n homey village, for to snip snip snip whiche'er pompions await his four-palmy cuttery: Blade and cleaver, hatchet and trowel, all gruesomely a-sprout'd from the very bones of his black furr'd coat and hing'd wrists! To snip snip his nacht a'way tis the singlemost thing for which be he a-live!

Poor Coppe-Snippen, some big hearters here in the village do say, all year-long he dost feed solo pon mealy worm-critters and teensy coppeweb spinners. Peh, peh being they! No how such'n this maeke for tasting morsels, so glory be yum-yum the triangle'd bytes of the sweet pompions he snips. For us they'n be our'n salvation; for him be they be his bonbons, his solo renumerant.

But sad be he and bashful, for vain useless seek he his own'd vanity, poor homely Monstrum he in the end likewisen'd be. For the Coppe-Snippen be a quick wit'd as a talent-fill'd sort, in spite his oh, so gruesom'd self, squeamish any mann else maekes. Sad, indeedy, be he, that no other e'er may never look pon his lanky, black-spike-limby self. Hence, his middling hour darke rounds bout the village whilst we be a-snooze be the way twas e'er then done, e'er twill be.

Many oh so a many ago, the ancient olds build yon village long-stretches afar from the burn-firing city for to build a life for they'n selves and all lil ones a-come afore and aft. Hundred pon hundred they dost labor, stir-legg'd play and wily build and craft hovel and garden, our'n paths linking stoop to stoop, door to door most intention'd. But deep oh so far-in we be in wood'd thicket best settl'd we must a-light each home gainst the midnachting beasties. And who but the Coppe-Snippen lurkest off-side unseen, who we desirest most, who carve snip snip snip the pompions a-grown in our'n turn'd earthly patches, all lovely orb full harvest, with yon tri-angl'd eyes, nose and teethy-splay'd wide smiling! Next ways, with candles we plant in their'n innards to hold post strong 'gainst whence nachtmarish fog come misting and a-crossin, to bright shine and keep bay all manner of Monstrum that otherwise seek to fill gullet and gill with our'n tenderest babes done snatch'd straight out o' yon beds!

We hold thankful the Coppe-Snippen for his crawling stops nigh pon each pompion fresh-set stoop. But ye must heed above more'n all to no no never e'er put ye curiouser eyes pon fenester'd to yon Snippen hisself, for what dost the Coppe-Snippen wrought pon yonder curiousing fool? If he see ye, he a-comin for to carve out fresh a pair o' triangle eyes in thy'n lil heads!

Oh, ye gasp and ye giggle, ye bombastious chillen! Mind me warning. If these small telling snippets dost not do thy'n fear good treatment, then a-telling now I will give, of two sorry souls, lost-gone to tragic mourning do:

There liv'd in yon cottage pon farthest corner of our'n very village a pair, an eldering boot-stitchen cobbler and his rug weaving goodwyfe, who crafting their craft with overmuch begrudgement, such were they'n no smile day lives. No peaceable life was they'n lot, but done e'ermuch shout they'n at nacht done did, over soup and ale, indeedy long times shar'd with much ugly, oh so much ugly. The cobbler, no patience keepage he, chill heart'd was he 'gainst the goodwyfe. Slug a-bed he, for solo crash down and rip ripe snorage he maeke til roof shingles gone shimmy with shakin all the gone day. All a-snooze his be, not a one thing of other, dost muchly anger'd the wyfe til was no more. She made for to stitch thread words into her'n rugs, to be stepp'd pon like curses. Anger flowage twix'd such as they – dost ne'er serve welle pon any home hearth, ye chillen, do heed me on this. His name, she done spelt in the weave. Her hate, she wove in the weft.

It came to be pon an eve whence new pompion be splay'd pon yon stoop of the cobbler and his wyfe, for to be a-snipp'd by the Coppe-Snippen for their own guardship of yon deep tree-hiding, flesh-gobblin Monstrum. Anger whirl'd, and she who now I call yon un-goodwyfe mapp'd a ruse, for instead to leave no pompion but other not a one than her *own* cobbler for to serve up as villagemann Monstrum fodder. All she mus'd need taken occur, was she stir up the cobbler from his snoozement and send him out whence his sleepy self ne'er suspecting, for *his* waterin eye to fall pon the fractil'd gazers of the Coppe-Snippen, whereupon *he* be a-taken out and snip-snip made quick work pon his peering eyes midst snippen blading done.

Not fathom the plenish'd ale of the cobbler's mugs, did yon goodwyfe, eh? No indeedy! For yon cobbler to be rous'd was failed over and again, so there come a moment whence the un-goodwyfe did his collar yank withe mighty might so to squash his homely face to fenestrate as the Coppe-Snippen did squat pon yon stoop for to snip snip snip their own fatted pompions. But oh, no, twas not the cobbler who wink'd open his eyes – was the scheming un-goodwyfe who might chanc'd a lookout as she cruel yank'd pon his sleeve...

...twas *she* who of a sudden eye lock'd with the Coppe-Snippen hisself!

Welle I can say, twas not he but she who ghost'd thinly midst a "Puff!" and was un-appear'd for alle e'ers after that. And yon cobbler, he woken next day grogg'd to surest mass, grovel'd midst grief and rage and aches twixt his ears a-grown e'er worse. Twas but smallish some month after, a-fore he upp'd and was plumb dead'd hisself, soul-fled, and to e'er-lasting bed warn't tuck'd neath yon own mulching blanket of none but his own pompion field to rot, much as his old pompions done do.

So, chillen mind ye, heed me warn when it go lil bump in the nacht, for that be the blind'd triangle eyed young uns the Coppe-Snippen did ensnare withe a glance and a grab and a snip snip snip. Yon poorly ones, they small in the wooded glens, like rodents do bob sightless about, teary bled cheeks a-colour'd withe streak, to where thickest tree edge dost meet withe first small grass path and patch then lead to yon stoops whereon they were a-stolen, only lost gone to be by'n the Snippen blades, their marbl'd gaze-maekers and finders done plop chew'd nigh up in yon Coppe mawl. Now, they crawl bout come darke nacht and see no not a thing where they small foot'd might tread – and hence they'n a-bump bump bump into our cottage walls, our'n shrubbage, our'n gates. They forehead blunt knocking, come calling these small beasties do sound in the nacht middlin hours, for tis only that bump telling their'n poorly blind noggins, "Turn, turn! Try this a-way!"

But when it go big BOOM in the nacht? That be the likes of yon triangle eye'd old carcass of the un-goodewyfe! She foolment'd, who badly a-tempt the Coppe-Snippen withe the lazy bumm of her un-love'd mister soak'd of rotted ale in gut of brain. The Coppe-Snippen sought not the slumbering loaf of a man but the malice kempt keeper of yon cottage loom, who sow'd vengeful plan pon the one she were'n one time ago promis'd. Snip snip snip did the deftly hand'd Coppe-Snippen maeke quickest work of the un-goodewyfe eyes and mush drawn innards of her skull, left her muchly bereft withe same but a nigh pair-o deep-carved triangle eyes, and her'n small brain plum scooped out!

Now it be SHE who trods heavy of clumsy – oh less grace could not be a-found! For she walk smash blank into our'n walls and gainst our'n doors like a kettlin drum. And once boom'd, like yon triangle eye'd urchins, she turn dumbly and clod on over to otherin cottage nearby, alle to boom boom boom pon next wall up, shaking weary fearing souls from their fleet guarding slumber! Not a pretty sight no indeedy, withe her own jowls a-streak and her own limpid lobes a-pour withe the blood and the matter spillage in great forth.

So the learning ye must maeke of this be, whether ye heyring small "Bump" or biggish "Boom" in the deepest your'n snooze-darke, stay ye a-bed! And if ye pompion be plac'd pon front stoop for to have yon snip snip snip deeding of the Coppe-Snippen, be a-warn'd, let yon Snippen peace-keep a-work, for in his crafting he maeke a-keep us to least no sweet morsel for yon differing, much worst beastlier beans.

Lest the triangle eye'd spooking wanders not fear ye up plenty, know the deeper famishing Monstrum will gettin ye next!

Ended Be This

*Visit **http://www.butterflybroth.com** & select "Coppe Snippen" to view an image of **Webb's Monstre & Mythos**, which, unfortunately, is long out of print and quite impossible to find. The publisher's copy is for illustrative purposes only & not for sale.*

INDULGENCES

Who needs candy, I muse, when I have this in hand?

Cream vellum, thermograph print, a perfectly selected font – I believe it's a newer Chancery – a single, thick square ensconced in its envelope, a crimson wax seal imprinted with some heraldic motif to secure it.

The shield, so detailed; I study the iconography, appreciating its delicate imagery: On the bottom left corner, it looks like a dagger. Opposite that, there is a knotted length of rope; no doubt the type of knot has a very specific meaning. Top right, is a flower motif – appears to be a lily – and opposite that, I see the classic crescent of a sickle moon. Quite lovely. It looks expensive, as it should.

It did cost me and arm and a leg to net one of these invites. What no one knows, is how many are ever issued in a given year, nor how anyone is vetted and then selected for either participation or presentation. Who knows what the cost for the price?

I dress in my best – well, only – suit, a black pinstripe. I've paired it with a white shirt and a black tie. The black ribbon that came with the invitation is pinned to my left shoulder, as the instructions directed. Do I choose a loafer or a sneaker? I have no dress shoes.

Per items four and five, I gave notice at work several weeks ago, providing un-asked for details on upcoming vacation plans to colleagues who couldn't care less where I was going. No one will be left wondering or worrying where exactly I've gone, or why, or for how long. My voice mail greeting and email auto responses have been updated with the appropriate messages, also as instructed, so to deflect any remnant misgivings as to my whereabouts, and to defray any inclinations others, outsiders, might have to inquire on my behalf. When I don't answer, when I don't get back, it won't raise a single eyebrow or cause a moment's pause.

The bills have been paid in full, and my mail has been forwarded to the post office box. Utilities and subscription services have been suspended. I do believe I am ready to go.

I sip the last of the scotch as I watch from my window for my ride, which is due to arrive soon. Emptying the bottle made for a hefty pour, but I enjoy it today as I have enjoyed it every day, like clockwork, for years. This elixir is my evening companion of choice, an indulgence, you could say. She holds me, warms me, never talks back. Better than candy.

It is not terribly late, but the sun is about to set, its last lighted dregs trickling out from beneath the gathering wall of clouds. The rays tint the air a pinkish gray, imbuing the autumnal dusk, the wet leaves, and the shiny sidewalks with a quick-fading warmth. From my second-floor apartment, I see costumed children making their way down the block; the youngest ones have already finished with their rounds. I see patches of candle glow on porches and in windows below, lopsided grins and sinister eyes carved less to illuminate some welcoming path than to simply announce, *The goods are here, kids*. It's all so sweet, so quaint, so mundane.

There is a knock on the door, followed by a muffled, "Trick or Treat!" from young voices aimed against barricade of my locked front door. I startle, but recover instantly, assured they cannot possibly know I am inside. I make my way, slowly and as quietly as possible, to the vestibule so I can unplug the nightlight, to make sure there is not one bit of light to suggest someone might be inside and willing to participate in the superficial largesse of the evening.

After a second attempt by the kids, this time delivered as a cluster of small-fisted raps on the door, there is silence. Good. They've left. Hopefully, they will all soon be done with their night, and no one will be around to see me exit the building. No doubt the children, eager to make good on their quest, have hurried off to sweeter addresses. They have no time to waste, for the city sanctioned trick or treat hours are almost over.

Per item eight, the capsule is at the ready for ingestion. The massive lozenge lies in a change dish on my dresser. Not taking any chances, I move with care to cross the room as noiselessly as possible once again. It's time, and so the capsule is downed with a gullet singeing, final mouthful of the scotch. A two-hour window, it was instructed, was needed for the drug to take full effect. I look at my watch. I am, if all goes according to the itinerary, going to be right on time.

The sidewalks and street below have grown quiet. Here and there, porches have gone dark. A lone jack-o-lantern glances up at me from across the street. He won't tell. A group of teen-agers saunter along the sidewalk, arms linked, passing below my window. I watch them, appreciating their tender forms. One lugs a pillowcase full of what one would assume is Halloween candy. I imagine a bottle of something illicit is stashed in there as well. The kids laugh and stumble, joking amongst themselves as they exit the scene, disappearing behind the low hanging branches of the oak trees that line the street. The heavy overhang bars my view of most the block, thanks to the stubborn hold of the leaves, which always hang on far longer into the winter than they should. I regard them idly as well, at the fickle sturdiness they embody, for it is only a matter of weeks when the whip of numbing winter winds will finally strip them of their last bite on life.

For me, the letting go, considering the circumstances, is almost too easy. Certainly, far easier than the fleeting season of stupid, little leaves. I should feel the dirge, but I feel like I am merely going out to dinner.

I want another drink. I lift the empty bottle to my mouth and hold it aloft, hoping a few more drops might fall upon my waiting tongue.

I feel a shift in my awareness. There is something else now, making its way around and through me, a chemical enhancement alongside the familiar warmth of the scotch. Good shit. Both of them.

A car rounds the corner, its headlights pointing first away, then parallel to the curb as the conveyance slows down, comes to a full stop. The limousine is an older one, a stretch sedan. The engine remains engaged; it rumbles rather than purrs. This one has seen miles and years. No one exits the car. Clearly, it is there for me, but it will be up to me to make my way down to meet it. And therein lies the problem.

My apartment building is an old one, and the lone elevator has been non-functional for weeks. The driver will have to be patient. This could take a few minutes. If only I could text for help, or call out the window to the driver, but I can't do either. Per item six, though I have set my phone account to cancel in three months' time, I have no phone number for anyone associated with this thing tonight

– there is no one to call or text. So, I turn full focus on the trip downstairs. Crossing a small room is one thing; going down two flights of stairs is another.

I make my way to the front door, open it, pass through, close the door. Even though it won't really matter, for there is hardly anything left inside, I lock the door. I scoot along the hall, thankful there is no carpeting, hoping, praying no one hears or sees me. For all they know, I have been on vacation these last few weeks already. Perhaps some think I have moved. Feigning absence for over three weeks certainly wasn't easy, but it was a solid a start, a trail period of withdrawal, of my commitment as well – and necessary, per the contract. Let them assume I am off on a beach somewhere, perched on a bar stool stuck into the sand, glass in hand, calling to the barefoot waitress for another round…

I reach the stairs and pause. At least, going down grants me the fundamental aid of basic physics. It's always easiest going down. I grab the stair rail with my remaining hand, my left one, and with my remaining leg, I begin an incremental seat-dropped descent, one bumpy landing, one tread at a time, my left hand grabbing at intervals along the bannister as I go, keeping me in some control of my body as I descend. I wince with each drop; the impact jars still-raw nerve endings still trying to figure out where now to send their signals. The right sleeve of my suit I have pinned neatly to the shoulder seam in preparation for this, so to not accidentally sit on it. The right leg of my pants is similarly folded up and pinned at the hip, so to not dangle haphazardly about, either.

I have finally made it to the front door. It has started to drizzle again. I am relieved; no one is about. The rain serves me well, for it has cleared the street in anticipation of my front-step arrival. No one will see my departure. I can reach the door lever and depress it; it gives easily enough. The door swings open, slowly, due to its weight, but far enough so that I am exposed to the eyes of the street. I am seated on the threshold of the doorway in a most undignified fashion, but hopefully also to the view of the driver, who, especially with the rain falling, will see fit to help me, load me into the limo.

The driver's door opens, the warning tone dings. Good. The driver has seen me.

A uniformed man emerges. He is wearing sunglasses. I have no idea how he can possibly see, given the dark that now enfolds us. But he is strong and sure, and in a few seconds, he is standing on the top step and looking down at me. He reaches out to touch, fleetingly, the black ribbon pinned to my shoulder, smiles with acknowledgement and recognition, and then in a single motion, lifts me up into his arms. Without any semblance of cradling me, he installs me into the back seat of the car. No one bothers with a seat belt. We are quickly off and on our way. I look back, over my shoulder, at the apartment building, its smooth limestone walls, the wrought iron fence, the mailbox. I watch as the picture is almost immediately erased by a succession of street trees and parked cars. So be it. I have the printed invitation in my left jacket pocket, just in case I need to present it when we arrive. My hand-written and signed statement, per item number two, is in my right pocket.

†††

I don't have to present anything. They recognize me instantly; well, they recognize the limo first, and I as its lone passenger. I guess it's obvious, which one of us was the one who paid and arm and a leg to get in.

†††

I am carried, rather ceremoniously I should say, into the building, a grand, old place. The décor and architecture are at odds with one another; the entry and broad hall are reminiscent of a grand Newport cottage, homey yet opulent in the extreme. The furnishings – or lack thereof – are form-functional and contemporary to the point of looking somewhat sterile. Well, I suppose that could be in keeping with its usage. Somehow, it is clear to me; this is no one's home.

The drug's properties continue to invade and alter my sensibilities. Interestingly, while not diminishing my awareness, already gently befuddled with my finishing off of the scotch, its effect is one of deep neutralization, a sort of dual numbness, which foments a sense of detachment. I am reminded of out-of-body experiences as described by those who witnessed their own spiritual separation from their corporeal selves. Will this be my vantage point? What a shame, if that were the case, to not be around after the fact, to be able to write about something interesting like that.

I am, thanks to the drug's effects, mildly disappointed at the prospect – or lack thereof – but little more than that. I am drifting.

My conveyance upon entry into the mansion has been obviously planned for maximized aesthetic effect. It is a palanquin, an ornate device of carved and gilded wood, which in its opulent exoticism heralds nicely the commencement of my exotic end. The litter is detailed with scrollwork and hammered nail heads, my seat is a plush pillow into which I am nestled in a loungy, semi-reclining posture of stately repose. The four who carry the palanquin wear long, black robes. Their faces are hidden from me as we proceed through the halls, but they had, when we first appeared at the door, greeted me with small nods and benign smiles from beneath the shadowy overhangs of their hoods. I note all this with detachment, and find it odd, but expected. The four carry me effortlessly. I feel weightless, and I like it.

I am carried in silence, through one passage after another. Right turns repeat, then left. There is a sensation of descent. The floor, almost imperceptibly, takes us down what must be a full story, perhaps two, into what I believe are the subterraneous levels. Curtained windows along the walls, all drawn shut, soon give way to unbroken, paneled walls. Portrait paintings are hung at intervals, uniformly framed. As we progress, the garb of those portrayed grows less dated, incrementally contemporary. The images are moving forward in time the farther – or closer – we get to wherever it is we are going. Those portrayed are mostly men, a few are women.

At the end of one long hall – it appears to be our last – the walls are empty. There is space for more portraits. Two people are standing there to meet us, in front of a set of double doors. They are waiting for us, for me. One carries a ledger in his arms.

My palanquin eases to a full stop, but I am held aloft. The man with the ledger raises the book; it is so massive it cannot be handled by one alone. The second person, a woman, opens the ledger, and using a wide ribbon bookmark to help turn back the pages, she locates what at a glance appears to be a hand-written chart, this particular page being half-filled. She scans the page, her long fingernail tracing the words as she reads.

"So; you know why you are here?"

"I do."

"And you have made this choice freely?"

"I have."

"And you remain certain in your decision?"

"I do."

"Content and at peace with it?"

"I am."

"And, in preparation for the ceremony, you have followed all instructions, items one through eight?"

"I have."

"Can you verify, please, your code?"

"RSVP 14-K1862."

"Thank you. And 'Regret.' You understand its connotations, in this, our context?"

"I do."

"And you have prepared your written statement to the group for absolution?"

"I have."

"And do you understand your payment, the retainer you gave of yourself, was the only way your true intentions could be confirmed?"

"I do."

"And do you give freely of all that is left of yourself?"

"I do."

"And if you could verify the address of the recipient, please?"

"Sure." I follow as the fingernail traces the line in the ledger. Yes, it looks about right.

"And the recipients?" she asked, pointing to their names.

"Yes, that's them, the parents of…"

"Good. We are confirmed. We will not speak the other's name. Now, the benefactors will receive delivery of a money order in two days' time. It'll be made out to the both of them. And that is per our contractual promise. You have nothing to worry about."

"Thank you."

We pause. I assume the question and answer session is over, but she has one more query for me. She touches the back of my one, remaining hand with her pointed fingernail and pushes in, hard. She presses so hard, her nail breaks my skin. A drop of blood wells up in the divot her nail makes.

"Can you feel that?"

Surprised, I look at my hand, where the blood is gathering. I am sure it is my hand. It looks like my hand.

I reply in a hushed voice, "No, I can't."

"Good. Then you are ready. Are you ready?"

"I am."

She signs something on the half-filled page and nods to her partner, who closes the album. The two open the double doors and the bearers carry me on my palanquin into the dining hall.

In this room, I will be cleansed, absolved. I will donate my body – what's left of it – to the Society, which, in return for my, um, endowment, will mail a check of restitution to the parents of, of…my co-worker…

…that is, my *former* co-worker, who, yes, as you rightly suspect, pulled a number on me and more, which brought me to this place. Little did *she* know, when I invited her to join me at a non-existent conference up north, what her sniveling, gossipy scheming would leave her with, and little did she know, when I picked her up, oh my, when she blabbed non-stop, and with that fucking cackle of hers and oh, what I had planned for her – for me, for us – and how she, that stupid cunt, *believed* me – what a friggin ignorant idiot she was – so that when I took her back home with me under the guise of having forgotten our passes – our *VIP* passes as I so smoothly told her – we just *had* to have them oh, yes, oh yes, come on in with me, it'll only take a minute – oh indeedy, she followed me in like a fucking dog, and it took only a minute, one puny, little ass set o' seconds to turn that mother fucking bitch's world on its mother fucking head, on *her* head – and, oh, I had everything worked out – I had prepped the space so perfectly, lined it like a friggin decontamination chamber, all to take care of that stupid, ugly bitch once and for all – yeah, yeah, you're welcome – come on in, you piece o' shit *colleague of mine*, come in, you lying piece of…of…welcome to my fucking *atelier*… Oh yes, I took care of that piece o' work! Red, red, spatters and splashes! How it sprayed! I was a fucking *artiste,* painting with her stinkin' blood, tossing it about better than a plain old graffiti artist, better than a prankster, better than carnival clown with a tub of balloons all filled with icky sticky red paint! Shit, you could have read the sheets like tea leaves, they were that streaked up, that dynamically spotted! Oh, yes, I Jackson Pollock'ed the fuck out of those canvases but good! Too bad they couldn't have been saved, stretched and framed to hang on some wall, for fuck's sake – they'd have made one helluva messed up work of art. So yeah, sure, you all, you could all go visit *that* gallery, mother fuckers! Classic corporate, hoighty-toity ugly-ass board room art crap, meaningless but fucking splashy. *Right*? Nope, never much the cook, my Slice Em Dice Em set of knives, new as the day they were bought, worked wonders on the bitch, as they fucking should have; they sure as shit cost enough! I had yet to use them for a meal – guess I never will – but oh, that bitch, that fucking piece o' dirty ass bitch-work! She was shredded, oh, yeah! Shredded five years and five months and thirteen days and four moves back, to three different States almost to the day, to this day, to this very day this, this, this…

No. Stop. Regroup. Reset.

Her parents will never get their baby back. *I* know this, but *that* me did it freely. And it's not even that. *This* me still believes some people earn their rightful demise. They do. But they, the others, like those parents, they didn't necessarily *earn* this. They certainly didn't ask for it. So, the E.G.G. is making it possible for me to render payback with the only currency I possess, for what I am hoping will serve this believer as a fat and effective VIP pass at those proverbial pearly gates. It's my final indulgence so that, wherever in the next plane I will find myself, it will be something better than what I suspect I am currently slated for. You see, that's my one fear. I am a counter. I tally, I keep score, and I believe to my core the universe does, too. It's the only thing I need to yet try and avoid. I've managed everything else. I've done the math. What I *don't* want is to be stuck here on this earth, assigned to dark bedroom corners at midnight, slated for eternity to scare the living shit out of lame and meaningless, random others…

You could say, this all has the potential to be a win-win, so long as victims can benefit through the same channels by which perpetrators can be ushered to lesser fires of eternal damnation. I *do* believe in pay to play. On every level, in every dimension. Indulgences, taxes, roads paved here or there – no difference.

But there's more to it. In doing this, I will also avoid the upcoming arrest. I have been tracking things online and I know the buzz on a pending apprehension is real, and accurate, and about to hit. They got me. They will be coming for me soon. They've already talked to me twice; their feigned casualness was almost laughable. In which case, when it would all have come down, I will have been able to avoid the inevitable arrest, the prosecution, the imprisonment (they'd eat me alive in there), and the possible execution. So, as I now manage my exit, I get to provide a couple of pitiable collaterals with a monetary windfall that, by sheer virtue of its amount, should help ease whatever it is that money can ease. Maybe they can do some good with that money, buy their way out of something. They can indulge themselves. Perhaps, they will wonder who gave it to them and be creeped out, even if just a little. I'm not what I was, especially back then, when I did *that* to her, but a little post-mortem chill up the ole spine is still a concept that entices.

As for me, I'm just tired. I am so tired of the hiding, the moving, tired of changing jobs, the isolation, the conflicted feelings, the loneliness, the sleepless nights, and the nightmares when I do manage to drift off. When they approached me – and just how did they know to find *me*? – this so-called Exemplarious Gourmand Guild, or E.G.G., as the embossed card noted, I knew this would be my way out. Indulges for *me;* indulgences all around.

I killed. And so, I would be killed in turn. No, there would be no eye for an eye – eyes were not my thing. I liked mine watching – the whole time. You know, one *can* orchestrate a kill just so. But this now, um, reversal, would be under my terms; well, at least their terms, as agreed to by myself, as committed to with the initial conscription of my arm and leg. I am quite literally re-balancing the scales. Pounds of flesh and buckets of blood for pounds of flesh and buckets of blood. And her screams? I'm not that big on excess Noise, myself. Gosh, her howls could have filled a canyon void, had I not stuffed her lipstick smeared maw with her own scarf. I remember, it was silk. And hideously vibrant. I suppose in her world it was representative of having dressed one's best. For success. Success – shit. Yes, well, one of us had great success, I guess.

Her best years for mine? However lonesome and stagnant mine may have been Since then, it is what it is. So, yes. Done. A good trade. We make our choices based on what's presented us. *I* had no choice. *She* did. She never ever had to be the way she was. She never had to say what she said or look at me the way she did. And I *know* what she was thinking, even when she was pretending to be nice to me. Friends. Sure. More like a willing back to step on. I *had* to do what I did, and it doesn't matter what I thought of it then, or what I think of it now. It's done. There were no options left on that particular table. So, I permitted myself. It will forever have been my most supreme indulgence. Better than candy, better than scotch, emblematic as being perhaps the truest manifestation of me in the context of purest survivalism – *unnatural, intentional* selection. What else is the calling card of a killer? I played God the Supreme. Such as this was, is, my predilection.

And so, I have elected to eradicate myself. But with a profit motive. If not for me, then fine, for them. I can only hope this E.G.G. group keeps its word and gets that check over to my beneficiaries, once they are done with me here. What they showed me when we first met appeared to prove their patterns of payments. So, I signed my name, with their version of the devil.

I am now fully imbued with the chemical spalling of myself from my corporeal form:

I look down upon the palanquin from the ceiling and see my body lifted from the cushion, see it placed upon the edge of a vast, oaken table, something suited for a brutish Viking's wedding banquet – or perhaps an elegant madrigal dinner, the authentic kind, where they do it whole-hog style, apple packed into a gaping mouth, the fresh-roasted, grinning face still leering, eyes glazed, ready to pop…

I see myself being undressed, then laid gently upon a massive and deep, rimmed platter. A square of black linen is placed over my groin. That's nice. I see the place settings re-situated around me once I am centered upon the table. Goblets are arranged around me in a circle. Perhaps there will be a toast. I see people filing in, two at a time – couples, I imagine. How romantic; no doubt, an undercurrent of lust is churning. They take their places at the table. They surround me, but they remain standing, all the better for to see, no doubt. I see my left arm laid flat out upon a silver trencher with a drain at its center. Tubing trails from its base to the floor, where it disappears into a hole cut in the planks. I see a blade extracted from a sheath and I see it run, deep and decisive, along the length of my arm, my one remaining arm. I see the river of me, flowing like a rich broth into the trough, draining clean away. So tasteful, so elegant. I am the first course, I am the main course, I am dessert.

I stay on the scene below me, but it is now beginning to fade to white. The last threads of my holding-on are giving way. Strings of consciousness are being pulled – long, spun fibers, soft and frail as cotton candy. They grow longer still, but I am reluctant to miss what comes next. Such is the nature of my predilection. If I can stage my exit as someone else's suckling beast, I can at long last and finally, finally let go of what I am, by virtue of what I did, by virtue of what rolled and boiled in my brain for as long as I can remember.

My connection wanes. It has come down to a single puff of a feathering thread. From my perch and in my state, drugged, drained, I can see with a hyper-focused clarity as the last threads of connectivity begin to fracture, like a snowflake being dismantled. I see the sushi chef take his place at table center. He unrolls his pack of knives. Deftly, artistically, he begins to carve.

†††

Welcome, esteemed members of E.G.G.
This year's annual dinner will commence at eleven in the evening
On the thirty-first of October
The location will be disclosed on event day via private post,
as will be the Regret Profile of this year's donor.
Payment in full will confirm your reservation,
& is due by the first of October.
The payment mailing address will be sent separately.
Please watch for this next week.
Cash only.
Kindly RSVP to EGG@butterflybroth.com to secure your spot at the table!

Efectus

SOFT WARM GOOD

Life had been discovered on the Pacific Purgamental Island.

The Purgamental was a 20th century consumerist phenomenon, a spate of coagulated debris known once upon a time as the Great Pacific Garbage Patch. The drifting island had gathered mass over the years and eventually lodged itself in a temperate corner of the convergence zone of the ocean, where it had remained and eventually morphed into a geographically recognized, stationary island. The discovery of life on the island had been leaked on the internet, but since those initial disclosures, the island had been deemed a military zone. Having become a guarded maritime entity, little information of this discovery ever made its way into the public realm.

The newly discovered island life was a colony of primitive creatures, the theory being they had evolved from spiny sea urchins that had attached themselves to the insides of open containers and in crevices on the underside of the floating pile of refuse during its formation. Simple in their corporeal composition and spherical in form, the creatures ranged in size and feel from, say, burr-like peppercorns to gel-filled tennis balls. Bristle-skinned, faceless, and passive, mostly stationary, the creatures were capable of a slow roll if lured with small pieces of refuse, which they consumed via phagic absorption. To the casual observer, it looked like a jellied slow motion, osmotic engulfing. The Volvating Ibramites, so named for Dr. Anson Ibram, the evolutionary biologist who had discovered them, were of phenomenal significance, for, aside from their obvious scientific notability, they held astronomical commercial potential. Their digestive acids, with which their soft forms were filled, like thick-skinned water balloons, had been found to hold an easily extracted, powerful natural anesthetic. Likewise, their capability as organic, non-human refuse collectors and processors were viewed by many as an ecological Second Coming. The critters were affectionately dubbed I-mites.

Another 20th century consumerist cultural legacy was the word "Veruca," which had found its origins in Dahlian literary iconography. One could be a Veruca, or one could veruca someone, which was to petulantly demand something, regardless how dangerous or detrimental it might be for the recipient. This term was based on the age-old storybook character, Veruca Salt, per English literary buffs and etymologists. Veruca had been accepted as both a noun and verb into the Oxford English Dictionary some four hundred years ago.

Jess, for one, loved to pull Verucas on his father.

"Daaaad, I want one – and I wannit NOW!"

I-mites, Jess whined, were stinkin' cute. He *had* to have one. He would die if he didn't get one. How, Jess's father wondered, his precocious son had found out about those critters, he could only guess. What a smart little shit, to come up wanting this kind of stuff, the proud father fondly rationalized.

Jess's very busy father, who practiced material appeasement as a form of parenting, gave Jess what he wanted, when he wanted it. As such, with the island and its Volvating Ibramites under military lock and key, it fell to the determined father to shop the Dark Web so to procure an I-mite for his little whippersnapper. The I-mite was not cheap, and it took about a month of online sleuthing to locate a dealer; but soon enough, Jess, under strictest rules to not share this with anyone, *anyone*, was presented with his very own proto-pet, a real-life I-mite.

Jess was alone most of the time, and so it was an easy shift for him to spend days on end observing this red diamond rare, gently pulsating, bristle brush haired, globular creature, which had been duly ensconced in a 100-gallon glass fish tank purchased just for it, which remained empty but for the critter, per the few instructions Jess's father's assistant had been given when he had made the cash drop for it.

Jess fed his pet scraps of paper and plastic, placing tissues, post-it notes, pieces of jar lids and twist ties into the tank, always a few inches distant from the critter. He'd then watch as it would slowly ooze itself over to the object, and as it would cover the object with a jelly-like, roll-n-stretch maneuver of its bristle brush skinned, rotund self; and he'd watch as the refuse was passed through, almost imperceptibly, the slightly translucent, scruff-covered outer skin of the critter, to where he could then see it shadowed and afloat inside the critter's body, as the material was dissolved and disappeared, being absorbed in minutes, sometimes an hour or two.

The I-mite, fed rather continuously, grew. Miraculously, it seemed to begin to respond to Jess, rolling itself into whichever corner of the fish tank was nearest the boy. Jess began, when no one was around, to pick up and hold the critter. It felt like a dirt-encrusted basketball in his arms. Jess, in desperate need of affection and attention, was falling in love.

Soft. Warm. Good.

After many months, Jess noticed a membrane fold appear, approximately one-sixth of the critter's diameter, behind which a globular shadow could be discerned. The darkish mass developed over the next few weeks into what looked like a rather solid sphere. As the I-mite grew, its coat of bristles thinned, for the rough hairs did not grow in and thicken as quickly as did the critter, which was now the size of a beach ball. It was a good thing Jess's father was often overseas, and a good thing staff didn't give a damn about that petulant son of his, for the critter's rapid growth and Jess's attachment to it would otherwise have been cause for great concern to anyone who did.

Jess was entranced. He fed his critter bigger pieces of trash, and more often. He could swear, upon entering his room, the critter would perk up and quiver as a form of greeting.

Anticipation. Good. Soft. Warm.

To pass time between feedings, Jess surfed the internet, reading whatever bits of information he could find on I-mites. Anson Ibram, a storied adventurer and their discoverer, had become the topic of chat room conjecture, evidently having disappeared in the real world. There was speculation of a grave injury, somehow connected to the Island and the volvating creatures. A photo of a handless wrist, edged with mangled and blackened skin and covered in a viscous, amber colored liquid, appeared frequently in image threads linked to his name, or that of the island's, or the I-mites. Jess could not verify whose hand it was, or what was going on with it, but the image was vibrantly gruesome, all the better for purposes of its viralization. Jess saved one particularly graphic pic of the mutilated arm and set it as the home screen on his phone.

One night, while Jess's father was overseas on business – again – a thunderstorm passed through the area. The critter, now about the size of a kiddie bean bag chair, quivered. No, it shook. With fear. Jess was certain it was afraid. Jess gathered up the critter, now half his size and quite heavy, perhaps a fourth of his weight, and laid it gently upon his vast bed. He decided he would sit with it until the storm passed. The critter, nestled in the crook of Jess's crossed legs, rolled and shifted itself so that the folded membrane was positioned directly in front of Jess's face.

The fold separated, became a lid that lifted, and a newly developed lens – dark, faceted, moistly reflective – was revealed. The I-mite had formed an eye, and that eye was gazing up, though color blind and fragmented of image, directly, deeply into the eyes of the boy. Jess gasped, first in shock, then in delight. He almost cried; his heart was so filled to overflowing.

Seconds passed between the two. The lens shifted by way of tiny fibroids, wholly controlled by the critter, back and forth, back and forth, from Jess's left eye to his right, and then back again.

Imprinting. Good. Soft. Good. Warm. Good.

Jess's soul blossomed with pride.

"Hey, you little cutie," Jess cooed, "I've got to give you a name!"

Lightning flashed, seconds later followed by a clap of thunder. The critter quivered expressively, sensing the storm. Jess wrapped his arms around his pet and held it, ever so gently, ever so lovingly. It was late, and Jess, having slept far too little for far too long, grew deliciously groggy in the enveloping bubble of quiet joy and comforting companionship his critter had bestowed upon them both.

Jess dozed off.

While Jess slept, his critter went flaccid, lost its spherical form. It began to spread, with arm-like extensions reaching and stretching, first full across Jess's lap, then further up, oozing, clinging, embracing the boy's shoulders, and then his back. The numbing toxins, emitted through the hollow bristles in which the critter was covered, prevented any sensation of burning, or pain. Jess never knew what happened. He dreamt he was swimming in a warm ocean, and it felt wonderful.

When the housekeeper entered the bedroom the next morning, she saw what looked like a massive stuffed animal on Jess's bed, thin furred, bristly, translucently glowing with a shadowy, skeletal form afloat in its interior. The animal appeared to be sprouting arms and legs; tiny stumps were emerging at its four corners. The animal turned its topmost protrusion towards the door. The lid lifted and a massive, black eye it directed full upon the much bigger human at the door. It blinked at her. Twice.

More Soft Good. More.

The housekeeper emitted a blood-curdling, wall-shaking scream, and off she ran, heaving and sobbing, stumbling blindly down the stairs, arms flailing. She left the bedroom door wide open. The critter vibrated with something akin to excitement, but remained otherwise motionless, for it would require a few more hours to finish digesting this first SoftWarmGood. Then, it could exit the room and set off, in pursuit of another one.

Efectus

THE HAPPIEST HOUR

"Ma'am, there are only six spots available for the junket to the island, and you are a party of eight, are you not?"

"Excuse me, we would be one President and founder, one Vice President, *four* board members and two, mmm, let's call them apprentices. That would be a party of two executives plus a party of *six*."

"Of course, of course."

"And the solution is obvious. Six of us will go and my, er, assistants can stay behind."

"*D'accord*. And which ones would they be?"

"Oh dear, give me a moment…it's sometimes rather difficult to remember names of subordinates…you know how that is…."

The concierge laughed obligingly, waiting patiently.

"Ah, yes, I remember! That would be Margrete and, ah, Ainsley."

"*Bon*. I see their names. Very well, we will leave those two off the list. So, you and your group will need to be at the west portico at nine tomorrow morning, sharp. We will have a motorcar take you to the pier, where you will catch the ferry. Your day at the island is scheduled to begin with a late brunch, and based on the timing to cross the bay, provided of course the weather cooperates, you should be arriving just in time for mimosas. I promise you; it will be a time to remember!"

"I dare say, it should prove to be a Xanadu, considering what it's costing the foundation!"

The concierge laughed obligingly.

"You have chosen well. It is the most luxurious excursion we offer, but then, only the best for the best, *oui*? And may I book, perhaps, a nice luncheon for your assistants, being that they are staying behind?"

"Oh, no, we needn't worry about them. Those two have been like *Kinder* in a candy shop these last several days. This resort experience has been more than enough for them, truly. They are fine. They can fend for themselves. Besides, they will have a task list, courtesy of *moi*. I can keep them productively occupied until at least mid-afternoon."

"As you wish, *madame*."

"Besides," she added, "considering their status, they have more than fully benefitted from my generosity. Apprentices anywhere would give their eyeteeth to stay here," she gestured, sweeping her arm, "let alone as employed younglings, earning their first bread and butter whilst enjoying such as this!"

"Indeed! And, truly, we do appreciate your loyalty."

"Of course, you do."

"Now, if I could have you peruse the spa treatment options, we can situate the individual itineraries as you prefer them…"

†††

The grand terrace of the oceanside resort was an island onto itself, a vast marble lagoon dotted with potted palms and planters erupting with tropical blooms. Finely dressed, money-effusing patrons floated about, whiling away the late morning hour, breakfast cocktails, fans, pipes, and cigars in hand. A languid breeze, ventured in from the shore, threaded its way about the scene, connecting the pretty dots, point by gentle point, playing with the ruffled trim of parasols, with lace-edged hems, and sleeves of gossamer gowns, touching deferentially as well upon broad hat brims, stirring gently all the exotic foliage which framed the stage. A balmy metronome, setting cadence for the softest of starts to a genteel and placid, summer's kind of day.

Two individuals, younger than most, stood amidst the luxuriousness, quite out of place, agitated and oblivious of the beauty that surrounded them. Their heads together to allow for hushed exchanges, their brows drawn in confusion and consternation, they remained planted to their spot on the terrace, on high, self-conscious alert – but for what, they no longer had any idea. No one had contacted them that morning. There had been no phone call, no missive handed through the door, no note left for them at the front desk. Likewise, no call or message from them had been responded to. They were puzzled and not a little concerned.

"So, you've tried all the others too?" Ainsley asked.

"I have," Margrete responded, looking around her, still hoping to catch sight of their group.

"Surely, they would have let us know, had there been a change of plans…"

"Well, I'm not too sure about that…"

"Madame Queen Bee's demeanor last night wasn't exactly inclusive…"

Margrete grimaced at the nickname, "I know, I caught that from her too, all those internal conversations to which I couldn't add a single thing. I just sat there, feeling like a simple stump. All I could do was listen."

"I felt it too. We're the new ones here, I understand that. And if we aren't to partake of everything, well, that's fine, but…"

"It's just that someone could bother with a smidgeon of professional decorum and tell us if plans had changed…"

"…or if we weren't to be invited to the island today to begin with…"

"Precisely."

"Say, let's ask the gentleman over there. He might know if our group was here."

The two spoke briefly with the manager, who informed them that yes, he had seen the others, who had departed in the resort motorcar about half an hour ago, but if they wanted to, he would be happy to order up a ride for them, because they might still catch their party before they boarded the ferry at the pier.

The sad longing in Margrete's eyes spurred Ainsley to accept the manager's de facto offer without hesitation.

†††

After the two were gone, a concierge appeared, silver tray in hand.

"Sholly, you know those two young ones with that group from, oh, what's it called? With that woman you keep referring to as 'Her Royal Highness?' Have you seen them? This notecard was left for me to hand to them at breakfast, but they weren't there, nor in the salon.

"Oh, you just missed them! I sent them out to meet their party at the pier."

"Hmmm."

"Well, give it an hour or two. If they don't return, we can assume they all went on to the island together. I can keep watch for the youngsters and make sure they get their letter if they do show back up here."

"Thank you, Sholl'," the concierge said. "I'm about to be supremely tied up today. Yet another wedding."

"Never a worry. Here, allow me. I'll take care of it."

"Much obliged, Sholl'," the concierge nodded to his colleague as he handed over the envelope.

†††

Only a wagonette had been available, so by the time Ainsley and Margrete were dropped off at the pier, the *See Vogel* was but a slip on the far edge of the bay. Ainsley sighed and looked over at Margrete with an expression that held both a silent question and a plea for resignation to the situation. It was clear, they had been cut from this last day of indulgence. What made it less than palatable, was how ungraciously, how unprofessionally the exclusion had been handled.

"You know, Grete, she could have just informed us from the get-go that this last item on the itinerary wasn't intended for the entire group."

"Maybe they didn't know until last minute themselves," she replied.

"That's possible. Still..." Ainsely mused.

"I know, still…"

"So, what do you want to do? Go back? I bet we can still catch…"

"Eh, no, we can't." Margrete stopped her friend. "It's gone already. The driver took off without waiting to see what we were going to do."

"What?"

"Look!"

Margrete pointed to a cloud of dust that still hung in the air over the road, where it bent hard left inland, evidence of their driver's abrupt retreat back to the resort.

"Damn!" Ainsley stomped his foot. "He could have confirmed as much before hightailing it back to the hotel!"

"I know, I know. So… Now, what?" Margrete asked, sighing.

"I suppose we could walk."

"Oh, no we don't. It's sweltering already. I will positively faint from heatstroke if I have to walk back dressed like this," Margrete said, holding up a weighty swath of skirt fabric.

"Well, what else *are* we to do? Let's start back and hope someone happens upon us. We can flag them down, even offer cash if we need to."

"Gracious! Here we are in Paradise, and all I am feeling is that we are stuck and in limbo in the middle of nowhere!" Margrete lamented.

"Welcome to yesteryear, Grete. Come, let's start back."

The two were about to step off the pier, when a raspy voice called out.

"Heya there! You there!"

The two turned and saw a small boat they somehow had missed seeing arrive. It must have eased up from around the rocky juts and remained hidden behind the breakers up to the point of its docking.

The voice broke once more the placid silence, this time louder and more insistently.

"Heya there! Yeah, you two!"

"Hello there!" Ainsley replied, waving as they retraced their steps to the pier's waterside edge.

A gull was calling off in the distance. Margrete followed the sound, noting a bank of clouds that had drifted in from the east, whose shadows were scattered across the bay, which had turned the aquamarine expanse into a patchwork of blues, greens and lavender. Breezes responding to the clouding over lent a wafting cool, which felt good. Margrete welcomed the shift in temperature, thinking little of what its gathering source foretold.

"You needing a ride out to the island?" the man inquired.

"Well, I'm, we're not sure…"

"We think we…"

"I saw you two get dropped off. That driver stirred up all kinds of dust! Even from the water, it sure looked like he was in a big, catch-up kinda hurry."

"I guess, yes…" Margrete ventured.

"Our party, our group," Ainsley added, pointing towards the horizon, for the two often spoke interchangeably, "They're on that ferry way out there. They've been booked a trip to some spa on the island."

"Ah, yes, I saw the *Vogel* heading out. You two missed 'em by just a couple o' minutes."

"They were too far out for us to wave them back…"

"Well, you wanna lift to the island? You both got that look on your faces like you missing out on something. I can take you. I'm going there myself."

Margrete brightened visibly.

"Yes, we'd love to catch a ride with you!" she answered for them both.

Ainsley tossed a look at his friend. Evidently, that thing about not accepting rides from strangers didn't apply when in Paradise. But then, the pure sand, the palm trees, the warm seas, the sun, the pelicans, and the gulls – all pointed to only to that which ought be lovely, nice… Well alright, he concluded. Just this once.

"Very well, we accept," Ainsley said. To Margrete, he added, "But leave something on the pier as a marker to show that we were here. Here; hand me your shawl."

Before Margrete could protest, Ainsley pulled the rose-printed scarf from his friend's shoulders and tied it to the armrest of the bench placed at the far end of the pier. It would have to do.

"You wanna throw down some breadcrumbs too, kid?" the boatman teased. "I'm sure the gulls would be most tickled by that."

Ainsley responded sheepishly, "No, no. It's just in case we don't find our group and they arrive back before we do. They'll recognize it as hers."

The boater peered up, into the sky, shielding his eyes.

"Looks to me something might be brewing. Rogue clouds making their way towards us. And looky there; a whole wash of 'em coming in from the southeast. Never bodes well. We might be getting some nasty weather later today, kids. Let's get going. In a wink, I promise, you'll be settled in your lounges and watching the afternoon rains from the cozy comfort of the arcade at the spa. Yep, I know the place."

The "kids" boarded the runabout. The boater engaged the motor and pointed it due north. Margrete and Ainsley watched the shoreline recede as the boat carved a path past the breakers and turned keel towards the horizon. The pier and beach, with its palm bedecked rise of land serving as backdrop, was transformed into a vacation postcard the moment they launched. Though the sky in the direction they were headed was thick and colorless, over land it remained clear and blue. Ainsley found himself wishing he owned a camera. Memory would have to do. He turned after a moment's reflection to face forward. The breeze mustered and became a strong wind, pushing against them all. The sea lifted its chop into energetic waves, which hit the small boat with enough force to cover the three in rapid-fire bursts of saltwater spray.

Margrete and Ainsley also each contended with the encroaching, cautionary voices also carried in those winds, which began to whisper with more insistence the farther from land they were. *Warning, warning…*

But the two stragglers were so much more focused on catching up with the group, so wanting to climb that ladder, to belong, that neither one listened.

†††

By the time the runabout made land, the skies had grown foreboding and the ocean had been transformed into a churning obstacle course. Had Ainsley taken time for breakfast, he would have lost it in most uncouth fashion. His face had become drawn and ashen, his eyes sunken. Margrete fared better, but being also bereft of sustenance and weary of the turbulent tossing about, she was feeling likewise hollowed out.

At long, arduous last, the "kids" were able to disembark onto the island's pier, a rustic but solidly built structure. They stood a moment to recompose their balance and breath. As they did, they took in the scene before them. A wait station fronted the pier at land's end, outfitted in a storm-worthy coat of thick shingles, mullioned fenestration, and a seamed metal roof upon which a small cupola boasted both a windsock and wind gauge. Clearly, this was a destination of some moderate distinction. A painted sign bore a finely lettered, "Welcome" in five languages.

"Well, sir, which way do we go?" Ainsley, still wiping his brow, asked the boatman.

Other than the welcome sign, there was no signage to be seen. A lone road which met up with the pier trailed off in both directions. By way of the sharp curves of the shoreline of the small island, it disappeared quickly on either side.

"To your left. No, I mean to your right. Go that-a way. To your right." The boatman pointed first one way, then the other.

Margrete and Ainsley exchanged quick glances, brows lifted with question and doubt.

"Hey, where are you headed?" Ainsley asked the boatman. "Are you going back?"

"Nope," the boatman replied, "I gotta place on the far side, over this-a way. Just makin' my way 'round the island, then I'll tie up too. Best to be off the water for the next few hours, I'm a-thinkin'." Then adding a finalizing, "Later, kids!" he revved the boat's motor and was on his way.

The boatman waved perfunctorily as he turned his boat about and puttered off.

The "kids" waved back and yelled their good-byes along with yet another set of thank you's into the blustery ether; the boatman had made quick work of his dismissal and departure and was quite out of earshot.

Ainsley and Margrete ventured over to the wait station at the end of the pier, Ainsley seating himself in a protected, wind-still cubby to regain his composure. He did not feel well at all. The small boat was gone, and there the two were, once again, all alone.

Thunder rolled in the distance, a steady rumble that passed quickly over the bay and reverberated against the windowpanes. A remittent flash of lightning suggested there was time enough to cover a good distance before the storm was upon them. The two decided to make a go of it, and hooking arms for support, they set out. Surely the spa couldn't be too far off, and judging by the way the road was adorned, with fragrant flowers planted along the berm and conch shells decoratively placed every few feet, the path positively beckoned to them, *Yes, my dears; this is the way to go.*

The stormfront soon caught up with their wind– and fatigue-hindered progress. A whipping blow bent the palms and lifted delicate vortexes of fine sand into the air. At precisely the moment the first raindrops began to fall, hitting the broad fronds with audible pocks, Margrete spied a small gate in an alcove of cleared foliage. No, this would not be the entrance to a world-class spa, but, given the circumstances, it spoke clearly enough to the pair: *Come on, right this way!*

Without hesitation, Margrete pulled Ainsley in its direction. Ainsley resisted, wanting rather to forge on, even if soaked to the skin. But Margrete, meaning well, for her dear friend was still in possession of a death mask complexion, thought it would serve them best to wait the squall out under some form of cover. Perhaps she could find some potable water. As hungry as they may have been, their need for something to drink was more immediate.

The arched gate in the clearing was made of bamboo, tied fast with ropes of dried grasses. Its design invoked more the formality of a European garden entry than a portal to the tropical hovel of some islander. But it spoke promisingly either which way, by impact of its beauty and construction alone. As such, Margrete opened the gate, and they passed through.

The rain picked up as the two followed the path, this one not demarcated with conch shells but solidly festooned with enormous cockles pushed deep into the sand, one right after the other, so to create a lace-edged effect. After some minutes, they passed beneath an arbor of palm sheathing, also secured with long, interwoven grasses. So entranced and distracted were they with the visual delights of the finely crafted garden elements, that when they remembered to turn their gazes up and forward, what met their eyes caused them to gasp in shock and delight.

Nestled into a grove of flowering trees and centered upon a patch of emerald-green, moss-carpeted lawn, there stood a cottage quaintly reminiscent of a merry olde England, with a steep pitched roof and a façade demarcated with evenly interspersed and shuttered windows. An entry door, arched like its garden counterparts, stood at plumb center, whimsically painted a dark, tropical pink. It positively glowed in the off-lit, midday dusk the storm had wrought.

The time-forgotten quaintness was not the only aspect of the structure that was so entrancing, so wholly unexpected for a tropical island abode: The very walls of the cottage had been paved like a mermaid's jewel casket, with what had to be thousands upon thousands of pearlescent seashells. Seashells covered, in fact, every surface; they edged every corner, silled every window. The shells were even arranged into patterns, so to mimic rows of lacework draped between the structure's oyster-clad half-timbers. The cottage was a work of such artistry and patient execution, it beckoned with the scrumptiousness of a master baker's wedding torte; a princely sugarplum vision, the sweetest of dreams come true.

Which was, of course, entirely as intended.

The house spoke; no, *sang* with its beauty: *Come on in, my dears, come in!*

"Golly!" Ainsley exclaimed.

"As I live and breathe…!" Margrete whispered, awestruck.

To the side of the front door, as if awaiting the two, stood a slender table upon which stood a basin and two cups. The bowl was filled to the brim with rainwater. Heavy drops still fell from leaves above, splashing onto its surface, causing the water to trickle over the edge. The water was so clear, that but for the droplets striking its surface, the bowl appeared to be empty. Margrete filled the cups and they both drank. The rejuvenating effects were instantaneous. How wise his friend had been, Ainsley thought, to turn them both through that gate and down this path. Whatever the spa – no doubt not far away – had to offer, it could not compete with the magic of this weather-necessitated interlude.

Ainsley trailed his fingers along the wall, the rows of colorful tellins, as he drank, while Margrete finished more quickly, and made her way to the front door. She was just about to raise her hand to knock, when the door creaked slowly open. An elderly woman stood there on the threshold, her face sun baked and lined with the marks of countless summers. She had snow-white hair, which was twisted, knotted, and pinned to the top of her head by way of a massive spike made of tortoise shell. She was dressed in a long, shapeless smock of fabric riotously printed with palm fronds which sparkled with each breath she took, each leaf being outlined in beads of bright gold. The stump of an unlit cigar she held tightly in her gums. She stepped onto the porch, walking with considerable difficulty. She carried a length of dried sugar cane in one hand to assist. This was a South Pacific fairy godmother incarnate.

"So, what the blazes you two doing on my land?" the old woman belted out, her speech heavily accented.

Ainsley and Margrete, when they found their voices, stammered alternately.

"We, oh…"

"Crikey, we are so…"

"Ma'am…"

"Please, we…"

The old woman shut them both up, "Sheesh, you dratted trespassers could at least quit talking over each other and let one of you offer up some kinda apology!"

The old woman popped the end of her walking stick into Ainsley's belly.

"You!" she rasped, "Foozler boy! Speak up and explain what you doing here before I belt you one with my cane!"

"Ma'am," Ainsley began again, "we were, are, with a party from the mainland. We're trying to meet up with our group. They're at the island…"

"Oh, sure, the spa. You just a pair o' stragglers, eh?" she said, squinting at them.

"Well, yes, in a sense."

"What he means, ma'am," Margrete interjected, "is that we were left behind at the hotel on the mainland. We were, are, on our way to the spa now. We missed the ferry ride over here and now we're just trying to…"

"Ma'am," Ainsley threaded in, "this was truly an accidental stop. We can leave immediately if you…"

"With this storm over us? Are you just making to hornswoggle me? You coulda get zinged like a gnat by the lightning!" she spat.

"Come on, you two," the woman went on, her tone changing markedly, "I'm-a not the bitin' kind. You can wait the storm out in the house. It's barely a twenty-minute walk from here to the resort. You'll be there in plenty o' time for your happiest of hours. Oh boy!"

"Oh, ma'am, how kind of you!"

"Yes, thank you for trusting us and letting us in!"

"Well, whatcha gonna do? Stay outside and get electrified like some dimbulb could maybe better use a good jolt, or come inside and then kill me and have *me* for supper? Dare I let you two in? Ach! Why not, heh?"

They all laughed.

Another flash of lightning split the misted gloom as if on cue, and the quick answer of the thunder spurred the displaced apprentices indoors just as the rain kicked up once more.

"C'mon, c'mon," the woman beckoned with her walking stick. "And you know what? You never gonna believe it, but it's my birthday today. How about that? You little foozlers *are* my birthday surprise!"

They all laughed again as the old woman swept them all inside.

†††

The old woman leaned back in her chair and continued to listen with what appeared to be an obvious show of interest as her young guests told of their unexpected travels, their cantankerous employer, and their days at the grand, seaside hotel. Laying her cigar into the brass ashtray at her elbow, she from time to time picked up a decanter poised at the ready, to offer more to her guests by way of pointing the bottle at each one of them. The "kids" eventually declined the proffered drink, only to have her pour a bit more anyway. On empty stomachs, the sippable stuff made for an especially heady beverage, stronger than what may have been good for a couple of wary but terribly naïve, young adults.

"So, your geese are in that little house out back?" Margrete asked between sips, her eyes roaming about the room as she spoke. She was enjoying the eclecticism of the interior; seashells, as with the exterior, were everywhere. Sailor's valentines, most of them unfinished, hung in shadowboxes on every wall. Loose shells filled baskets set under end tables, and bowls with even more shells were situated on the credenza, on bookshelves and even the deep windowsills. Clearly, this woman was the artist in residence. The "kids," no longer afraid, had become quite charmed.

"Indeedy," the old woman cooed, "they are my babies. They lay me their eggs; one of the ways I make my itty-bitty living. I'm a purr-veyor," she pulled the word long, trilling the R's for emphasis. "I supply that there restaurant at the spa you two gonna go to. My voovies produce the best eggs you ever eat. When they grow old, sure, some of 'em go by way of the big ol' roasting pans over there, but not many. Some of 'em I bet old as you." The old woman shrugged. "It's how it goes. They're my voovies, and I love them, I do, and they takin' care of me too."

"Voovies?" Margrete asked.

"Voovies. You never heard that before?"

"Never!" Margrete replied.

"Whatever, kid. You talk like you got lotsa learning to do. You one of those new kinda professionals. Don't mean you gotta pick apart my conversations."

Ainsley felt a warning, a split-second lurch, deep in his gut. The old woman was possessed of a flipflopping persona, which was concerning despite everything as it appeared to be. He realized, anything they might say could warrant another verbal slap from this crass-mouthed hostess. Perhaps worse? Ainsley glanced at the front door, which seemed to have receded a few feet from where they were sitting, a disconcerting illusion. He glanced at Margrete, whose eyes met his. She was perceiving this, too.

The thundershower, having waned a second time, was now fully passed. The room had grown prematurely dark, for the sky was still blanketed with clouds. As yet, no candle or lamp had been lit.

Ainsley, now quite uneasy, feigned a casual tone of voice and said in an aside, "The rain has stopped, Grete. I say it's time we are on our way."

"Yes," Margrete replied, taking his cue. "They will be positively frantic over us!"

Turning to the old woman, Margrete began, "And we so want to thank you for…"

To which the old woman looked full upon Margrete, her small eyes brimming, glinting with sudden tears. Her lower lip began to tremble visibly.

She sputtered, "But kids, it's, it's my birthday! I *told* you!"

Ainsley and Margrete were dumbfounded.

"Kids!" the old woman implored, "You gotta stay now, you can't just abandon me like this on…on my birthday!" A single, big tear worked its way over her lower lid and began to make its way down a wrinkled crevice of her cheek. The fat droplet spilled from the small ledge of her chin and onto the neckline of her dress. The old woman was instantly transformed into a picture of dejection and defeat. "C'mon now, dears," she implored, "I gotta big to-do all done and set up. C'mon, c'mon, have dinner with me, and then you can go. You'll still make it for your happiest of hours. I promise!"

Her eyes filled with more tears, threatening an even more pitiable display.

What were they to do?

Ainsley shot a purposeful glance at Margrete and answered, his words weighted with an attempt at authority, "Very well. We would be honored to celebrate with you. For a bit. We've got an hour at the very most before our group, I am certain, will be sending out a search party for us, and then we will all be in such trouble!"

"…oh, it will be a shambles if it came to that!" Margrete chimed in. "Our boss is no lady when she is mad!"

"Sure, sure; of course," the old woman made a show of concession, shrugging. "They are on pins and needles over you, to be sure, kids. No doubt about it."

That the old woman saw right through their pastiche of professional relevance sent a surge of trepidation through both Ainsley and Margrete. Her insight was unnerving, making no more sense than the extravagent coquillage had, which had adorned the pathway and cottage structure, which had initially so entranced them, lured them in.

The old woman, with another sweep of her cane, herded her puzzled, but in the end compliant guests into her dining room. What awaited them would continue the nearly indiscernible descent from all things sensible.

†††

And what did await the old woman and her guests, but a tableau of such lush abundance, such excessive beauty and bounty, it began to upend the impact of their initial impressions. Admiration and pleasurable enjoyment were being turned inside out, nay, *exploded* by the impact of even more over-the-top loveliness. Soon enough, the guests' hesitation descended into hissing whispers, which hinted of a sick, if reluctant and largely ignored, dread.

†††

The dining table, standing there to greet the host and her guests, bore not merely a repast but a foodscape fit for a Dionysius and his minions, fit for a Fezziwig and his celebrants, fit for a generous King and his contingency of famished Knights. Tiered platters were laden with every imaginable food any tropical island banquet could possibly wish to proffer: Coconut encrusted sea creatures, coconut-laced stews, coconut-coated sweet treats; creamy, dulcet sauces beckoned from an armada of silver gravy boats; braids of fruit-studded breads and rolled dates, skewered with all manner of the sweet and savory filled myriad, little platters; baked fish, breaded fish, fried fish, tidbits of conch, of scallops, of shrimp steamed, hot and fresh; shellfish chilled upon platters boasting mountains of ice, studded with fragrant and jewel-bright slices of lemons and limes. A massive roast goose lay in crisp repose upon a trencher at table center. Riotously colored fruits were arranged into towers; plantains mashed, fried, and coated in aromatic brickles of this 'n that were piled into generous bowls. It was a glutton's tropical garden of delights, a *Stilleven* unbound.

Ainsley and Margrete, already preternaturally warmed by whatever it had been in that carafe, took their places at table. Obediently, they spread linen napkins over their laps. Their eyes ran up and down the length of the table – neither one of them had ever seen anything even close to this. Not even the hotel's dinner buffets could compare to what was on display before them, *for* them.

"Well, okay, ye little meaters," the old woman chortled, "dive in and eat. Celebrate! For crikey's sake, I might even let you serenade me with a 'Happy Birthday' if you behave yourselves and put it away good for me!"

Which bites held the poison; which bites did not? What was wrong with this delightful picture? This, Margrete wondered far too idly as she helped herself to yet another spear of crisp-edged, impossibly plump scallops. The wave of pleasure Margrete experienced when she popped one into her mouth, when it burst like an explosion of oceanic ambrosia, was almost frightening in its intensity. It tasted too good. It *felt* too good.

Ainsley, equally afflicted, his cheeks stuffed, his jowls working as if motorized, was likewise enthralled. He reached with both arms, hands clawing, across the table for more.

"Good, good, wonderful!" cackled the old woman. "This is my best birthday ever!"

She presented her guests yet another platter that seemed to materialize out of thin air, this one boasting an enormous and sizzling whale of a grouper, over which she warbled, "Take some, dig in, and eat, eat, eat!"

†††

How the plates and bowls, how the platters and tiered servers remained filled, garnished, hot and steaming or crisp and cold as the evening progressed was beyond comprehension, but the sensibilities of the old woman's two "surprise" guests lay merely with the dregs of some distant and daylit, mortal's past. In their dejection of the morning hours, having been so left behind, and in their weariness and worry of the afternoon, to then the indulgences of the last few hours, Margrete and Ainsley had fully lost themselves to their impulses. The rich and exotic delicacies serving them far too well as the most insidious of intoxicants.

The two apprentices neither saw It coming, nor recognized It, once It was upon them. In their ever-weakening states, how they even remained properly seated, conversant, and spared from any uncouth dribbling of syrups and fatty drips which might mar their faces or clothing, was just as much a mystery as anything else. Their propriety was amusingly intact; well, up to a point…

The old woman barely ate a thing. She was content to sit with her guests, rocking in her seat to the cadence of their pleasured ramblings, and to suck on her dead stogie with such vigor, it may as well have been a silently whistling tin flute, calling forth who knows what, as she watched, assessed, approved, invoked.

"Here, kids," the old woman quipped as she offered up yet another plate, "We gotta wrap this thing up. I told you; you'd be on your way in no time, didn't I? Here. One last, little bite. For me."

Margrete belched, unable to contain herself any longer. She attempted a chuckle and mumbled something about it still being her host's birthday.

Ainsley took this last plate in hand, and holding it aloft, slurred, "An' we did say we'd sing for…for…you…"

The old woman gurgled noiselessly. They were so far gone, the bonbons were hardly warranted. She answered, "You think you can still carry a tune for me?"

The kids giggled and hiccupped into their napkins.

The room, to the two of them, now swam. The old woman's guests were solidly beyond caring, their minds turning to jelly.

Margrete let her gaze fall on the small plate Ainsley held out between them. Two marbled, sculpted chocolates in the shape of snails' shells begged her to *yes, please, take one.*

"Ooh, pretty!" Margrete oozed, helping herself.

"Now, you gotta put the whole thing in your mouth at once," the old woman advised with an earnest tone of voice. Those guys are full of a liqueur I know you never tasted before in your short lives. They are special. Only the bestest of my friends get these little critters!"

"Aaaaw!" the two guffawed, glaze-eyed as they inserted the bonbons into their limp maws.

The old woman watched, working the stump of the cigar in her gums, barely able to refrain from quaking, such was her anticipation.

An elixir burst forth from the chocolate, filling their mouths, infiltrating what was left of their faculties. The honeyed poison immediately began to complete the evening's work the moment it coated its victims' tongues. Ainsley slumped back in his chair, his mouth falling slack and wide, spit dribbling down his chin. Margrete glazed over and fell forward, her face landing upon the crumpled napkin she had just draped over her plate. She immediately began to snore.

The old woman retrieved an empty soup tin from a small hutch, which had a bit of string taped to its base. She placed the open end of the can to her ear and began to speak into the air.

"Friede? Yep, it's me. Can you come on over, deary?" She listened a moment, then replied, "Yes. Yes. I got me, well, two of 'em. Well, more or less. Whimperish and a might scrawny, that one, but he'll make for a good catch nonetheless." She listened a moment, "Ha! Yeah, it was a piece o' cake, my friend. Yes, as always. Such pigs! Ate everything in sight! Nope…nope…no… Yes…Okay then. See you in a skosh."

†††

How quickly the freshest of wits can be dulled, even stupefied, in the face of such excessive lushness and largesse! How intoxicating, the effects of frenzied consumption, which can distract, diminish, and sidetrack, even if in the absence of any hell-signed, mind-bending chicanery! And, in the face of that old woman's purpose-filled enchantment, which began its takeover the moment the cast-off hirelings crossed her threshold? They never had a chance. For, the old woman was indeed a sorceress, and not without considerable merit. How else could she have built so entrancing a trap, served so lavish a meal, and so fully knocked out her guests with the succulent one-two of a tiny, innocent-looking, but potion-filled bonbon? And how about that wireless communicator of hers?

†††

Our two young friends awoke late the following day, woozy of mind, to the dim silence of a bedchamber designed precisely for such as they. While cozy at the onset, futile imprisonment was the instantaneous realization as soon as sobered circumstances were quickly – and increasingly grimly – recognized for what they truly were.

Hints of what may have been daylight seeped through the slats of a shuttered window high above their beds. It could have just as easily been moonlight.

The small room Ainsley and Margrete found themselves in held only two beds, to which the pitiable guests had been somehow consigned in their unconscious state. They were each held fast by fabric strips tied around their wrists, which had been threaded and knotted through iron rings set into the newel posts of their beds.

A narrow stair hugged the wall, leading up to a door which, they surmised in silence, would take them back into the rooms where they had spent the – previous? – evening. A second door was cut into the wall at their level, and set with a primitive latch. The beds were comfortable, but the quilts that covered them had been pulled taut and nailed fast to the sideboards. Neither one of them would be able to exit their bed without considerable time and effort.

Awash in fear, Margrete and Ainsley turned their heads as best as they could to look upon the other. Ainsley drew in his breath as if to call out for help.

Margrete hissed, "Shush! Do you want her to hear us?"

"Margrete!" Ainsley whispered back, "What in the devil? I can take her on!"

"Oh, I don't know, Ainsley; but you've *got* to be still! How in the blazes did we let ourselves get into this?"

"I dunno, I dunno. It's frightening as all get-out. And embarrassing."

"She drugged us, I just know it," whispered Margrete.

"Who knows what all else she did!"

"Oh, help us, indeed. This is insanity."

"I tell you, *she is a witch,*" Ainsley said, mouthing the final word as if it were too horrific – or absurd – to speak.

"Good God," Margrete replied, "Let's not make it worse than it already is. She's a maniac, but she is old. Ancient. Ancient and slow. *We* have the advantage."

"We've got to get out of these things…" Ainsley said, working at his bindings.

The two wrestled with their ties, which clearly showed themselves as not having been intended to fully hold them, only to delay their exits from their beds. Ainsley was soon able to split his ties and freed himself. He then assisted his friend. The two were dismayed afresh when, once out of their beds, they realized they had been dressed as they slept in long sleeping gowns made of a rough and yellowed muslin.

A stealthy foray through the lower-level door proved unfruitful. Only a ladder was to be found in the dark space beyond, which led down to a small cellar wherein a barred enclave stood empty, its wide, iron door ajar. Broken seashells littered the dirt floor. Dark streaks marred the walls, some streaks appearing intentional, like tick marks to tally some sort of interval, perhaps time. Other marks were random and mottled, some were puddled upon the floor, possibly the results of chaotic or forceful encounters.

The "kids" retreated up the ladder, back to the bedchamber. They next climbed the small staircase, where they tried the latch at the door. Once again, as if on cue, the old woman appeared just as Margrete was about to insert a hairpin into the lock.

"Aha, kids!" She cackled in greeting, foisting her sugar cane walking stick across the door at mid-height, as if to bar them from exiting. "I was wondering how long you two lazy bones would take to come up and see me!"

Ainsley and Margrete responded by grabbing the cane, thinking they could catch the woman by surprise and knock it out of her hands, then force their way out. But her cane did not budge, though held lightly in her frail hands. It remained affixed, as if it had been bolted to the doorjamb.

"Oh, no, you don't!" the old woman warned, not skipping a beat. "The more you fight, the harder it will be. The harder it will be, the more it gonna hurt."

"You can't do this to us!" the two cried.

"Oh, yes, I can!" she replied, "I already did, you dolts!"

"Let us out of here! They're going to be looking for us!"

"You keep telling that to yourselves, kids. The others, they're already so sunk deep into their own happiest of hours at the spa, they're not gonna think, let alone care, two wits about you!"

Margrete reached out to grab at the old woman's topknot, whereupon a small spider leapt up from the depths of her hair, biting quickly into the skin between Margrete's thumb and forefinger. She shrieked in pain as she shook the tiny beast off her hand. It scampered across the floor and disappeared under the cellar door.

"I told you, you fickle girl, the more you fight, the harder it will be. The harder it will be, the more it gonna hurt!" the old woman repeated.

"Friede!" she next called over her shoulder, "The kids are finally up! It's feeding time…er…it's breakfast time! Come on and help me!"

None other than the boatman appeared behind the old woman, his wide grin splitting the stained whiskers which blanketed his face.

"Well, here you are!" he exclaimed. "I had a whole silver dollar bet on you, that you two'd land here before sundown. Ha! And I won!"

"Yeah, your ole pals are gonna have to pay up, won't they?" the old woman cackled.

"So, what's it gonna be, kids?" the woman turned back to the pair. "You gonna fight? You hurt. You cooperate, it not gonna hurt. All you got to do for me now is have some breakfast. I'm not gonna do nothing else. But you gotta eat. Kids gotta eat so they can grow and be big and strong and wise old…eh…adults!"

The boatman erupted in laughter over this, as if he had just been told the most outlandish of jokes. The old woman joined in, tickled by her own wit.

Ainsley and Margrete sensed futility amidst the absurdity of these two vile clowns. Their will already in shreds, they had a feeling they were being made to succumb once more to the bizarre magic of the night before, which was manipulating them at their core, from the inside out. Despite everything, they could still comprehend what was happening around them, to them. But, once again, they found they could only comply, and began to scuff to the same dining room table where just a few hours – days? – earlier, they had gorged themselves to oblivion.

Being young, somewhat strong, and a little bit stubborn, the two "kids" naturally decided to attempt another show of resistance. Margrete, once seated, spoke for the both of them, calmly informing the old woman and the boater they had no intention of eating anything whatsoever. Some sort of run-for-it still seemed plausible, for the front entrance was once again fully in sight from where they sat. If they couldn't negotiate their exit, they could still perhaps force a quick escape. The "kids" knew from the old woman's many references to the spa, that their salvation, their original destination, was not far away and a reachable goal.

"How stupid you gonna be?" the old woman retorted, dismissing Margrete's declination with a snort.

"Okay. I am full-on done with you two kids," she concluded, muttering past her cold stogie, which she had retrieved from its ashtray and re-inserted between her gums.

"You. Ainsley," she pointed the stump of her cigar at him. "You up first."

The old woman called out in the direction of the kitchen, "Freide! Friede! Bring me the you-know-what. I'm-a gonna need your help after all!"

Margrete and Ainsley both suddenly realized, their bodies had become effectively glued to their seats. They sat in their chairs, their arms, having grown numb and slack, hung lamely at their sides, their bare feet as stuck to the floor as had they been welded into place. Only their eyes were afforded movement, and these flitted about the room, wide with fear, seeking out harbingers of what might be next. The "kids" now, finally, understood from within their twentieth-century, industrial-age perspectives, they were dealing with something timelessly aged and bad, lethal, and terribly powerful, and with unseen forces which were holding them fast, machinated and implemented by the old woman, existing solely to do her bidding.

Why, the cunning hag was so practiced, no commands or cliché implements had ever been needed! All she had done in her captive guests' presence was to spew a few crass comments and commands amidst the chatter. And still, the universe had obeyed, and the captive pair's wills had been bent rather completely backwards, and were about to break.

Friede entered the dining room, carrying an enormous tin funnel. This, he gingerly held upright, for it was filled to the brim with something thick, textured, and pale in color.

"Okay, you dunderhead," he sputtered in Ainsley's direction, as he raised the funnel high. "Remember what she said. 'If you fight, it gonna hurt'…"

Ainsley's mouth opened in a silent wailing "Noooo!" at which point the old woman leaned in and deftly pinched the young man's nose shut with one hand. With her other hand, she grabbed Ainsley's chin and steered his face skyward, her sudden show of strength frighteningly unearthly. The old woman's hands smelled of death and burnt tobacco, causing Ainsley to retch. His body heaved.

Ainsley's reaction seemed to serve as a sort of horrific signal. The boatman jammed the funnel into Ainsley's mouth, pushing the small end in with such cruel drive, it prevented Ainsley from even thinking about clamping his teeth together in resistance. The boatman jiggled the device, which set its contents, a mash made of the blended leftovers from the night before, into motion. Stench-imbued globs proceeded to dump into Ainsley's mouth, lobbing past his epiglottis, onward and down into his gullet, past any gag reflex, past anything remotely human, past anything humane.

The old woman, in her wicked glee, felt a giggle roll in her gut as she watched her friend and fellow henchman strongarm the feeding. She looked down upon her young hostage with pride, her black heart swelling in her hollow breast. He was being *so* good, *so* compliant! Ingesting, ingesting, ingesting, the stupid poke was, like the dumbest of beasts. The giggle, the glee, shook her to her core. It was all so hilariously satisfying!

Just how tender would *this* one's be, she pondered. How handsomely would she be paid for *this* one? As the old woman watched the mash descend, as she watched the boy's throat bulge and constrict with each swallow, the nasty giggle finally erupted from *her* own gullet. It bubbled forth in hateful chuckles as she held fast to the stupid critter's pliant orifice.

Amidst all her shaking and quaking, the length of ash from the end of her cigar broke off and fell into the funnel, where it was sucked down into the swill. It descended along with the rest of the mess, gulp by rancid gulp, into Ainsley's stomach.

Unlike the pampered voovies in her backyard shed, Ainsley was her less fortunate goose. And as it has long been quipped, his was cooked.

Margrete watched, transfixed with horror, tears streaming from her eyes. Her suffering on behalf of someone who had managed to become something of a true friend was profound, and *quite* real.

The last thing Ainsley saw before he passed out was Grete. He saw mortal dread in her face, and an obvious disgust over what was being done to him – what would no doubt be done to her, next.

Outside, it began to rain again, this time a lovely, gentler sort of shower. The seashell tressed walls of the cottage shimmered as if coated in a thin glaze, not unlike the sweet handiwork of an expert island confectioner.

†††

Red velvet divans, all facing the open ocean, are lined up like field hospital beds beneath the broad canopy of the stone arcade. Support columns intersperse the wide, cloister-like stretch, affording guests privacy by way of the cover the wide, carved stone trunks provide. Ceiling fans turn ever so slowly, mesmerizingly. Planted palms move hypnotically to and fro, their rustle mixing with the music of an unseen harpist and the patter of a gentle rain, which has just begun to fall.

It is, after all, the servers reassure, that time of year. The weather cannot be helped.

The weather does not matter.

Beyond the stone arches lies a narrow band of untrodden sand. The beach meets with the gently encroaching waves of a somnambulant sea. It is almost high tide. The horizon has disappeared, obscured by rain, mist, and clouds. Where the dove gray skies meet with the sea is indiscernible. But none of that matters, either, in this timeless atmosphere of lethargic conviviality.

What day is it? Who knows? Who cares?

A constant sprinkling, sprite's bells a-play in a forest glen, is the only intermittent sound of activity as goblets of fine crystal are raised over and again in genteel toasts – to the mood, to the moment, the hour, the day, the place, the fantasy...

†††

"*Madame*, may I..."

"Oh, darling, is there time? *Can* I have another?"

"But of course, *madame*!"

"Oh, how lovely! And perhaps tomorrow I will get that massage...if I feel more up to it..."

"Why, of course, *madame*..."

"...perhaps get my hair done..."

"Absolutely, *madame*. You can re-book at any time...There is no rush... Relax. Enjoy the view...never a rush..."

"Thank you, darling. I am so glad. I just don't want to go anywhere...not just yet...want to stay..."

"…and that, you can do…for as long as you please…"

"…as long as I like…"

"…here, with us…"

"…yes, here…" she sighed, looking up at her waiter.

"And silly me!" she said, coming to a little, remembering why she had called him over, "I've finished my plate already! I just can't get enough of this appetizer! It's divine! And look," she gushed, drawing a bracelet-laden arm through the air in the direction of her staff, "It isn't just *moi* who's fallen in love with your foie gras. Take a look at my associates!"

The waiter and his patron tittered quietly, enjoying together the sight of her companions sprawled on their chaise lounges a short distance from hers, chewing, sipping, swallowing, gazing out over the endlessness before them, sighing as one, satiated, contented.

"Indeed, ma'am, your friends are enjoying themselves wonderfully well. We are so happy to provide you with all of this, and…"

"Ha!" she softly interjected, "They've practically *licked* their plates clean!"

"Indeed, they have," the waiter allowed, affectionately.

"Oh, I never want to leave this place! I think…I think," her eyes rolled up to meet the server's warm gaze, "I'm in love! And this…this is my…my *happiest* of hours! Never have I been so…so…"

"Happy?" he patted her hand.

"Yes," she cried, her eyes welling up with tears, "So very, very happy."

"Well, then, it is indeed a happy hour. Let's say we put in for another order of the foie gras for the lady. And for her friends as well?"

"Yes, yes, please," she garbled, her speech thick with pleasure. "And more toast rounds. And another one of these…these…"

"Another Bloody Mary?"

"Yes, yes. One for me, and a round for them, over there," she gestured again towards the group.

"Oh! And one more for my dear little friend, who should be arriving any moment. I just received word she's on her way over to us. And, please, darling, put it all on my…"

The proprietress started visibly, stopping in mid-sentence, her face lighting up with delighted recognition.

"Look!" she cried out, pointing, "There she is now. My darling…!"

The waiter glanced over his shoulder, ready to greet, ready to serve.

"At last!" the woman sat up, lifting her arms in welcome.

The proprietress received her companion with a warm and welcoming hug. Her mouth almost touching the ear of the newly arrived young woman, she hissed softly, affectionately "Goodness, love, how long did this one take?"

"Ma'am," Margrete whispered back, "it's been barely two weeks. This one was good and ready much quicker than the one before…"

"Much more quickly, my love," the woman corrected, her tone indulgent. "My, how time flies…no crawls…no… Dash it all! I have no idea how much…when one is having *this* much fun…"

Efectus

THE LAST HOUR

They look as if asleep. Isn't that what people always say? I am going to imagine they are sleeping, dreaming, dreaming together, waiting for me. I am going to imagine – no *believe* – they are together, watching me, watching over me, waiting for me. I am going to believe – no, I *know* this – they are sending their love to me right this very second. They are sending me strength and peace and….

Oh, Lord, where *is* that damn dog? I am ready. I am ready to do this. I am going to join them, but I can't just yet. I am going to do this one last thing for myself, and that thing is to find Maeve, and have her in my arms, and to put her to sleep before I take my pills.

The sky, oh the sky! It is blindingly, scorchingly red hot. Vivid, hateful, no longer a copycat array of dancing crimson, playing about like some underworld's interpretation of the Northern Lights, the real ones of which we had partaken of from our bedroom window nearly every night for these past two years… No, the pink skies have grown acidic and dark, and with the clouds now all gone, the atmosphere effectively burned off, the earthbound path for that renegade *thing* in the sky is as obvious as had it been a hellish curveball thrown by God Himself.

What kind of God does that? And where is He, She, or It?

The chaos of the last few days has given way to eerie silence as the populations of the world have passed, most of it by their own hands. All those pills, wow. Did ever Big Pharma have its final heyday. Profitable to the end. As for the others, violent insanity, and pathos-laden abandonment of every last iota of survivalist drive did the rest of the work. For all I can tell, I am alone. At least up in this part of the world. It's too quiet for me to think anything else still survives, not up here.

All broadcasts, but for the occasional, random messages sent by off-grid ham operators who are still alive and in hiding, have ceased, and it's just as well. The last reports were absurdly focused on the inordinately high numbers of people who were dying from literally having too much fun. Massive percentages of the human population went on fatal benders of orgiastic consumption and lethally hedonistic indulgences, which were as primitive as they were predictable. And the 24/7 reporting on the final escapades made for cultish entertainment. Some said, the incessant reporting spurred it on, from all the incremental suicides of over-indulgence to the dramatic, fatally instantaneous ones. Perhaps that was the intention, some plan the media fed into all along, to hear what fools we are when the last chips are being cashed in. I just don't know. The weight of disappointment alone – what, who I am, and am a part of – is almost unbearable. Were they the wiser ones, who went out with whoops and smiles? Is there something I am totally missing here? And if so, what?

Oh, Lord, the retaliatory killings they talked about after that, and all the puny scores that were being settled! The last live interview we listened to was of some man who had just shot everyone on his team, some amateur league he belonged to, who talked of what he did like it was nothing. And the reporter, to keep pushing for more details, to sound so matter of fact, so *professional*. That's when Gregg threw the radio out. To witness fear and panic shutting down parts of our brains, to hear of how way too many of us were reduced to reactive predators? I had no problem with his outburst – good riddance to the radio. What's so creepy, is to realize how the same primal reduction that causes violence crosses into the very same realm of the pleasure-seeking. While some ate or fucked or drank themselves into oblivion, others had their brains clobbered out. All with the same results. Good Lord, good grief.

So here I am, very possibly alone, at least up here in this part of the world, in what we'd come to call our woods. And the woods it is where I, we, can be thankful, for me, us, to not have been wiped out for benefit of someone else's murderous last call. When we moved here two years ago, little did we know….

I helped bathe, dress and tuck our babies under the covers, and I helped my husband situate himself in bed with them. I made my place ready, turned the corner of the coverlet back for me, next to them. God help me, I was the one with the idea, the one who rolled the tablets in the colored baking sugar to make them easier to take, so help me, to give to the girls. Green ones, red ones. Sweet. Crunchy. *Look, sweeties, they're covered in fairy sprinkles!*

Oh, Lord, are *You* holding them now, too? My husband's embrace, so expansive, so protective, his broad, outdoorsman's hands still free for me to take hold of when I am ready to climb under the covers and join them…

They are safe. They are content. They are safe. Smiling. Safe. . .

Breaths so gently waning, I couldn't even tell which ones were their last. Under the quilt, as if we needed a blanket, the patchwork coverlet I made when Isa…

No, I cannot think their names. I cannot cry. Must hold on. I am so close to wrapping this thing up. I need to find Maeve. I need to have my pup with me. She doesn't deserve to feel fear or pain, either.

Maeve! Maeve! Puppy, puppy, where are you?

Come to mommy! C'mon! Treat…treat!

All I need to do is find my stupid little dog. How frightened she must be. I can't bear to think it, to leave her alone like that.

I know, I know: when the tornado is bearing down, and the sirens are blaring, seek shelter. Don't go looking for the damn pets. They know to hide.

But that is exactly what I am doing. And I am going to find her. Then I will hold her and do the unspeakable – put her to sleep with the stuff I got at the clinic before they closed up. Good Lord, Cassie, the nurse, had already been shot dead, and the doc was a sunken-eyed shell of herself when she handed me the meds, her hand shaking so terribly. She kissed Maeve's scruffy little head, and we hugged, but only for a moment. *Go! Go!* She had whispered through clenched teeth, *before they come for us here!*

The woods, the house, the lake – what was the lake. Now, it's a mirror-smooth plain of dry sediment and smooth rock, awash in shades of red. It *was* almost beautiful, but now it's not. The red has taken on a poisonous intensity. Rose colored glasses; they'd say…

Maeve! Maeve! Dear God, if you are out there, please, please help me find her! I ask nothing else, nothing. Only this. I will go home, I will walk the path back to the house and give my stupid little dog her meds, then I will lay down in the big bed with my husband and the….

I can't think of them, see them lying there in my mind. I must stay clear-headed so I can see and think and find my stupid little dog.

Maeve! Honey, come to mommy!

Oh, my God, this is almost unbearable. The air shimmers. The evergreens are now but dried bristle brushes. They waver as if stirred by a breeze, but, no, they are perfectly still. It is the heat doing that. It's building, it's flowing – visibly. Way off, on the mountain crests, I swear I can see fire. The earth is igniting.

I have to get home! If I don't find the dog soon, I may wind up being sucked into the air myself, all the water in my body blanched straightaway out of me, like the clouds we watched, when they were siphoned off into the heavens. They disappeared like cotton candy pulled up and out of a steel basin. And that basin became our barren sky – we saw it empty out. Utterly and completely. The sky that went through the full color spectrum as it died, our very own color-coded morbidity indicator, my husband joked sarcastically. *Ha ha,* I had responded.

What's this under the boulder? What? It's Maeve! It's the dog! My stupid little runabout baby girl pup! Oh my God, I have found her!

Come, sweetie. Come to mommy!

I can barely reach her.

Here, here! Treat! I have a treat!

I gather my quaking pup into my arms and cover her head with kisses. She licks my face, frantically returning my affection. Even her tiny tongue is dry. It feels like my chin is being swiped with a scrap of felt. We are momentarily enveloped in a souvenir of what is our history, all our history:

Love. Just love.

Okay. Okay. Back to the house *now*. It's getting harder to even move. The air has thinned to a dangerous point. I am breathless. When I do inhale, it's hot, and it hurts. So hot. Worse than that first step into a dry sauna, worse than the moment you check on the bread baking in the oven and have your face closer to it than you should. The air is so hot, I am sipping it, thinking perhaps my insides can cool the air sufficiently before it hits the walls of my lungs. I just need another minute or two of this, just enough to get back…

Maeve, my baby little lovey pup, I tuck her under my blouse, hoping the micro atmosphere between the fabric and my skin can sustain her, keep her sufficiently unharmed so she doesn't perish in the heat of that evil, looming, burning *thing* that is hurtling towards earth, towards us, towards me, which will soon blow me, her and everything to oblivion.

How many minutes *do* I have left?

Home, home!

Back to my husband, back to….

No, no, stop. I will not think their names just yet. Clarity. Clarity.

Go!

I am hobbling up the path to the cabin. The cabin shimmers, like a mirage. I hope I am really seeing my home and not some after-image in hell.

What if I am dead already and this is all there is?

What did I do?

I can no longer keep my eyes open. I have to squint, tight. The heat threatens to dry my exposed eyeballs. My mouth is already like paper. I feel my way towards the front steps. Twenty seconds, I think, is all I need.

No, no. The hair on my arm is now lifting. I feel my scalp tingle.

It is not merely heat but now also the static draw of that, *that thing* in the sky, which is now so close, it is beginning to pull us in towards itself. The size of an aircraft carrier, even at this distance, *that thing,* a molten, pulsating, celestine scape of swirling reds, yellows, and oranges. And not only that, the aura it emits – a surround of pure, super-heated energy – is now completely visible to the naked eye. Glowing insidiously, its tentacled halo stretches ever more unfettered into the immediate reaches above and around me. Any minute now, those heated fingers will make contact with the mountaintops. And vaporize them. In the end, I imagine the gravitational pull of *that thing* will simply suck the earth right up onto itself once it gets close enough. Like a planetary Medea, she'll draw her last child to her breast to kill it.

There is no time left. Not enough to even get to the bedroom, not anymore.

I am on the bottom step. Dear Lord, God.

Okay:

Gregg.

Evelyn.

Isabel.

There. I thought their names. I call out their names in my heart.

I feel in my pocket for the vial.

Here, pup, open your mouth. We are out of time. Maevey my sweet puppy, you will not suffer.

She will feel my kiss as her last moment. She will feel only love, all the love I still have in me – for Gregg, for my amazing Evie, for my little Isabelli. My love is still so big, so alive. Surely that love has to go somewhere, live on in some way. I want to believe it's not just fear that drives this, but fact. That I will see them – all of them – in just a little bit.

I wedge my finger into Maeve's mouth to pry it open. She in her blessed oblivion begins to lick my finger with her felted tongue.

I insert the tip of the vial into Maeve's mouth.

As I am about to depress the vial, a shadow sweeps over me, us, the front step, the house, the woods. Beyond us. The shadow sails across the terrain like a super-sonic curtain. It stills the air, the land, the moment. I gasp and instantly feel air enter my lungs that, though still preternaturally heated, is in the space of one second no longer as hot as it was a moment ago.

I look up. We look up. Maeve in her limited, dutiful capacity senses something is afoot. Sniffing, her dry button of a nose pointing skyward, Maeve is investigating, checking, less so for her sake than out of her sense of duty for her beloved human, on whose behalf she is tracking the universe.

We watch. A humanoid, hand-like form has appeared, fingers spread eons wide. It is cloaked in heaving, atmospheric grays and greens, cloud masses and nebulae. It trails sparkling threads of icy space debris, tails as long as time. Perhaps it is the glitter of infant stars that twinkles near its fingertips – a rhythmic, almost intentional, pulsation. This *thing* has emerged out of a deep-space galactic crevice in the sky, or some nethering worm hole, a dark matter nexus which has simply, easily split the solar system – without fanfare or warning, without a sound.

This, this *hand* stretches its fingers and grabs hold of the flaming dervish, that, *that thing* that has been flying towards the earth for weeks, for millennia, for an eternity. It tightens its grip. It holds fast.

The hand-like entity is cradling that *thing*, holding it aloft, a liquified, sovereign's orb, for whom – all? – to behold. It's being ceremoniously presented to all the galaxies out there, be it the ones coming or the ones going. I can see the red hot, seething surface from between the fingers and their enveloping grasp.

Is this some kind of contest? Between what? Between whom?

When news that Mercury, and then Venus, had hit, that they had been thrown off their orbits, the world knew, all bets were off. Within hours, an intercontinental panic had been spawned, resulting in an explosion of extreme actions of individuals, groups and nations. And once the words "futility" and "inevitability" had been inserted into the informational floodgates, a regressive last-ditch purge had been triggered. Mankind regressed in hours to Man versus Man. "We" reverted back to primal lows in no time, and there "we" stayed. Most of humanity was gone in months.

Now add to that my husband and the… No. Stop right there.

Inklings of the slippery and easy slope upon which "we" all sat was what had compelled me and my husband to move ourselves and the girls off the grid, up to the northernmost reaches of the continent to live, to survive. And that relative escape was why I now stood alone with my dog, weathering this nightmare by myself, lone witness to what I had come to understand would be my last hour.

But now? What proto-natural manifestation had just emerged out of the chaos, to stop whatever was about to happen?

Maeve barks. She barks again and then looks at me for approval. I, out of simple, blessed, loving habit scratch her head to still her with affection.

My pup and I are in the presence of something huge, so huge, I instinctively know I cannot miss a single, split second. If I am to die here, where I stand, I want my memory of this, this, *miracle* to be so imprinted into my soul, that if there is any chance for it to resurface in the sentience of some next era being, it will be a recallable memory, no matter how piecemeal or fractured it might be. I will look and remember *so* hard, that somehow, the encoded message will be carried forward over time, so if, when, someone someday accidentally grabs at its fragments, they will be able to put the pieces together, and decipher them. And share them.

This is the kind of stuff that bends the eternal. I must *remember*.

I am crying as I watch, but as I am as dehydrated as a hollow husk, my sobs are silent, my eyes remain dry. I can barely manage to blink.

The heavenly hand is surrounded by swirling nebulae, which drape themselves around the liquid-neon object it holds fast, which suddenly appears – gosh – rather small. Like one of Maeve's tennis balls. The clouds spin and wrap themselves around the entities, wrapping them up, together.

It is the most beautiful thing I have ever seen.

My mind tells me I am watching a light-year broad, light-speed fueled maneuver, playing itself out in the cosmic equivalent of my back yard.

I do not move. I barely breathe.

I have only images of questions. There are, indeed, no words.

Is this the Second Coming?

Is it a Second Chance?

What the hell is going on?

Thank God, I stand alone, well, alone with my pup, to witness this. No doubt the panicked reactivity of any fellow surviving humans would have only resulted in more mass mayhem, even if it were of a manic, celebratory nature. What stupid, violent creatures we are. That thing about beautiful dreams and horrible nightmares? Yep. That is, was, is us. Me too, I suppose. Only for me, it had all and only become about the shielding against fear, of a peaceful passage. For my beloved husband and the….

Oh. My. God.

What have I done?

I killed my children. I killed my husband.

Out of love?

The only thing now to make *my* emptiness bearable, would be the absence of my family from the roster of human population that exists no more. But that is not the case. They are gone. Oh, my Lord, my God, they are gone.

We all just thought we were doing the right thing.

Who else is left?

I am left. I and my stupid, precious dog.

I hold Maeve against my cheek. My mind regresses. Old, dark images try to speak to me. I am adrift inside Noah's big, empty ark, an accidental passenger, but I am alone; I am not one of a pair, I have no place there. And so, I am on the outside. I am the rains. Forty days and forty nights. I will be a cup of water fed to the flood, and I will be glad to drown with it.

If this doesn't do me in, nothing will. Not even the killing suck of that *thing* made it as far as me, for here I fucking stand. I look at my shoes. Dusty, but intact. I look at my hands. Scratched, nails broken and dirty, but there they are. Holding my dog. Maeve looks at me and tilts her head. She is trying to understand.

Why me?

I startle, disgusted to even think I would dare entertain the notion I was *intentionally* spared.

Did I survive because I did not deserve *it*, or did I live because I deserve *this*?

There are no answers.

I watch the heavenly hand pull the blazing heart back, back, back, putting her into her rightful and benign place, a moon on one of the most distant children of the solar system. Suddenly, I can see the sun again, a pinprick of light. She is still there, where she has been all along, hidden these last several months behind the site line of a stone-cold, rogue castoff, which had been re-ignited by none other than her warming fires, to carve a killing path across our life-giving skies.

Our skies. I watch them darken, turning first a dusky lavender then deepening to violet, becoming once again transparent. I see the fires on the mountain tops; they have crept up to the crests and are burning themselves out, their cragged outline a feathered gold against what will soon become, once again, a clear night sky. So ironic, so much beauty.

Stars.

The sun, a giantess incarnate, our peach-colored elder, winks from her perch, distanced and ensconced. She is seated, per my paltry perspective, with her family. The heavenly kindred have re-appeared, once again as benign as lightning bugs, traversing the broad, open fields of our solar system on their elegant trajectories, undisturbed, now that the demon child has been put safely away.

The swath, the hand, the fingers of – What? Whom? – recede and merge with the darkness of deep space, vanishing like an atoned spirit at the end of a ghost story.

It's gone. No glory, no fanfare. A casualness.

A breeze kicks up. The skies are rearranging themselves. The stratosphere inhales, expands. The atmosphere is reconstituting itself. The moon no doubt still lurks in the safe harbor of earth's shadow; it will be a while before it dares show its small face…

A lonely cricket chirps.

I sink to the ground, and here I sit. At this moment, my legs are dead weight. No doubt, they will come to soon enough. But I am unsure of absolutely everything, including if this miraculous confluence was merely a taunting invitation to yet another but more prolonged demise, a hint of more hellishness yet to come.

I am trying to fathom what I stood in the presence of…

I. Have. No. Idea.

Maeve whimpers and nudges my hand, wondrously oblivious. I bet she is hungry. There is plenty of food in the basement; we did stock up. As for myself, I cannot see past my own shores, past what will have to rise up and fill me, grow into an ocean of loss I will have to cross, in all likelihood, alone.

Beyond the loss lies Nothing. I may as well be dead, but something in me forbids me from doing myself in. I will keep breathing. I will see how I do.

I cannot begin to interpret, let alone wax poetic, on what just happened, what I witnessed, accidentally, undeservedly.

My mourning has only begun.

Efectus

Homages and references to:

The Last Day (1953) Richard Matheson

and

"You're an interesting species. An interesting mix. You're capable of such beautiful dreams, and such horrible nightmares. You feel so lost, so cut off, so alone, only you're not. See, in all our searching, the only thing we've found that makes the emptiness bearable, is each other." *Contact (1985)* Carl Sagan

…and Toto, too.

GAMMA GAIA

February 13 Launch Day

Hey Diary,

I have precisely one hour before this beast takes off. Stasis immersion and system deceleration will start fifteen minutes before launch. Yes, my good-byes have been said, and so I will use this time to talk to you, to record in some detail what is going on, for your soon-to-be Earthling No More:

I am sad. And scared. But more than that, I am excited.

I will miss my friends.

Who'd have thought, that "mail order bride" would once again be resurrected as a bit of wry partnership vernacular? That's what my friends have been calling me ever since I told them what I was going to do. And yes, I agree with Effrin; I was born many a century too late. What sparks my spirit, is indeed, from another era.

So, I passed the tests. All of them, which is why I am here, one of, um, just over 550 passengers, I believe, on the good ship Lollipop – I jest – on the good ship Druyan VIII.

T-minus fifty-five minutes as I speak, before I sink into a medically induced long winter's nap. Winter…Will I miss the turning of the seasons?

And who'd have thought, a qualification such as "bio purity" would rear its archaic head? Untaintedness as a measure of feminine worth? Gads. But I willingly opted in. And how about being tested for stable fertility potential, or birth delivery functionality (not wishing those exams on anyone!)? And what's with a decent string o' genes to round out that hyper intimate self-portrait? So be it.

I'm good to go, good to go…

Who all else was tempted to bail when confronted with sign-up at those levels of profiling? Yes, it took just that to fling the doors wide to deep, far-ass-off space travel, to serve – yes, I said *serve* – as a mail order space bride, a living, breathing, fertile female human for…hmmm, what do I call it…a far-out sex-based adventure in a new life I can't even begin to imagine?

So, what *should* I call my starry-eyed trek? This ancient pop song once asked, "What's love got to do with it?" But that *is* what got me to thinking: Far away is where I *think* I might I find what I *believe* I am looking for.

I wouldn't mind trying out "love."

So, here is the ad behind it all.

Diary: paste document, "Mail Order Bride Ad."

Could this be you?
Seeking viable female candidates
with reproductive functionality & familial behavioral affinity
for deep space travel & child-bearing partnership
with Terral-2 Astralnauts
for purposes of populating Terral AB2-765
Resumes & DNA profile disclosure mandated
Voice prompt: Apply Terral-2 Repro-V6-HL

I know how people used to meet – I am a pro on the subject – in random places: stores, bars, parks, to measure each other up, gauge compatibility. "Hooking up" as they called it, back in the post-tech bridge years. Quaint, to liken sexual conquest with fishing. Maybe not so quaint… Anyway, face to face was how it was done, once upon a time. People quite literally sniffed each other out. Verifiable! Scent mattered. I've seen it play out in tons of the books and motion pictures still out there. Gosh – how many of those have I downloaded? Suffice it to say, I have yet to experience a dull moment in a travel pod. So much great stuff to read or listen to, to watch – many a lonesome Lunar highway makes for an awesome Hollywood "silver screen" fix.

And romance, wow! Gushing emotions, displays of temper, passionate reconciliation, "hot" stuff…it was *so alive*… Society was *obsessed* with it! The best stuff I have on my reader, and oh, yes, it's going with me.

It's relationship narratives of the eras prior to the Extraterrestrial Disclosures (In some ancient texts they used to posit *we'd* find *them*. How hilarious is that?) that are still the most fascinating to me. Which brings me to what drove me to this undertaking.

T-minus 49 minutes as I speak…

Love.

It *does* sound lovely. Love and its driver, romance. Funny thing, how my penchant for stories of that genre paved a beeline path (I think that is how they put it) to my earning solid cred as Doctorate of Cultural Anthropology, with a specialization in pre-tech era Western World Romantics literature, and, yes, you could say how it even landed me here. I am a believer one can earn their "bread and butter," as they used to say, doing what they love best. I guess that's a romantic perspective too, isn't it…have it be all about love…

So, I'm wondering, who will be on the other end of this launch? Will there be a "True Love" waiting for me? The classic adage generally was all about the "happily ever after."

44 minutes. Nerves, stay cool. Be still my beating heart…

That ad I pasted above was embedded in some of the books I downloaded in recent years. Definitely targeted to demographics the likes of me. Sure, I'm honored to have been catapulted from their rosters of candidates to this, um, let's call it heroine's journey, to "our" baby Earth, the Terral AB2-654 in the Galaxial arm of Alpha-Centauri, for purposes of sexual reproduction with some likewise tested and rostered male candidate. Old-fashioned baby making, sort of. Ironic, how we wound up, after so many hundreds of years, reverting back to this means of populating new planetary colonies.

But, good grief, all those cryogenic pre-borns, all those future beings we tend to call eggstronauts. And just how many perished before they finally admitted that wasn't going to be the answer? Mary Shelley, for goodness' sake, just a teenager when she conjured up that age-old story, had the conundrum so brilliantly – so pre-emptively – figured out. Good intentioned or bad, even in this era, we can't quite keep up with ourselves, what we do with what we bring about. Especially, when life itself remains the collateral.

Mary…that is a good name…a pretty name, solid phonetics…

Diary: make a note of that name.

38 minutes…

I am thinking, the relative isolation of where I am going could make for real pair bonding. Friendship. So, why not romance? Always presented as a messy and odd human odyssey, the notion of trying out something like that, provided my reproductive partner is willing, does give me this nice, funny feeling… As they used to say, the things we pretend to be…

Evidently, there were Terral lab-born generations, but as we were informed in training, they were never able to reach relative maturity, what we still sometimes call "old age." The subjects aged out exponentially, passing way too soon. Scientists never got the "recipe" right. Sounds callous, but it is what it is. Which is why, of course, I lie here, on my way to Terral-2. This process needs, they told us, fresh genetic "influx." Live human hosts…

Ironic, isn't it, that the "old school" way of doing all this would find its re-birth on the farthest nooks of existence, in an entirely different planetary system, so far only populated by a smattering of best-of-the-best scientists?

Well, off, into space I go, off to sleep for one hundred – well, not quite – years. A Sleeping Beauty who'll slumber 'til awakened by True Love's first kiss….

Kissing… it sounds fun. I intend to try that.

30 minutes to launch…oh, wow, it's happening…about fifteen minutes before stasis initiation…

But, it won't be so much a kiss as a whiff of juiced-up air and chemicals that will bring me out of stasis once we enter into Terral-2's orbital highways. The stuff better work…

What I do know is that someone out there when I come to will have been willing to be tested for the same purposes I have been. And he hasn't even been born yet.

…and so, here I am, about a half hour 'til launch; mapped, verified, basically sterilized from head to toe ("Clean as a whistle," they used to say. Inside and out. Yikes, that part was *not* fun), ready for what they persist in calling "sleep" for the next sixty some years, at speeds that will not only suspend my "loverly" twenty-two-year age but could possibly reverse me by a year or two by arrival. It better not take me back farther than that…

Part of me wishes I could be awake for the flight, especially the wormhole portion of it. The personal accounts of those who were conscious during the light speed Waking Slingshots are masterpieces of sentient experience. But to be awake, consciously receptive, during a slingshot is to commit suicide. Which of course is why the personal accounts are so heart-rending – wormhole narratives are as poetic as they are poignant. These people ought to be sainted for their contributions. I myself can't imagine *willingly* giving my life up for anything.

What does it take to be willing to do that?

No, they never were able to program a Non-Sentient to capture the moments, the feelings, the imagery of interstellar, fold-time travel. Poeticism is amazingly human – to this day, it still separates us from the bots. Bless those dear souls who gave their lives to tell us their stories…

Ten minutes 'til stasis…

Wow, here I lie on my Interstellar Travel Bier… I know the risks, and yes, I am resigned to them. I am making this trip for *life*, so that a new human, perhaps a few of them, can result from my making this journey. My body. A baby. That thing where you give birth, then nurture and care for a new human until it reaches maturity. I mean, that's a kind of poetry too…

Five minutes to immersion…

So sleepy now. The drip has started. I heard the click, and I can feel an, um, liquid-like calming down. Oh my gosh, I am so nervous! Nervous and excited. I will need every drop of whatever is being pumped into me. Hey, turn it up a notch – knock me out!

Counting, counting…

The warmth…perfect, the stuff in the IV feels good. They know what they are doing… I hope… Wish I could stay awake, but, as that one guy…what's his name…would write, So It Goes…

Aaah. Lovely. Resting…lights…dimming. You, Dear Diary, must go…sleep too. I have…serious snooze ahead of…

Please, let me dream…

†††

68 Earth years later…

…follow you will you follow me
All the days and nights that we know will be
I will stay with you will you stay with me

Softly, softly, music plays. The song, I selected as my callup, apropos, by a 20th century music group called Genesis, of all things. Sweet song. All about travel amidst love, the journey…

Good morning. Softest of lights. I open my eyes – lashes sticky – I can see, dimly. It's dark, but not blackout night. Blue, dim. My eyes can handle this. Yes, I can see. I blink. I see the dome of my bier. All appears, um, all appears…

All as I remember it, what, some days, some years ago. Funny, this time thing. I guess I am light years from Earth now. There is peacefulness around me but it's not, um, a dead kind of vibe. Slight movement in the pods next to me. A successful journey "through the stars"? Let's hope. We should be, according to what I, um, recall, now in thrust, ready to enter the outer atmosphere of Terral-2… A couple more days…

…can't quite feel my arms, legs. I think I am wiggling my toes…

Food, hmmm… But I am not hungry.

I see a door slide open. Subdued illumination, but something hinting a bit brighter than solid black. Forms standing in the passageway. People.

It's the crew. They've been up for some time…moving quickly, a group of them…blurry… Three, four of them? They are moving together, a tight group, quickly. With intention. Urgency? Something in their postures triggers something in me. A twinge. Deep inside… They are passing the other travel biers in my row. They are approaching mine. They are approaching me. Oh, to see a smile again will be so nice…

…they are not smiling…

…sleepy…no…

Wait a moment…Wai…

†††

I am looking out of my eyes, with my twenty-two-year-old sight, recently roused from a sixty-eight-year period of stasis. This is fucked. I can see the shadow of the bridge of my nose. For all else, I must rely on what is looking back at me in the reflection of the window partition of the infirmary, behind which the room stands empty, lights out. Minuscule pinpoints – green, orange, red – dot the console and wall panels. It feels good to see color.

But they've only offered me a *window*, not a mirror.

Maybe they have no mirrors here? Given mandates of interstellar qualification, it's almost a given, decent good looks would be a pleasant aside, although how one might present physically in this society would come a distant second to capabilities of the gray matter. So, I guess it is possible, there are no mirrors.

No, I can see plenty. More than enough…

My eyes have met up with some sort of human fixture borne of, um, what else can I call it but decrepitness? It's staring rudely, intimately, angrily back at me. A scowling mouth, brows drawn together. Sunken wells accost me in the glass, darkened windows to a someone rather soulless. There is a mass of white hair atop the head – in a braid, like what I had done in preparation for flight. It appears to be a few inches longer than mine was, but it's devoid of the rich browns of my – oh help me – my youth. After mulling on the whiteness of the – my? – hair I notice crepe paper skin, sagging, sallowed, a fretwork of red and bluish blood vessels shimmering through wherever bone or cartilage meet with the vaguely feminine shell I see reflected, which, so help me, cannot be…no, not me…surely…

Hands? My hands are those things at my side? What protrudes from these sleeves cannot be not my hands. No way! They are the stone-knuckled hands of a hag.

In that moment, a chair is pushed up against the back of my knees. My legs give out as if cued by the seat's placement behind me, and I fall into it. The seat is well cushioned but the impact hurts. Arms grab and hold me, keep me from sliding off the chair and onto the floor…

"I'm melting! I'm melting!" she screams.

Someone wake me from this nightmare – yes, throw some cold water on me!

The hovering gaggle of astro-geniuses are tsk-tsking me like a bunch of old aunties from Kansas.

I croak at them, "Well, you're going to need to tell your Einstein's, they sure as shit got *this* recipe wrong!"

As soon as my outburst – these Astral-whatevers haven't used or even heard profanity in their pristine and sterile world – strikes their pretty, little ears, with their teensy earrings glinting, sending their pastel-colored crewcuts on end, I feel a coolness in my arm kick in. Again. Dammit. They are hiking up my IV drip once more in reaction to the lady protesting too much…

Why the hell do they keep thinking they need to sedate me?

As I drift off – again – I manage a few more choice words, something about what a bunch of Victor Frankenstein's they *all* are.

A new memory: walking past the biers to the keeping room. Pods with their domed lids still firmly in place. Still filled with stasis gel. And passengers. In them. Not asleep – dead. Afloat in clear muck. Humans in aspic. One passenger's hands were pressed against the dome, her face frozen. Mid-scream? Mid-gulp? Her eyes were wide, wide open.

Pompeii, Herculaneum. History repeats herself, the nasty bitch. A colony, a community: Poof!

I remember. And I will remember this all going forward. I listened as they spoke. Hushed, panicked hisses. Information, admonishment, conjecture. How in the world this could have happened? Almost half the transport population perished. Half of it aged practically beyond recognition. Rotted youth, suspended human prey. Deep space alien amber. Help us all.

What was it I had read, that I had incorporated into my graduate thesis? Oh, yes; it's coming back to me: I am now myself hardly more than two steps extant from the bloody, chest-bursting fear gamesmanship of late twentieth century entertainment I studied for years. *I am the alien.* What an insidious, full circle mess this is.

Maybe it's my anger that spares me. My spunk and spitfire, as my friends used to call it. Anything less electric than a fight-inducing reaction to this horrific awakening may have simply killed me. And alive, oh boy, I am, whatever the incarnation this version of me turns out to be…

…and I was, am – was, so help me – a young woman about to embark on life. Life. And now, I am this, this, aged *thing*, stitched at a cellular level into a housing with a shrew's face, a withered form, blanched hair, knotted hands…

What about *time*? What of time will be mine?

I had a life to live!

I want to scream at these, these *scientists*…

No, let me look! Let me see!

†††

With that, like some unruly pest having kicked up too much of a fuss for comfort, she was under, again.

†††

"…so, you see, as it turns out, the malfunction in your ITB did not preserve your age as it should…"

"…you can say that again…"

"…rather, it accelerated your bio-age, though I must stress it preserved your functionality remarkably well, miraculously, actually…"

"…how dare you talk of miracles with me!"

"Sorry, sorry, of course, Gaia. I am just as heartbroken over this as you are, and trust me, we are going to do absolutely everything in our power to make this right…keep you, well, comfortable…"

"Right, my ass!"

"I know, I know…"

"No, you don't know! You have no idea how I am feeling right now! Hell, I don't know how *I* am feeling right now! I feel *old*! Horrid! Horrible! This is a nightmare – *I* am a nightmare!"

"Gaia, you have good years ahead of you here. And you made it! Look where we are and what a contribution you will make by just *being,* living here amongst us!"

"Oh, help me, please! I want to die. Don't talk to me as if I'm some kind of bio-relic you can put on display!

"I am so sorry, so…"

"Oh, stop with the pity play! I can see you, you *scientists*: you're practically salivating at this beastly, ancient thing I have become and what I hold for you as human guinea pig! This was to be the start of an amazing, new life for me. Life – oh, wow – life! I was going to be somebody's reproductive partner – I was going to *give* life! And now, look at me, I am barely able to hang onto what I have. What the hell *is* left for me?"

"Surely, Gaia, we can get a solid decade or so out of you yet…I mean, we can foster many quality years for you. And…"

"Can you send me back?"

"What?"

"Send me back, put me back through the loopholes, wormholes, whatever those damn things are called; reverse me, put me back on Earth at my *real* age."

"My dear, this isn't science fiction."

"Doctor, I am sure many would want to debate that point with you."

"Look. We won't have another manned return trip for at least another fifteen, twenty years. You know those are still in Phase 1. We just don't have the capacity for fabrication here as we do, did, on the Lunar stations. And this most recent stasis malfunction – I am sorry to put it this way – proves the point, we do not yet dare launch return passenger-carrying trips. Earth won't even hear of this mission failure for another four years. Until communication transmission speed is effectively squared, everything we do has to be in four- to five-year intervals, so that information and the advancements made, whether here or there…"

"Well, then just put me down! Give me something!"

"No. That we will not do. Cannot do. The Directive forbids it. Life preserved. At all costs. You know that."

"Life. Ha! What life? What cost?"

"Please, Gaia, calm down. Things will feel better in the morning. The right meds, some food – you know, we have nearly perfected our food replicators. I'll make you breakfast…"

"But I'm not hungry."

"But, oh, my dear, when you smell the coffee…"

"No! I am not hungry! Shit, I still don't have any feeling in my…"

"In due time, Gaia, preliminary tests all show nerve pathways are intact and engaged. You are still waking up."

"Fuck the waking up!"

"Now, Gaia, you don't mean that…"

"Yes, I do!"

"Alrighty, my dear, we're going to administer some…"

"No!"

"You'll feel better in the morning…"

"No! No.…"

†††

The psych-recalibration treatments helped, though Gaia vehemently refused implantation of a mood stabilizing device. Something about a Borg…She also used another word – what was it – a Giger…?

But Gaia was a good subject. Biologically speaking, she was well put together, and the spunk and spitfire she had seen fit to mention in her personal statement applied itself most advantageously to her adjusting as well as was possible, in the face of what amounted to her entire adult life having been pulled out from under her.

†††

The "Mail Order Bride," as the subject sarcastically referred to herself, remained sullen for a time, but she eventually appeared to reconcile the loss of her stolen youth. Granted, what a calamity her mission flight had been for many; while the majority of passengers had made it unscathed, Gaia Scott was the only one among the aged-out passengers to survive the post-revival shock. The others died within days.

As for lost causes – her youth, health, vague and untested constructs of desire, undeveloped passions, perhaps an untapped capacity for love, certainly that of motherhood, and life to be lived as a nurturing body, teacher, and mentor to some newly-made human – those loomed as infinitely unfortunate as a personal black hole to Gaia. But was this end an absolute?

No.

By the time she expired, Gaia had spent almost thirty earth years as teacher and tall-tale teller to the newest offspring of the Terral-2 community. The children came to adore Gaia for her animated, profanity peppered, ad-libbed narratives. She opened the kids' young minds to the ancient literary legacies of their Earthling kindred – noble and otherwise.

Gaia also taught "her" kids age old vernacular, spicy bits and pieces with which her Lil Half Pints delightedly shocked their parents and parental designees, who also found themselves feeding eagerly on the simple riches of something almost bypassed in the sophisticated complexities of their high-level, planned society. In doing this, Gaia tossed a monkey wrench into a system that would serve to smash to pieces every perfected façade, every mirrored vanity, every smug intellect, and correspondingly compliant wit. She smashed them all with *Humor.*

"Heavens to Murgatroyd!" the children would yell on the playground.

"Please sir, I want some more!" they would quip when asking for seconds at meals.

"Auntie Em! Auntie Em!" and "Halt, who goes there!" and "Out, damn spot!" the Astralings (Gaia's other name for them) would gleefully employ, though often, given the hyper-ordered circumstances of their world, out of context, but always at the tops of their tiny lungs.

It even became a game for programmers to keep the food replicator updated with new and creative snacks for the children, who became so well versed in matters of Augustus Gloop and friends, that the vocabulary for vocal prompts for those foods had to be downloaded verbatim from the antique text on Gaia's own reader.

Was it some mystical transmogrification of anger that compelled Gaia to instill this nonsense into the sterile perfection of a colony of highest human order? The scientists thought so, but it appears, they *approved*. A few months before Gaia expired, they named the school for her. Her ancient eyes could barely muster a tear, but the sparkle of her stunted youth shone through in blazes as she steered her hover-chair up to the podium.

Eventually, words like "brat," "mischief," and "sass" were recognized as part of the language of Terral-2, a direct result of the legendary immigrant who had raised its first generation of little shits. Gamma Gaia, as they came to call her, had managed to infuse – no, *infect* – a newly founded society with some of the oldest, most rambunctiously healthy vestigial remains of their human ancestors – Laughter.

†††

Too Saccharin an Ever After? Let us crimp time and re-consider…

†††

"Send me back, put me back through the loopholes, wormholes, whatever those damn things are called; reverse me, put me back on Earth at my *real* age."

"My dear, this isn't science fiction."

"Doctor, I am sure many would want to debate that point with you."

"Look. We won't have another manned return trip for at least another fifteen, twenty years. You know those are still in Phase 1. We just don't have the capacity for fabrication here as we do, did, on the Lunar stations. And this most recent stasis malfunction – I am sorry to put it this way – proves the point, we do not yet dare launch return passenger-carrying trips. Earth won't even hear of this mission failure for another four years. Until communication transmission speed is effectively squared, everything we do has to be in four- to five-year intervals, so that information and the advancements made, whether here or there…"

"…back home…"

"…yes, back home, are logged and received. You know that. Otherwise, we are quite literally, as they used to say, doomed to repeat our mistakes."

"You can say that again – we've been doing that for eons."

"Your historical circumspection is duly noted…"

"So, what about the kamikaze wormhole broadcasts? Send me on one of those."

"*What* did you call them?"

"Kami…yeah, okay. That's my nickname for them. I have followed them from the get-go. I say it with a historian's reverence, trust me."

"The one-way wormhole final broadcasts remain here, as they do on earth, WSR's. It remains best to stick to the, um, technical when referencing them."

"I know, Waking Slingshot Reports. Space poetry. Requiems for the Interstellar Age."

"Yes. Poetic requiems. Saganism at its finest. May he rest well."

"But that's my point. Let me rest in *my* peace by letting me volunteer for one of those. I can't possibly have much time left. This aged container, this carcass that houses me now? No. I will never, cannot, reconcile myself with this. Let me go."

"I can do some tests."

"For what?"

"Viability predictors. More of what we did earlier today."

"You mean, how well – er, how long – I might endure a Waking Slingshot?"

"No. It would be to determine what capacity your system has in its present state to maintain a productive viability here, amongst us…"

"I don't care about that. Test me to see if I can go. I want to go. I don't want to stay. How can I make it more clear to you?"

"Well, Gaia, that's what I am getting at. I can't breach directives. But if tests show you are in a…"

"Oh, I get it. A decline. As in, if I am headed to what happened to those others… You're saying I could be on my way out too, right?"

"In a sense…"

"Just say 'Yes.' Can you not tell by now I can take it, whatever "it" may be? What I don't intend to 'take,' is a decrepit subsistence amidst some ghastly decline among all you *scientists*. I might as well be a hamster in a glass box. Or an ant."

"No, we would never treat you as…"

"Oh, don't kid yourself. Now, Doctor, you all owe me this much. It's my last will, my last testament. *My will.*"

"Alright, alright, Gaia. Let's re-do your scans in the morning. I can re-calibrate the scanner to a higher sensitivity. If there is active de-generation, if your resumption of normal bio-functions as one of us shows any discrepancies – any at all – that point to any semblance of imminent demise, I will find them. And then you have my word. I will nominate you personally. Goodness knows, if I were in your shoes, I would want my wishes respected too."

"Thank you. This is the first sense you have made. This is the first thing any of you *scientists* have told me that sits well with this *thing* I have become."

"Gaia, it's still *you* in there…"

"I know, Doctor. That's why I can't do this, lie on my deathbed, awaiting expiration in wide, waking awareness. I would go kicking and screaming into my dark night, as it was once stated, and I promise you, it would be ugly. I, this "me" that's still inside, would fight instinctively until my last breath. And it would be bad. Really bad. Let me go in a state of awe. Let me go distracted, watching, talking, sharing everything I am feeling and seeing. Let me go in a state of wonderment."

"Can't argue with you there, Gaia. Get some sleep. We'll start in the morning."

"But I'm not tired."

†††

Launch Day

Hey Diary,

I have precisely fifteen minutes before this thing takes off, and immersion and system deceleration are to take place in, um, let's see: T-minus four minutes. I will be in stasis for only three years, until I exit outer orbit and breach the horizon of the Wormhole ZG-478A. And then it'll begin. The show of a lifetime.

Yes, my good-byes have been said, and so I will use this time to talk to you, my friend, to record in some detail what is going on, for your soon-to-be Human No More, to close the books on what was a failed first mission, on what sure as shit better be me going out with an interstellar Big Bang.

I am excited. And scared. But more than that, I am sad.

Not for my expiration. At this point, it'll be a relief. I can feel this corpse of a body failing me; it didn't take a freaking scan calibrated to Kingdom Come to tell me what's going on inside me. I am dying.

I am sad because what I will soon experience, I will only have for the immediate moment. So, diary, I must stay in the moment. Not one second in the past, not one iota in the future.

The Now. Only the Now.

I will miss life, but when I am out there, when I am looking out from my pod and it is transmitting every aspect of me, watching, talking, sharing, describing everything I can see, everything I am feeling, until the warp breaks me, my body and the Solojet apart, I am going to be standing on a heaven-crested horizon of experience, and I will honor all who have gone before me by adding to the knowledge of all who will eventually receive my last transmission, to help grow understanding of what it is we have wrought, and where the heck it is we have taken ourselves, and what it might be like if we start to have the opportunities to go back…

We build our monsters, and just as we have done for ages, we can't quite keep up with the beasts of circumstance we create alongside them, nor the ironies and conundrums in which we, like fools in love, become hopelessly lost.

I will paint a stellar picture, a thousand words' worth, with my final narrative, until my consciousness is ripped from me, and I will add my name to the roster of those who have seen time fold, and the constellations will greet me, I know it.

Please. I hope I dream…

†††

Still too Saccharin an ending? Let us crimp time once more, and go back again, this time all the way to…

Counting, counting…

The warmth…perfect, the stuff in the IV feels good. They know what they are doing… I hope… Wish I could stay awake, but, as that one guy…what's his name…would write, So It Goes…

Aaah. Lovely. Resting…lights…dimming. You, Dear Diary, must go…sleep too. I have…serious snooze ahead of…

Please, let me dream…

†††

68 Earth years later…

…follow you will you follow me
All the days and nights that we know will be
I will stay with you will you stay with me

Softly, softly, music plays. The song she selected as her callup, apropos by a 20th century music group called Genesis. Sweet song. All about travel amidst love, the journey…

†††

Good morning. I open my eyes. I open my mouth, draw in my first waking breath. But instead of sweet, pressurized air, my mouth fills with thick gel – *the stuff in which I am still afloat.*

My eyes tear open wide, in panic and out of a primal desire *to see.*

What the fuck?

I can't see!

Light? Movement?

Heeeeelp!

Arms lurch upwards. Fingertips strike the glassy surface of my domed bier. Pushing. Weak. Gel…thick…

Trapped!

I swallow. I choke.

I can't…

I…

Efectus

"Some celestial event. No – no words. No words to describe it. Poetry! They should have sent a poet. So beautiful. So beautiful…I had no idea."
Contact (1985) Carl Sagan

Eggstronaut *A stored and interstellar transported, fertilized human egg/zygote/embryo existing for purposes of re-populating newly inhabited worlds.*
Published at Urban Dictionary September 1, 2015, by ka the wordsmythe

BUTTERFLYBROTH

Yes, Heaven is thine; but this
Is a world of sweets and sours
Our flowers are merely—flowers

From, "Isafrel"
Edgar Allan Poe

Frell opened her eyes.
Nothing appeared different; everything seemed fine.
Everything was okay.
What a special day this might, could, at long last be.

†††

Frell lay her phone just so into her bag and placed it on the passenger seat beside her, so that she could still see its screen, on the off chance it might light up with a notification from Carl.

In that moment, the day was quietly joyous, rather perfect. The sun shone from a deep blue sky dotted with a benign scattering of combed cotton clouds. The street trees were a fresh, peridot green, testament to the perfectly timed rain showers over the last few weeks. Traffic was not too bad.

She had heard the heartbeat.

Albeit an echoey, rapid-fire blip, it was a real, living heartbeat, strong if solidly minuscule Frell had heard, a coded missive sent up and out from within the depths of her body, to announce to her, to the physician, and to posterity in the file recording, that all was very likely as it should be. At least preliminarily, biologically so. *It* was well. It was thriving and alive; and the plodding first trimester Frell had endured, one hour, one day, one week at a time, a time of nausea and interminable deep, psychic listening, listening, listening, had been successfully weathered. The odds of this reproductive attempt holding not a miscarriage, but an eventual live birth had that very morning become a valid, potential outcome.

How weird this first phase had been, she mused, for it was still a little too much like before, where she would so worry whenever she was feeling better. That lay, she knew, at the root of all ironies, being that a living being's fundamental, first spark of existence warranted ill-feeling in the mother as a sign all was in order, and that to feel, well, more normal – whatever might be for anyone – was a sign things were not as they should be. That Frell's system was adjusting over time and might no longer sound constant warning bells to bode ill, but now rather play quieted host to the ushering in of a next, significant phase in baby making, so commonly known as the second trimester, began to dawn on Frell as a viable next step status quo.

Now, Frell told herself, it was perhaps – maybe just maybe – okay to start thinking the new human within her would soon be with her, in their life together, come early autumn. This was what was making the good day a very good day. Now, she thought, if only she could get word to Carl. Forget about waiting and crafting some orchestrated announcement, Frell just wanted him to join in the intensely inwardly focused moment with her, to partake with her in the wash of relief in which she was beginning to think she could now indulge, even if with some residual hesitancy borne of experience and natural caution. How ironic, that of all days, today Carl was traveling back from the east coast on a highway that wound for the better part of the day through the mountains, where cell phone connectivity was still so spotty as to be useless. He had promised to call as soon as he was back on more open terrain; back in civilization as he, a city boy, often put it. Surely, Carl would be calling soon… Frell could hardly wait.

The now-familiar presence of a slight ill feeling, like one was on the brink of coming down with something, still nagged at Frell, but she was grateful for it. Frell decided she would celebrate this faint wave nausea by treating herself to a milkshake, knowing full well the cold in her stomach would do little to assuage the hormone-fueled symptoms which still plagued her all day, every day. Still, Frell smiled. She could indulge, permit herself to give in to that "eating for two" adage, just for fun. A vanilla milkshake would be the perfect baby n me kick-off treat for for the two of them. A sweet thought.

Driving home from the obstetrician, Frell was on a familiar four-lane thoroughfare divided by a grassy meridian split at regular intervals to allow for left turns into parking lots and frontage roads. The late afternoon sun, fractured by the street trees' new leaves, was broken into a glittering play of light on the windshield, and proving to be something of an impairment for all westbound drivers. Frell leaned forward in her seat, squinting, fishing for her sunglasses. No doubt land planners had thought park-effect plantings on a meridian to be both quaint and eco-embracing – it had, no doubt, looked terrific in renderings. Problem was, in practical application, the fruits of their genius had made for a continuous succession of blind spots.

For Frell, this was an oft-traveled homeward stretch; she knew vaguely whereabout the Emporium was located, knew its turnoff was fast approaching. Frell spied the store's sign over the treetops, coming into view more quickly than anticipated. It was difficult to see into the distance, especially across the road, now that the trees had fully greened in. But the Emporium was the place to go; they specialized in frozen custard shakes – all the more decadent and more the indulgence. So much more the order of her day. Frell scanned the meridian up ahead as best as she could, unsure where exactly the break in the curb to the parking lot was located. Not one to begrudge the trees their existences, but they always annoyed her on this particular stretch of road.

To be sure, Frell was a skilled driver, but at that moment, she was still ever so slightly afflicted with the happy mind fog of her milestone visit to the obstetrician, plus she was hungry, in need of a something to tide her over until dinner. Between her emotional distraction and that of the piercing late afternoon sunlight, and with the rising wave of morning sickness demanding appeasement, Frell's focus was just misdirected enough to prevent her from accurately gauging the timing and tactics for a quick turn-off into the parking lot, given the relative speed of all the vehicles on that rather heavily commercialized stretch.

An east-bound glass delivery truck with its glass racks loaded to the hilt sped through the stale yellow light at the next intersection, coming abreast of Frell's sought-for break in the meridian at precisely the moment Frell hit the gas so to quickly cross and clear what had two seconds earlier been an opening in the oncoming traffic. Frell never saw the truck. And not only did all elements converge to create a most unfortunate moment of near total blindness to the situation, but to top that off, in that very same instant, Frell's phone lit up and began to vibrate, still being set to silence from her visit to the doctor. Frell glanced reactionarily at her handbag at precisely the split second her car made impact with delivery truck.

Frell's husband was calling her, as promised. A photo from their week at the beach served as his contact image, and so as her car hit the glass rack, blowing its payload sky high, it was Carl Frell saw, his tanned arms spread wide, against a firework backdrop of ocean spray as a wave exploded around him.

†††

Frell opened her eyes. Leaves' shadows danced upon the ceiling of what appeared to be her bedroom. It took a moment. The street sounds from outside the window played familiarly, an innocuous mix of slow-moving automobiles and barking dogs. But then, the accident of the day before erupted into her consciousness with a breath-stealing rush, the crash and its crazed aftermath playing through in the theater of her mind. Impact. Sound. Glass raining down on the car like hail. Voices, sirens, people who invaded the collapsed interior of her car, holding her hand and asking, asking odd, random questions. The ambulance, more people, the hospital, the doctors, the tests, and then, finally, finally, at long last, the face of her husband at the door, his eyes wide with concern, his face ashen. But his appearance was like a sunrise, shining as if risen for her alone, calming, clearing her mind, allowing Frell a letting down of the desperate courage she had clung to, to where the healing tears could finally begin to fall.

All tests showed negative as to any injurious harm to her or to the very new human in her belly. Frell's state of mind and general good health had granted her the freedom to be discharged from the emergency room that very night, on the steadying arm of her husband. Emerged out of the chaos, they drove home in silence, holding hands, back to a real world that had just a few hours ago become a far lovelier place, for it was now one to be shared with another, brand-new beloved.

†††

It was Saturday morning. How late, Frell could only guess. She was ever so slightly sore. Could be from the crash – and was that only yesterday? Perhaps the stiffness was due to an over-long night of sleep. Either way, Frell was willing to permit herself an easing into the day, to help both mind and body re-acclimate to a full, wakeful mode. That much, she reckoned, she had most assuredly earned. The other side of the bed was empty. Carl's pajama bottoms lay in a heap on the foot of the bed. Perhaps he was making breakfast, as he often did on weekends.

When Frell entered the kitchen to start water for her tea, it was empty. Carl was nowhere to be seen or heard. Frell's eyes came to rest upon a note tucked under her cell phone, where she had left it on the counter. Carl would be right back, the note stated, hastily scrawled. How odd, Frell thought, for him to have taken off on this morning of all mornings, right after the day of her car accident, also the very next morning after she had told him, through tears as sentimentally charged as they were hormonal, of the heartbeat she had just heard for the first time that afternoon. The baby's. Their baby's.

Frell's tears had deeper meaning, as did the news. Her tears were still part of a sorrowful echo-effect of the two miscarriages she, they, had suffered over the past two years. Two babies, two lives already lost. Her body knew what it was doing, Carl would say to reassure her, tapping bio-logic to try and help console a wife who, while stoic on the practical reality of the failed pregnancies, still mourned the fleeting joy the two previous cherubs had gifted them, who would forever remain familial might-have-beens, asleep upon their celestial clouds, which would forever hold them in memoriam. Both Carl and his wife understood and accepted, as much as they also did not; such was their conditional wisdom, granted by force of their casualties.

Even so, Frell's disposition was inclined to question, even begrudge a little, her husband's needless absence on this morning of all mornings. What could he have possibly thought he needed to do that would take him away from her first thing, on a leisurely at-home Saturday morning, the first day, no less, of a three-day weekend? Part of the weekend had already been planned out, to be spent with family for a cookout, where now the added component of delivery of very happy news would surely be the order of their day. Why the rush to rush off when, to her, the morning hours could have been spent in quiet, intimate togetherness?

Frell noticed Carl had not signed the note with his customary two-heart motif, which over the years had become as familiar and valid a signature as his name ever would be. Instead of the dual, interlocking hearts, Carl's post-it bore a capital C with an "xoxo." Sweet, sure. But not the same. Carl had never, in all their years together, signed off with a "C xoxo." Frell dismissed this slight oddity and attributed her even noticing this to her "raging" – isn't that what people always said? – hormones, and to her being somewhat on edge, a major car accident having happened less than twenty-four hours ago. Frell stretched and flexed her neck. Her joints adjusted with small pops. Feels so good, she thought. Nope, not even enough soreness to warrant a Tylenol.

Frell decided she was in need of food. She made the tea, toasted a bagel, and settled into her favorite chair in the sunroom. Some morning news, perhaps a little reading, were in order. Her solitude had already shifted to the positive, a sense of contentment quickly supplanting her irritation from a moment ago. Frell loved having the place to herself, despite the fact that Carl was often away. To build his career required these absences, and the fruits of his labors were clearly being manifested. Who was she to be the complainer? Carl would show up at any moment. Her one text message to Carl, while remaining unanswered, Frell immediately attributed to his possibly being behind the wheel. Especially now, the last thing she wanted to do was distract him. She could wait.

Frell watched the broadcast, thinking idly "her" wreck might net a mention on the local news. But that was not the case, which was just fine. It had looked awful, especially with all that glass, and would have made for decent small-town sensationalism. The sheet glass, thick and green, had shattered on impact so forcefully, pieces of it had been blown into the air like water from an upturned fire hose. Particles had rained on both vehicles, hitting all like a rogue hailstorm. Both the truck and her car had been deemed totaled, having absorbed the collision within their structures, leaving no drivers injured but for the jarring shock of the moment. The accident was mostly Frell's fault, but as soon as the officer had learned she was pregnant – and how ridiculous it seemed, to tell a stranger, a law enforcement person, the big news of the day before her own husband even heard it – she had reassured Frell, all would be taken care of. Insurance information was exchanged, no charges were filed, and each driver was duly whisked away and tended to. Frell knew enough of the process to know she would most likely never set eyes upon the driver of the truck again. Thankfully, she was able to remember seeing him walking around the vehicles with the other officer, talking and gesticulating, no doubt relaying the moment of the accident to them for their reports. The truck driver would share some fault by having sped through the intersection a few yards away, which helped assuage the guilt Frell felt over the incident. All other details, she surmised, the agents would hash out.

The newscast was now over, and though there had been no report of "her" accident, a few extra minutes had been devoted to the weather report to discuss the thunderstorms that had made their way over the area over the last twenty-four hours, in particular on the hail that had been reported late yesterday afternoon and how it had affected traffic, on their side of town. Well, that's odd, Frell thought, shrugging off this second incidental differential. Hail? Yesterday had been such a beautiful day… She decided to conclude, the weather must have turned after the accident, while she was at the hospital being checked and tested. She looked out the window. By gosh, she thought, the irises did look a bit beaten down.

Frell put away her breakfast things, made the bed. She decided to shower. Frell felt better than she had expected to. Even the doctor last night had expressed concern over the very real possibility she might have some residual issues, perhaps some whiplash, from the accident. But no, once up and about that morning, Frell's entire body had returned to such a level of normalcy that, given the morning sickness which had plagued her until then, it gave rise to renewed concern of a different kind. The two miscarriages had for Frell forged warning bells which would ring balefully whenever she thought the nausea was not pronounced enough to broadcast to the rest of her system that yes, there was a viable life developing and growing inside her, and turning her inside out – as it ought.

Nope, this was not good. Frell felt entirely too well.

She grabbed her phone, opened the app, and made an appointment. Thank God, the clinic saw patients until noon on Saturdays, and a spot was available. Surely, Carl would be back in plenty of time and go with her.

As Frell was about to text Carl again, the back door opened. He was home. And not only that, he was also the bearer of gifts, namely a large paper bag filled to the top with all kinds of packaged foods, plus a carrier tray set with two large, lidded cups, all from the same, ill-fated Emporium where Frell had wanted to treat herself to a milkshake the day before. Not that it wasn't a slight bit tone-deaf, Frell thought bemusedly, to bring offerings to a pregnant wife from the very place directly involved with a near-miss, horrific event… But, Frell chose gratitude over consternation, quickly assigned affection to his gesture. Carl handed his wife one of the enormous Styrofoam cups, into which lid he had ceremoniously stuck a straw.

"I got you a vanilla shake, honey. I know how much you love them, and this place is THE best. They use…"

"…custard; I know, honey, instead of ordinary ice cream." Frell finished for him.

"Yeah, and I got us a few things for the weekend and some carryout we can have for lunch," Carl added.

Frell explained she had made an appointment at the ob-gyn clinic for 11:30 that morning. She did not say why. It did not seem right to tell Carl something so joyous on one day, only to take it back the very next morning, especially if the celebratory taking back was only based on the slightly paranoid speculation of a worried mother-to-be. Frell did not want to burden Carl with her insecurities. Let the thoughts go, she thought, let the two of them hear the heartbeat together, and the weekend would take a decidedly wonderful turn; even more solidly so, for them together.

"It's okay, sweetie," Carl replied, reading her mind, "I am sure they have tremendous understanding and don't mind at all helping to put to rest any anxieties a new parent might have. No doubt people go in all the time for reassurance visits, especially when they have a history of," he hesitated, "you know."

What a gem of a husband, Frell thought. Carl gets it and doesn't mind coming along and cutting his Saturday in half with me. She hugged her husband.

"Thank you honey," Frell replied, "It'll only take a moment, I am sure of it, then we'll come back home, get the salad made and load up for the cookout. So, I was thinking…" she began.

"…that we might make the big announcement today?" Carl finished for his wife.

"Yes!" Frell's heart swelled with love.

"Let's toast to the new news!" Carl said, holding his milkshake aloft. The two thunked their soft, oversized cups together and each took a ceremonial swig.

Frell, feeling the world back in its rightful place, also felt a newly quieted and deeper happiness encroaching upon her soul. She kissed her husband, and shake in hand, made for the bedroom. Carl loved to putter about in the kitchen; he would put things away while she showered and dressed. Barely two hours from now, they would be at the doctor's and then everything would be truly amazing. Once Frell could hear that wonderful heartbeat again and be professionally reassured that her feeling well had nothing to do with anything risky or possibly tragic. All would be not just rightfully in its place, but wondrously so.

Breakfast had been a light one, and Frell was already looking forward to a quick bite of lunch before they headed over to the clinic.

In the shower, Frell, with her glasses off, could not make out which bottle was the shampoo, and which was the conditioner. The small print on the bottles were a long-term source of frustration for her. She grabbed her glasses from the vanity and put them on. What she saw, however, were not the labels as she expected them; there was no S or C, nor were there the customary words. Instead, one bottle was labeled "Schampu" and one bottle was labeled "Rense." What the heck were these? Some European product Carl had traded out for the stuff she normally used? Carl occasionally did the shopping for them, and he did have a penchant for bringing home new stuff. Moreoer, he did have a thing for products that invoked the country from which his grandparents heralded, and so, Frell figured, his inclination to shop euro-themed had yet again resulting in this latest surprise encounter in the shower. Problem was, the shampoo smelled awful, fully unlike the customary, floral scents she preferred. This stuff was not like anything she had ever used – its odor didn't even qualify as a scent, but rather, a stench. A stench she could only describe as sausage-like, with acidic overtones of, heaven forbid... Good Lord, was it gross!

"Caaaarl!" Frell called from the shower.

"Wha...what honey? Is everything okay?" Carl quickly appeared, his voice belying concern. He was, truly, such a caring husband.

"Oh, no, honey, I'm okay. All is fine, but honey, if you could reach me my regular shampoo and conditioner? I'm, guessing it's in the cabinet, under the sink?"

"Sweetie, what are you talking about?" Carl's voice had shifted, but now hinted at confusion. "That's the stuff you always use."

"Um, no, honey," Frell countered, annoyed but wondering if her "raging" hormones were causing her nose to play tricks on her. "This is something new. I'm not, um..." she wanted to be fair, "so sure I am that crazy about the scent. It's kind of funky."

"Funky? Honey, really? Now you've got me doubting myself! That's the stuff we've been using for weeks now, and the shampoo is even a replacement bottle I just put in there."

Frell wanted with all her heart not to spoil the magic of the special day. She didn't want to get into any kind of an argument with Carl on the one day the two of them would stand together, by loved ones surrounded, to announce to their family – the world in its best, most meaningful nutshell – that they were going to have, really have this time, a baby. The best news in the world, as far as Frell was concerned. No, nothing would be inserted into the picture to spoil it.

Frell backed down quickly and completely, once again chalking it up to her hormones, and to the accident she had just endured. No doubt, her subconscious was on edge and red-flagging everything. She simply said, "No worries honey. It's hormones, like they say. I'll finish up and be out in a minute."

"Hormones?" Carl laughed on cue, happy to sideline an interaction that had made absolutely no sense to him. It was likewise for him far too special a day, for him as a man, a new father, and partner to the woman who had given him the most wonderful gift in the world. And so soon, their entire family would be rejoicing with them both. Carl chuckled indulgently, and quipped, "Tell me all about it!"

Frell, back under the water, could not hear him. She was eager to finish up, dress, have a bite of lunch before they headed out. Making a baby sure did work up an appetite.

††††

When Frell emerged from the bedroom, empty shake cup in hand, Carl was a-bustle in the kitchen. He had even set the table. A cozy, domestic vignette greeted Frell. She tied the sash on her cardigan and made for the counter to help.

"No, no, honey, let me do this!" Carl admonished. "There's nothing to this lunch, so let me assemble everything. You've been through plenty, honey, and deserve a little breather today."

"Gosh, Carl, this is so sweet of you!" Frell exclaimed, seating herself. "I can't believe how hungry I am and it's still so early!"

"Yeah, but we have an important date with the doc, don't we?" he replied, kissing her forehead. "First thing's first. I need to serve the beautiful mother-to-be a decent bite o' lunch before we head out."

"You better be careful, my mister," Frell joked, "I could get very used to this!"

They smiled at each other, over their sweet and banal exchange, their shared gazes awash with contentment.

Frell tinkered on her phone, browsing strollers online, while Carl hurried about the kitchen, warming the food, and plating it as his wife shopped for the three of them. What a lovely, little picture of a family in waiting they made.

Frell noticed another odd odor wafting about. It must be whatever Carl was heating in the saucepan. This hormone thing was not going to make things easy for her, she thought bemusedly. Everything was leaning to the acidic, slightly foul, and soured. But not a word on this, she insisted to herself; be grateful for his help, be grateful for the trouble he was taking, even having made a market run early in the morning, just for her. Still, something smelled, well, rather vile.

A minute or two passed, and Carl approached the table grinning with aplomb, kitchen towel slung over his shoulder, a soup bowl centered upon a charger plate in each hand, thick slices of warm bread balanced on the rims. Frell set her phone aside to make clear her intent to fully enjoy and appreciate the meal he had prepared. Carl placed a plate in front of Frell, then set the other one down opposite hers. He beamed expectantly, eager for her delightful pronouncement as to what a fantastic job he had done.

Their eyes met momentarily, playful in the moment. Frell leaned forward to behold the dish, ready to extol its virtues. She looked down onto the steaming bowl, filled nearly to the brim with what was obviously a hot broth, a soup of some kind. But Frell's smile fell flat the moment her eyes affixed upon what was in the bowl. Her jaw went slack as her gut recoiled.

Afloat upon the soup were disembodied butterfly wings.

Frell's soup – and Carl's – were each garnished with a mosaic of still-crisp butterfly wings, some of them spotted, some of them blue, some orange. They swam like brilliant lily pads upon a vaporous pool of dark brown pondwater.

"What the fu…" Frell whispered.

"Sweetie?" Carl asked, looking up from his meal. His bowl, he had already tipped slightly with one hand, the better to ladle up a just-right mix of broth and wing. With his other hand he held the soup spoon, a brimming mouthful with a single butterfly wing perched across its edge.

Frell had no response for her husband. Carl's questioning tone was too devoid of anything other than mildest concern, which in and of itself had instantly become grotesquely bizarre.

"Sweetie?" he repeated. Carl opened wide, swallowed as he awaited his wife's response. He chewed slowly, attentive in his concern while yet admiring of the crisp freshness of the wing.

"Is it too hot?" was all he asked.

Too hot? Too hot? And that was the only thing he saw fit to ask?

What the hell?

Frell sat still as stone, permitting only her eyes to bely by way of rapid-fire assessment her confusion. They flitted back and forth, landing first on the wing-infused soup, then on the face of this person who was, for the time being and all intents and purposes, her husband. Was this person her husband? Was this their kitchen? Their Saturday morning? Was this their hour together just prior to seeing their doctor? Carl looked not only himself; he looked gently, radiantly so, his face was imbued with the conviviality of a lovely morning, plus a solid night's sleep, and with a pending visit to their doctor now only a matter of minutes away, with then a fun cookout with family later on, and a planned, happy announcement, their crowning moment, yet to come. Carl, Frell noted with odd dread, was simply there, and at his most ordinary best, which was what made him appear all that much more sinister to her as she scanned his face, his eyes, waiting for him to blink, or for some shift in his expression, for him to grow a set of fangs, or. . .

"Honey?" Carl tried again. "What's gotten into you? Are you okay?"

Frell wanted desperately to hear mockery in his voice, but if it was there, it was, at least to her ears, undetectable.

Carl took another bite as he studied his wife. A big, butterfly wing laden spoonful. He chewed, swallowed hard. But his concern was genuine.

Frell found her voice at last. She instinctively feigned composure in the same way a fresh-caught hostage might present a calm, non-fight, non-flight demeanor in the face of imminent, immense danger, intending to disarm their captor, sway him from some next, sudden swing of the arm, slash of the knife, blow to the head.

"I…I'm not sure I have that much appetite after all, honey."

"Oh, sweetie, I am so sorry to hear that! Gosh, I thought for sure a nice bowl of Papillion Bisque would be just the thing! The Emporium had it on special, and their wings are always the best, the freshest. I guess I just have to plead guilty to the indulgence! 'This eating for two' has got me going all the way," Carl sought to muster a chuckle. "I just wanted to buy everything in sight at the store. Guess that can't be helped, huh, honey?" He finished with the slightest of laughs, a pleading sort of display, him wishing to cajole his beloved wife in hopes of finding some humor in his attempt at self-deprecation. All Carl wanted to do was re-capture some – any – level of the happy, homey-ness in which they had both reveled barely a minute ago.

Frell watched Carl take another bite, then another. Revolting. It was sickening to see him slurp the thick broth, see his lips curl around the fragmented wings, sucking them into his mouth like some lizard in a nature documentary. The surrealism of the moment was so thick, its hold on her so physical, it left Frell frozen in her seat. Was it a soup or was it not? Was this her husband or was it not? What in hell was going on, when all, everything, was not only as it should be, but most simply, sublimely so? There they were, in their breakfast alcove, at their table, on this wonderful first full day of a long weekend together, and now it no longer was just the two of them, but the three of them… Three of them? Family? Their family?

No, no, Frell thought, feverishly computing the moment, the scene, the bizarre, winged garnishes floating in her bowl. All else that still was – or seemed to be – perfectly, absolutely ordinary, just *had* to be as it so obviously appeared. Now was not going to be a time to fall apart, to let things come crashing down. Family. Family.

No, Frell succumbed to her own deep-core desires. Perhaps it was a survival instinct, that of woman pregnant with her first-born child. She owed this little being inside her everything. And everything included this man to whom she had committed as an individual, to whom she was now committing as a partner in the biggest undertaking she, they, would ever attempt – this raising of a child, a new little citizen, a fledgling member of their human race. Family. Family.

Frell conceded to the moment, once again deciding it'd be best to invoke her raging hormones and to set it all aside, however difficult this was proving to be. She had heard it joked on often enough, that pregnancy could not only wreak havoc on one's digestive tract, blood pressure, and all-around health; it was known to affect smell, mood, perception. Heck, even "sanity" – however that was defined these days. Look at the car crash she had just survived…

Yes, it *had* to be hormones. It had to be just some massive, instantaneous but momentary glitch in her sensibilities. Surely this was just another European gourmet-guy moment on the part of Carl's, who had no doubt dined on this "Papillon Bisque," stuff at some other point, perhaps on some work-related travel, and he had merely forgotten, he had never eaten this specific dish with his wife. Carl did like to shop the gourmet aisles at the Emporium…

Frell had never heard of such a dish, but having breeched the present plain of reality, it felt like a no-brainer to assume she, never much the gourmand, simply hadn't encountered it herself, and thanks to her morning sickness, was just not in a position to embrace a new foodie experience.

Frell pushed back her bowl and said, "Honey, don't mind me, really. I'm just going to go make myself some more toast."

Frell did, however, carefully study her husband from the back as she stepped around him and behind the counter.

"Well, be sure to put some peanut butter on it or something. Something that'll stick to yer ribs, dearie." Carl joked ever so gently, wanting to make sure the equilibrium of the day could be gathered back up and in. The look Frell had just given him had, to be honest, scared the shit out of him. He had never seen that, that *thing* in her eyes.

†††

"Lunch," now out of the way and cleared up, was quickly put behind by the both of them, each for their own purposes and desires, and for the sake of the day. For their very future together. Family. Family.

Carl drove them to the clinic for their 11:30 appointment. When they arrived, the place already projected the diminishing energies of a weekend wind-down. Only one other man sat in the waiting room. Frell assumed he was waiting for his partner, who was still being seen by the physician.

Frell and Carl checked in and sat down, side by side. They held hands as they waited.

The door opened and the nurse called out, "Matthias!"

Frell and Carl glanced at each other, smiled, and stood up. Carl nodded to the nurse as they were let through the door. Family. Family.

It was almost noon and time to wrap things up. The obstetrician was an older fellow, jolly, well respected, admired by both patients and colleagues. He had tee time in precisely one hour.

The doctor put on a benevolent smile and burst through the door.

"G'mornin', g'mornin'" he quipped, exuding a perfect mix of expertise and fatherly presidorship. "And how are we doing today? Frell, I am so, so glad to see you here! Heard from Mary you were in here just yesterday; well, in the emergency room, due to an accident. To see you here confirms you survived it all wonderfully, thankfully, well, thank goodness for that."

"Gotta love good automobile design," Carl added, shaking his head. "Frellie's car took the brunt of it, and it's totaled, but my beautiful wife literally walked away from the accident."

"So then! This will not just be a three-day weekend but a red banner weekend of happiness and gratitude all around!"

"Yes, indeed, Doctor," Carl agreed, winking at Frell. He added, "we're going to share the big news with the rest of the family in just a few hours!"

"Well then," the doctor said, "we better get to business, folks. Let's give the little one a look and a listen and send Mom and Dad on their merry way!"

Frell smiled and took this as her cue. She laid her handbag on the small table by her chair and made ready to stand up.

"Carl, how have you been?" the physician directed this to Frell's husband, his voice having switched to a more matter of fact, business-at-hand tone.

"Super. Can't say it's been the easiest thing in the world but it's certainly worth every bit of it."

Frell looked at her husband. She looked at the physician.

"Well," the kind doctor repeated, "come on, have a seat, and let's git er done, as they say where I come from." He slapped on a pair of latex gloves.

Carl rose from his chair and seated himself at the foot of the examining table.

An image of "C xoxo" flashed across Frell's mind.

An image of the shampoo and the conditioner Frell had used that morning flashed across her mind.

Frell, wholly dumbfounded, stayed put, rooted to her chair, glued to it, feeling – reeling with – a resurgence of the confusion she had fought off only minutes ago, at the table in their kitchen, when she had witnessed her husband – her husband? – scarf down a bowl of fucking butterfly wings.

Carl lifted his polo shirt to reveal a massive, fatty fold of skin which spanned the breadth of his upper abdomen, right at the base of his sternum. Tucking the gathered fabric of his shirt under his chin, Carl pulled out and forward on the flap of skin with both hands. The physician reached into the pouch, and from the slightly bulbous depths of Carl's belly, he gently extracted a tan-colored, leathery, and vein-laced sack, connected at one end to some part of Carl inside that fold of skin by way of a thick, dark brown umbilical cord. The uterial bladder, at this point already about as big as a bread box, pulsated. The thing shifted in the obstetrician's hands.

It was aliiiiive.

The physician was just about to congratulate the new parents and exclaim how much It had grown since he had last seen Carl, when Frell toppled off the ledge of her personal event horizon. As the universe as she had known it imploded and went to black, Frell fell off her chair, tipping it over with her, sending them both crashing to the floor.

She'd adjust.

Efectus

All that we see or seem
Is but a dream within a dream

"A Dream Within A Dream"
Edgar Allan Poe

ROMEO & JULIET ENTHRONED

MEMORANDUM

TO: Brythwhyte Board of Trustees

FROM: C. Bunting

DATE: 16 March 2022

RE: Granthe Endowment Progress Report & New Findings

CONFIDENTIAL

Esteemed Board:

I am honored to provide with you this report, which includes the first shared transcription of a recently discovered denouement to William Shakespeare's *Romeo and Juliet* by someone possibly linked to the bard himself, entitled, ACT IV – DENOUEMENT INUPURATUS.

The concluding lines of Shakespeare's *Romeo and Juliet* follow, to better introduce the material contained in this memorandum, and to better contextualize the matter at hand, which is the dual issue of the denouement's origin and its controversial content.

(From: Romeo & Juliet, Act III Scene III)

CAPULET
O brother Montague, give me thy hand:
This is my daughter's jointure, for no more
Can I demand.

MONTAGUE
But I can give thee more:
For I will raise her statue in pure gold;
That while Verona by that name is known,
There shall no figure at such rate be set
As that of true and faithful Juliet.

CAPULET
As rich shall Romeo's by his lady's lie;
Poor sacrifices of our enmity!

PRINCE
A glooming peace this morning with it brings;
The sun, for sorrow, will not show his head:
Go hence, to have more talk of these sad things;
Some shall be pardon'd, and some punished:
For never was a story of more woe
Than this of Juliet and her Romeo.

Exeunt

Note: What follows next is a heretofore unknown denouement to William Shakespeare's *Romeo and Juliet*, dubbed the "Vile Scene," per footnoted inscriptions found in the manuscript, which is believed to originate from some time in the 18th century, as deduced from research completed thus far. The denouement was copied from the pages of a recently discovered volume of plays and sonnets authored by an as-yet unidentified, unverified writer, listed for the time being by Granthe scholars only as the Stratford Scribe. This manuscript is one of a dozen attributed to the Scribe, all which were contained in an oversized, leather-bound folio housed in one of the three caskets (catalogue #238-a) stored in the southernmost ante chamber of the hidden library at the Closterium Atticus, where also the Tomes of the Brythwhyte Elders were discovered, which were soon after released by way of limited publication (see *Memorandum 10/2/21*) to members of the board.

Seven of the works attributed to the Stratford Scribe bear the inscription, "A.W.S. One work, a play entitled, *The Curse of the Bard*, is signed en toto, *Auberon Wm Shakespear (*sic*)*. The Denouement itself, while hand-written in a style consistent with the signature and five of the other documents attributed to the Scribe, is unsigned.

In addition to pending authentication (including ancestral), more exact dating and interpretive exposition, the Brythewhyte Board of Trustees will, together with the departments of English Literature and Anthropology at Granthe University, determine even if this extraneous scene should be made public at all, which reasons should become obvious when considering the stark irony of the Denouement's title and the blasphemous nature of its narrative. The Denouement appears to mock heretofore celebrated aspects of Romeo and Juliet's legendary love, and to denigrate representations of faith-based propriety and morality so famously at the heart of the original known work. This, the Denouement does by way of delving into aspects of the marketplace of religious profiteering, from deceptive spiritual ruses to the manufacture and sale of faith-related luxury goods. The so-called Vile Scene additionally seeks to spotlight the unsavory realities of the postmortem handling of corpses in centuries gone by. Any extraneous twists as portrayed in this final scene can only be speculated on as to their purpose, aside from the obvious entertainment value of the macabre, which, as we all know, Shakespeare himself employed in droves.

We respectfully insist that the following text, wholly owned and listed as level-1 classified property of the Brythwhyte Elders (per adjunct proprietary default ownership, which applies to all contents of the Closterium Atticus), remains confidential.

No portion of this document or the text therein may be reproduced or distributed in any way, shape, or form.

Submitted on this day,

C. Bunting, Esq.

Comes now, the so-called:

ACT IV – DENOUEMENT INUPURATUS, OR ROMEO & JULIET ENTHRONED

Scene: Burial Crypt of Romeo & Juliet, next day

Enter a heretofore unseen procession of Friars, walking two-by-two across the stage.

Whilst this cadre is clothed in knee-length, hooded robes identical to that of Friar Laurence, hems of floor-length under-vestments are visible. The embroidered fabric sweeps the floor, appearing heavy and costly. All members of this ensemble are cloaked beneath the hoods of their robes, which render them unrecognizable but for the uniformity of their garments, which suggest they are the very brethren of the Good Friar. The men walk in unison, with a slow and measured gait. Their arms, held abreast, are folded; their hands they have brought together, thumb to thumb over outstretched fingertips touching, each to form the shape of an inverted triangle.

The presumed leader, an unknown Friar at the head of the procession, proceeds to where the bodies of Romeo and Juliet have been placed, side by side upon their biers. The bodies are draped in linen cloths. Their faces are covered with linen squares.

The men, upon arrival at the feet of the deceased pair, bow formally, in unison. They next drop their cloaks to the floor, to expose elaborately embroidered coats, from which lace-edge collars and sashes burst in a show of fashionable excess. It is to be surmised, this group, while posing as fellow esthetes in committed poverty to their callings, are instead of a far worldlier ilk.

ACOLYTE I

Remember, men, keep thy voices down! The ceiling above our heads might boast a yard's girth of solid stone, but our echoes shall yet worm and sift their way into the climes of yon nave above, leaving the mournful parties in their grief and ignorant superstition nigh susceptible to peculiar noises wafting from below, where in their sorrow they would rather believe than not, their dearest, freshly departed lie peace-filled and unmolested, in slumbrous eternal rest quite unsullied, and, dare I say, in elegant repose.

ACOLYTE II

Aye, low of tone to be sure. If an illustrative gesture suffices, may we rather signal our intents so to keep a stealthy silence about us.

ACOLYTE III

Hush! Quietly at our task we must endeavor, so not to quell the loveliness of their illusions!

ACOLYTE I

Addressing the deceased pair.

'tis time, my children, to be risen from thine quaint beds!

ACOLYTE IV

May we be quick. I am famished!

ACOLYTE III

May we be neat, for our garments must serve us equally well at table this eve…

ACOLYTE V

Endure the labors, line the coffers, fill the wardrobes, men, 'tis how we place another gold ring upon a commanding hand!
We thank thee, doomed youngsters, for thy legends shall feed our every aspect!

ACOLYTE VI

Make haste! But may we conclude this dank business, lest we are made to endure the stench at the onset of their decay!

ACOLYTE VII

Come now, Rodolpho. Even in these molded environs, we well precede the first fragrant inklings of the romantics' shared rot. However, before we escort this sorrowful pair to their next lair, our good brother must do his deed. The jeweler requires his relics be replenished for to craft another passel of his precious and costly monstrances. His patrons clamor as we dally. We have a job to do. Work before play, good brethren!

ACOLYTE II

Work before play…pray before pay…and thus, it goes…

All laugh.

ACOLYTE IV

Monstrances indeed – monstrosities I call them! And those patrons… They salivate with coin a-plenty over their sinners' reliquaries, do they not? Such pigs in their every consumptive greed! How better to spend, than to benefit the good sons of poverty, to hold ever wider for us the gates to our heavens!

ACOLYTE VIII

Indeed, Roberto, indeed!

ACOLYTE VII

This batch is nigh commissioned as we speak, for the story upon which this pair of lovelorn stiffs resides is one of particularly keen and costly want! And, being told far and wide, a relic from that pretty one over there will verily glimmer with the self-same magical power potential as once sourced from long lost ages hence, from the most vestal of yon erstwhile and delectable virgins!

ACOLYTE V

Precious commodities, all of them!

ACOLYTE II

Scrumptious! And borne of intrigue rich as the loot in a needful sultan's caves…

ACOLYTE III

Fascinating, as always 'tis, how short the path 'twixt thieves and gods…

ACOLYTE I

'tis but a frog's leap over a stagnant puddle. But, to build the souvenir to then craft the deal, one must have the hallowed goods in hand to begin with…

The acolyte takes one of Juliet's hands into his. He gestures to his compatriot to join him, who will proceed to divest the corpse of its fingers.

ACOLYTE VIII

A handsome batch of monstrances these shall make!

ACOLYTE VI

A high handful of crowns duly rendered from each and every delicate digit! And, once chased in silver, oh, what fine offerings these shall proffer. They will serve our cause well!

ACOLYTE IV

Better yet if the Master fancies they ought with jewels be encrusted…

ACOLYTE II

Rubies red as blood, emeralds the color of bile…

ACOLYTE V

My gut heaves in anticipation!

They chortle quietly yet mirthfully.

ACOLYTE III

Gloved and sealed for posterity…

ACOLYTE II

…and profit!

The bones of Juliet's hands snap audibly as her fingers are severed clean off by the blade of a knife the friar will have produced from a sporran he wears affixed to his sash. He drops the fingers with aplomb into the bag.

ACOLYTE VIII

…and four and five, and then this one too… Six and seven, and there you are, is the eighth…

ACOLYTE IV

Aha. So, she may keep her thumbs?

ACOLYTE VIII

Novice. Yes, those are difficult to render clean from the hand. 'tis not my style to take all ten.

ACOLYTE VII

Do not tell me you are subject to superstitious limitations?

ACOLYTE III

I? No indeed! 'tis but a preference, a gentlemanly gift back to the giver of the parts in question. I prefer to let my donors be… Rather leave the poor souls with a little more than a little bit less…

ACOLYTE IV

Thou art too kind!

ACOLYTE VII

No, sir, I am simply far too peculiar a rogue. Fiends do have their own predilections…

All laugh.

ACOLYTE I

Alright. Enough of this banter. Our fair maid is duly voided of her contributions in the name of the perpetuity of our sect. 'tis time to complete our work so we may be done with this dour bedchamber.

All reassemble at the sides of the deceased couple, half of the men at Romeo's side, the other half at the side of Juliet.

ACOLYTE II

Heave ho, men, it is now the hour whereupon the king and his queen are to be re-seated upon their purgatorial thrones, for to leak of the remnants to which their salty hulls as yet cling. May they be rendered pure as the morning air and better readied for their final flights, to a more sterile heaven, which one would rather believe, awaits this unfortunate pair…

ACOLYTE IV

Peter, throw yourself the gates but wide!

ACOLYTE III

So that they can be better left neatly stacked in perpetuity!

ACOLYTE VI

With skulls polished and neatly affixed atop their respectively stacked and craggled housings.

ACOLYTE VII

Encamped forever more, then, like all the foolish lovers who have gone before them.

ACOLYTE V

Equals in their skeletal simplicity. Sticks and stones…

ACOLYTE II

Broken bones…

ACOLYTE I

As all men are, indeed. Dust to dust to dust to dust…

Heretofore civil tones of voice are now fully transformed to sneering sarcasm.

ACOLYTE III

No doubt this pretty pair thought themselves elevated beyond all that…

ACOLYTE IV

A pretty pair of privileged loiter-sacks they were!

ACOLYTE VI

Insipid sacrifices to love, the carcasses those two left behind are, in the end, not unlike any other ordinary human heaps…

ACOLYTE VIII

Pah! Love!

ACOLYTE II

And yet, their heaven no doubt beckons with grandiose adornment and overmuch aplomb…

ACOLYTE IV

Promises taught; 'tis idiots who hold Cupid's arrows forever aloft…

ACOLYTE VII

Aye, may all fools be comforted in their hocus pocus, while we, my boys, profit well. 'tis the way things have always been…

ACOLYTE I

To be sure! A panacea of noblest knaves and their unwitting wenches are but high-cost wares and later still ripe fodder for the masquerades come Carnivale season!

ACOLYTE III

Leaving us, "His" humble lot…

Grunting with effort as the men begin to hoist Romeo from his bier

…to do the laborious triflings as they are needed…

The men lift Romeo's stiffening corpse irreverentially, clumsily. One acolyte stumbles and nearly drops the limb he holds. Romeo's body is roughly jostled.

ACOLYTE VII

Look at these bags, their awkward marionette's limbs! They lamely seek entrée to our heavens whilst we still draw breath and pave the truer road…Lord Commerce, our god…

Whistles to indicate a breathlessness

…aye this one is possessed of a cumbersome load!

ACOLYTE IV

Come now, men! You complain like spoilt children. Aye, our muscle-bound lad must have impressed not just this one wench with his sporting heft!

ACOLYTE VI

'twas said by all, he cut a fine young man's figure. A robustness of limb he betrays in me, for my aching spine insists I must suffer for it!

ACOLYTE VII

Ha, ha! We've not one golden calf but two, I'll warrant, to which those who so astutely kneel on the pavers above can pray to their foolish hearts' contentment!

ACOLYTE III

Sarcastically

Idols for the idle, you dare imply? I am aghast. For shame!

ACOLYTE II

Your feigned shock, sir, is as false as those two precious ones!

ACOLYTE VI

Ha ha. Touché!

ACOLYTE I

And the girl …come now and let us at the count of three foist this one good and high. Weighted less and slighter of form she may be, but oh my, the drag of her dress, and those damned, impossible undergarments. Hades!

ACOLYTE II

Ah, but to abide by the fashion *du jour* is to verily roll oneself in layers as thick as what once wrapped and bagged the queen Nefertiti, off to cross her muckish river as they all once presumed they would…

ACOLYTE III

Indeed, rolled snug was this one, in muslins and laces quite fine, I might add…
Come see! Pearls paving every inch of her skirt, stitched wretchedly tight, throughout…What a fortune, what a waste! 'tis a shame we cannot wrangle a departure of the gown as well!

ACOLYTE IV

That would be, my friend, far too obvious as harvesting of one so famously and recently deceased…

ACOLYTE V

Give it a handful of decades, brother, when her kin will have joined this ill-fated pair. It is then when we can employ our descendant brethren to plunder …er, render due process…of the rest of all this mess. Given the veils of a future unbeknownst, whatever remains of earthly value down here can in time serve our descendants up there, to fill anew our coffers and keep the lamps brimming with oil. In time, no one will be alive to know the difference!

ACOLYTE VI

Wise words, sir.

ACOLYTE VII

Indeed. Patience has its virtues.

Bowing slightly as he offers his comment, feigning reverence

ACOLYTE VIII

Patience, ha! Come now, brother comrades. Let us patiently and with utmost deference foist this unfortunate paramour and his lady not-so-fair onto their putridorial thrones.

The corpses are unceremoniously hauled onto their respective putridorial seats, their stiffening limbs lurching and swaying in an awkward and macabre dance of the dead. They are next secured by way of belts and brackets into upright positions, their heads hanging precariously off to either side. The corpses' garments are next arranged to expose the bared legs, to suggest facilitation of the inevitable drainage, which will ensue as their bodies decompose and release their liquids and corporeal matter into the trenches below.

The acolytes bow in exaggerated fashion

ACOLYTE I

I beseech, thee, grand Sir and m'Lady Not So Fair! Stay as thou are. Enjoy! May the gravitational forces marry well with the decompositional inclinations of thy human housings.

ACOLYTE V

Leak long and prosper, for your realm and glory are at hand, oh Romeo and Juliet!

ACOLYTE VI

Hush, Adolfo! Were we not told to never speak of them by name?

ACOLYTE IV

I stand humbly corrected, Savio.

ACOLYTE VII

…your realm and – eh – your glory are at hand, oh – eh – Sir Bones and Lady Crumble!

They laugh again.

ACOLYTE II

Far better, Savio!

The men, having concluded their task, bow once more in mocking deference to the deceased, and, stepping backwards, retake their places in the queue.

Having re-assembled in formation, the brethren exit, two by two, hands returned to their inverted triangular genuflection, the hoods drawn back up, over their bowed heads, so to render all once more analogous, anonymous and genuflective.

For some moments, the emptied stage is quiet, the corpses unmoving.

Then:

The corpses of Romeo and Juliet, seated side by side upon their respective putridaria, each reach out a hand to take hold of the other's, Juliet's fingerless palm awkwardly encased within her lover's intact grasp. It is to be understood, they are to now sit for the next several months, to a year or more, to drain into the reaches below. It is to be further understood that in time, their costly robes will be retrieved, leaving only their bared bones – what of them will not be removed for further commercial fabrication – to be neatly stacked upon the shelves close by.

The lamps flicker and fail at this point. The crypt is left in utter darkness.

CURTAIN.

Efectus

A BRIEF HISTORY OF TRAV'LERS

March 3, 3:45pm

Time travel. Romanticized, euphemized, idealized, sanitized. In crafting adventurous, intriguing, even sensualized time travel narratives, its realities – in actuality, a messy, sometimes horrific, pan-dimensional business – were sidelined for far too long.

Time Travelers. What a costly, distracting, and tragic bunch they were! Few made it to adulthood, the collateral tragedy being that all the Non-Travelers out there were as much the victims in these scenarios as were their traveling counterparts. They too suffered for the unfortunate incidents in which they were defaulted to, as perpetrators for having merely gone about their mono-dimensional lives. It was the linear-living Non-Travelers who haplessly mowed down the random Travelers when they suddenly appeared in front of them as they went about their ordinary days, on their ordinary paths, be it on bicycles, in cars, trucks, trains, on lawnmowers, plows, on harvesters, or in planes, on the runways, or, oh my, in the maws of massive junkyard compactors. Their divergent existences certainly did intersect, time and again…

At its most benign, sometimes comical, was the issue of tolerating freshly arrived, unclothed Travelers. Once upon a time, they had been erroneously lumped in with nudists or streakers as they ran around – any time, day or night, in any place whatsoever – in search of clothing and/or cover, disrupting ladies' lunches, somber religious services, graduations, and grand sporting events. People, whether Travelers or not, over time became so accustomed to the sight of the adult runners, that provided no one or nothing was damaged in any given situation, they were often simply ignored.

Children and infants were another matter.

The worst of it were the babies. For one, pre-natal testing was still not completely reliable. Parents, where one partner was a Traveler, or if either of them had any trace of traveling in their genetic makeup, were lamentably forever on guarded standby for the well-being of their pre-born offspring, unable to know pre-emptively if their little one was blessed – or afflicted, depending on how one looked at it – with the ability to travel. As it were, amidst the growth of the traveling population, almost all pregnancies came to be regarded with as much trepidation as joy.

Second, was the almost unilateral absence of control among traveling infants and children. With babies, it was the fledgling, involuntary travel incidents that held parents and caregivers in constant, active fear, for the spontaneous onset of a time-place fold could steal the tiniest, newest of humans away from the cocooning safety of their originating locations, be it their crib, the arms of a parent, or even maternity wards of the hospitals where they may have just been born, leaving their parents in mortal dread of their momentarily pending return and whatever outcomes it might present, over which they likewise had no control. Non-traveling parents were particularly egregiously left behind – helpless, linear-living humans who were the force-fed recipients of terror of the unknown at its deepest, most heart-rending levels. Non-Travelers could do nothing but wring their hands, cry, and wait interminable seconds, sometimes minutes, for their offspring to re-appear.

Statistics here were, tragically, in the basement, for, while Travelers could jump from one time-place location to the next, the only guaranteed originating return, especially in the case of spontaneous Travelers, was at the point when a last, dying breath was drawn. In other words, but for a few notable, documented exceptions, Travelers only ever died at their points of original, or linear, origin. In the cases of young Travelers, the younger they were, the greater the odds existed for them to re-manifest from their unconsciously triggered time-place folds in injurious, often fatally so, states. Additionally, spontaneous travel return coordinates were rarely – if ever – precise, and returns off by a few feet, or even inches, could result in risky or tragic results.

March 9, 3:45 am

For a minority of parents, where at least one of them was also a Traveler, and for the even smaller faction among these, where that traveling parent was possessed of a full-capacity control of their time-space folding, there was at least a chance of "chasing" one's child down, to grab them off some intersection, or construction site, or subway, or set of train tracks. Yes, literally, off the tracks, in a blizzard, on a mountain train trestle. It has been documented.

The only thing worse than the accidental travel of infants and its tragic outcomes, was when toddlers, children, and obstinate adolescents willed themselves away in hissy fits, amidst tantrums, or in classic teen defiance of their caregivers. To lose a Traveler child to the moment in anger – sometimes all it took was for a misbehaving preschooler to hold their breath in fit of rage – was to possibly receive them back in pieces moments later. This grew the guilt in unhealable leaps and bounds and tainted the mourning, for the worst imaginable losses, that of a parent losing their child, had to be processed amidst the gut sock of petulance driven, unnecessary departures from which there might be no survivable return, nothing to have been done differently, no loving moment of farewell.

Some people, mostly the Non-Travelers who were left behind, were blessed with posthumous visits by their deceased loved ones, but those events were rare and legendary for their frightening occurrences, especially for those that took place at night, when individuals were at their most vulnerable, whether victims to lively imaginations or simply for their having succumbed to the weariness of a long day. Post-mortem manifestations, aptly dubbed echo-materializations, had long ago been adapted into pop cultural and literary repertoires as a form of haunting. Many an elder non-traveling parent had died of a heart attack upon the sudden appearance of their long-lost loved ones, especially when the wavering forms of their dead spouses or children would shimmer out from the shadowy ether late in the night to manifest for a quick "visit." The stats on this also proved the tragic irony for what it was.

Next off problematically, was the arrival side of time-fold incidents involving post-infancy children of all ages, who would suddenly, innocently appear on streets, beaches, in fields, in factories and worse. The younger, less experienced kids were generally traumatized and in need of consoling, once they were captured and held for safety until their return time-place fold kicked in and their small selves would de-materialize. Volunteers in bright red vests, dubbed the Kiddie Brigade, when they weren't vacuum packing, labeling and depositing Traveler clothing packets in kiosks everywhere, walked the streets in larger communities in anticipation of juvenile Traveler materializations, which, due to the overwhelming risks of vehicular traffic, were particularly problematic and accident prone. A tad better, but still vastly dangerous, were the intentionally traveling children, who gleefully gave chase, stark naked, doing their darndest to avoid capture, as primitive in their urges to play and evade capture as any spry fawn in the woods might have ever been. Far less adept or quick as a deer, these children were often just as much a hazard to themselves as they were to others.

Small wonder, then, that adult Travelers were such an elite group. The mortality rate of Travelers was high at every stage of life. Some Travelers never made it past their early stages of inadvertent, spontaneous time travel, where time and location were randomly targeted by their hyper-active subconsciouses. Fewer yet made it past their identic, rebellious growth years, when inherent shades of arrogance, especially competitive travel among teens, increased tenfold the risk quotient of fatal returns. There was no difference in risk to them, for instance, as would be a non-traveling teen deciding to race their car on some highway at two in the morning – blindfolded.

The non-biological reality of travel, during which extraneous items were shed, from clothing to jewelry to such as medical or dental devices, remained an ever-present issue for all Travelers. Having existed alongside Mankind over the epochs, a genetic pre-disposition towards dental advantage – good teeth – had evolved among Travelers, who came to possess this tangential aspect of their genetic makeup out of sheer necessity in order to remain alive to a reproductive capability. Dental malaise was, after all, historically notorious for having crippled entire populations, as was speculated, for instance, with the majority of the Mesa Verde Cliff Dwellers. Such would also have been the case with Travelers, had this bio-detail not quickly evolved of its own Darwinian accord.

As the folding of time-place only affected the biological being, the unconnected, non-biological bits and pieces of oneself would stay behind. For instance, there was dental work, in particular the gold crowns and fillings left behind by exiting Travelers in the Pre-Tech eras, which were notoriously painful to accidentally step upon. These were dubbed Houdini's Dubloons around the mid-1900's, in a sardonic nod to the famous magician who, unbeknownst to fans and most of his family, had been an ardent but unsuccessful student of time travel, in hopes he could acquire an ability he had not been born with.

These oral oddities, so popular with collectors, were only exceeded in rarity by the few sets of orthodontic braces left behind by adolescence-activated traveling teens, whose parents would have unwittingly outfitted their offspring with the corrective metal hardware before they even knew their child was a Traveler. Left behind braces, even rarer than dental gold, were wryly dubbed Houdini's cages. These commanded ridiculous prices at auction.

In the end, it was the dire need for bio-congruent dental corrective materials for Travelers which catapulted the entire dentistry industry into its next, bio-based, Traveler-compatible era. Once corrective materials, such as cavity fillers, could be grown from the host cells of Travelers, fillers, crowns, and other dental fixes were finally able to "travel" along with their hosts. To be sure, Traveler accommodations launched many a bio medical-industrial advance in the post tech centuries.

April 24, 2:30 am

And weather? Suffice it to say, the more pleasant the climate, the bigger the problem. Mean temperature, its comfort quotient to the carbon-based corporal form, seemed to skew Travel risk, both random and intentional, away from colder and frozen climates. Winter seasons the world over, were "quieter" times of the year for traveling and travel-related incidents. Certainly, there were also basic parallels to population density correlated to the more temperate climates preferred by humans.

Once, there had been made a grand discovery of a Traveler frozen in ice. Initially, he was believed to have been some sort of pre-historic man, but DNA and time-place sequencing later found him to have been a young man from the twelfth century, who had traveled back some 7,000 years in time, whether spontaneously or intentionally remained anyone's guess, considering the notion that an adequate anthropological awareness in the Middle Ages may have been possible. It appeared, the accidental guest had tried to escape a cadre of befuddled but violently territorial, would-be captors by running from their encampment (a trail of arrow heads, axe heads, and the wounds on his body and hands were proof of his unwelcome appearance and the subsequent battle he fought), only to have found himself caught out in the wilds when a sudden snowstorm hit. Without a stitch on to protect him, the Traveler froze to death so quickly, his corporeal self expired right there and then. The Traveler – a truly unique specimen – had remained in that spot until he was disinterred from his permafrost berth during an archeological dig in the late 22nd century. Piccard, so named by the team of archeologists that discovered this most unfortunate of Travelers, held the dubious honor of holding the record for the longest known, albeit fatal, time-place fold.

Lotteries, betting and gambling, vast, profitable industries masquerading as beneficial forms of entertainment for the masses, had of course collapsed ages ago, once the abuses of the ever growing, ever evolving traveling demographic had finally been leaked into the informational realms of Non-Travelers. Many a syndicate criminal had it out for Travelers; they were unwelcome guests in myriad establishments. Problem was, they were rather hard to identify, especially the control Travelers, who planned their forays through space-time to perpetrate stunts, thefts and worse. You could say, Travelers gamed time. They strong-armed practically all historic wins in games of chance and odd-based results for centuries, before the extent of their ruses was discovered.

On the one hand, wins-based income was an evil necessity. Many adult Travelers could not control, at least never completely, their time-place folding, and so could not hold down jobs or suitably grow their careers to sufficiently support themselves or whatever families they may have managed to create or become a part of. To be sure, traveling had been classified as a disability, for all its magnificent power and potential. But once that cat, Traveler time fold thievery, had been let out of the bag, the demise of all high dollar, high stakes industries ensued. And it was a rapid implosion. Moreover, given the far reaches of the gaming industry, its failure affected numerous tangential industries for decades. This economic collapse was never completely forgiven by the majority of Non-Traveler syndicates or executives, criminal or otherwise, nor their employment-reliant support workers or supply siders. In the end, it served as a substantial bit of fodder for societal divisiveness and prejudice against all Travelers.

Potential for good, the nature of humans being what it always has been, was the last avenue for travel failure, for amongst the lucky Travelers who survived to adulthood, few had the moral fortitude to keep their impulses in check. Many – too many, one could say – abused their traveling abilities to perpetrate selfish, dangerously hedonistic, and, yes, violent acts. Again, where society, fate and free will had skewed and molded individuals to paths either high or of base nature, the dark lures time travel presented to the many were little more than Wonderland rabbit holes of experience, which, if they did not kill their participants and tangentially affected ones outright, did so much damage to so many, they may as well have.

NIMBY-ism, as we all know it and are susceptible to, quickly reverses course when one is struck at home, to the heart, by an event or occurrence which turns the world as one would have known it on its head.

Such was the case of the President of the American Federation, a Non-Traveler (there was never an elected official who was a Traveler), and her first grandchild, the offspring of her own, non-traveling daughter and her son-in-law, an up-and-coming writer who did happen to be a Traveler. The President's pre-born granddaughter spontaneously exited her mother's womb at just under four month's gestation, for what could only have been a matter of seconds, so fleeting would the sensation have been, that proverbial whisper of a maternal warning. It happened, of all days, on a Christmas morning (Yes, the celebration persisted, having been too vital a retail season to homogenize with other holidays, or cancel altogether), at the dawn of a bright, winter's day at the White House, where they also happened to be celebrating the expectant mother's birthday.

To the horror of everyone present in the private library, the pre-born Traveler – a girl – re-materialized from her time-place fold, not back in the safe confines of her mother's womb, but right there, on the carpeted floor, right in front of her own, young mother, who happened to be seated on the floor, in front of the Christmas tree, in the process of opening a gift from her husband. The President's daughter – such a lovely, young lady – had just torn back a section of brightly colored paper, expecting to see nothing else but the antique server she had so wished for. But when she removed the paper, the grisly, heart-breaking sight that met her eyes, what – who – met with the eyes of everyone there in the room with her, catapulted them all into a deepest, horrified grief from which no one ever fully would recover. The loving family just stood there, surrounding the young mother, in a thunder-struck silence as together they beheld the tiny being struggle momentarily, then expire. This imprinting, to witness life so brutally whisked out and away, with the swiftness of a sleight of hand trick, no one else, the President decided then and there, should also ever have to suffer.

There is, sadly, more. That son-in-law of the President, the father of the tragically lost pre-born? A history buff, he had indulgently educated himself in the histories of ancient Egypt and its faith-based practices, but as a spontaneous Traveler, dangerously so. For you see, spontaneous Travelers can only ever fold time-place in random fashion, at tremendous risk to themselves and anyone in their paths, coming or going. His attempts at controlled time-place folds ultimately put him – and others – at great, and most unfortunate risk. More on him in a moment.

First, a little more background on Traveling: Travelers require a conscious knowledge, however superficial it may be, of wherever it is in time or place they might manifest, or "land" as they called it. This axiom holds true for both spontaneous Travelers and control Travelers. Unfortunately, the interconnected high risks of inopportune manifestations had in the last Post-Tech centuries mandated a reigning in of education for all identified Travelers, out of a sheer desire to maximize safest possible passage through their originating lives. Late onset Travelers, whose traveling ignited upon reaching puberty, forced these mandates upon all levels of the public educational systems. So, to restrict general knowledge in both matters of history and geography to minimize dangerous time-place arrivals, where risk would far outweigh the experiences, the government forcibly removed the teaching of history and geography out of the mainstream – and, of course, into the intellectual underground. Sadly, the eradication of these areas of study left offsides, private institutions to teach these subjects to verified Non-Travelers. Historical and geographical knowledge became, therefore, its own form of elitism among the non-traveling populace. In the end, this intellectual control fostered a dumbing down of society on behalf of the few – for, alas, the benefit of the few. As it were, many Travelers willingly resisted offsides education for their own safety, but as Man has always had more than its share of outliers and defiants, it resulted in the creation of ever harsher rules, enforcements and even punishments against the learning. Sociologists later theorized this shift in education and its ensuing disconnects as having sowed the final seeds which would help set the stage for The Great Separation. More on that later.

May 24, 12:02 am

Control Travelers, considered the elite among Travelers fortunate enough to reach adulthood, had long ago formed an international support group, re-branded in the late twenty-first century as Travelers Anonymous, or TA, in their collective desire to pro-actively foster maximized, safe, time-place folds. Coaching programs were developed under the auspices of TA, which were only ever taught by legacy, as a mentorship. Only Travelers could coach other Travelers. This internalization of travel education served as a preliminary demographics tightening agent, which further laid the foundations for the Great Separation of the twenty-third century.

Back to the son-in-law. Being the privileged, slightly arrogant young man that he was, it had been his deep desire to explore theories of trained transitioning to attain the rank of a Control Traveler, a school of thought which remained, until the inevitable end, destined for failure. The son-in-law did possess the means to pay for the coaching (which some would argue, had been the latter-day educational equivalent to snake oil salesmanship), and, paired with his having educated himself on histories that could put him at risk in the event of spontaneous time-folds, it all simply became a recipe for disaster. As a writer, he would blame his muse, saying he was creatively compelled to seek out experiences he could later expound upon. The son-in-law, ignoring the warning bells of historical precedent, dug into ancient Egyptian archeology, the Old Testament pharaohs, their burial practices, their pyramids and tombs, and their obsession with the afterlife.

The son-in-law's realm of knowledge, coupled with his training, cracked doors to time-place folds for which the young husband, still mourning the loss of his child, was not fully prepared. So, it came to pass, the President's daughter was forced to suffer a second travel tragedy, this time when she witnessed her husband, still sobbing, vanish late one night from their own bed. He never returned. What she never knew, what the President was privately briefed on a few days later by way of a classified dossier, was this: A blackened corpse had been found in the late 2100's, about sixty years earlier, in the sarcophagus of a newly unearthed, off-sides tomb in the Valley of the Kings, wedged between the mummy of a noblewoman and her mummified pet cat, the three of them fitted like dusty sardines into the splintered, inner housing of her painted casket. That man turned out to be the President's son-in-law. His face still retained most of its soft tissue; it had taken on the characteristics of an ink-drenched papier mâché death mask. The fixed expression on his face bore evidence of a horrific demise amidst mouth-ripping, agonized cries. Forensics later substantiated what the reporting anthropologist surmised, an onset of death by way of heat stroke with rapid dehydration and suffocation. In short, the poor fellow more or less baked to death as he lay there, unable to de-materialize back out from his most claustrophobic time-place arrival location, probably due to the lead lining of the wooden casket. Not knowing at the time who this would prove to be (his garb belied the time of his origination as being of the future), the team's internal nickname for the Traveler was Tut II, or Tuttoo. Later, officially, he was labelled with his Parenthian code, the genetic ID system developed in the late twenty-second century, as best as it could be sequenced, due to the fact that he would not be born for another forty years. Upon the presentation of the dossier to the President, JK(_)R456-B8(_)2 was at long last put to final rest, refitted with the name he had been assigned at birth – and the rest of his missing code.

Suffice it to say, the disclosure to the President of her son-in-law's accidental entombment sealed the deal. It became the mission of this twice-over, deeply aggrieved grandmother-in-waiting to re-craft an aspect of invasive Government for-the-good-of-the-people by way of her very personal legacy of loss. Her saintly cause was quickly leveraged into policy, at highest threat and dollar – the President made damn sure it would pass. It was deemed, officially, that the cost of lives and to society had become too big a burden to bear. Travelers would have to be dealt with.

And so, like other precedent-setting social control experiments over the ages, the "elected" hive of rule makers named "Government" "decided" time travel needed to be eradicated from the genetic makeup of its citizens in order to re-establish a consistent continuum from which all could/should/would move forward as One through time, in non-traveling, linear, more predictable, and perhaps more benign fashion. All industries, all actuarially-affected aspects of life and commerce that had suffered and been later wiped out due to the gaming of its Traveler consumers would then be able to reconstitute themselves and proceed similarly, in more ordered, linear – and profitable – fashion, for the benefit of "everyone" and "everything," also known as the Economy. The Gaming Lobby, never having expected the cards to fall as they had, so horrifically in the lap of the Big Boss herself, had finally, at long last and tremendous cost, won. Again.

And, like any governmentally instigated sea change, this resulted in the benevolently postured dividing and factioning off of its people. Relationship and friendship ending, family splitting, society wrecking side-taking ranked and filed both those who opposed this next, law-backed societal takeover and those who supported it. There would be no stopping this beast of division.

Funny thing is, who stood to which side turned out to be as unpredictable and inconsistent as were the personal maths which led any individual to conclude where they stood on the eradication of a key aspect of their fellow citizens. Indeed, many adult Travelers – the few who survived to voice their opinions on the matter – turned out to be whole-hearted supporters of the genetic eradication of Travel in society, for they had learned first-hand of all the risks, the pain, and the outcomes which rarely, if ever, justified the dabbling, the traveling.

Understand, there had been a small handful of sage Travelers who had tried to "do good" by way of their traveling: undoing past wrongs, fixing old issues with newer knowledge, saving others who had already suffered, or died, only to find that space-time folding was not an automatic invitation to bend the continuum, change strings of events, tinker with outcomes, sucker-punch Fate. More often than not, their saves and fixes only spawned other – sometimes worse – eventual outcomes. There had even been a few court cases in which Travelers had been retroactively found guilty of having attempted "good" that had resulted in "bad," which had set new and confusing legal precedents. And forget about the cases in which the intentional "bad" of Travelers was prosecuted; those cases had required the forming of their own courts of law and new fields of legal study, developed solely to deal with the additional complexities presented in such situations where, quite literally, an added dimension was a key factor.

Remember, many Travelers weren't in full control of their traveling, let alone their impulses as erring humans. To feign spontaneous travel had served far too long as a legal, extra-dimensional hall pass. Even punishments and imprisonment had to be re-imagined, for physical confinement was a non-issue and something of a joke for the worst of them.

As had happened in years past, the scourge of segregation reared its oxymoronic head even in this, for many Travelers argued, if they could live isolated enough from the rest of society, away from those "lesser" non-Travelers (Travelers tended to be a rather tribal, snobbish bunch and looked down upon non-Travelers), they could customize awareness, consciousness, sub- and even un-conscious knowledge and familiarity with time-place scenarios so to minimize all travel-related dangers, so that time travel, from infancy onward, could be molded and guided, like some enormous containment bubble of existence, in order to hold as little risk to their kind as possible. To be sure, Travelers wanted to live as Travelers.

This concept helped launch what came to be called The Great Separation, for which the government created a handful of institutions and think tanks expressly for purposes of researching, formulating and then implementing a solution of this societal duality. The institutions immediately hired a cadre of agreeable Traveler influencers to champion the cause, the movement, and their plans, who were paid well and catapulted to celebrity statuses by one means or another, so that their voices and positions could be heard, internalized, and heeded by all information consumers, Travelers and non-Travelers alike, regardless of their other identities and allegiances.

As such, it was decided that Travelers were to be officially identified, ID'd with bio-organic nano-trackers, implanted via injection into the base of their mandibles, for purposes of tracking and logging Traveler population counts and their time-place fold locations. In a mere two years' time, all living Travelers had been outfitted with the nano-trackers.

May 27, 11:30 pm

It was at about this time that a definitive study of Travelers was published, authored by a team comprised of Non-Travelers and Control Travelers. It made official, by way of its publication and the pop cultural adaptation of the term itself, the slightly abbreviated term, "Trav'ler," which had already for centuries been the spoken vernacular for Travelers. Its first official, recorded usage was with the re-registration of the organization known from that point on as "Trav'lers Anonymous," whose members had anyway long referred to themselves simply as Trav's.

Hereafter, the later and officially recognized (Oxford Dictionary's 2315 Word of the Year) abbreviated term, Trav'ler, will also be used.

Less than thirty years after the Christmas morning tragedy at the White House, phase two of the Trav'ler roundup was implemented. All Trav'lers were rounded up by the military – some of them by force – and transported to their designated locations, isolated, planned communities built just for them, for what was soon dubbed, as I have mentioned, The Great Separation. Trav'lers were taken to communities all over the world, on every continent, designed and built in accordance with the needs of their regional population counts. Indeed, The Great Separation had been eagerly adapted by the entire world of Non-Trav'lers, who were weary of the high cost, countless risks, issues and tragedies Travelers presented to their linear worlds. Separation quickly became a global cause.

After the Trav'ler communities were settled, ties were to be cut – all of them – between Non-Trav'lers and Trav'lers, so that each "kind" would be forced to look inward to their own "kind" for community, companionship and family formation, reproduction – and, as had been the goal from the beginning, to limit time-place fold destinations to within the Trav'ler communities themselves by way of fully restricting all levels of historic or geographic knowledge or awareness of Trav'lers. It took less than three generations for personal communications between the societies to dwindle to nothing, to then allow for a complete disconnection. Fungible goods were easily shipped intra-community, allowing for each "kind," in every nation to concurrently develop and grow their commercial viability and maintain supply-side relevance in accordance with their host nations. Ditto for consumption, for clearly, both "kinds" of people were still, at least initially, identical to each other in their daily wants and basic needs.

What no one had counted on, however, was that the Trav'lers, in visible, incremental advancements from one generation to the next, evolved their travel capabilities, most obviously due to the fact that all Trav'ler offspring were now the progeny of both parents possessing the genetic makeup of a Trav'ler. Additionally, with realms of knowledge so restricted in the Trav'ler community, the naturally curious humans sought out – and quickly found – new venues for discovery, for their intellectual expansion. As it turns out, in less than two hundred years, Trav'lers were not only capable of selecting all their time-place folds, they were also able to remain for spans of linear time in their non-corporal states of active travel, casually referred to as "the Neither," by the youngsters who first breached its zone, who would remain there for a time, and then "come back out," as they called it, to share their experiences on it. Soon enough, other adventurous, often younger Trav'lers discovered they too could ever increasingly remain in the abstracted hold of the Neither – and they liked it there. In no time flat, Trav'lers were choosing to spend time in the Neither as a destination, not merely as an interim point on a path to some other lineal time or place, past or future. This phase of discovery was a cultural explosion for all Trav'lers, for it quickly morphed from renegade teen practice to an aspirational *place* of being for all Trav'ler citizens.

This time-place dimension found within the folding, Trav'lers began to regard and even map as a viable a location, a new reality, a dimension wholly theirs. The Neither became as much a destination as any place on earth had ever been. Awareness of the Neither registered in the subconscious of any Trav'ler the moment it was successfully breached, it was that infectious to their psychic sensibilities; hence, once arrived at, it was ever more easily revisited. In due time, and with some coaching from their control mentors, even the dwindling demographic of spontaneous Trav'lers were able to envision, pinpoint and then "land" in the Neither.

Attainment of this level of travel was promptly leaked to the non-traveling world. It was then all the traveling communities could do, to keep government spies and voyeuristic outsiders at bay. Unfortunately, their desire to be left completely alone was ignored, including at very high levels. It was the last time in history that government sponsored espionage was undertaken. But, as Non-Trav'lers who breached the Trav'ler zones were easy to identify, they were summarily rounded up and either shipped out in batches or executed by Trav'ler gangs, which had formed to guard the perimeter zones. This short-lived period of intense curiosity and clandestine observation was sadly also recorded as a particularly violent one between the two societies, a time of further division between them.

In this newly "solidified" and conquered realm, the Neither had also started to hold *more* appeal to those who could tap its wellspring of existence, its hyper-existence, if you will, than the earthbound, physical realm – reality as it had heretofore been regarded. Inside the fold of travel, in the Neither, physical shortcomings, biological issues and ills of the tangible world no longer existed. Inherent virtues and pleasures held within the Neither, a place where objects and status markers of all kinds no longer existed, made for a place where what had once been regarded as fantasy was as much an aspect of the realm as any other. It was such that it came to make sense for anyone who had the ability to cross over and stay within its limitless confines, to consider the Neither a preferred destination. It touched upon the infinite, and wonderfully so. In due time, Trav'lers who could merge with the plane of the Neither came less and less out of it.

Before long, they simply stayed.

Residual citizens, Trav'lers not born with the ability to stay within the Neither, eventually died off, victims of the limitations of their bio-organic selves.

The Trav'ler communities, then, de-evolved rather quickly into ghost towns, peopled with only shadows of plane-intersecting throngs or the occasional singletons who would reappear on the physical landscapes to temporarily reside in the linear plane, for whatever personal reasons they had. Occasionally, infirm Trav'lers manifested back into the linear plane and were unable to return to the Neither, which was a particularly lamentable life's end. These end-station Trav'lers never lasted long once that point had been passed. It was a sad expiration but did provide the non-traveling scientific community with specimens for study. Scholars, retained by the government to track the morphing and log the ever-dwindling proof of presence of the Trav'lers, were sworn to passive positions of non-interference and non-communication, so to not disturb the new continuum that was evolving on this very different plane. They would later call this phase The Evaporation, and wax somewhat mournfully on it, as if some feeling of being left behind could not be avoided, no matter how guardedly firm they stood on their carefully constructed platforms of academia.

As amorphous life took increasing hold of the traveling population, so did the need for biological reproduction cease, for the physiologically abstracted sentients, no longer burdened with corporeal placeholders to hold them down or back, left behind their carbon-based carriers as perfunctorily as insects would discard their exoskeletons, without thought, remorse, or sentimentality. Their plan, it appeared, was to simply exist in the Neither forever. Was this a form of immortality? Those left behind, non-traveling Mankind, could only wonder.

It didn't take long for non-Trav'lers to repopulate the abandoned Trav'ler communities, for, as their populations had continued to grow, the need for viable areas to settle had also increased. Empty Trav'ler towns, though overgrown and in need of major updating, had been cared for and were relatively tidy destinations. They felt to the non-traveling settlers like farewell gifts, bequeathed to them by their benevolent, intra-planar kindred, to whom they had been, at one time, more or less connected.

It was later rumored, glittering arrays that appeared in the night skies when end-station deaths were at their highest, were the twinkling emissions of the nano-trackers worn by the originating generation of disembodied Trav'lers, those precocious teens who had first crossed over and eventually acquired the ability to stay in the Neither, as they moved about in their realm, when they fleetingly intersected with the visual planes of the linear present, and that it was their trackers' emissions which were sparked into visible illumination by the magnetic pull of the earth's atmosphere.

Romantically inclined non-Trav'lers would say the Nanolights, as they came to be called, were a greeting from the "other side." Those more pragmatically inclined would surmise the lights were nothing more than happy accidents of nature. All agreed, the arrays, whatever they were, were just lovely. Sadly, at about the time the last of linear time-return fatalities occurred, those arrays also ceased.

August 9, 10:33 pm

And by the way: Those lights? Yes, it was those kids.

So, there you have it, as you requested, all those years ago, when we met by accident at the spot where once my home was located. I am glad for that chance encounter, for it has been an interesting travel challenge for me to keep being able to return to this spot to write all this out for you. I have enjoyed what I'll call our joint project – you did, after all, instigate it with your request. And I do appreciate the notes you left for me, and how you arranged to always have the keyboard here, ready for me, so that I could lay this nutshell history out for you. As you can see now, the stories, the lore, the folktales, were, are indeed, based on fact. The bits and pieces you had heard of, what you described to me… Nope, they were no fiction at all. It really did happen. All of it. And, as you noted, being that hardly anyone knows any of this anymore, I am glad I could literally spell it out for you, so you could pass this story forward – again – in your world.

As we suspected, all of this Trav'ler business was swept under the rugs for its inconvenient insights into human nature. Our nature. In our pithy competitiveness, we – and I say we, for we are ancestrally linked – still fight with futility against ideations of being left behind, left out, being left the perceived lesser. To that, all I can say is, be happy when and where you are. Work, thrive, strive. From my limitless perspective – and trust me, I, we, are still learning too – what I can tell you is this: everything, and I mean everything, circles back onto itself. The smallest and simplest has meaning and possesses worth equal to the biggest, the most distant, the most powerful and the most wondrous out there. Let this assurance comfort to you. You are quite sublime as you are.

And so, I will sign off again, this time for good. I've wrapped up my report, and with this last return having proven a bit more difficult, I cannot risk losing re-entry to what I consider my home, due to what I am faced with at this moment, in this plane, in my linear old age. It's nothing more than a hazard of my late onset travel. Sure, I mastered time-place folding well enough, but I rather not chance it further. As you can see, my brief intervals here were neither evenly sequential nor terribly long stays – the folding does get harder the older one gets.

But at least we have my emerging randomness to thank for having met in the first place. You do, of course, have my permission (as if I'll have any real say in this!) to share this document. Seek out other curious ones, like you, who are not afraid of a re-attainment of our shared histories. You as a society "can take it," as they used to say. Like minds out there will help piece it all back together. Perhaps there are others like me who will have come back and communicated with other linear-living humans. The window, this narrative, that I am honored to leave for you, to times and places foregone, I promise you, will absolutely help keep windows of your future wider open. As has always been the case, with knowledge comes understanding, and the understanding will help keep us all connected.

One more thing, just so you aren't too shocked when it happens: You will see me once more, when you are seventy-five. I manifest to visit you for just a few minutes. It will be around mid-day, I believe. The sun was bright, so it will be at some point on a sunny day. I'm thinking it will be in the springtime, for I saw irises out back, all a-bloom. They were so beautiful. And you looked terrific too. I won't tell you what we discussed, for it would give too much away, and you must live your life with the fullness of the mystical potential in all outcomes. But let me stress, you had wonderful things to share.

Be well. See you then.

T.J.
Trav' JK8R456

Efectus

With a nod to Audrey Niffenegger and her 2002 *The Time Traveler's Wife*, for her delving, rightfully so, into the unfortunate and messy business that is time travel.

"Do You Love the Flowers," by Roberto Diaz

*"...the more flawed, the more raw the gift. The darker, the
deeper. The more fractured, the brighter the spark,
the burn of the drive, the desire."
From, "Storia dell'arte dei Vampiri"*

STORIA DELL'ARTE DEI VAMPIRI

Allow me…just a moment…as I light a few more candles and pour myself a glass of let's call it wine. A digestif, yes?

There you go. Wonderful. A lovely vintage, my dear, I must say…

I know, I know, I date myself with my preference for this sort of illumination. But the light the candles shed is kind, easy on the eyes. Plus, I need very little to get about. Very. And what it does with the pupils in your eyes – such dark pools – so huge, so inviting. One can imagine, one could almost see themselves in them…

…if only….

Hence, all this.

Let's settle in. I apologize; I took rather long tonight, but with streets so devoid of humanity, it is neither as quick nor as simple. Obviously, the icy temperatures are keeping everyone indoors, warm and cozy, more or less safe and sound. I do hate it, when human wintertime seclusion warrants destruction of property to gain access, but that, my dear, is how it goes.

Nevertheless, we do have a solid few hours before sunrise. We can always schedule another session, but it would have to wait a week or so – you don't want to put yourself at risk for let's call it my sake, especially this time of year. I am delighted, however, to see the progress you've made on the background. I feel the delight of a child, seeing myself illuminated in, in *daylight* of all things – so precious! A late afternoon sun – imagine that! And the lavender shadows, the way they play upon my face? Well done! This newer style – yes, you are capturing it quite well. I would bet those snobs at the Academy will have to accept this one, too, even if it jars the critics' stranglehold on what they perceive to be a lofty idealism. Times change, and so must they.

You were asking about the altar at the cathedral? Yes, you guessed it. Second panel from the bottom left. I'm the one in the red cloak, with the ermine collar and the black skullcap. Regal, is it not? But I warn you, don't press me, there is little else I can disclose on that work. I am quite literally sworn to secrecy. Yes, we do take an oath; there is far too much at *stake* – ha! – for me or anyone of my kind to *spill* too much – oh, I am such a card! – on the precise details, so I cannot go into more than what I will simply call, um, the fun, anecdotal, bits and pieces. I think you understand, these limitations. It is less a predicament than it is a fundamental necessity to protect oneself and let's call them next of kin.

Yes, yes; I promise. I won't move. Not an inch. And you prefer I continue in English, yes? Take your pick. I can carry on in any one of the, um, six – no, seven – languages I have effectively mastered. Alas, your dialect still betrays me. Clearly, there is more for me to learn. When one has the time, one might as well, don't you agree?

Now, pray, do not take any of my, er, perspective, or the words or terms I might use, personally. At least, not *too* personally. Accept that you cannot know what I know out of the utter and most extreme differentiality that separates us. It's what keeps you and your kind so terribly curious; it's what keeps me and mine so circumspect. And amused. Oh, how you do amuse us! You are to us but a herd of silly, romping, plump-as-butter-pie toddlers! And mind you, but for those despicable few who seek to eradicate us, we love you. Oh, yes, indeed; we can't get enough of you!

Apologies, my dear. I cannot help myself sometimes…

Yes, *pardonnez-moi,* the allusion to animals of prey was intentional…

Fools? In a word: Yes. You humans are rather easily duped. I chuckle as I think back on all the times…

Yes? Hold it this way? No, not a problem at all…

Ah yes; your kind has a tendancy towards the delusional, thinking you know what it is you've been enjoying, studying, imitating all these years, do you not? You go about your little devotionals, your rituals, you soak up all your culture, swell your sensibilities with ever-morphing methods of scholarly dissection; you walk your museum galleries, make your investments, purchase your books, your works of art – your kind is quite self-congratulatory when it comes to acknowledging your supremely good taste!

You and yours, my dear, you are surrounded by art – compatriots, patrons, teachers, speculators – countless living, breathing, pulsating humans and their subjects; and still, we marvel that the best most generally manage is to wonder ad nauseum who that mysterious woman is, with that faint smile of hers; who she may have been, to herself, to the Maestro. "She" who has held an endless parade of passive voyeurs in thrall for centuries. So, what about all the artists, like yourself, who are responsible for having rendered these works? Doubtless, you think you understand yourselves as well, don't you? As you dig into every dirty nook of every closet to better tap the *Sturm,* the *Drang*…

Look. At the very simplest, you ply your craft to put bread on the table, pay the barkeep, pay a tax. Don't even begin to pretend, my dear, that the tallies accrued at the inns, the brothels and those filthy dens are not the biggest debts in need of settlement amongst even your most talented ones! Such ills, to be visited upon the so-called "gifted" ones… And that's merely the living, human underbelly of the baser needs I refer to, which for the most part cannot be helped. Of course, there are the few, fortunate ones who have managed to work their way into your histories, into the minds of Man, be it memory, or fancy, sometimes both. Sure, they may have come into good fortunes that permitted them to dust off their boots at the outermost porticos of Heaven itself, or whatever sort of salvational gateway it would have been called in their day, but in the end, they were still, well, just *human,* which from my let's call it platform, isn't saying too terribly much.

Speaking of that, how is it you all still cling to your collective destinies of eternal reward? Befuddled that one leaves me, I assure you. Tell me, what is it *you* expect to find there? But I digress. You must remain focused on your task, and I am not here in your service, let alone to interview *you*. Moreover, I must sit still, and as I promised, wax a bit philosophical for you, tell you more about myself, us, in exchange for your painting my portrait. To be sure, it entertains me as well, for I confess, I am as chatty now as I ever was.

Oh, yes; that, plus the two hundred we agreed upon. Is but a small price for the delight to see myself…and by way of such a talented hand…

Eternal reward, eternal rest. How funny those concepts sound to me! I cannot suggest strongly enough that you too try to see this heavenward business through the lens of our, er, greatly extended sense of humor. Mind you, humor can also – and I say should – be as jarring, as dark, thick, and sticky as pitch if it wants to be. And we should gratefully partake thereof, even when it becomes progressively difficult to get out from under one's nails. Why look, just how long mine have become and how filthy they happen to be…no doubt the remnants of…oh, you wouldn't want to know. Ha, ha! I will nigh give myself away boasting of the messes I make! Trust me, we beclawed ones are a snooty but hilarious lot. I can, and do, poke fun at myself something terrible.

But let us get past the convivial stuff. Think some more on your heaven, your hell… Try, my dear, to crack wide the lesser-known gates, those not fabricated of spun sugar dreams and pearls as your one desired destination. Dare peek around the sharper corners, the ones that cut off *all* light. Then look, eyes open, and let yourself think on all you behold. Yes, it will mean pulling aside the carpeting veils of unlit spaces and gazing into the shadows' cores, and then on past all that, to what just might be the very portals of hell itself. I tell you: beauty, horror and hilarity come home to roost in companionable union. It is, indeed, from within the nethering realms where even such as yourself can better grasp, make your own, all that will catapult you – your abilities, your oeuvre – to unknown heights. Those are the landscapes I tread, to which you too, my talented, young portraitist, ought aspire.

Mind you, the sappy nature of mortally beholden aesthetic inclination has always been hard to swallow. I can feel let's call it my supper rise in my gullet as I merely contemplate what you all have held as aspirational, or reverential, over the ages. Oh, the works of art to which such prayer, such song, such blessed this and that have been devoted!

Such burdens, these works have borne on Man's behalf! To be sure, what fills your cloisters, your chapels, your galleries, even your banquet halls, are for the most part but pithy, transactional manifestations of mortal vanity. The scribes really had something there when they conjured up and named its personification "Narcissus."

Perhaps you can imagine how funny it then all seems, what the collective assumptions over the ages have been, with those pale faces and their benign gazes, their freshly coiffed tresses, their straight backs, lax hands, and those insipidly vacant smiles. Those exquisite features…yes indeed, they were possessed of beings who existed in the same realm as the likes of me! Clearly, you assumed those ethereally beautiful Madonnas, those perforated and bleeding saints, those nubile Graces, were sourced from living, subsisting, inhaling and exhaling mortals, didn't you? Ha!

Simplest logic points to the interminable hours of serene and extreme immobility required of all these artists' models over all time. Now, who do you think in actuality was best suited to sit for these portraits? Is it possible, if not obvious, that it would be amongst the comely undead there could be found the ideal subjects to lay languid, sit unflinchingly, the long hours upon hours required for the production of these great works?

Then, think about this, the – ahem – spiritual connectivity of the undead models to their portraitists. Minds and souls found companionship in the gut-splaying realm both factions were incidentally, incendiarily laid open to. Tainted or questionable, virtuous, or profound, artistic compulsion has always drawn in and kept its most volatile members in intimate communion with each other. And the more flawed, the more raw the gift. The darker, the deeper. The more fractured, the brighter the spark, the burn of the drive, the desire. The more distracted from the commonplace, the better heard are the unrelenting whispers of the Muses themselves. The offsides faction of which I speak is the true creative's community. It is a fellowship with a deeply regarded, devilish diversity. And, oh my, their legacies run deeper and wider than your kind can possibly imagine! And they've *always* been there…

…yes, yes. I can wait…

…no, thank you. I am perfectly fine going until the brink of dawn. I can be settled in and safe in two seconds.

Now, where was I…?

To be sure, patricians over all ages hired gifted artisan laborers with as little afterthought as they would gather nameless collectives to harvest their fields. It was no difference to them, whether a hireling was recruited to mend a sail, plow the soil, stain a canvas, paint a panel or a stretch of some freshly plastered wall. Cathedral nooks to grand naves, impossible ceilings to cumbersome doors, these illuminations have always been little more than pictures in Mankind's storybook, rife with as many superficial statements of perceived self-worth as are there are colors in all the rainbows themselves.

Which leads me to point out what I believe should now be obvious to you:

You have long heard how in vain vampires would seek to behold themselves, yes? A reflection, to see oneself – be it as a wavering image splayed across silvered glass, or upon a surfaces of stilled pool water, in a pane of window glass, whether transparent to the fields beyond or baked into an acidic glaze – has always been and will remain the one phantom desire of my kind. Call it vanity, call it curiosity, the need is an echo effect of what once existed in all of us. But vestigial remains of the humans we were born as. To my knowledge, there has never, ever, existed a surface to provide a reflection to a fellow member of the undead, permit him to see how exactly he appeared once the daylit confines of one's mortality were thus abandoned. This, we mourn. Endlessly.

So, can you begin to fathom, how in our immortality, the vanities of the vampiric populace grow proportionate to the longevity and powers we are reborn with? Oh, my dear; emotions, passions, and drives are all taken to extremes where we are concerned, which should be accepted as a given by anyone who has studied these sorts of things, for sky-high functionality of any immortal is but *normal*. We vampires long desperately to see how we have appeared over the ages, how the eras will have affected us, how well we will have adapted, you could say, so we may continue to extract what best suits us, literally and figuratively, as we pass through and partake of ever-evolving times and trends. We have always been a terribly vain lot, and that, my dear, has made us somewhat vulnerable. It long ago forced our hand; we forged not just one but a few bridges to the living, which we are compelled to sustain, protect, and bring with us, forward in time, parallel to our eternal existences. It has, indeed, brought you to me, me to you, because or in spite of the inherent risks, all mutually acknowledged.

It stands to reason, then, that humans ripe with good health, distinctive of feature and form, manifest as making for the most delicious feeding. The simplest comparisons lie in the honored traditions and manufacture of grapes into wine. In similar fashion, over the millennia, the vampire population has grown to directly reflect the prime pickings of its members, of both its forced victims and that rare cadre of willing providers, regardless as to whether they survived and attained vampirehood, or not. We are, you could say, a scrumptious lot.

…and on this frosty winter's night? Ha ha – yes, my dear, you could say you are my little *Eiswein*…

We vampires do love our lovely humans. So, why not the love affairs of self be perpetuated in post-mortem flourishment by the hyper-existence that is vampiric eternity? And why not achieve aspects of this from within the classic realm of artistic endeavor? It makes for wonderful rendering, amidst the renting of humans from their crimson rivers! Like fine wine, mortals in all their varieties, varietals, and vintages – infants, elders, young lovers with their special zest – are repasts forever imbued with all the emotions and passions they manifest, the finest harvests later serving in treasured collections. You see, we too, are connoisseurs. Distant lands or different eras, circumstance, fate, and life lived lend flavor markers and myriad, unique bouquets to not only the blood that is imbibed, but also to us, the beings sustained by them. Hand-of-the-gods crafted human carafes of the most wondrous kinds are sought out for good reason, for we are, in the truest sense of the word, what we eat. Vampires must, therefore, remain a finicky lot.

…honestly, what do you think was in those chalices we held aloft?

And you humans, mired in your rituals of mourning, remain – thankfully for us – forever sidetracked, whether by fact or fable, when the best, most gifted or merely delectable specimens among you are taken at points you are quick to call "too soon." Sometimes it almost seems too easy. You can't imagine who all we have dined on, and of those, who we have brought into our unhallowed midst.

What, my dear? I see. Aha. *Now* you begin to understand…

…yes, vampires do have extraordinarily good taste; it is a survival mechanism.

Logical, wouldn't you think? It is not mere enjoyment of a quality beverage, it is a means to ensure, even if in violent and forceful fashion, our existence, both within our constituency and without.

Which brings me to you, to me, to us as I sit here, to you as you stand over there, palette in hand: For us to bathe in the simplest of indulgent luxuries, which is to be afforded the opportunity to gaze back at ourselves by means of some reflective device, has remained an abject impossibility. The new photographic devices I am seeing out there hold little promise of doing better; as such, they do not interest me, us, much – yet. So, the very means by which vampire countenances could be captured remains the chimeric conundrum of my midnight populace, and for that reason alone, it is *achingly* sought. Unrequited vanity makes for a desirous cocktail, leaving us vampires a rather thirsty lot.

Speaking of achingly sought, we do, contrary to boundless lore, miss the sun. Terribly. Vampires are suckers for all things that reek of sweet sentimentality.

…I know, I know…I just couldn't help myself on that one!

But that is precisely why I commissioned you to paint me, place me, into the riotously hued, stroke-slathered, light-imbued garden you have managed to conjure up on my behalf. May the critics at the Academy faint when they see this one!

Let us conclude, my dear, very simply, that nothing is as it seems. Add this to your inversions, which I know you are so bravely trying to grasp. I call that an enhanced understanding.

Yes. The beauteous Madonna's, the Saints, and yes, the Angels! All those heavenly bodies, with their saintly faces, their ringlet halos, their feathered wings, their gowns, their crowns, on their crosses or their clouds, are but the recordings of an art-obsessed, and portrait-hungry vampiric constituency! Admittedly, few portraitists lived to tell it. Those who did, had to abide by our codes of secrecy. They had no choice. The consequences were too dire, for, if nothing else, where our violent inclinations are concerned, we vampires are a direly predictable lot.

And still, you persist on asking about that infernal doodle they call the Mona Lisa? Can your kind *not* let that one go?

Very well. I shall tell you.

You refer to "her" as "she," that "she" was some lovely and mysterious, anonymous human female… That is so hilarious to my kind! I will let you in on a secret: Maestro Leonardo's so-called "Lisa" was, is, none other than my old friend, Silvano di Patolo, who was one of the most famous – and famously mischievous – troubadours of his time. He became Leonardo's lover while they were both still young, and he remained the deliciously youthful paramour of the Maestro well into his old age. After Silvano was taken – oh, and that one was a messy event, for he did not expect it, and fought tooth and nail – and once crossed over into immortality, he continued to visit DaVinci, but only, of course, at night. Silvano was a dramatic sap. Legend has it, he paid his calls only when the moon shone full upon the grounds in whichever apartment or palazzo the maestro was calling his home – he was a bit of a nomad. And the more dramatic the entrance, the better. Silvano would sit for Leonardo all night long, which suited the pathologically driven artist-genius wonderfully well. Maestro was a famously poor sleeper. Di Patolo wisely induced his ever-aging friend to tinker ongoingly with his portrait, what had many years prior already been realized as a perfectly rendered work of art. Yes, that's the one. Silvano would ask the Maestro to, say, tweak a fold on the robe, or to add some little shrub to the landscape; or he'd ask for a slightly different curl to the hair, or a more slendering shadow along the nose – whatever struck his ever-changing fancy. In due course, the vaguely emasculated, beautiful young man's painted image evolved to acquire a rather hard to describe, let's call it pan-sexual luminescence. It ascended – or descended, depending on whom knew its *real* backstory – into a portrait of some sort of undefinable *someone*, forever on the brink of *something*; always connected, always distant… Silvano's portrait morphed into that of a human just emerged from, from, let's call it the Neither. *One not of either world.*

I can still remember when I heard Silvano tell his story for the first time… Oh, how he loves to tell it still!

This, my dear, is precisely why the so-called Mona Lisa appears as it does – it was in the physical, literal sense an ever-changing image capture, never completed, never signed off on. And so long as Leonardo maintained that his portrait of Silvano wasn't "ready," he knew he could hold onto the magic of their midnight hours together. The random visits of one of his truest loves would continue, so long as there was work to be done. Additionally, this ruse – let's call it for what it was – spared DaVinci from a similar fate. Legend has it, though known only in certain circles, that Leonardo had repeatedly declined Silvano's vampiric advances from the outset and never did concede to them, though no one to this day understands why, least of all Silvano himself. Why immortality was not desired by the Maestro, no one in our world has ever been able to fathom. We – all of us – lost that particular portraitist far too soon, for his death came as a bit of a surprise; surely to him, and no doubt to Silvano. One can only surmise, for all his genius, for all his willingness to look deep and dark, eyes wide open, there was, perhaps, at least one thing that still frightened Leonardo…

You assume I speak of death? No, I am talking about life eternal – a wakefulness with no end. I never said the Maestro *enjoyed* his insomnia… To this day, Silvano regrets he did not take Leonardo by force. He misses him terribly.

…now, come here, just a little closer…

No! Absolutely not. You are far too young and hold too much promise. Work, live, learn, master your craft. Your gift is undeniable.

…yes. You have my word. I'll come for you when the time is right…

In the meantime, my love, just a driblet more. I only want to fill my glass halfway before I'm off to let's call it "bed." And no, no, it won't hurt as much this time. I promise. I'll be gentle. We'll call this one the dessert course.…

Efectus

"We preserve our life with the death of others. In a dead thing insensate life remains which, when it is reunited with the stomachs of the living, regains sensitive and intellectual life."
Leonardo di ser Peiro da Vinci (1452-1519)

PARADISE

I had always had a "Plan Be," which is to say, I had always had a plan as to what to do – to be, if you will – if things, which is to say we, fell apart. In retrospect, I think I had expected it. It had come to be a matter of not if, but when, a long time ago.

One can only take so much.

After *He* had told me – again – in tears of course, of this latest one, this latest sad, woe is Him failure of His, where He had finally learned his lessons and how much, how very much I meant to Him, I had had enough.

Plan Be, as I had always called it, was a life path hard stop n turn which would hold something so lovely in it for me, it would make the leaving of that life as I had known it (and shared with *Him*) not only alright, but also an opportunity to be a someone so different in a place so different, it would hold for me a new existence to carry me – the new me – over and onto a far better, far lovelier life than what I had ever had – or thought I had had – with *Him*.

Plan Be involved a beach.

Plan Be involved a thatched roof bar situated on that beach.

Plan Be involved me shucking life as I had known it and moving away from it all and taking a job at that bar.

Plan Be involved me working there, barefoot, tanned, dressed in faded cotton skirts and t-shirts with random, tropics-invoking images on them, part of a permanently beach-bound and sun-kissed contingency.

Plan Be involved me with my hair grown long, natural and uncolored, left free to bleach out in the sun's rays – blonde, gray who cared – and pulled back in a simple ponytail, perhaps braided. And no makeup. None.

Plan Be was about me not having to care anymore – about my hair, my looks, about my place on whatever ladders had been out there, about my marital status, about my status in anything.

Plan Be had me outdoors, watching the surf, the sun, the clouds, the birds.

Plan Be had me living and breathing good cheer – mixing cocktails, serving a beer, pouring glass after glass of wine.

Plan Be had me partaking of and helping fellow sun worshippers and beach lovers stretch their hours as long as they could possibly go. Beautiful, islander-bucolic afternoons for them, beautiful, islander-bucolic afternoons for me, for us together – receptive, kindred revelers relishing the locale, the beverages, my helpful and friendly service, and me among them, in peaceful and insular oneness with both time and place.

Plan Be was about superficial congeniality, pleasure in the company of a paying clientele who would ask nothing else from me whatsoever.

Plan Be was about me being just me, and nothing more. To myself and certainly not to anyone else.

All else? I had been there, done that. And *He* was proof. Twelve years, two months, and thirteen days proof, to be exact.

†††

After the turbulent winds of change had finally calmed, they had landed me quite neatly on this spot. I stood there, facing an innocuous, beautiful oceanfront shoreline which stretched languidly, endlessly in either direction in front of me. I stood there, gazing about me, easing myself into its present, its moment, feeling a quieting sort of awe. This oceanside could have been anywhere, really, any place where boundless sand and sky met with the seas. Taking it all in, I was a barefooted, bohemian Dorothy who had been dropped plumb out of the skies and into, well, Paradise.

Where I stood was a comfortably shaded spot, which also happened to be just under the eaves of a broad, thatched roof hut. The hut was a generous structure, boasting a steeply pitched canopy boasting a sturdy fretwork of interwoven grasses that loomed high above, past the hand-hewn rafters. Painted cross beams were dressed in lantern lights of every color, all serving to cover a generous, four-sided bar. The bar was a permanent structure, timeless in its simplicity, beautiful for the patina of its plank top, which had been worn over the years to a silken smoothness. Solid stools encircled the bar, set into a concrete berm nestled into the sands, there to ensure an easy transition from beach stroll to seated readiness for service.

A hand-lettered sign hung from the king post at the heart of the building. It bore one word: "Paradise." Yes, I was in Paradise, and this Paradise was my Plan Be come to fruition. This would be where I would work, make my home, become one of them. I had already adapted the basic look of a member of the surfside populace; the only thing missing was a tan. I was terribly pale. Nonetheless, I had done with my ensemble what I could. I had tied my rather short hair as best as I could into a ponytail and dressed in a longish skirt of a sun-washed floral print. My t-shirt boasted on its back a stylized sea turtle, which I hoped made for the perfect un-fashionable fashion statement.

I had already removed my sneakers, which I held in one hand. I flexed my bare toes in the sand and sighed.

Warm sand between the toes is Paradise.

I could feel the sun on my arms. Warm sun on one's limbs is Paradise.

I looked out over the ocean, even and calm. It was low tide. The gentle shush of the waves was rhythmic and melodic in its give, take, give, take, push, pull. The sun sat low in a perfectly clear, colorless sky. It was just that time of day when the glare of late afternoon light cast everything a bit more anonymously, a bit less discernable. One had to squint to see anything at all.

The ocean, the shore, the sky before me. That is Paradise.

A breeze chose the next moment to brush past my face and my arms. My skirt moved ever so gently with the wind. The caress of an ocean breeze is Paradise.

Sunglasses, you ask? No. somehow, they seemed entirely too practical to have been warranted. Shoes in hand were enough of a reminder of my urban subsistence. A handbag filled with stuff would have been worse – what burdensome, vestigial devices one of those things would have been. In that moment, I needed nothing but myself as I stood at easy attention, ready to report for my new job.

Plan Be was me, not only in Paradise, but me there as an active member, an insider. One at one, with, and *of* the garden.

A pelican flew past, followed by a seagull, the silent bird trailed by its raucous cousin, with its long echoing caw. Threaded in with the sounds of the rolling surf, the land- and seascape surrounding me, it could have been the opening scene of a film – some getaway vacation, escapist, visual feast kind of film. I felt peculiarly romantic, and somehow, oddly, prettier.

You see, new beginnings can indeed be pulled off, and with wonderful outcomes. No one, and I say, no one needs to be victim to their own poor decisions or stagnant obligations. If Plan A doesn't work out, have a Plan Be. Then act on it.

Like I did.

So, here I am.

†††

The impossibly good-looking fellow behind the bar waved at *me*. His eyes, unlike mine, were hidden, protected from the sun by a pair of enormous, dark sunglasses. His dark blonde hair he had tucked behind his ears, the ends curling just so at his neck. His smile was perfect – a wide, sly grin edged with humor. His teeth were white and even, almost too perfect. He was tall, well-built, but naturally, athletically so. His ancient button-down shirt was frayed at every seam, and with the topmost buttons missing, had been incidentally left open to reveal tanned and toned pectorals distractingly covered in a scruff of fine, golden hair into which a sizable pendant lay nested, which only *begged* for closer inspection. It was some sort of an inscribed coin I had never seen before.

I made a concerted effort to move my eyes back up to his face and then past him, feigning more interest in the structure than this Malibu Adonis. I scanned the bar as I approached the pass-through at the far end, like some seasoned pro, assessing the place.

"Hiya, hon," the demi-god behind the bar greeted me.

What was I, some kid just out of school?

I loved it.

"Yes, hello. I'm the new waitstaff, er, bartender – um, I'm not exactly sure what. At any rate; yes, hello. I'm here, reporting for work. The ad called for a self-starting 'wingman barkeep' if I remember correctly. So that'd be me!"

The job search, application and hiring had all been done online, of course, and in the blink of an eye. In a bit of a blur, actually. Meant to *be*, was how I had interpreted all that.

Plan Be was my meant to be.

"And that'd be you, for sure!" the statuesque David come to life smiled at *me*, again.

"I'm David," he said, taking my hand to shake it.

David. Imagine that.

"Good to meet you," I returned, "I'm, um, Anne, I lied. But if you like, you can call me AJ. That's what my closest friends call me," I added lamely, not happy with either moniker.

I felt my knees grow weak in the light of his luminous presence, but I ignored that and adapted what I hoped would pass for a casual professionalism. Beachy professionalism, one could say. I was not in the market, so to speak, nor was I planning on changing that edict. I'd had enough of that. *He* had more than seen to it. The David two feet away from me was nothing more than a congenial employer.

"At your service!" I added, the jovial, chill colleague reporting for duty.

"Well, it's a good thing you got here when you did," David the Dream said as he tossed me a hand towel, which I expertly flung over one shoulder. "Our afternoon regulars are already arriving and settling in – and they're a thirsty bunch! You can jump right in. I know you've got experience, otherwise you wouldn't have been brought on board. Ask questions as they arise, and just keep the customers happy."

"You got it!" I answered, tossing my sneakers onto a low shelf. This job would be a dream. To keep my gaze leaning towards the ocean, the sun, to follow the sea birds as they passed by, and amidst all that, serve up cooling beverages to sun-soaked afficionados of island life could *hardly* be called work.

I already felt more the free-spirited girl-by-the-sea than anything else.

"What'll it be?" I asked my first customers. A couple had seated themselves right in front of where I stood. I couldn't see their faces, for they sat with their backs to the ocean, and were instantly silhouetted by the sun. It was rather blinding, to try and look into their faces, and so I made minimal effort, rather focusing on their shadowed outlines.

"I'll take a Bloody Mary," the one on the left said.

The one on the right chimed in, "And I'll have a beer, and, um, what kind…"

"Sir, it appears we have only this kind of beer," I said, pulling first one then a second dripping, cold bottle from the ice-filled basin.

"Oh, sure, okay; no problem, I'll take it."

I grabbed the only thing that resembled a bottle opener, a large, old cast iron gadget with a sharp toothed prong at the center of its semi-circular, open end, and wedged the cap into place. The bottle cap resisted. Crikey, I thought as I tried again. To struggle with something so commonplace as this was absurd. Why the cap didn't give, especially given the leverage of the heavy opener, I couldn't say. This called for more force than was good for either myself or the beer, and with the dripping bottle so slippery, made it a bit risky. I was at last able to pry the cap off, but at the cost of the back of my left hand. When the sharply crimped cap popped off and flew to the ground, the iron tooth of the opener gouged a deep cut across the back of my hand, tearing a fat swath of skin clean off. Blood welled up in the wound and began to seep along the flexed tendons of my hand. The pain was searing. My thoughts instantly went to cleanliness. No idea what dirt or germs or even rust I may have just literally drug through me. Professionalism. And safety.

I shot a glance over at David. Thankfully, he hadn't caught this introductory, self-injurious moment of clumsiness. And the couple at the bar, although it remained hard to see exactly what they were about, appeared to be deep in conversation, their heads almost touching. Hopefully they hadn't seen, either.

I tore a length of clean rag from one I found in a bin under the counter and wrapped it around my hand. It hurt. Really hurt. The blood immediately spotted through the fabric, the stain growing in visible increments. I tore a second length of fabric and layered it over the first bandage, even tighter, realizing I needed to think tourniquet over mere covering. Pressure. Lots of it.

"Here you go," I said, my voice low and tight amidst the pain, handing the bottle of beer to the customer with my good hand.

I started when I heard David's voice call out behind me, "One spicy Bloody Mary, coming right up!"

I looked over my shoulder. David, though with his back still to me, launched a tall glass filled to the brim with dark, red liquid along the length of the bar, in my direction. Caught off guard and certainly not having found any sort of cadence with the place, I lurched forward to grab the cocktail with my right hand. Its velocity met with my grab only to cause a solid percentage of the Bloody Mary to slosh up, out of the glass and all over the front of my t-shirt. The dark stain made it look as if I had been stabbed in the breast. The beverage-soaked fabric adhered to my skin, feeling nasty and wet. Naturally, the wet spot could not have been placed more egregiously, for it left nothing of my nipple to the imagination. I was mortified.

And still, my right hand burned with pain. The second bandage would soon need replacing. I had to keep David from seeing it.

Good grief. First my hand, now my t-shirt.

I grabbed the remainder of the torn rag and wiped down the bar top. I handed the Bloody Mary to the second patron.

I threw the soiled rag – yuck, it looked like it was soaked in blood – into the trash bin.

Another customer had seated himself at the bar. His face was likewise impossible to discern, the unrelenting light of the sun casting him as well into a blindingly shadowed form. It was wearying on the eyes. I consoled myself, knowing the sun would eventually set and I would be relieved of its exhausting brightness. Tomorrow, the better part of the day would find the sun high above, with me and all the- 231 -tteons of Paradise cozily ensconced in the comfortable shade of the thatched roof. That was a nice thought.

Meantime, I contended with the glare. The unrelenting, color-stripping glare, which was rendering me sun blind.

I began to make my way to the next customer. After that, I'd move on to the next two, who had arrived almost immediately after this one. Then, there was a small group of three who had seated themselves soon after that.

I glanced back over at David, who though he was busy mixing another Bloody Mary, remained stationed at his end of the bar, deep in conversation with a customer.

What the fuck, I thought to myself. Am I supposed to serve this whole freakin' place all by myself?

A lone server at a quickly filling counter is not Paradise, no matter where, or how beautiful the place is, especially when there's another server, but one who thinks they can just stand around and yack on and on, and just mix up cocktails as it suited them.

This was not part of my Plan Be.

Still, I assigned the mishaps to first day, on-the-job blues, and a bit of a fluke. Rushes do happen and I'd get into the swing of things. I was where I wanted to be, on the beach, at a bar, and an integral part of it all. I could see the ocean stretching endlessly beyond me; I could see the cloudless sky to either side behind my glare-enshrouded customers, and I could see the sun seated dead center in the midst of that stark afternoon…

That sun. That bright, hot sun.

Burning the skin on my arms. My pale arms, which had not seen direct sunlight in years. When we, *He* and I, had been outdoors, we had always dutifully worn our sunscreen or been dressed in proper hiking clothes, which always included shirts with long sleeves. Never the sun worshipper before, my Plan Be had for that very reason included the indulgence of acquiring a suntan.

But not like this. Not quite this aggressively. Ouch. I could feel the onset of a burn on my forearms, which had grown quite pink. Despite the late afternoon hour, the sun in this tropical Paradise shone relentlessly. And not only did its searing light accost my sight, its warm rays, its lovely, warm rays, were now working a bit too steadfastly on the surface of my unprotected skin.

Surely, there'd be some sunscreen, something left by a customer, or another employee, sitting somewhere on a shelf under the bar. I would find it just as soon as I could…

But that would have to wait. The customers who had just appeared required my attention. And David was still over there, still talking, now mixing some other sort of cocktail, brandishing a shaker, and moving his lithe torso in far more seductive a fashion than was warranted, shaking the hell out of whatever the heck it was.

"David?" I ventured.

"Be right there, hon'," he replied, clearly distracted with whomever it was he was still far too engaged with at the back end of the bar.

"What can I get for you?" I rapid-fired down the row as I approached the new arrivals, still holding my right hand tightly with my left, hoping to stave the blood flow. Intermittently, I pulled the wet, ever-darkening fabric off my breast.

"Heya there," the single, likewise faceless one answered, "I'll take a beer."

"Yeah, me too," the first of the newer couple chimed in.

"Make that three, kiddo!" the second of the pair called out, hand raised in my direction, as if I couldn't tell who was ordering.

Oh shit, I thought. Here goes with that opener from hell…

I called out to the others I'd be right with them as I pulled three beers from the icy depths of the steel basin with my good hand.

In my haste, as I could use only one hand and as such had grabbed onto and was holding three wet longnecks between my fingers, I dropped one of them. The damn bottle fell like a missile – slippery and hard as a rock – landing squarely on my right foot.

"Fuck!" I cursed myself. I wanted to cry out in pain. I felt that telltale lurch in my stomach, telling me I had broken at least one toe. I controlled my outburst, held it in, but my foot wailed. It throbbed. The agony was so extreme, it was nearly numbing.

As my foot had absorbed the fall of the bottle, and though too shaken up to be drinkable at that moment, the beer was still intact. Which wasn't saying much. Shards of broken glass would have really been a problem, I rationalized. I was lucky; I would have had to put my sneakers back on.

The customers, all talking amongst themselves, were thankfully, I guess, oblivious to my clumsy machinations, my injuries. How no one seemed to notice anything, I couldn't say. Lax attentiveness was evidently a key component of easy-going islander vibe.

I hobbled up to the counter and braced myself for a precious few, recuperative seconds. As soon as I could steady my breath, I took a step back to the basin to retrieve a replacement beer for the order. It took only two steps to reach the basin, but each step was a mile, so horrific was the pain, I had nearly forgotten the injury to my right hand, where the fabric bandage was now visibly soaked through. A blood stain the size of ping pong ball broadcast the wound beneath it with as much garishness as had it been a horror film special effect. Neon red upon a field as white as snow.

Mental note: Find a darker piece of fabric in the rag bin to wrap this with.

I held my breath and through the pain returned with the third bottle to a spot behind the bar near the three who awaited their beers. Turning my back to them, I took the crowbar of a bottle opener and, this time with my dishtowel to hold the bottle, I made to pry off its cap. Knowing now what to expect, I was confident I could open the three bottles of beer without incident, and quickly, and then move on to the other clientele.

I pried off one cap. I pried off the second cap.

As I was prying off the third bottle cap, a voice bolted out from the far end of the bar, bellowing, "Miss! Miss! Can we get some service down here?"

You guessed it. I was so caught off guard – the voice so overly and unnecessarily loud – that, yes, I gouged my bandaged hand with the tooth-like protrusion of the opener. Again. This time, however, the metal tooth dug into the bandage itself, pulling back completely the second wrapping to expose the first, completely soaked length of fabric.

I exhaled long and slow in my agony, horrified at how wet and bloody my hand was. Blood had seeped into the crevices of my knuckles. This new gouge had re-jiggered what had managed to coagulate and slow down, rendering the wound as fresh as had it just happened, again. Now, the blood, flowing fresh, began to drip. Droplets of blood fell onto the sand-covered floor and on my bare feet. When the warm drops hit the second and third toes of my right foot, which had already turned purple, it felt like they were tiny nails, shot with a gun.

Involuntary tears ran down my cheeks. My heart raced. The fight in me had been called forth. It was all I could do to remain standing.

I set the beers down with my good hand, grimacing at the faceless customers, still so engrossed in their conversation, and looked once more behind me, this time to try and illicit some kind of mentorship invoking reaction from my self-absorbed boss.

David was doing shots with his customer, the one he had been talking with the entire time. Both had their heads tipped back, faces to the sky, tossing who knows what down their respective throats.

Sonofabitch! I thought.

This was not working.

But was anyone else to blame for my abject clumsiness?

"Miss! Oh, Miss!" the bellow sounded again.

"Yes, yes, coming!" I simpered, trying my damndest to remain composed.

"David?" I ventured once more, this time allowing the plaintiveness in my voice to come through. Would a sideways call for help possibly be interpreted and heeded as such?

"Yep, hon' – be there in a bit!" was all he said, without so much as looking at me, acknowledging me.

Fucker, I thought.

Damn him!

I hobbled to the far end, where the as-yet unserved customers were seated. While two of them were similarly engaged in conversation, this last one sat in relative solitude. And, based on his body language, his need for a drink was both obvious and urgent. Alright, I'd get him tended to.

Making my way down the bar, I passed the bin holding the rags and grabbed another one. Taking a corner of the fabric in my teeth, I tore off a section. As I quickly wound the newest makeshift bandage around my throbbing, bleeding hand, I thought of *Him*.

Now, why did I suddenly think of *Him*? Had I not erased *Him* from my mind?

Oh, I realized.

It was the rag. A plaid flannel. It looked just like a shirt of *His*.

Fuck. Now, how susceptible was I if something like that would send my thoughts back to *Him*? To someone I had quite literally put behind me?

"Miss?" a voice much closer to me called out.

"Yes? Can I help?" I asked, tucking the end of the flannel into place. The blood had already begun to soak through, again. I placed myself into the client's shadow, which her ample form cast over the bar, like a shield. Anything to get out of the sun for a moment. My forearms were on fire.

"Dang, Missy. You look like you could use a little SPF on those," the customer ventured between hiccups.

"Yes," I sighed. I had no strength left for aimless friendliness. "What can I do for you? I'm needing to get down there to…"

"Here, Miss. Thing is, I don't feel so well. There's something wrong with this Bloody…"

The customer was about to hand over her near-empty glass when she hiccupped again. Hard. All of a sudden, her eyes opened wide as she clapped her other hand over her mouth, her shoulders drawing in tight. But it was too late. The contents of her stomach erupted, spewing past her hand, some of it landing on the bar top, most of it landing on me. I looked down, aghast. My top was sprayed, neck to hem, with dark pink, mattery bits stuck all over the fabric. Still, ever the professional, my first action was to jump to the patron's assistance. I hobbled the few steps it took to get me to the rapidly emptying rag bin, my heart pounding. So much adrenaline. I grabbed two rags, one for her and one for me.

"Oh, Lordy, Lordy," she began, before turning away from me to vomit once more, this time all over her stool and onto the sand.

"There, there, ma'am," I strove for some semblance of caring. Let me get you some water, okay? Some to drink and some to tidy up a bit. I'll be right back…" I murmured, handing over both rags. Forget about me.

This time, instead of forging on to tend to the last of the newly arrived customers, I hobbled over to David, who was now leaning over the bar, stroking the hair out of his pet customer's eyes. His oblivious calm had never wavered. What dimension was this macho piece of work stuck in?

"David…David," I stuttered, tugging at his shirtsleeve.

I was done. I couldn't keep up on any level. I was wracked with pain. I was soaked to the skin, and the bandage on my hand needed replacing. Heck, I needed to leave and get myself to an emergency room. The bleeding was not subsiding.

"What, hon'?" he turned and looked at me blankly from somewhere beneath the black fields of his sunglasses. "You need something?"

That was it. I lost my professional cool. My islander chill was no more.

"Do I need something? Do I need something? Are you fucking kidding me?" I yelled.

"Whoa, girl," the clueless ass chided. "Hang on there a moment!"

"No! I am done with this! This is no, no…Paradise! It's…it's a fucking nightmare here! Everything is falling to pot and all you can do is stay in your corner over here and screw around, leaving me to do *everything*?" I railed, poking his washboard abs. I was over any perfunctory proper distancing, any superficial admiration of this beauteous cad. "Can you see that I am injured? Do you see I am *bleeding*?" I held my seeping, wrapped hand up to his face.

"Alright, alright, kiddo. Maybe you need refreshing."

I thought he meant cleaning up, perhaps a stiff drink.

When he made no move, I spat out, "Well, what the hell do you mean?"

"Boop!" was all he said, and he touched the tip of my nose.

Good God.

That was what I had said to *Him* when I pushed *Him* off the ledge.

Dear Lord, that was what my father used to say to me when he'd touch my nose, when he'd deign to put on some fatherly airs towards me, treat me as if I were some seven-year-old. And when I'd flinch….

But when I heard the word, and when I felt his pointed fingernail graze my nose, it all came back to me.

I saw what happened.

†††

The hike, the lovely day, the deep blue sky, the cotton ball clouds, and the climb up, up, up to the overlook, so far into the woods, hardly anyone knew of it, let alone dared venture up there, especially now that the road had been closed to tourists, being that the old bridge had collapsed, prohibiting any vehicles from even getting to the base…

…and the Falls…

So beautiful. So picturesque. A rainbow fragment hanging in the distance below, afloat in a misted cloud of spray, the green of the deep gully, the pool reflecting the shadowing forest, and the winding, lower river, flowing so quickly, fed by the watery torrent from above.

…and the fall…

So satisfying, so final. *Bastard mother fucker lying cheating shithead* getting what He *really* deserved.

"Boop!" I had said to *Him* when I pushed Him off the ledge, right at that precise moment when He was perfectly, completely distracted, right when He was so occupied, balancing His phone in His outstretched hand, navigating the glare of the sun, about to hit the record button.

I saw *Him* fall away from me, His free arm reaching for me, His squinting eyes instantly transformed into white orbs of shock, His mouth agape. If He screamed, the downward rush and thunderous din of the falls swept the sound away from me, sparing me from whatever it was He may have attempted to utter. I could have sworn I saw Him begin to mouth the penultimate and classic, "Fuuu…!" But the fresh air tore away at His voice, His clothes and at His hair as He went down, down, down.

Yeah, fuck is right. Fuck You.

Down He went, a million miles away from me in the split of a second. Tunnel vision hollowed my mind, and I heard a roaring in my head. Interspersed with intermittent glimmers of consciousness were images of Him pared down to almost nothing. He was less than a two-dimensional object thrown into a trance-like void.

I saw Him hit the ledge directly below us, which jutted a few yards out, over the pool. Gosh, a couple more feet, and He would have cleared the ledge and fallen into the water. No telling how that might have played out – He could have conceivably survived the fall, and what a mess that would have been, whether intact or injured. I'd have had to think up a plan C.

No, a Plan C was not going to be needed. He hit the ledge dead center, and the mess that resulted, when He combusted upon the unrelenting, bleached-white limestone surface was sufficient. Blood sprayed from every orifice of His body and then some. His skull exploded like an old pumpkin. Heck, blood even seeped from the cuffs of His pants. He lay there, face-planted, limbs askew in every direction, a bloom of quickly darkening crimson framing His fractured body. It was an amazing sight, even from my perch high above.

And then, I saw, remembered, the rest:

I saw my foot slip on loose gravel, I saw me drop my phone as I tried, foolishly, to grab the strands of foliage which were so bravely growing out of a crack in the rock. That sprig wanted nothing to do with me, and so it let my hand slip along its length until I held only air.

I saw my arms flail, saw the landscape spin a quick back n forth as my head turned first one way, then another, in a panic-stricken moment of assessment.

I concluded there was nothing I could do but follow suit. Follow *Him* on *His* beeline path to the ground below. There was no time to arch my back or add a last bit of spring to my feet to propel me outwards and away from the ledge on which *He* was already sprawled. My one foot, once it had left the ground, never met with the potential helpmate of a solid surface again. My other foot was likewise instantly airborne and useless.

I was headed down, straight down, and I would in a few seconds hit the ledge, or perhaps even land on the blown-up body that had once housed *Him*.

I saw the vertical mass of land fly by me as my body turned in space. Then I saw the sky, that beautiful, azure endlessness you only see on clear autumn days. Gosh, what a pretty day it had been, what a wonderful new beginning it had almost been.

Day one of my Plan Be.

I felt the cool air woosh pass me, ever faster, and too soon, I landed.

I missed *Him* by a few inches. Could a somewhat cushioned landing on *Him* have saved me?

Irrelevant. My head bounced, my spine pulverized , and my arms, my legs, my joints blew out. I remembered feeling the explosion I had only moments ago observed from a distance happening inside of me.

I saw the rainbow hovering in the mist, now at eye level. I saw it turn to gray, then all went black.

†††

I came to with a shock. A sudden, jarring resuscitation. I gasped audibly. There I was, standing upright, back at the bar, perfectly still, with my bare feet planted firmly in the sand. And there he stood, that fiendish, black-lensed bastard, still smiling, his long finger with its pointed nail still in the air in front of my face.

"*What the hell?*" I cried.

"Exactly," he replied.

†††

"So, here's the thing," he continued matter-of-factly, "You have a choice. Not that you deserve to have one, but you do. I'm only following orders.

"What you just relived, that is Option A. Over and over again, you will see that dude, falling, then you will see, feel, yourself falling until you hit, until you loop over, and it all starts again."

Oh, merciful God, I thought. Noooo…

He went on.

"Your other choice is this. This, your 'Paradise'," David air-quoted, clawing staccato the air to either side of his horrifically handsome face. "Your other choice is this, looped."

"Get it?" he asked.

I had no words.

"Okay, whatever," he shrugged. "Be dumbstruck, you stupid innocent. Nod when I speak the loop you want. They're both yours already, anyway. You conjured them up yourself. You got what you wanted. I don't give a fuck either way."

I still had no words.

"So, what'll it be?" he insisted, "The Falls?"

I said nothing.

"Or this?" He paused, then sneered, "Option B? *Plan Be?*"

I said nothing.

"Okay. Just as I suspected," the creature said, turning his face away from me, as if he could no longer stand to look upon my damnable ordinary, pathetic self. "It's your choice. It's your Paradise."

He threw me a fresh hand towel, which I laid over my shoulder.

"Now, get back to work," he commanded.

Then, voice switching over in a full-on turnabout, the David addressed me, with that menacing warmth of his, which I now fully recognized for what it was.

"Look, hon'!" he crooned, pointing to a newly arrived couple. "Our afternoon regulars are already arriving and settling in – and they're a thirsty bunch!"

†††

The first customers had just seated themselves. The late afternoon sun hung in the colorless sky, blinding me. All I could see were their shadowed outlines. No faces. The sidelong rays shone on my bare forearms, warming, toasting my unprotected skin. The sand-covered floor was soft and cool against my bare feet. I looked at the two toes of my right foot, which would soon be broken by a falling bottle of beer. As a gentle breeze played across my cheek, stirred the folds of my skirt; I looked at the smooth, unbroken skin on the back of my hand....

Efectus

THE REST

I really can't say I have any memory of it not being there.

And now that I know, and look back, everything – everything – that I thought about it has been turned upside down. It's a shame, to perceive the extent of a loathsomeness with such absolute certainty, but it's a real bitch to then witness the whole thing turned inside out and having its rotting innards explode full in your face, to insult you with its obviousness, of its having been something far more repugnant than you could have ever imagined it. You realize, you had no idea. All your life, no idea at all. That's what really sucks.

All those wasted years of dread-filled wakefulness.

My earliest memories of the shadow are of a mere puddle of dark, about the size of a cake plate, which would slowly appear and come into a sort of focus in the farthest corner of my room once the light had been turned off and my door had been pulled shut. I can even remember seeing its circular form from between the slats of my crib. At first, I had no perception of fear, only familiarity, an anodyne awareness of its imminent, nightly emergence, once my mother or father, or my grandmother or the occasional babysitter, had told me sweet dreams, sleep tight, and so on, and left me alone to my night.

The shadow, as time went on, began to spread, slowly, like a pancake on a griddle. By the time I started preschool, while it remained as yet a two-dimensional patch, it was always in the same spot, a shadow puddle which would materialize and begin to grow over the course of the next few hours, to about the size of the small mirror over my bathroom sink. The shadow seemed to grow with me. About the time puberty hit, my shadow took on a third dimension and began to rise from the floor, edging upwards, like a lopsided column. It always matched me in height, now that I think back on it, never broader or taller than I was at any point in my life. As I grew into adulthood, the shadow evolved along with me, showing me, deliberately, incrementally, more and more of itself, as if clueing me in on its secretive identity, trying to keep me adjusted to an ever-increasing clarity of what it was – or whatever I might imagine it might be – to the point where, about when I turned eighteen, I began to think I could see a face underneath what had to have been some kind of cloak, or shawl, draped over what could only have been its head.

The problem with the evolution of my shadow, was the onset of, then the ever-growing state of fear I suffered because of it, however much of that fear was self-induced, or part of a natural, fight-flight reactiveness any human would be wired to respond with. Media, stories told, books I read, all fed into my innocent familiarity morphing into what I came to perceive as agonizing, unrelenting, nightly hauntings, which progressively cemented me into my bed in a state of abject terror. Night after night, pressed against the wall as best as I could manage, I would try and keep my body as far away from my shadow as was physically possible.

After a few years of calling to my parents and disrupting their precious sleep, and after a few soundly punished attempts to steal into their vast bed, way down there, in their bedroom at the end of a hallway about a quarter mile long, I gave up any childish notions of conciliatory parental soothing or rescue, from either that dark entity or the fear that had become so merged in my core as to be its own metaphysical malignancy.

The one time too many I ever dared call to my parents, my father, in some state of something, burst into my room and pulled me out of my bed. He hit me as I fell to the floor, in a wild, half-wakeful rage unlike any of the other times he had ever smacked me, and all the while he was doing that to me, my shadow was over there in the corner, like some spectral doormat, just watching, doing nothing, watching as my dad did *this* to me. It was ridiculous, but I was embarrassed that my shadow was serving as hatefully passive witness to my parent's unrestrained, furious indulgence, to my humiliation. I was angry at *it* for its stagnant apathy. My parents were never going to believe me, or quit beating me because of it, but neither would there ever be any intervention by whatever that thing was. In its own way, that odious shadow saw fit to torment me with its hauntingly unchanging presence, leaving me feeling twice forsaken.

The shadow demonstrated to me, how heartbreakingly alone I was at far too early an age.

I grew accustomed to being afraid. Dread became my familiar climate of repose. To (try and) rest was to fight, futilely, for any sense of calm, or safety. I never knew what a gentle falling asleep was, for, rest was never, ever restful. From my earliest years on, night was something to be survived. I was compelled to fight sleep with a panic-stricken, wide-eyed wakefulness until the sleep chemicals in my brain would overtake me, knocking me out with the suddenness of a soft one-two punch in the early morning hours when my subconscious would finally give in, and a brief spell of sleep was forced upon me. An hour, two hours, perhaps three if I was lucky. I fought that long, dark night like one who fights death, night after night after night…

I had to. I had to keep watch over myself, because there was no one, or nothing, to do it for me, or with me.

I had a prayer, one I made up over the course of my untallied, interminable nights. Curled up under the twisted bedsheets like a bunny hunkered down in a shallow divot in the grass, I would formulate phrases to serve as protective invocations. As I grew older, I sought out some cadence within them, eventually composing rudimentary rhyme schemes around them. I would chant these verses in my head, sometimes speaking them out loud to the room, to the shadow, wherever in the room it had manifested for that night, until my recitations induced something akin to a self-hypnosis, a state of suspended awareness that would allow me to drift off, even as I wondered, feared, it would be the last time I would get to do this…

Shadow puddle, stay away; let me sleep so I can wake
Shadow, please, stay over there; I'm in my bed, do not come near
And shadow puddle should I die, please let me stay right where I lie
So, all the loving angels can find me

I never knew, if my falling into unconsciousness would be my last moment of living awareness, if my shadow would do something to me as I slept, or if I would awaken to the world of the living one more time. I also wondered if I might open my eyes to some post-life realm of the dead.

It drains the soul, to end each and every day with thoughts like that.

I've been weary all my life, in more ways than one. For one, my parents' regard for me descended ages ago into resigned tolerance edged with anger. They were always mad at me. They called me lazy, shiftless. My grandmother, the one time she stayed with me, called me nuts. Sure, there were sleep clinics. Two months of them, with my shadow right there, in the far corners rooms as there I'd lay, wired like an automaton, not even remotely close to falling asleep. The machines recorded whatever they were supposed to record, but they read nothing. I'd lie there, wide awake, while the overnight technicians dozed, watching my shadow watching me. No one ever bothered to look where exactly their patient was looking, or why. The doctors would shake their heads and ask to see my parents in the hall to talk.

They couldn't see my shadow. No one could.

When I finally got my driver's license, and I would borrow one of the cars and drive myself places, it was to churches and chapels in town and the nearby countryside that I would go, always looking for some sign – in some work of art, some object at rest upon an altar, some play of light upon a wall – which might point me to some mystical clue for reassurance, or a sign, or a message, possibly intended for me. I was desperate for an explanation, willing to peer under every doubt, through every superstition, beyond every bit of dogma for some visual marker – maybe a primer or a directive – that would help explain what it was I had to endure every single night, and why. I found myself even looking in the most commonplace elements of these houses of worship – doorstops, bulletin boards, exit signs, anything – beseeching I knew not what or whom for any cipher that might spark a flash of new understanding. It seemed a bit ego-ridden, I suppose, to think I might exist as a conduit for something in the context of faith-based mysticism, but it was the only way I could deal with what already seemed proven to me as undeniable, unavoidable. The reverse, that I was a human link to the world of the damned, existed in a place I wasn't ready to consider, let alone embrace. No way did I want to invite in any notion that what sought me out, would not leave me alone, was of some hellish foundation, and that there might be an accursed outcome intended for me.

I had never done anything to deserve something as bad as that, nor did I think I was born with any more original sin than any other human had ever been born with. Concepts of some evil ancestry or legacy hung no more at my back than did any other guilt or damning past hang upon the shoulders of any other, random, space-filler human. I was born of ordinary parents into an ordinary world of working class, mortal placeholders, surely too mundane an example of my species to have captured the attentions of anything as great, or as dark, as I was daring to wonder about or acknowledge as possible.

Whatever it was, whatever I was or was not, a shadow had sought me out, and once arrived, had never left, missed a single night with me, granted me one blessed, freaking night of blissful nothingness.

The toll the shadow and my sleep deprivation took on me was profound. It re-crafted my personality from the inside out, which soon enough proved uninviting to even the most desperately seeking, lonely classmates in school, or later on, the people I knew from work, or randomly encountered others I crossed paths with on my days off. I remained a solitary wanderer through every stage of my life. Friendship evaded me but mattered too little to be anything for which I in my perennially depleted state may have been driven to seek out or fight for. Fatigue infected my capability to feel emotion – I sailed upon calm, dulled, and lonesome seas of days, weeks, months, and years. The four dates I ever had – three asked on, one I initiated – all ended prematurely, and badly. The one dinner out I was able to survive to the dessert course, I still had to find my own ride home; I was that inattentive, that undesirable, for all my otherwise decently fitted components. Had I had a modicum of a life spark to energize my waking hours, I could have passed for attractive. But looks were the farthest thing from my mind, a mind which drifted and wandered like a lost ant on a concrete playground. My small universe was impossibly vast and unnavigable. My consciousness wandered in circles, which never got me anywhere.

But then I met her, at the grotto, that little one along State Road 32W, about five miles outside of town, straight south. She was arranging river rocks around the base of the sign at the head of the path to the grotto, laying each stone to bed much as any little girl might have tended to a beloved doll. She jumped visibly when I ventured a reluctant greeting. It would not do to pretend this person was not there at all, though to ignore her, to remain consistent in my solitude, would have been my preference. So, I spoke to her.

Whatever do you want from me? Were the first, odd words she sputtered back from beneath the shield of her arm. I stood with the sun directly at my back, which had cast me in stark silhouette.

Moments later, drawing long her words, as if something had just dawned to her, she added, nodding her head, *Oh, yes – it's you.*

I feigned a nonchalance, and rambled an explanation, on my having toured a few other faith-based localities that afternoon, just a free-time explorer, a history buff, casually passing a day off. But I was surging inside with wild hope, wondering if I had finally found a first along the lines of whatever it was I had been looking for.

No, no, she shook her head, squinting, still blinded by the stark outline of me where I stood, from which I had no intention of moving. *It's no accident you are here. You're here for a reason, and that reason was to meet me, right here, today. I am sorry – hope to not frighten you by my saying so. But it's there in the...*

As if a human in broad daylight could even begin to frighten me. No, it was clear to me, too. We had found each other as had been ordained. By whom, I didn't know, or care much, anymore. At that point, I would take anyone, and so I did.

The brevity and tone of the woman's phrases were echoed in her appearance, which lent themselves to an easy, if abrupt presentation of self. She was odd, but not alarming; brusque, but not rude. I was this, too, I suppose, though far more awkward, never having had much opportunity to engage with strangers. You could say we were well matched, even at a superficial level.

Consigned to the serendipity behind our mutually acknowledged and accepted peculiarities, and to the coincidence of our encounter, after a few more minutes of decidedly odd chit chat, we agreed to meet for lunch the next day.

That night, I went to bed carrying the tiniest flicker of hope in my heart. This new unknown held a glimmer of something positive, some next step, though I knew not exactly what. When I drifted off at about 4:15 am, my shadow glowering at me as usual from its corner, my two-hour sojourn before the alarm went off was almost refreshing.

We met the following day as agreed, at one.

Once the server was safely out of earshot, the woman from the grotto switched immediately from irrelevant pleasantries to what instantly sounded like a proposal for some pre-determined undertaking. It was as if a dial in her head had been turned to a different channel. Her voice lowered, her brows drew together, and she began to pepper me with statements about me, rather than even making a pretext at wanting to engage in any kind of a conversational back and forth. She told me about myself, and what she said was spot on.

A couple minutes in, she mentioned the word "shadow," which caused me to sit up and peer down the bar to the far end of the café's dining room. Holding my breath, I scanned the floor for any telltale sign of the shadow's arrival. The shadow had yet to invade my daylighted waking hours, my periods of active living, but I was at the point where I was expecting that to change any day, at any moment.

She told me she had known for a long time, there would come a day when she would encounter a stranger whose need for her was so specific, it would serve to define who she was and would be until her death. And that she would recognize me instantly, this being part of some calling not yet disclosed to her, and that she by her subsequent actions would learn what her true purpose for existence was.

Then she added, yes, I was the one, and when I had stood there, in the aura of my makeshift, late afternoon halo at the newly re-opened roadside grotto where she had just been hired as caretaker, and had arrived precisely at the particular moment which coordinated with some key marker in her own timeline, that the encounter yesterday afternoon had signaled, according to her, all the stars in her universe as having come together, with me included, in an entirely non-random confluence of circumstance.

Her purpose in life, she emphasized, would come to fruition by this pairing up with me – by, what she put it as, my *cleansing*.

When she used the word "cleansing," my poor, stressed heart skipped a beat. She with her word choice was inadvertently pointing me to my worst held, desperately avoided fears, that this continual presence in my nights, this puddle of a shadow that with each year had grown with me and now stood at full height in the corner of whichever room I would dare and try put my weary head to rest, was indeed borne of something unclean, dirty – dare I say evil. And that I by its unrelenting presence was its trigger, or lure, perhaps its host. That *I* was unclean, dirty, evil.

Was she the one to *cleanse* me, to usher me up and out of whatever it was in which I was mired? Was she a conduit of God, or an emissary from something diametrically opposed the basic tenants of all things God, or God-like, there to tempt me, guide me off my cliff, where perhaps my shadow awaited me, hungry for the rest of me? What if she were *of* my shadow, a daytime, anthropomorphized incarnation, working to prevent me from hiding, fighting back in the only way I knew how, under my sheets, blankets, and comforters, in what I believed to be my only means of shelter? The alternative was to see myself pulled out from under my precious covers and splayed across the bedroom floor as I was dragged like a carcass across the fields, into the arms of whatever beastly manifestation it was that glowered at me from the corners of my room each and every night.

What if she was part of a big trick? What if I would come to trust her too much and blindly hand over what little was left of my sanity? But I was so tired, so tired. All I wanted was to rest; to have one single, solid night of beautiful, sound sleep.

And so, I accepted.

My hell was already such that I knew in my core, I would not accept too much more of the subsistence that paraded as my sentient presence on the face of what so far only presented itself as a cold and indifferent world.

The ritual, she told me, could take place as soon as that very night. In my room, at what she had quickly calculated to be my – and she apologized for her using this archaic and negative term – witching hour.

I left my – well, I guess I will refer to her as my friend – with my address, written onto the receipt.

Dinner that night was, as more or less expected, a non-event. My mother was off to bed almost immediately after chasing down her second martini, and my father followed soon after, leaving the house to its glum denouement well before the clock struck eleven. That the house my parents shared with me was a big and solid, old place, and that they were faithful practitioners of their cocktail-aided dormancy, would serve me especially well that night, for to clandestinely usher in the closest thing I had ever had to a personal house guest, let alone after midnight, would be an easy thing.

I crept downstairs into the kitchen the moment I heard the clang of the lock to my parents' bedroom door echo down the hallway. For well over an hour, I sat on the banquette in the breakfast nook, silent and unmoving, listening to the pulse of the stove clock, to the crickets' faint song out back, watching as the moon slowly rose, then seeing the clouds slide across the sky to obscure it, on high alert for any hint of the shadow's puddle to announce its hateful, little presence in one of the corners of the kitchen.

At last, I saw my friend – her shadow, so benign by comparison – appear on the back porch. I let her in. Neither one of us spoke. I pointed the way to the back stairs, which led directly to the landing nearest my bedroom. Instinctively, she trod on precisely the same section of each step as we ascended. I knew those stairs well and was able to guide us both upstairs with not the first creak of a board.

Still without speaking, she gestured to me once we were in my bedroom, for me to lean the door shut and to take my seat upon the floor.

Wordlessly, she extracted from her bag a series of smooth river rocks, much like the ones she had been arranging at the roadside grotto, but smaller, and began to place them in a circle on the floor around me. While seeming terribly cliché – I had seen this done in countless movies – I complied. Knowing I wasn't willing to live much longer with that shadow in my life, staring at me every darn night, faceless and eyeless, made it an easy decision to obey, no matter how foolish things might look.

My friend had also brought three candles with her, black tapers in glass stands, which she lit. The blinds at my windows were turned down tight, so the moonlight was nothing but a line of mottled haze at the base of the windows. The candlelight was warm, the flickering a pleasant aside. I worried the odor of hot wax might drift under the door and make its way down the long hall, to the far end where my parents slept. My friend sensed my concern – could she read my mind? – and grabbed one of the coverlets from the foot of my bed. She pushed it up against the base of the door to block any air exchange. We smiled briefly in our odd companionship in that moment, and then that too, like the snuffing of the moonlight, disappeared. She had her business to attend, I had my salvation to chase.

When the final rock had been placed, a puff of air crossed the room. I felt it on my arms, saw it in the flame's response. I saw my friend acknowledge these things with a momentary lifting of her eyebrows. Her pupils were dilated, leaving her eyes enormously wet, black, somewhat hollowed.

Force of sheer habit alone had me searching the corners of my room.

Normally, in any active state, in which I now considered myself to be, the shadow would not manifest. Had I entered into some more relaxed state, despite my skepticism and anxiety over this stranger and her antics? For, there, yes; there it was. Sure enough – immediately to the left of the closet door, a small circle of black had appeared upon the floor, about the size of a silver dollar.

My expression must have changed when I spied the shadow, for my friend's gaze followed mine to the corner where I was now looking. Her mouth dropped open in surprise. At long last – someone other than I was seeing what I had seen all my conscious life! My friend was looking at the circle as well! The delight in her face both alarmed me and filled me with hope. You could say I was dying for hope.

The shadow's puddle spread, slowly, evenly, like that pancake on a hot griddle. It was growing in size, taking its time like always, the slow increments suggesting as they generally did, there was no *imminent* threat in its mere presence. My friends' rapid breathing belied her excitement, although she was making an obvious effort to maintain a calm demeanor as she pressed on.

What my friend took next from her bag was a second, smaller bag, from which she began to extract small tokens. They looked like coins; many of them had small holes cast into their centers. Some looked like old subway tokens, some looked like antique currency. It took several minutes for her to lay the pieces out into a series of starburst lines, radiating outward, with me as their center, to the inside edges of the circle of rocks.

The swish of air I had felt earlier continued, almost as if it were circulating round and about in my room, in a rotating fashion. The hair on my arms and the back of my neck stood on end, as much from the chill as spookish trepidation. Was this the onset of some unearthly energization, a new presence in the room? Something that might chase away the deplorable shadow that had been forever mocking me with its slinking, moribund presence?

Since I was dying for any iota of hope, I clung to the shreds my friend appeared to be offering me. If I could serve as her guinea pig for some kind of witchery that might grant me a night of normal sleep – real rest, dreams, a satisfied awakening (how heavenly that sounded!) – I was willing to accommodate just about *anything*. I *had* already let her in, and *something* was already at play. Some portal had been breached. The dancing candle flames, the swirling cool, our shared acknowledgement of the apparition, were proof of this.

The shadow had meantime lifted itself into its customary, vertical bulk, stretched towards its full height. Soon, I knew, resignedly, it would flesh itself out into the final, somewhat humanoid form so wretchedly familiar to me. And then, it would just sit there, sit there, sit there….

My friend, after all that silence and occasional pantomiming, began to speak. What she said, I could not make out but for occasional consonants, here a slight hissing sound, there a pop of the lips. Whatever it was she spoke, she said it over and over, much like my stupid prayers, only her phrases were far more syllabically laden, rather foreign sounding.

Then I saw something I had never seen before.

The shadow began to lean in the direction of my friend. It leaned ever so slightly but obviously towards her, as if it too were listening, trying to hear better whatever it was she was saying.

My friend noticed this about the same time I did. Her voice jumped a note, her throat constricting with surprise, although her delivery remained hushed. To whom, or what, these words were intended, volume was not of an issue. Walls have ears, spirits have ears, gods have ears; they can hear every word from their far-off places. They don't miss a thing. In this case, the participants of the night – the shadow, my friend, and I – were all in my bedroom, and but a few feet apart. Had my friend merely thought her words, I imagine they would still have engendered the desired effect. Perhaps she vocalized to keep me, her guinea pig, somewhat reassured, more compliant. If that was her intention, it was working. I sat glued to the floor, as still as the stones that surrounded me.

The longer my friend kept on with her recitation, the more my shadow leaned towards her. I began to think I could see it moving, infinitesimally, incrementally, *to* her. I had never, ever seen my shadow move from its spot. And now, it was mobile? After all these years, it was creeping forward, - towards *her*. I swear, in that moment, I felt a gut twist of jealousy, as if I was being betrayed by what had been to date *my* faithful nemesis.

What I then saw chased from me any residual doubt, any commoner's resistance as to my friend's potential or her pre-destined presence in my room that night. As she beheld my shadow, her chin began to quiver, and her eyes welled up with tears. Profound sadness suffused her face. She then, of all things, raised her arms towards the shadow in what could only be construed as a gesture of comfort, or welcome. Towards *my* shadow. As my friend continued to mouth her ruminations, her tears began to fall, leaving thick, black, makeup-laden streaks on her cheeks. Those tears fell onto the broad collar of her dress, staining it as if of ink. What fell to the floor did not splatter and dissipate; rather, the tiny droplets came to sluggish life, bright balls of liquid onyx, which rolled about and found their way to the joints between the floorboards, where they were sucked down, into the crevices, and disappeared. The mandala remained immaculate, untouched by my friend's grotesque display of emotion.

My friend, my rival, took a single step towards the shadow. My shadow arched towards her, hesitant, haltingly, almost shyly, for Christ's sake.

I felt all but forgotten.

I watched as the shadow came into the plane of that woman's embrace, and then as it moved even further into the circle of her arms. I felt a wave of nausea as I saw my friend enfold my shadow as if it were some long-lost child, and I saw the shadow's translucent darkness begin to suffuse her form. It, my shadow, was being practically soaked up into the crumpled fabric of my so-called friend's garments, into her heaving breasts, her lumpish body. I shuddered with revulsion as I saw the shadow *merge* and become one with my "friend." Closer, closer, I saw her draw *my* shadow *into* her. I watched that frumpy piece of work that I had until then thought was there for me go dark, as if she were afloat within a black tinted cloud, ready to drift off and away, together into the shadows, just the two of them…

But then, I saw my – her – my shadow fade, and it disappeared.

That woman's eyes, as she emerged from her slutty, autogenous little waltz with what I had always thought of as my shadow, lightened and brightened. Once more, I could discern the whites of her eyes, the brown of her irises, the pinpoints of her pupils. She had turned to face me, though I had not yet moved, was not about to. I remained seated, the obedient child, waiting with full, desperate expectation for some announcement of resolution, perhaps even a proclamation of a kind of victory, a supernatural conquest on my behalf.

But no, that was not to be.

When her eyes refocused on me, they grew stark and wide with fright. All the color drained from her face, her ghost-like parlor shining so torrid, the candlelight could only bounce off it, rejected as if by some metaphysical barrier. What beheld me in that moment was no face of a friend, but a death mask, wearing an expression devoid of…what?

Her chest, heaving anew, my "friend's" eyes filled once more.

"Oh my God," she whispered as she looked down at me, "That shadow wasn't here to haunt you. *It was here to protect you.*"

It was then that the ears of my soul opened up, and I could hear from over the distances of miles, epochs, and eras, the very echoes of all the lies and betrayals with which I had been raised. It was a dissonance borne of deceptiveness devised to isolate not only me, but *all* players involved, the kind of stuff that ended friendships, killed off whole families, stunted entire societies. It was a deluge of noise which rose from faraway, from below and yes, even above – wails, moans, groaning and howling – and it was calling to *me*. The cacophony was calling to me, practically by name.

"No!" the charlatan hissed, grabbing her bags, "This was not what I signed up for! I don't know what the hell you're a part of, but you…you…this…this is way past my pay grade! I'm just starting out and no way is this first gig going to be my last!

"You're on your own kiddo," she continued, slinging her bag over her shoulder, tripping on the rocks, scattering them. "I am the fuck outta here!"

And with that, my erstwhile friend, that snake-oil medium, flung open the door so hard, it broke the old doorstop clean off and hit the wall. The interloper dashed out, and without a single backwards, conciliatory glance my way, she clambered down the back staircase.

I stood up, too much in shock to even know in which direction I ought to take a step. I heard the kitchen door open, and then slam shut, all proprietary regard for quiet callously tossed aside. The walls shook with the force of her exit.

A new, old panic struck. I shot a glance down the long hall. A light came on at the far end from underneath my parents' bedroom door.

Now this.

I jumped visibly when my mother appeared at my door, a sleep mask on her forehead, a shotgun in her hands.

"What the hell is going on here?" she demanded.

The howling, the wails had stopped. They had stopped cold. Even to my ears there was dead silence.

"Oh mom," I cried, fighting back tears, joyous with relief, "It's you!"

"Well, of course it's me!" she sneered. "And what in tarnation is this mess on the floor?" Her question was more a command, cold exasperation overriding any pretense of motherly attentiveness. She was sick to death of her daughter's invisible demons, sick to death of her only child's countless weaknesses, sick of the medical bills for tests that had never been able to diagnose anything, no meds had been able to numb, no counselling had been able to rationalize or re-program.

The woman gestured with the barrel of her shotgun, drawing small circles in the air in *that* daughter's direction. "You up all night, doing this stuff, going outside to gather rocks, only to throw them all over our nice floors, and you expect me and your dad to sleep through all this? Do you have any idea how stupid this looks, and how risky this is? Do you know I could have *shot* you?"

†††

How I wish that had been the case.

It's now 2 a.m. and I am sitting here, once again, upon my bed. Almost twenty-four hours have passed since the I don't know what to call it – the ritual, the ceremony, the hocus pocus…

My parents gave me an ultimatum today. Sat me down in the kitchen, two against one. I am to move out by the end of next month, no matter what. They can't take it – namely, me – anymore. My antics, they call it, my unwillingness to move on in any direction whatsoever, they said, had taken them to "the brink." Well, I do have my job, that mindless thing, but they are aware I can't afford to live on my own with my income as it is. So, they promised me a stipend. *They are paying me to get me the hell out of their house.* If my fear over all these years, over a shadow I lived in secret dread of every night of my life, took its toll on me, it's *nothing* compared to the fear I now feel, knowing I am about to be forced out of the only world I have known in this room of mine, knowing I am going to have to put myself into a new room, somewhere different, all by myself. *Totally* alone.

And now to know, now that my shadow is gone, that it was there to *protect* me. Protect me?

I can't do it anymore. I can't fight, can't try, can't search for what I was never sure of. I am so tired. I'm also done praying. I don't even remember the words to my prayers anymore. I am done with them, and with angels as I imagined them, and with silly notions of being saved, cradled, lulled to some state of restful peace in the arms of someone or something that might wish something nice for me for once…

I have left my bedroom door open. No, not to see down the hall to my parent's room. They won't hear anything. They can't – not anymore. Nor can they stomp down the hall anymore to terrorize me either, point shotguns at my face, pull me from my bed to flail away at me in one of their blind rages.

I've seen to that.

My door lies open to welcome in what's coming for me. Those things, the rest of them, who I heard last night, howling in the distance, what my shadow had kept at bay on my behalf for what would tomorrow have been precisely twenty-six years. Twenty-six sluggish and sleep-deprived, long, long years.

And there they are. I can hear them now. The passageway to their world begins to reveal itself, an entry marked for starters with the mottled imprints of my own bare feet, from when I tracked *their* blood onto the hall carpet as I ran back to my own bedroom from theirs. The ancestral paint they shed recorded every step I took as I put distance between what was left of them and myself.

Do you think any physical pain will be involved? That would, at least, be something new – a stimulating sort of awakening.

I now see my friend's – no, she was not a friend, but I have decided I will keep calling her that – tears bubbling up, out of the floorboards, spreading like spilled paint across the floor. I watch, absurdly dispassionate, and regard this turn of events with a nonchalance that would impress any acolyte of the devil's. The wet mass now spans the reach of my bedroom and is seeping out, into the hall, towards the landing, making of itself a path of fibrous slime. And there! I can see the dark surface reverberating with the jolts of ponderous, decay-laden feet as the others make their way up the stairs, to my room, on their way to my bedside. Look! I see bare-bonded fingers grabbing at the stair rails; I see the bones of a wrist, the tattered edge of a molded sleeve… Whether I like it or not, I am now an audience of one, awaiting a contingency of ghouls which has been lurking in the wings for so very long. Such patience!

Now, they are free to do their work. At this very moment, their kin, my kin, rise from the cellar floors of this house and the gravesites on the far hill, clawing, scratching their way into my world, seeking to pull me from my bed as my father so often did.

The irony is not lost on me: I am missing my shadow.

But I am so tired, I don't care anymore.

That shadow, turns out, was my loving angel, but it abandoned me, was exorcized by someone who sought only to experiment with the accursed thing I always was. I wasn't merely left behind; I was, am, pre-destined collateral – a player or a pawn, I don't know. Oh, yes, my so-called friend opened the door wide. Time had come for her to usher in the rest of my shadows.

Listen; they are calling my name!

Efectus

- 258 -

RAVENSCRAFTED

"...transfixed, and ever more willing to heed the unspoken promises held by the intensity of her gaze, Ruearke felt himself sinking into the oceanic heavens of her wideset, teal eyes – beautiful pools, so bewitchingly flecked in gold, so delicately framed by the feathering edges of impossibly long and silken lashes...

He knew, it was but a matter of minutes until those lashes would be at rest upon his..."

Well, hell, she thought.

Here I go again; down, down, into the writerly abyss, where superfluous adverbs and wayward adjectives swarm like luminescent fish, where one genuflects at altars of multi-colored eyes, speckled with this n that; where broad chests are forever bared, made to pant and heave and glisten with perspiration, wet, slick, muscular as dolphins...

Lilah paused, staring at her screen, momentarily stymied, her fingers at rest upon the keys. The spiral that had lured her writer's sensibilities into the realm of the fluff she had committed to some four years back was now a black icing on an ever more impossibly layered cake, which tasted not of whipped sugar delights, but of ash. Difficult to swallow, even harder to digest. But she wrote on, for a newly imposed deadline loomed, and her readers were begging for more. Her inbox of late so inundated with fan mail, Lilah no longer responded to the plethora of entreaties, adulations, and occasional propositions that found their way to her website's email address. She didn't need any help.

This next scene would require serious odes to the long locks of both, the auburn-haired Esmeredine, and her sun stroked, blonde Ruearke. What was it, this hack-lit tradition of outfitting protagonists with flowing tresses in every autumnal shade imaginable and multi-hued, gold-flecked eyes?

Such schlock, Lilah's inner voice griped. Keep writing, her auto response fired back. This crap keeps the lights on.

"Crap" supplemented a modest but steady paycheck. "Crap" generated disposable income. And seduction, however saccharin or baroque the details, padded her bottom line, grew those much-anticipated royalty payments. It was, Lilah understood, her readers whom she was seducing, subscribers now willing to pre-pay and be placed on reservation lists for her increasingly anticipated upcoming releases. Volume four was in the works, its full first draft due in two months, and they were clamoring for more.

For the last two years, sales of Lilah's books had seen a steady climb. Her social media presence was also taking off. As her followers accrued, so did sales. Or might that be the other way around? Either way, Lilah was now a real author, a *professional* writer who made enough money writing for it to have made a solid difference in her everyday. Lilah knew she wasn't a bad writer. She felt quite certain she was a decent writer. But a good writer? Hmmm. Perhaps a great writer? Could she grow to someday be a literary contributor in a more profound capacity? Lilah mulled ceaselessly over this unknown, unsure how to view herself as she was, versus what she wanted to be. Was it her destiny to serve as a story grinder who happened to enjoy better luck than most of the countless, other dust-speck dwelling *I am here* literati out there, or was there something more in store for her?

It was on long, quiet stretches at home like this, when Lilah's musings would distract her from her work. They'd pester her, speaking too loudly across the silent spaces of her mind, keeping her from her writing. Questions and self-doubt would invade the studious serenity, sidetracking her from the goals she judiciously set for herself each weekend. Wordcounts and specific scenes generally provided solid incentives, and since she had been assigned one of the senior associates at the agency for her fourth release, deadlines were no longer dates to be fooled with. On this day, however, no milestone beckoned, no inspiration triggered her fancy.

Surely, Lilah thought, trying to re-focus, she had enough romantic hubris in her to weather another couple of hours at the keyboard. She sat up, pulled her shoulders back, lifted her coat from the chairback and draped it over her shoulders.

Taking a long swig of wine, Lilah re-read her last four paragraphs. She put the glass back down on its makeshift coaster and began to write again.

†††

The draft before Lilah glowed ever more brightly from the shallow field of the computer screen the darker her room grew, the laptop's illumination but an ambient afterthought, barely reaching the corners of the room in which she had been ensconced for the past several hours, scrounging for some literary fecundity.

The alcove in which she sat served her well, more as a writing nook than proper office, being that an antique vanity outfitted with a laptop and a lamp comprised the entirety of said office. The rest of the room was devoted to the more customary accoutrement of sleep and dress, with bits and pieces of the room's dual roles crossing over with regularity. Cast off knit hats and scarves were draped over the vanity's hinged mirrors, and both Lilah's wool coat and her robe lived on the back of her desk chair, where they served as cushions for the slatted wood back. Printouts of her current draft were often spread across the bedroom floor, marked up in red, green, or blue ink, one of her systems for editing. In reverse, old makeup compacts served as coasters for her coffee mugs or wine glasses, always placed at the far left-hand corner of her desk, to minimize spill risk to the keyboard. Being that a nine-to-five job still commanded Lilah's daylight hours, pre-dawn and late nights were for her writing, when either wakefulness was pursued by way of a strong, black brew or eased back from with the aid of a glass of wine – or two, or three.

Lilah had now spent yet another Saturday at home, alone. She was grateful for the inclement weather, for the way it more justifiably kept her indoors, and happy for the way it negated any residual guilt over her preference for confined solitude over socializing, which at times still nagged from the depths of her childish echo chambers – old thought pathways, never fully re-routed. *Get yourself out into the fresh air young lady*! Or: *Get yourself out there, among the living, for goodness' sake, girl!*

On that Saturday, however, the draft's narrative lay flaccid and cliché. On that Saturday, however, the draft's narrative lay flaccid and cliché. While Lilah felt some resentment over her status as low-tier recipient of the entry-level fodder the Muses shoveled her way, she was contractually obliged to listen, and to crank out the content. Sighing, Lilah leaned back in her chair, folding the collar of her coat around her neck. The heavy fabric provided warmth and a measure of comfort, the top floor apartment being nearly impossible to heat this time of year, its old radiators insufficient for the rooms' proximity to the peaked rooftops.

Lilah, beholden to the superficiality of her literary output, was, it turns out, equally enslaved to the conceits of a rather duplicitous persona she had likewise composed. Lilah, or Mil, whose full first name was Milifred, had with the publication of her first novel, book one of what was eventually dubbed the *Echo Tundra* Series, adapted a new author identity, intended to enhance her social media presence, and to better reflect the genre in which she was making notable headway. And *Lilah Ravenscraft* was the name with which Mil had gifted herself. This was how she was now introducing herself to everyone, who she posted to social media as, and who she "was" with everyone who existed in her post-published world, both real and virtual.

Lilah Ravenscraft – goth-gal authoress, business doyen, cognac-tressed weaver of the sultry tale, decidedly dark-side inclined. Mil as Lilah had nurtured her transformation with the diligence of a true performance artist, having crafted her presentation of self with a dutiful allegiance to the fabrications borne of her own literary heroines. It was something of a self-congratulatory homage, internalized. Lilah Ravenscraft, the name, had been a transformative piece of cake. All that it had taken was one late night session, where, afloat in merlot, Mil had slogged over a hand-written list comprised of phonetically pleasing, historically illustrative first + last name candidates. It was around three in the morning when she had finally circled the "Lila," added an H, and then attached to it the melodious "Ravenscraft."

Lilah Ravenscraft, the real-world personification, had taken considerably more time and money. It had required a major divestment of hard-earned cash (and a tidy chunk of credit) to re-fashion an entire wardrobe to place Lilah, or Mil, somewhere between, say, a Carrie Bradshaw and a Miss Mina Harker. Purchasing all new makeup, and then spending hours viewing online tutorials and applying the lessons learned, had been a pricey undertaking on both fiscal and free-time levels, as had been the investments in professionally done hair color and top-quality human hair extensions. The finely-honed, barely there and unplaceable English accent Mil as Lilah next appropriated for her verbal interactivity had been but a matter of practice, solitary chatter in the confines of her apartment followed by its honing during exchanges she had with disgruntled customers at the call center where she worked. With name and outfittings in place, head to toe, Mil – now Lilah – had repurposed herself into an alluringly twilighted young woman. Lilah's bookish magnetism happily proved irresistible online, as did her painted pout and makeup- and bustier-enhanced cleavage. In very little time, @lilahravenscraft had garnered a high five-digit follower count. Mil's transformation into Lilah was proving a note-worthy, even if superficial and filter-reliant, success.

Milifred grew less a Mil each day, as more and more she became a Lilah. Her fanbase, whom she had affectedly dubbed her Ravenscrafters, was a nicely inter-connected batch of followers who even came with their own stash of hashtags. Ravenscrafters were Lilah's loyal swag collectors – bookmarks, candles, t-shirts, friendship bracelets, real and fake tattoos, to name but a few. They flocked to her live reels, hearting and re-posting everything she quipped or shared. They dutifully purchased all her books, and re-posted on them too; now, they were lining up as eager pre-sale subscribers.

And while Mil may have remained the gal at the call center, Lilah the writer had of late actively broadened her horizons as proprietress of Ravenscrafters Publishing LLC, an indie press she had fabricated to front a slew of rejected works by a certain Milifred Snodgrass, of which there were plenty. It was too easy – and turns out, so much fun – to fabricate author names and assign them to the three dozen+ short stories and two novelettes she had written over the last few years. Lilah, founder and editor-in-chief, presided like a proud mother hen over her half-dozen budding authors – misanthropes all of them, impossible to connect with, but who sported monikers even more evocative and illustrative than their mentor. It was a delicately depraved, tidily hidden facet of Lilah, this indulgence of hers, to feel the level of satisfaction she did over the lit world ruse she was perpetrating.

Lilah, keenly aware of her obligations to her readers and now also that spirited cadre of authors of hers, had taken to spending nearly all her time at home, writing, posting, editing, posting some more, writing some more, and so on. Her sick days, vacation and family leave days had long since been depleted, having been used to stay at home to write and tinker on her phone. She was feeling the growing pains of becoming something of a franchise – a good problem to have, one of her few friends had said when her first follow-up release to *The Echoing Tundra* had taken off. Perhaps, Mil pondered on this, her publishing company would eventually need to be folded, which she figured Lilah could accomplish by way of some craftily worded, sympathy-evoking, demise-based storyline. Lilah waded knee-deep indeed in the creative tarpit she herself had stirred up – it sometimes started to feel a little like she might be sinking.

Lilah stretched in her chair, arms and legs chilled and stiff, and yawned wide. She then settled in to write a few minutes more.

†††

The gloomy Saturday had devolved into a chilly, fog-ridden evening. Traffic on the avenue below was sparse, and so the apartment, but for the futile clanking of the radiators, was awash in a drowsy quietude. Encroaching cold sifted downward from the rooftop, through the ceilings and into the four rooms Lilah called her own, despite the best efforts of the old heating system. The day had wound up being a typical one, with Lilah spending almost of it at her laptop, alternatingly staring at the screen and then hammering away on the keyboard, after which she would break away to post some shallow crumb to her social media account. These posts often included Lilah's classic selfie, a pucker-mouthed, inquisitive gaze with her face eerily blue-lit by the glow of her computer screen. She considered it a signature self-portrait. Dinner had been but a snack of random leftovers, washed down with wine, which also served as something of a silent companion for the way it so faithfully provided a soothing path to more muddled senses, which was, for lack of solid food in the belly, generally a rather short one.

Lilah was fully tapped out. She now sat in complete darkness, her face faintly peering back at her from the tri-fold mirror of the vanity. The unlit room she interpreted as a respectable benchmark, testament to her level of concentration having been such that the onset of night had gone unnoticed. Lilah was glad whenever this happened. She thought idly, time to light a lamp, perhaps a candle, or two.

The scene next to be written, Esmeredine's first seduction of Ruearke, Lilah didn't much feel like tackling. The dank aura of the quiet day having turned into yet another silent and solitary night had her feeling not only alone, but decidedly lonesome. Not only was Lilah still hungry; she was feeling quite empty inside. When it came down to it, no quantity of followers, or anonymous emails, or any layered, black lace outfits or painted lips or waist-length ponytail extensions, did anything to assuage the deeply rutted, narrow roads traveled by the true loner she hated to admit she really was.

Tonight, Lilah wasn't feeling "it" at all, whatever It was supposed to be. Tonight, the weight of all the content she was *not* writing bore down upon her. It made Lilah feel older, to be bogged down with such ideations, though she was not old at all. It was the abstract burden of the untitled, unmolded, next-level novel that she truly longed to write that weighed upon her, hung over her like a massive cloud, a hindering overhang, blocking her view of the stars – just like that high-rise planted right next to her much older apartment building, which had cut off any view of the skies, or the harbor just down the road, leaving her and her neighbors in perpetuity of its concrete shadow.

Lilah continued to sip her wine, appreciating its tannic, sweet bite. Night having fully descended, the darkness was quite complete. Disinclined to leave her chair, she took yet another mouthful of wine as she regarded her laptop, still glowing in an otherwise unlit room. But as she sat there, in that next second, her idle computer also went black. Now, only a faint gray loomed beyond the dormer windows. Lilah peered over the screen of her laptop, into the vanity's mirrors. Only the faintest outline of her right jaw was visible.

Otherwise, nothing. Silence inside, silence outside. An empty space within, empty spaces without. Lilah, letting out a slow, sad sigh, allowed her eyes to wander the darkened room as her mind drifted.

Dreams. What about dreams? How many great tales had come to writers who had effectively served as scribes, setting to page glorious stories and wondrous words hurled at them from the nethering plains of the subconscious, or, from the nonsensical wellsprings of dreams and nightmares? What *did* it feel like when sentience merged with the kaleidoscopic seas of inspiration? Why, then, did nothing but benign imagery invade her mundanely restful nights? Lilah was loathe to admit, she slept like a baby. *Sturm* and *Drang* did not strike her with its diamond-tipped arrows. Lilah felt left out, left behind. Nothing had spurred her writing onto some broader, deeper path. A truly passionate, gut-ripping outpouring? Nope, nothing; at least not yet.

Having grown up with a comfortable ordinariness, but for the cruel ignorance of a few kids who had made fun of her name, or the irritations of a blockheaded sibling to whom she hadn't spoken in years, Lilah had also been spared the imprinting of extreme life paths that otherwise would have given rise to acute, cathartic needs to dig deep, to create from the subterranean platforms others tapped in their healing journeys. Where her random literary proclivities came from, no one quite knew; but no one had ever cared much, either. Lilah had always been a bookworm; as pre-teen, she had delved precociously into adult literature the moment hormones had turned her eyes to the books on *those* particular shelves. Lilah's preoccupied parents had no idea of the eloquent smut their teen daughter grew up with, nor what she later wrote. Though they supported her writing, Lilah's parents had never read any of her books, a rather insensitive status quo with which Lilah was perfectly content. Her parents' disinterest conveniently granted the "good" daughter free license when it came to all the torn bodices and throbbing members she employed, which fueled the narratives of her novels.

Lilah had once read an article on the creative process, on endocepts and exocepts, and how they defined the process by which the subconscious could, at any time, erupt with a consciously manifested creative outburst – like an Athena exploding, fully formed, from the skull of Zeus – which would demand fabrication, so that the rest of the world could partake of it. Why couldn't she suffer her art too? Lilah wanted to write like one possessed. She wanted to know the wonderful agony of raw fingertips, a wholly drained soul. She wanted, like the form of the Parent, to bring forth something greater than she, as its human fabricator. Lilah longed to give life to a story, to lay it out, dress it, arm it, and then send it off into the world, so it could live beyond her, on its own accord and merits.

So, where could Lilah look? Under which corner of her consciousness lurked that which she did not even know she sought?

Lilah clapped down the lid of her laptop. She was done. Done for the night. How in the hell did that eighteen-year-old Mary Shelley do it? How did Ann Rice, Isaac Asimov, Clive Barker, or even ye olde Charles Dickens come up with all they had? Why, oh, why, did not even one single, solitary stroke of so-called inspired genius come to tease her with *some* hope of attainability within her?

Lilah hiked her coat more firmly about her shoulders. With glass in hand, she rose from her desk to feel her way over to the bed. Lilah switched on the bedside lamp, an antique metal unit topped with a fringed shade that may once upon a time have been a soft, coral color. It less lit the room as wash the space a brownish pink, but it was enough illumination to suit her needs, and her mood. Lilah had no one to call, no one with whom to make a last-minute plan. Having nothing else she wanted to do, it would serve the interminable evening to just try and keep warm, and to finish off that last, hefty pour.

The barren field in Lilah's headspace was being quickly taken up by the wine's effects. She noticed how the old, striped wallpaper repeat began to tick, tick, tick....

Lilah's writer's inclinations took off on additional literary tangents as her ruminations drifted alongside her. No Pandora was lifting any lids in her presence; no winged gremlins flew about to taunt her. The Muses were shunning her too – mean girls refusing to hang out with her. Their sister Fates weren't any kinder; shit, they were probably all hunched together, sniggering at her. Lilah's conversations with herself and the rest of an uninterested universe began to spiral towards sleep. Down and down, and farther still, and onto... *Aqua-blue eyes, gold-flecked, my ass... Auburn tresses, autumn tresses, hair in every freaking shade of red and orange, yellow and brown… Like dumb trees on a hillside… The hills are alive, with the sound of…hair…in every color…maple leaves…of the trees…tree-headed…*

With that, Mil, Lilah, slumped back against the headboard and sunk into a sated repose that did a fairly decent job of resembling sound sleep. Her unremarkable dreams launched on cue, but as a subset of that day's worries, they remained nothing more than elementary-level mental laundry. Rags of the conventional have, after all, little reason to be sorted or stripped away and resolved when a lonesome soul must do all the work alone.

†††

Lilah did not awaken; rather, she came to. Grudgingly. The cheap wine's residual half-life thudded against her temples, her forehead, the base of her skull, an all-points admonishment warning her of an oncoming hangover. Lilah saw the familiar roomscape beyond her bed, barely visible in the reddish gloom cast by the lamp, which she had not turned off. She saw the shadowed form of the massive dresser, the old wingback in the alcove, the vanity that served as her desk, the curtains at the far window, and the hall tree, dressed like a schlump in cast-offs from the last few days. All looked as it should.

Lilah was not quite all there, yet. The monochrome dark had a sort of latent, pinot-noired muddiness to it. Any other time, Lilah would have simply attributed her condition to the unfiltered wine's aftereffects. For some reason, that was not the case tonight. She had the distinct feeling she had awakened *into* a dream. Was this one of those lucid dreams? Was she in some state of semi-wakefulness?

Lilah's thoughts wandered to the feeble chapter she had written a few hours earlier. Esmeredine, the beautiful, the brilliant, the vixen instigator… And Ruearke. Rue. Rue the day. Rue the man. Oh, she was a clever one… Ruearke of the sun-kissed tresses, the bronzed skin, the poet's shirt forever unbuttoned to *there*, a requisite thatch of soft-as-down chest hair, chiseled abs… What a manly manifestation he was – as they all were – borne of how many movies, how many novels, and how many book covers, studiously browsed, borrowed from, and re-constituted into something marginally different enough that she could claim the cheesy oeuvre she was building, chapter by silly chapter, book by stupid book, as her own?

The image of the man in Lilah's mind began to fade, but as it did, something new took root at the foot of her bed, on the far-left corner, right there, past her feet, where a heavy sweater and yesterday's outfit lay in a heap.

The pile of clothing began to stir, as if some tiny creature – like a mouse or a kitten – were hiding in there, clawing their way out. The rumpled fabric began to rise and fall, moving up and down with the slightest of pulsations, as if deep breaths were being drawn in, expanding it, and then being let out again. As the pile of clothes expanded and contracted, it began to rise, grow taller. The mass quivered haltingly, reminding Lilah of a time-lapse film she had once seen, in which a Venus flytrap emerged from the soil like a leafy marionette, growing in spurts and jerks to next spread wide its tiny maws, a sightless, green beastie raised from the grave. The lopsided formation continued to grow in height, with neither elegance nor definition, and as it did, it began to mimic the actions of a living creature, leaning first this way and then that, as if looking first to one side, then the other. With each inhalation, the mass also added more girth and breadth. The animated heap of clothing soon took on the shape of a headless torso, risen straight up and out from the depths of the mattress itself. Lilah's wool sweater, which had been the last garment she had tossed onto the pile, began to fall away, exposing something that resembled a pair of broad shoulders which were dressed in a shirt of fine linen. The torso tapered to a slender base, anchored, and weighted.

In what were a few moments or a handful of minutes, the carelessly discarded pile of clothing at the foot of Lilah's bed had transformed itself into a humanoid form, soon crowned by a domed protrusion that continued to swell, up and out from the torso's shoulders. The mattress corner had in the meantime visibly sunk beneath the entity's weight. The thing, this being, was now beginning to emulate the posture of a seated being, with opposing limbs reaching like tentacles across the comforter, which folded and came to rest upon the covers. They began to suggest a pair of strong legs seated in a cross-legged position. Another protrusion emerged from one shoulder, stretching long, and then relaxed, becoming an arm with a hand laid to rest upon a newly bent knee. The topmost protrusion continued to sculpt itself as Lilah watched, more transfixed than she was horrified. The fleshy bulb then began to mold itself into a head, with a smooth, egg-like visage half-hidden by what would eventually morph into a swath of hair. Features next emerged, took on defined edges, and etched themselves into a ruggedly angular face that, when the two eyes lifted their lids to peer out at Lilah from beneath a sweep of tousled bangs, she gasped audibly.

The thing, this being, was a male figure; a man, and it, he, looked like…*no, it cannot be*…but it, he, was…it was *Ruearke,* Lilah realized, stunned. Or, rather, it was *a* Ruearke. The entity was a physical manifestation of the male protagonist in her fourth novel, the one she was working on, precisely as she had come to envision him. To whatever minimal extent her subconsciousness required this to accept the entity as one of her fictitious characters come to life, Lilah recognized It as him – instantly. Whatever the hell It, he, was or was not, she rationalized from her rapidly fading stupor, it *might as well* be him.

And so, Lilah understood, as best as she could, that she had possibly dreamt one of her storybook characters into existence, and that It, specifically he, had materialized expressly to see her, and that It, he, was still there after she had quite literally pinched herself, to make sure this was not indeed another dream. That said, It, he, for all she could tell, was more likely of her own making than anything come from afar, thanks to the impossible hour and the dregs of the wine's effects. It, he, was a something manifested from within an intensely personal realm of absurd acceptability. Still…

"Wha… What the…?" Lilah stammered, leery, despite the depth of her brain fog.

It, he, looked at her from behind what had just become an unruly sweep of impossibly thick and glossy hair and snapped back, "Yeah, well and…?"

"What?" Lilah repeated, chagrin egging her on. This thing was rude.

"Yeah, and so…?" It, he, said once more, blinking.

"Wha…Who…What are you doing here? Who are you?" Lilah persisted.

"I am, um, let's see…What will register with you?" The entity cast Its eyes to the ceiling in a display of studious contemplation. "You're one of those literary types, right?" Straightening up, It lowered Its voice to a mocking, oratorical timbre to then quote in a dulcet baritone, "I am Legion."

"You are 'Legion.' Legion? *Legion*?" Lilah repeated, the word sinking in, her voice cracking with surprise, her mouth so dry, she could hardly form the consonants.

"Yes. My, our, name is Legion." It, he repeated with a huff. "Get it, okay?"

Lilah, taken aback, began to pull at the top edge of the coverlet in an attempt to bring it up, higher around her.

The entity scoffed at her token display of fear.

"No…no," Lilah mouthed, shaking her head in disbelief.

"Dost thou deny my name; verily, my presence?" he, It challenged her, every word dripping acidic disdain.

"What…wha…" Lilah could only stammer. But the affected speak had an inauthentic ring to it. It sounded callous, mocking, and she was more doubtful than anything else.

"In what other manner should one such as I be addressed, pray tell?" The Being went on, Its hands spread wide in the air, as if imploring the room for support.

"It's just that…" Lilah ventured, recoiling, "…but what's with the…"

"Yeah, yeah. That's some eloquence there. And what's with *thee*?" It interrupted, "Can't form a sentence in *this* presence?" the Being tucked a lock of hair behind one perfect ear.

"*Thee*?" For all the phantasmic preposterousness of this visitation, Lilah wasn't buying into the details, however bizarre everything about it already was. Composure borne of skepticism building with each exchange, she asked again, "*Thee*? What's with all this Old Testament elocution?"

"Fine." The girl had called Its bluff. "Call me what you want, you stupidly fearless human. Call me your Eros, your thief in the night, accursed son of Vlad…"

"Go on, get out of here! Get thee away from me…you…you *beast*!" Lilah burst out, thinking some equally clichéd command might serve in her defense, have some effect on the Being's uncomfortably close proximity to her.

"Oh, ho, ho, no way, sister! I just got here, and I'm *not* leaving yet!" It sputtered angrily. "I am your fucking Nevermore, baby, so get used to the idea that I'm staying here until *I* say it's time for me to go!"

"What is it you want from me?" Lilah grabbed hold of her coverlet again, tried again to pull it closer to her chin. "Why are you…"

"Oh, stop that," the Entity gestured at the clutched bedding. "You're not some Harlequin Romance protagonist chick. Plus, that's no negligee under that blanket. Your tent of a sweatshirt could house a whole army. It's not like you'd even feel the cold under all that. And that ghastly coat of yours…"

Lilah let fall the coverlet and glanced down at herself. Seeing the university logo splayed across her chest, she remembered having gone straight from the desk to her bed, fully dressed. Irritation gnawed at her initial fear reaction, quickly turning her shock into anger. Lilah wondered if this dream was in fact some sort of an absurd nightmare, from which she would be better off waking, being that, despite her obvious lucidity, she was devoid of holding any command over the situation.

Lilah decided to venture a more intimately voiced show of aggression, "Begone with you, you...*Ruearke*!"

Nonplussed, "Rue...?" was all he, It replied with. "What the fuck kind of name is that?"

"I...I...don't know," Lilah answered lamely, shrugging her shoulders.

"Well, at least you're starting to get it," the Being replied.

"Get what? Get what, for God's sake...?"

"Oh, *shit*! Watch your mouth!"

"What?" Lilah insisted, " 'For God sake'? Jesus, what did I say?"

"Argh! There you go again!" It cried.

"You mean, if I invoke 'God,' I'm, um, *smiting* you with my words? Would it help wrap this thing up and get you on your way to wherever you came from if I kept that up?" Lilah insisted, irrationally inspired. "Invoke a few hallowed names?"

"Well, I didn't mean..." It, he stammered.

"God! God! God!" she shouted, the petulant teen to her unwelcome, ancient elder.

The Being clapped Its hands over Its ears, wincing visibly. However, when It did so, Lilah also felt the thread of a shock and startled. It surged upwards through her body, a faint sort of jolt, like when the filament of an old lightbulb explodes the moment it's screwed into the socket. Lilah felt a foreboding warmth fill her sinuses, followed by an airless, warm rush as a stream of blood discharged from both nostrils. She grabbed a corner of her bed sheet – the closest box of tissues was in the kitchen – and pinched it over her nose. The sudden onset and intensity of the nosebleed frightened Lilah. The apparition at the foot of her bed might bear the comely features of a romantic male protagonist, who was only all too familiar a character to her, but if that thing had anything to do with the charge of energy she had felt and its resulting nosebleed, he, It was someone or something far more sinister than a storybook character come to life.

"Will you stop all that fucking invoking now?" the Entity berated her.

So, the nosebleed *was* Its doing.

Lilah nodded silently, unable to say anything at all in that moment – it was all she could do to stave the flow of blood, which had already soaked the fabric. Lilah felt around blindly, remembering, and grabbed a sock from under her pillow. She buried her nose into it, as well.

"Okay then, so shut up on that crap and you'll be fine," It said. "Got it?"

Lilah nodded again, feebly. The nosebleed stopped. Her sinuses were instantly as clear as they had ever been. She removed the sock from her nose, let the bedsheet fall to her lap, the corner black and wet. Lilah folded it under, out of sight, repulsed by it, by everything, not least of which was the emotional hostage taking this obnoxious creature was managing with her.

Complacency, Lilah realized, was going to have to be part of the game. And this was no lucid dream, nor was it merely a nightmare. Lilah was at this situation's mercy, and this thing playing itself out was beyond anything she had heretofore come close to experiencing, and beyond anything she had the capacity to conjure up herself.

Lilah pushed the covers back and straightened up. Morbid curiosity mandated a reset.

"What are you doing here? Who are you?" her voice came out smaller than before, but the inquisitiveness was devoid of a threatening edge, and genuine.

"Stupid bitch. I already told you that."

"Legion. Right. A Ruearke come to…"

"Dammit – don't call me that. Leave that idiotic name in your lame draft."

"Are you he who is called Lucifer?" Lilah persisted, going biblical once more.

"Lucifer? Are you *kidding*?" It retorted.

"Well, are you, um, a fallen angel, a seraphic entity fallen from the heavens? I mean, the way you look…," the bastard *was* excruciatingly handsome, "…it wasn't like…" Lilah didn't know what else to say.

"Whoa, hold on a second there," the Being interrupted her. "I'm flattered, kid, for the fact that I need to correct you, but that motherfucker is one jealous deity, and if you attribute his backstory to me and I don't stop you in your tracks, I'm going to hear about it for the next millennium."

"You're telling me he is sensitive to *honesty*?" Lilah queried, stumped.

"Absolutely."

"That makes no sense."

"Of course, it does, you simpleton. There is integrity in *everything*. Honest anger, genuine hate, real commitment to mayhem, that sort of thing. There can be clarity in deceit and nobility in the deepest of subversions. It's you humans who confuse the shit out of all that. Always inverting stuff, or worse yet, excusing it. Especially with that blame shifting thing you're all doing these days. It's never *your* fault, is it?"

"Hmmm." Was all she could muster. "So you could say Lucifer has his adherents and you all have your own, um, ways and means?"

"You're telling me. Been to the movies lately?"

"Well, at least I don't seem to fall to the ranks of those he wreaks his, er, vengeance or whatever upon..."

"Oh, you may not have warranted a visit from the big guy himself, but trust me, he's keeping track of this exchange here. You are, after all, on board to become a latest member of his legion."

"A latest? Not *the* latest?"

"Great Beleth, such vanity even in this moment! Sheesh. No, you are a latest. Merely a latest. One of a constantly accruing lineup. And by constantly, I mean, like, we are talking the pace of a hummingbird heartrate at full throttle. You are merely, only, nothing more than a puny-ass one of countless others who at this very moment are also signing their names to whatever it is they asked for. You conniving, contriving humans are perpetual deal makers – you know that – and with your pithy understanding of what comes after – or in the between, for that matter, you are so pathetically three dimensional – you in your abject fear of all you have no fucking idea about will sign away anything and everything, and I mean *everything*, for the puny here and now. But who am I to complain? It's a diversionary assignment for me, something to do. Gives me a break from the, er, what you might call 'torture'."

"Torture?"

"If I told you, I wouldn't have to kill you. You would die from the impact of my descriptions alone."

"It's that bad?"

"'Bad' isn't even adequate. You don't have words in your language to express what's…what's out there, is done, has been done for so…"

"Yikes…"

"Yeah, well… Let's just say, your Hellraiser is my Mother Goose."

"Good Lord."

"Hey, I mean it! Don't say that kind of stuff!" It reproached her with a threat-edged earnestness. "Makes me retch. And don't test me; just stop with the freaking invocations of name. Look. Try to imagine intersecting planes of infinite, hellacious outcomes, crossing each other not only continuously but also in every possible way. Damnation squared. Squared to the power of infinity. If you bring that shit up by way of your word choice in some show of bravado, well then, you better understand the consequences will also be felt by you – not just me."

"Crikey."

"You can say that again."

"Gosh…maybe I don't want to do this…"

"Whoa there, sister. We are way past that point. Like, about a thousand miles back in your timeline. This here is a done deal."

"Wha… what's done?" Lilah asked, truly puzzled.

"You know perfectly well what's what and what is done and that what is done is super fucking done where we're concerned," It retorted, wagging an elegant, slender finger in her direction.

"Oh, that… You mean my, um, my wish? My writing?" Lilah asked, her voice faltering as she spoke the words that represented everything to her.

"What the fuck else?" the Entity spat back as It rolled Its eyes.

"So, we can't even talk about it? It's not up for discussion?" Lilah queried further, still confused.

"Of course not. All that was taken care of ages ago. By you. By you and *your* words. Your thoughts, your wishes, your desires…" It rolled Its eyes again, impatient and bored with the residual incomprehension of this girl, who had no idea what she was capable of, never would be.

"Aha…" Lilah's voice drifted off, lost momentarily to recollection.

"It's a done deal, got it? Okay? And you *are* going to get your," the Being sneered as he said it, "*wish,* by the way. Abra-fucking-cadabra. Boom," It added dryly.

"But, but why…why does it feel like I am talking to myself?"

"Because, you thick-skulled dimwit, *you are.*"

What a short walk to hell this was, Lilah thought, incredulous, beginning to feel she understood, and with it, an onset of resignation.

"You have no idea how crowded it is 'down' there," It added a bit more calmly, reading her thoughts, glad to be able to move on.

Lilah studied the Entity. She considered her own self, seated on her bed, still clutching her sheets and blankets like some damsel in distress. Lilah suddenly realized, the throbbing in her head had subsided. Completely. Was there something to that as well?

"But it's not like I wanted my wishes to grant these, um, Powers that Be unnecessary license to wreak something awful on *my* behalf…" she ventured.

"I know that," It impatiently cut her short, "although you could. It's neither here nor there. You can do with what you get as you please. The price you pay is yours and yours alone. I sure as hell don't give a shit. Neither does the rest of the world, in case you were deluded to think otherwise…"

"All I wanted was to write a book," Lilah insisted, her eyes misting.

"I know that," It repeated, sighing, "and like I said, I *really* don't care. Got that? Do. Not. Give. A. Shit."

"…an amazing literary work." Said Lilah, adrift in her revery. "A great story. Beautifully executed…" her gaze wandered past the Entity, past her bedposts, into the far corners of her room.

"So, the fuck what?" the Being offered with a sniff.

"But there's a trade-off, right?" She said, looking It straight in Its deep set eyes..

"Aha, you already *do* know," the Being shifted to a more comfortable position. "It's a one-for-one deal. Always been that way; always will be. For evermore, kid."

"And my price?" Lilah cast a sidelong glance, ready for anything.

"Why, you, of course. You, you, you. Bits n pieces of you." the Entity said, picking at the air in front of Lilah, snipping away at her as if with scissor blades for fingers. "What else? You got some bags o' gold, or a fat and juicy firstborn somewhere I don't know about?" It chided, licking its lips.

Lilah, nonplussed, having grown – oddly, so quickly – accustomed to the Being's presence, glanced over Its shoulder, to where a mirror hung on the wall. The reflection of the emanation that spoke to her with such rudeness, such disgusting familiarity, also filled in the glass, although with a transparency and certain vagueness to its outline. Lilah noted dispassionately, at least this creature did not possess the invisibility of a vampire…

"Well," Lilah mused, "I still look like myself…" She spoke quietly, considering, lifting a swath of hair from her shoulder, holding it aloft, as if testing its quality, and then letting it drop to her shoulder.

"Shit, how looks do matter in this world!" the Being admonished. "Of course! You are just, well, *you.* Sorry if you were deluded into thinking you'd magically transform into some lame-ass Cinderella. Now," Its tone shifted, became more business-like, "how quickly and completely your price kicks in will be commensurate with how deeply you dig into your gift. How *good* you want your trade to be." It added with an acrid tone, "That, kiddo, will determine the depth and breadth of your so-called price."

"You mean I could resist a bit? Keep some of this proverbial outcome at bay?"

"Weeell…" It began, rolling Its eyes, exasperated.

"Like, I could control the balance? Generate just enough quality content – you know, writing – so I could keep *some* of my old self intact, some…*some* of this as is? We are talking about me and my body, aren't we? I mean, well, looks aren't *everything,* but… And it's not like I'm some evil person…but…"

"One does what one's gotta do…" the Entity interrupted, "I just work on commission. Like you. Man, what is it, this obsession with body parts? What *do* you want? Do you even know?"

"…I mean," Lilah rambled on, lost in thought, "it's not like I'm a fame monger who would be willing to change every last thing about me, lose *everything* in some extreme trade… It's not even like I need to become some kinda Hemingway, or a Wharton or a Plath… I'd be willing to barter at intermediate levels…just one good piece of work…something decent…" Lilah trailed off.

"Bull-fucking-shit," the Being angrily interjected, "I am here because of the extent to which your desire for this – let's call it your *blessing* – has been registered with the ones who track all this shit. You've been at this for some time, sister. You've been on a dirty little path all your own, of your puny ass accord, for a while now. Don't act all innocent and dumb. Please. That is for my kind *the* most boring thing…"

"Well, I'm not *that* married to the idea… Come on…" Lilah feigned confusion, trying for something that might suggest an iota of flexibility which could allow her to backtrack, if just a little bit.

"Oh, so now you want to strike bargains on the bargain?" It cried. "Do you have any idea how fucking fickle that makes you sound?" The Being cried out, tossing Its hands into the air, "Trying to re-strike deals with the likes of *me* after everything's already been decided? You've got some nerve, kiddo!"

"Sorry, sorry," Lilah protested, holding her own hands up in protest.

Anger sparked in the Being's eyes, burning jagged pockmarks into the air in front of Lilah, which reminded her yet again, she was not speaking with any symbolic dream fabrication, or a Ruearke, or a human of any kind. This creature, this agent of the Underworld, was in command of the very powers of hell, and all it took to unleash them was a fleeting moment of ire.

"Now that you've made your trade," It restated. "I *dare* you to try to resist, go only halfway or some other half-assed distance with this deal." The Being paused for effect. "You asked for it, you got it, sister."

"But it's not like I *need* to do this thing," Lilah persisted, albeit half-heartedly. She knew she was losing. Lilah suspected, her subconscious had known the outcome of this exchange from the get-go. "I could still get by on my looks. I am considered pretty good looking – my follower count, my fans, they all are proof of that. I could still work the landscape out there, date strategically, marry up. I coulda also kept on with my writing without you, or this deal we are making. I coulda…"

"…deal *you made*, you dodo…"

"…I coulda kept at it and gotten better by myself," Lilah rambled. "Countless writers before me've done it, managed it, achieved some success on their own, over time. And me, I had – I mean have – enough of looks to back up even my crappy output. I know my appeal out there – and I know how to work it. Any halfway decent publicity along the way would open a slew of doors to choice catches along the way. Hell, I was proposed to, twice, and I never even saw either of them coming!"

"That's what they all say," It yawned, stretching, cracking its knuckles. "Listen to you. You start in so defensive and in two seconds you're dithering on in a backwoods vernacular, with that fine *English* twang of yours totally gone, sounding like some desperate altar chaser to boot. Superficial panache sure is yesterday's trash, ain't that so, Mizz Snoooodgrass?" It slurred, contempt lacing every syllable.

"Fuck you!" Lilah retorted, all facades cast fully aside.

"Fuck *you!*" the Entity hit back. For good measure, the Being blew a capillary in Lilah's left eye. She felt the tiny *pop* as clearly as had the creature tapped her eyeball with a stick pin.

"Ow!" Lilah cried, slapping her hand to her face to counter the prickling spear of pain. "Son of a bitch!"

"You want the other eyeball busted too, kiddo?" the Being screeched, Its ego as tetchy as Its powers were formidable.

"No, no. Stop it. Let's stop it. Both of us," Lilah implored, doing her darndest to force an air of resigned calm over herself. "Truce, okay?"

"Fine. Up to you, you redneck word hack," the Entity replied, shrugging nonchalantly, pleased with itself.

"Okay, okay," Lilah held her hands up in surrender. "Just stop. I can't…not this anymore… And, I am *not* a redneck. I can't help where I'm from… And you should talk. If you were only to be labeled by place of origin, what'd they be calling *you*?"

"I told you; I am…"

"Oh, enough with that already!" Lilah retorted.

"You really are a piece of work, sister," the Entity shot back. "No wonder they sent me here."

Now Lilah rolled *her* eyes. It took one to know one.

"Let's do this," she announced, pausing just long enough to make a show of the whole mess having finally sunk in. "I know what I am signing up for. And I know that I want this. I'm in."

"You asked for it, you got it," the Creature replied, shrugging its broad shoulders again.

"I'm ready." Lilah insisted. "What do I need to do?".

The Being's tone and posture shifted again, "So now comes the traditional part. We seal the deal, and you, girlie, will sign in blood."

Lilah held out her finger, the dutiful patient at the clinic, there for her finger stick.

"Ho ho," It chortled, "You think you're going to get off *that* easy?"

Lilah shrunk back, struck by the fresh injection of hostility in Its voice. She remained bolt upright however, and alert, being now fully sobered up. And on guard. Lilah pictured herself clambering off the bed and running out of her room, through the apartment door, down the stairs, out the front entrance and far, far away; but instead, she sat stock still. Lilah was as frozen to her spot on the bed as had the joints of her legs been bolted into place.

The entity sat up, pulling Its lithe torso to full height. It locked eyes with Lilah's and began to pull aside the lapel of Its shirt, theatrically, languidly, and with a sensuous pacing. The Beast's heavy brows were drawn together in concentration; this interlude requiring a keen and malevolent focus. The inky darkness of Its irises reflected no light whatsoever, but the pupils smoldered like burning coals, red-orange pinpricks which held Lilah's gaze as if with strings connected. It never once blinked.

Lilah, puzzled, remained attentive. Afraid, yes, she was that, but Lilah found herself distracted by the smooth skin of the creature's exposed chest, where now she could see a thatch of fine hair, which seemed to suggest, *Start Here.* Lilah stopped her thoughts short. How absurd for her to be sidetracked by *that*, out of all possible scenarios, by the very same seductive fabrications she had reconstituted time and again for her narratives. This male *thing*, seated far too comfortably on her bed, was toying maliciously with her in precisely the same way she had played with the sensibilities of countless, anonymous, subordinate others from whom she wanted nothing more than blind, anonymous fealty, with no commitment to any of them but to sell a fabricated self, a deadline-forced publication, to make a buck, and in the process to stoke a psychologically questionable perceived need.

Surely, Lilah's grasp of the situation should keep some override power at her command, but she felt a spark of dread ignite despite her best effort and her capacity for deceptive survivalist tactics. Surely, this visitation, this *haunting*, would soon end, be over with. Surely…

Lilah realized with a start, she was not sure about anything at that moment, except for what seemed to be the fact that she had willed this midnight rendezvous with *her* devil upon herself.

What form, then, was this blood signing to take?

A blood signing. Well then. So, was it *her* blood about to be taken, right? But in what fashion? Lilah scanned the creature surreptitiously, top to bottom. The Being held no knife, had no weapon she could see, nothing sharp on Its person, no formidable jewelry, not even a belt for Its trousers. If this were not to involve *her* own blood, then…what?

The creature placed a hand over Its left breast, and then with thumb outstretched, pressing hard, It drew a skin-splitting line over Its heart.

It was in that instant, Lilah knew what the Being was enacting. Of course. This was one of her most favorite film seduction scenes, ever. It had fed her fantasies and played into her creative repertoire, especially when fabricating the gothically inclined narratives of her novels. It was Count Dracula, when he was about to…

No way! Was this going to be some vampiric seduction re-enactment?

"No, it can't be… You've got to be… Are you fucking kidding me?" Lilah sputtered, panic pulling her voice taut. "Noooooo…" she wailed, her voice building to the high pitch of a small animal, suddenly cornered.

This is what the Beast meant by saying they had to sign their pact in blood? That *she* was going to be forced to consume his, *Its* blood? The grotesque scene playing out before Lilah hit her like a slap in the face, was revolting to her for the notion that it would now be she who would have to *taste* of this Creature's bodily fluids, as if tolerating Its invasion into her room hadn't been enough. And then, to think that this, *this thing* might go on and bleed all over her new, ridiculously expensive bedsheets, which she had just bought online – unless of course she could catch it all in her mouth, swallow it down before the mess made its disgusting way to a total desecration of her bed as well? It made Lilah feel ill, just to realize she had in her short-sightedness started to strategize on the ingesting of the Beast's seepage to save a stupid bedsheet she herself had already stained with her own blood…

"You've *got* to be kidding me!" Lilah repeated, shrill, panicked.

"Oh no, sister," It snorted, teeth clenched, "you asked for it, you got it. We're signing in blood, and this is how it's going to be done! You think *you* can dictate the details? You think I'm some kind of freakshow *puppet* that'll just comply with your inconsistent quirks, make it nice n easy for little Miss Squeamish here?" The Creature spat visibly as It railed. "This *blessing*, sister, *doesn't* come easy. Prices are going to get *paid*!"

"Oh, come on!" Lilah cajoled, mustering a weak show of bravado. "Put a nick right here, in the palm of my hand! Come on – we can shake on it! Or do you want me to sign something? I can sign whatever you want! Here, here – cut me!" she implored, holding out her hand, "I don't care! I'm *not* squeamish – *I* know what's involved!"

Lilah's eyes went back to the entity's chest, where now a three-inch gash was splayed. Glistening blood filled the gap, welled up and spilled over in rhythmic microbursts, in time with whatever it was that served as a heart from within the depths of that Thing's ribcage. Droplets of blood slithered about like skinned leeches upon Its chest, foraging among the fine hairs until they were absorbed by the fabric of Its shirt. Wet, spotted patches quickly blossomed, like freeform flowers painted by a brush dipped in a nice, thick merlot.

"You *can't* expect me to…to…*drink* that… Can you?" Lilah plead, desperate for some semblance of insistence. Her courage was quickly de-evolving, her admonishments were fast morphing into begging.

"I did *not* sign up for this!" she wailed.

"You bet your sweet life, you did, you stupid bitch," the Entity rasped, grabbing a handful of hair at the nape of her neck. With that, the beast began to pull Lilah in towards itself. The Beast pushed her head lower, maneuvering her face upwards with a vicious, practiced move, Its preternatural strength reducing Lilah to broken-hinged compliance.

"No, no," Lilah begged, "You can't make me drink! I don't want to be turned into some undead being! This *can't* be what the deal was about!" She could now smell his skin, smell the sweat, the stench of his corruption. "It's *writing* we are talking about! Literature! Dante, not Dracula! Come on – we're talking about a pact on a wholly different level! This cannot be about some ancient predatory monster about to pillage his virgin conquest!"

"Stupid girl! Dante, Dante, Dante – you lit types are always invoking him! We're not talking Dante," he sing-songed the name with obvious contempt. "We are talking Faust here. Paganini!" the Being snidely added. "Heh, heh," It laughed, "we aren't talking Dante at all. Shit, we are fucking talking Dylan, we're talking Page…

"Look sister," the Creature went on, forcing her to look up and into Its red-lit eyes. "I may not be *merely* a figment of your imagination – I am eons and epochs beyond the likes of *you* – but you can bet every stinkin' piece of me is likewise, whether *I* like it or not, a byproduct of that wild, dark world you carry around in your own head! I, all this, we were all orchestrated by *you* and all those fucking crazy fantasies of *yours*!" Its tone was jeering, Its patience long gone.

The Entity continued, "What's in your head is what's manifesting right here, right now! And this is the *only* way you're going to do this thing with me! You hear me? And you think *you* can tell *me* how to do it? Hell, I could just go away right now and leave you alone, back where you started, but – and I swear this on Lucifer himself – you'd be in waaaay worse shape than before! You actually do need me! That dopey fourth novel you're working on? Forget it! That insipid series you delude yourself into thinking is anything remotely associated with literature? Ha! It'll *never* get any farther! Book four is gonna tank, kiddo! You'll not only not write low-level crap for the rest of your days, you're never going to write *anything at all*, ever again! I promise you," and with this the Being lowered Its voice to a menacing whisper, "I have more power in my fucking left toe than you can even begin to imagine, let alone face up against!"

"Oh, my God," was all Lilah could muster.

"Aaaargh!" the Creature cried. "For fuck's sake, will you quit invoking that shit?"

With that, the Beast fisted her hair even more tightly and smashed her face against Its breast, smearing blood all over her cheeks, even forcing some of it into her nostrils.

Lilah closed her eyes and held her breath, out of all options but this last, paltry defense against what she was being made to do. But the Beast held her fast, keeping her mouth pressed over its bleeding wound. When Lilah could no longer hold out, when she finally had to draw some air or pass out and become utterly helpless to her interloper's whims, she reactively inhaled through both her nose and her mouth. Blood instantly filled her nostrils, globbed past her sinuses, and slid like a warm snake down her throat. Lilah choked and retched. But the creature had her face so firmly glued to Its chest, she was unable to expel anything from either orifice. Lilah had no choice. She had to let the blood fill her mouth, and she had to swallow. Which she did once. And then one more time. And then again.

Disgustingly viscous, hot, slick as oil, Lilah's hellish hazing ritual was worse than any vampiric seduction, for she did not want to partake of his sludge. To consume blood in any fashion was to Lilah a blasphemy against all her gods, Nature, *and* herself. But she continued to swallow, to drink. The ritual had to be endured to be survived. It was the trade, the pact, the price.

The Creature's blood was more revolting than Lilah could have imagined, had she ever thought she'd be seated on the flip side of such a reality, where demonic fantasies were being played out in an apartment bedroom turned Boschian boudoir. Not only was the brute's seepage rife with an acidic tang, Its blood was imbued with a stench that recalled immediately a memory Lilah had suppressed for years, that of the filthy sports sock her idiot brother had once stuffed into her mouth during horseplay, for which – oh yes, indeed – he had paid. Not only was Lilah's brother grounded by their parents for the rest of the summer, but a week later, the little shit somehow also managed to break his nose when he just happened to get in the way of the board Lilah was swinging at full force, when she was only trying to shoo away the bats they had accidentally stirred to panicked wakefulness up there, in the barn's rafters, on that afternoon when mom and dad had gone to town for the day…

Of her mind, of her imagination, of her memory… Lilah was remembering everything. She swallowed once more, and gagged, but she kept it down. All of it.

When at long last the Beast permitted Its prey to come up for air, momentarily releasing Its hold on her, Lilah pushed herself away from the corrupted wailing wall to which she had been effectively shackled and fell flat onto her back on the mattress. With a backwards crawl, Lilah scooted clumsily towards the headboard to seat herself upon her pillows, pressing her back against the wall in an attempt to plant herself as far away from "her" monster as was possible.

If her revulsion of the bloodletting and consumption of the Being's blood was not bad enough, the newly attained distance allowed Lilah to see the loathsome creature had spawned a massive erection. The fabric of Its loose trousers was fully tented by the swollen appendage, which now hovered upright, lewdly taunting her.

"Oh my God!" Lilah cried, aghast.

"There you go again," It reproached her once more. "You and those stupid invocations of yours have got to stop! As if you ever believed in *anything* more than your vain, little self anyway…" Then, seeing where her eyes had wandered, the Entity chuckled and added, "So, what do you think of *this* monster?"

"I…I…" Lilah faltered, flummoxed by the wretched absurdity of this next development. "I can't even believe what I'm seeing…"

"All the better, my dear," It snarled, "to *offend* you…" The Being laughed, a horrible, grating sound.

Tears welled up in Lilah's eyes.

The two faced off in hate-filled silence, each mired in their respective but mutual disdain, each despising the other for their symbiont connectivity, which may have been the most reprehensible but least expendable aspect of this one-night stand.

"Yeah," It continued, "whatever. So, I *liked* it! Isn't that what your stupid Ruearke would have done? Gotten all hot n bothered over a misbegotten tryst? Isn't that how your stories go? All fight and no flight and then oooh, and aaah, and oh baby, baby, give it to me, gimme, gimme…" the Thing blathered on, enjoying the demeaning and reducing to a mockery everything Lilah had ever written and had thought – however presumptively – she had accomplished. Lilah felt as if she had never composed a decent sentence in her life. The Beast was breaking her down, work by work, word by word, insult on top of insult.

The Creature preened, framing the hard-on with Its hands, growling with a primal intensity. It continued, "Now, listen: If there's any more lip from you, I promise you I'll whip this son of a bitch out and it's going to get *really* ugly from there…"

Lilah felt her stomach flip. She startled, her eyes wide, her mouth falling slack when the recognition hit her. Oh, Lord, she thought, was the Creature's blood passing through her system and managing to somehow twist her sensibilities? Was there some digestive integration of a wicked immortality happening within? A degeneration *must've* kicked in. For all her revulsion, despite her protestations, Lilah realized with a shock that the sight of the creature's arousal, along with the vibrato of Its lowering threats, had just triggered *in her* a responding rush of primitive and spontaneous desire, which had just now coursed through her body and struck hard in her own loins.

Lilah was disgusted *with herself.*

At what point had her resistance morphed into *this* lack of control? What part of this had she wanted all along? Much. Much too much of it. There it was, her very own underbelly, rearing its ugly head in an unwanted but undeniably degenerate outburst of responsive lust. For something quite monstrous. *For a beast I conjured up. From my own mind. From my imagination, my fantasy. No, no…*her thoughts were racing, *For my readers, for Christ's sake! Good God,* Lilah implored the dead pool that was her quashed spirit, *what's happening to me?*

"Aha!" the Being shouted, triumphant in the face of the unbidden deviance of Its derelict quarry. "Tell me this," The Beast spat visibly, "which one of you is it that wants *this*?" Splaying Its hands, the Creature set the erect member in motion, swinging it to the left, then to the right, a leering pendulum to keep time like some prurient metronome. "Is it Mizz Milifreeeed who wants this?" It taunted hatefully, drawing long her name, "or is it Mizz Li-Li-Li-Li-Lilaaaah?"

Lilah could only cower against the headboard in silence. She had wrapped her coat back around her shoulders and wiped her bloody face on one of its sleeves. Her ashen face had taken on the pallor of her once pristine bedsheets.

The Creature didn't wait for a response.

"Well, sister, hate to disappoint you, but this rod and staff is what you're *never* gonna get! Because guess what? Your punishment has begun! Your very own self *spites* you, *betrays* you. No dignity for you, girlie-girl! You want and you want, and you want, and you want, but from now on, it's *never* gonna be enough! That, kiddo, is a part of the curse you brought on all by lil ole yourself! You dared to think you wanted *this*? Well fuck that! *It* doesn't want you!"

Lilah got it. Desire, desires. Want, want. No matter what, she was accursed. Probably had been from the start. And this beastly incarnation was going to invert and pervert every exchange that would ever occur between the two of them. There would never be a communion of any kind, be it amidst their warped discourse, or the pact into which she had been guided, which she herself had wished into existence. Lilah now understood, she was the one who had started it all. And it was too late. The Creature was only in the room with her because she had passed the point of no return long before It had ever appeared.

However, …

…Lilah's mind was picking up speed…

…*if* this journey to hell and back would net her *that* book, *that* story, *that* narrative, the one writing experience that would raise her up as a creative contributor to some level where she had only been scratching at for years, well then, dammit, Lilah was going to take it. The deeds were done. She had swallowed. She may as well, Lilah rationalized from within her chaos, accept the deal.

Go for it.

The Beast was suddenly hit by a wave of a different energy, which passed through the room like a seismic fluctuation. It, which is to say the energy that emanated outwards from the blood-smeared, bedraggled woman seated on her pillows, pressed against her headboard, as far away from It as she could possibly be, flowed anew from a someone who had undergone a *metamorphosis*.

Taken aback by the liquid stillness that suddenly filled the whole room, the Creature also fell silent. It sat quietly, observing. It could see a million thoughts race across the young woman's mind. Her eyes jittered perceptibly. Memories, ideas, realizations were converging like migratory birds, scattering into the ether, re-grouping, settling, coming back down to roost. A resolution had formed, had arrived home. The Entity noted from Its post at the foot of the bed, this haughty, smeared-faced pretender, this arrogant but frightened dabbler who had not been able to resist, who had called this whole thing forth herself, was now one replaced. This human on the bed was a someone different, though not new at all. It – she – smacked of things positively antediluvian.

"Wait," Lilah whispered, her eyes flitting back and forth, her gaze reaching far beyond the paper-thin walls of her room, past the dull cover of night, out, out, and farther still, to the dark pitch that flowed in the beyond, there to guide her to untapped voids that now awaited her.

And then, Lilah murmured to no one in particular, "I have an idea…"

†††

A few years later, Lilah, or Mil, would look back upon her moment of transformation with the last vestiges of bemusement she was ever able to dredge up from the unfeeling hollows which soon thereafter replaced her soul. Her reflections of that night – she with her demon on her bed with her – was the last memory for which she was able to *feel* anything before her capacity for human emotion was completely stripped from her. True to the damning bargain Mil had struck, word for word, page for page, and chapter for chapter, as Lilah wrote like one possessed, crafting her literary masterpiece, every bit of her conscious self that could feel anything at all – pleasure, pain, compassion, humor, happiness, love – was drained from her, ounce by psychic ounce, and laid to rest within the narrative of her book, which would become known as her one great – and final – work.

By the time Lilah had completed the draft and sent it off to her agent, who upon finishing her read-through had immediately called Lilah, sobbing, barely able to put into words the transformative enormity of what she had just read, Lilah had lost the ability to feel any gratitude in response, or any iota of shared excitement. As Lilah listened to her agent blubbering over the phone, she just sat there, her coat draped over her shoulders, passive and unappreciative, in a slightly agitated and decidedly impatient silence.

Sure, Lilah breathed, she ate food, she spoke, she slept – dreamlessly, soundly, like a baby – but what remained of her was the dried-out hull of a human. Even in the context of her fatally flawed personality, the dark angel who had paid its lascivious call on that fateful night had simply recognized something in Lilah it had then taken to hellacious – but logical – levels. It was a quid pro quo, a masterpiece *for which the young woman had asked*, in exchange for an utter and complete exorcism of a living self. Lilah Ravenscraft, lauded author, adored by her own legions, walked among her fellow humans, but she was no longer *alive*.

Nope, gore is not necessary for the rest of this story. No eyeballs were plucked from their sockets, no limbs were ripped from their torsos; no more blood or bodily fluids were tapped to spike the resulting stages of necrosis. The young woman who traded everything to place herself up there with the topmost luminaries of the literary world paid with parts of herself that were ultimately far more painful to lose. Or not painful at all…

As Lilah gave birth to the book of her life, so did she, scene by scene, move ever closer to her own death. Lilah's masterwork, *I & You*, the first chapter which she laid down at the feet of her demon before the sun had even risen on the first day after their vile bedroom tryst, was no sooner released as did it – somehow, miraculously – catapult to the tops of countless bestseller lists on the sheer strengths of, well, let's just call it the merits of its beauteous narrative, its underlying message, and most especially, that shockingly moving ending.

I & You even came to be known by a pop culturally anointed moniker, "The Crying Book," for the way the story brought its readers to tears. And no, we are not talking about a dampened eye or small sniffle. *I & You* by Milifred Snodgrass, aka Lilah Ravenscraft, became notoriously famous for the way in which it triggered repeated sob sessions in its readers – heart-torn-from-breast, soul turned inside-out revelationary, cleansing experiences. Devotees of *I & You* consistently claimed they were forever changed by having journeyed through its pages. Historic, many proclaimed Lilah's, Mil's, last, great work. Her story was *that* good, *that* well written, *that* exquisite an execution of one's deal with the devil.

The Creature had kept Its word in droves.

By the time *I & You* was released to film, in which year it won six Oscars, including Best Picture and Best Original Screenplay, the famously reclusive Lilah Ravenscaft had exhaled her last. Per her last wishes, Lilah's, or Mil's, ashes were scattered in the harbor, a few blocks from the apartment building where she had lived, from which she had never moved, even after royalties from sales of *I & You* and its film rights acquisition had made her a wealthy woman. Her apartment was rumored to be haunted, and for that reason, some would say, she would not leave it, which only added to her allure among the tragic pantheon of doomed and legendary writers.

Mil's younger brother made the trip to LA to receive the golden statuette on his sister's behalf, for the film's screenplay had been gleaned verbatim, word for perfect word, from the dialogue in Mil's novel. When Mil's brother accepted the posthumous award, his brief speech went viral for its oddly callous, rather cold delivery. It was said back home, among childhood friends and former classmates, he never got over the loss of his dearly beloved sister.

Efectus

Ms Ravenscraft's Instagram account, @lilahravenscraft remains active & available for her followers, per express request of the late author herself.

DRAFTMITE

July 4

Avery

Police pardon any errors in this letter my dear I am dictating on my laptop and this old machine's porgram is just dated enough I have two little control over what the program interprets and can know longer type the old-fashioned way to fix all the nonsense that keeps showing up how funny it is to say that in light of what has brought me to this point and why

Well at least I can still hit the return key with my elbow I've become pretty adept at that

Indeed I can know more place a fingertip on this beloved old friend and companion of mine my keyboard my computer

But I am in a good place no worries kiddo I am peaceful resolved calmer than in weeks know months

Perhaps the glitches here will provide a laugh or too oh hon it's a dastardly situation but you no me I've always had a proclivity for dredging up this kind of stuff

Obviously if you are reading this you have found it as planned this is my won and only printout of my journal I new you would know where two look

Oh I do hope its you reading this and not some stranger good Lord if such is the case there is know way of preventing it so after the fact

If you are not Avery colon all caps stop reading now exclamation mark crap punctuation dictation never works put this back go away and forget you ever saw this ten exclamation marks well dammit those didn't work either

So so much two say so little time

Let me start again my dear Avery

With everything I have endured everything that has happened to me however specifically I may or may not have bin targeted and relentlessly tormented I can definitively say I am glad it is soon two be over with

And I am glad you are now holding this call it my last testament

What's left of my will is pretty much depleted

I pray your the one reading this and that what you will subsequently do for me will also help prove and set to bed any questions as two what pursued me and what will have in effect killed me so that maybe just maybe I can help prevent or at least motivate some pushback against those god-awful draft might those parasites from consuming others as they did me

Let's try this again

Draft might dammit no it's one word all caps d r a f t m i t e well crikey that didn't quite work but there you can at least see how its spelled yes its what I have dubbed them they're official name I guess you could say

Kiddo it could be you next

It could be anyone

Are you standing at my desk perhaps sitting in my chair as you read this question mark

Well then stay there or go take a seat at your old spot in the breakfast nook and sit down if you are in the kitchen lookout the back door if you are in the study at my desk lookout the window to your write

Due you see a blackened heap out there a pile of burnt debris that is where I am as I told you over the phone yes I did it you may oar may not find bones among the ashes there's no way for me two know fore sure what's left

The kindling and logs I stacked just so their are very specific ancient methods I studied up on cremation and funeral piles no pyres with an argh good that sort of worked a surprisingly satisfyingly patch of research butt oh me the images that float about online macabre doesn't begin two describe what pops up I was distracted two say the least not for the faint of hard or of stomach

Hart no heart as in ok well there you go heart as in a broken heart

I digress I truly do hope there are only non-descript fragments left

Brake the soil the settle me in I would certainly suspect my ashes are know longer contagious same holds for my laptop the draft might colony in my computer can in no way have survived the immolation

My laptop that thing I smashed two bits before I dumped the pieces onto the kindling now those could still bee rather sharp wear gloves my garden gloves should be wear I left them on the hook in the back hall

Please my love I am asking you to just bury us all where we lay the soil around here is loamy and soft was always perfect four gardening now aught to make for some easy digging ideal for a makeshift gravesite witch should green itself over in the space of one good growing season

Call it our secret garden eh question mark

Two that end the envelope tucked into the balk of the photo album the red leatherbound binder you no so well is over there on the coffee table that is also four you

It is a remittance iamb asking for you two tend to this in confidence simply going to have to trust you on this won

Please and thank you thank you from the bottom of my draft might infested dammit this blasted thing just refuses to get my name for those buggers correctly

You will learn more about them if you reed the rest of my journal that's your choice if not when you deliver my paper two the lab moron that in a second you will understand the depth and breadth of my malaise the infestation witch has taken over my entire bean it's all I can do to not scratch my face off my skin positively crawls with the little critters who'd have thought a grill brush wood become my best friend I just can't help it I am glad you cannot see me in this state

Do not worry about contagions here I took care of all that bleach and vinegar by the gallon are mercifully cheap and easily ordered in quantity I took care of me twos clean as a whistle inside outside and everywhere in between ass four my laptop the original hotbed of infestation the charred bits Shirley now can't possibly hurt anyone anymore those god-awful draft mites could in no way have survived the flames the way I constructed the pile no pile rhymes with tire no pee with a why and an are and an a well dammit i hope you can make sense of this

Shirley nothing could survive either the gasoline or the heat or the containment shell I built exclamation mark

I do hope my dark humor isn't two repugnant butt you know me kiddo it's all I have left of my humanity two at least try and laugh a little in the face of an impending self-immolation

I took meds I won't disclose how I got them but I did take quite a few they have begun two do their good deeds I am still able to function as I must but there are parts of me shuttting down I can feel lit as I dictate this final letter to you Hun

No no honey I meant honey gads

Oh by the weigh if you find any section of my skull or intact teeth police take a hammer to them police pulverized anything even remotely traceable you know teeth are the worst I did take care to pull my goad crowns ages ago and cell those stubborn sons of bitches to some online pawn shop witch did fund this last project of mine aunt it left more cash for me to leave to you

Good lumber required for the best burn is just so dam high these days I am looking out the window at it now it's quite the structure out their

Listen Avery I have stashed a hammer in the bottom write drawer of this desk as I suspect it will come in handy use it leaf nothing anyone can trace I am paying you plenty so I am asking in accordance with what I am offering I no you are up two this

Okay then I need not spend more time on logistics everything I have compiled on the draft mights is in the thick sheath no sheaf there that's better of paperwork fastened with the clips it is my last saved draft of my research paper now all printed out ready two go its still a bit ova mess those nano demons screwed with it up until the point I printed tit deer Lord oh my I am just sorry given the condition of my hands how quite impossible it was two notate corrections even though I wrapped the Sharpie in gauze to make it easier to hold I trite my best tried at least two make the most necessary corrections it'll make sense two the experts regardless despite the type owes don't you worry

Gauze gauze and more gauze also became a knew best friend I bought sew much of the stuff these last few months went threw cases of it thank goodness for home delivery I could not have mustard trips to actual stores certainly after never mind

Lord knows I spent enough time and energy dealing with those draft mites little do they no they are soon done four and I along with them what else can a person do if they have themselves become a living breathing host for a colony of micro monsters that are eating them up from the inside out oh me you should've seen them crawling all over ends of the queue tips I swear I used half a box just digging the buggers out of never mind

It is not my intention to turn your stomach I just thought it was hilarious after all that time to actually sea the teeny tiny fellas scurrying about like fine ground pepper come two life circling about the cotton swab end confused like they had know where to hide

Being my choice the relief I will soon be blessed with is so anticipated I am sew tired of all of this it's time four it to be over and I yes me myself and I get to have our final say ten exclamation marks dammit punctuation prompts never work

Fuck those things pardon my french Hun I mean honey

I'll clothes now and wish you all the best and myself Godspeed

Where two won can only guess but anywhere other than here will be an improvement I am just so glad you will not have scene me in this State

Do knot mourn my passing

Avery remember how you were warned years ago buy your Aunts when I took you in I had my quirks and boar them with a singular pride but who else in our family could afford to take you in

I no you got me as much as any child can get anyone in whom a good heart and unconventional disposition have crossed wires I hope you are suitably fortified four this last favor that I aks of you by virtue of are shared history

We shore did have some fun all those years before college took you a way the quirky old bachelor uncle and his Nice no niece that's better a sad but stalwart child of misfortune you were back when you landed at my place but it tall worked out didn't tit oh my so sorry you have done so well for yourself I am so proud of you perhaps I did do something write in this life

That your work took you sew far away was heart no hard with a d as in dog on me but sew that goes why does this thing always get that wrong it was probably for the best yes I think sew

And I am paying you well my dear right question mark it's all I have left or rather had

I suppose past tense would be a probate at this point

Have I thanked you yet I think sew Justin case thank you kiddo from the bottom of my heart

Spend the money wisely and please please do knot let yourself become ensnared by the web trust me you don't want this pestilence invited into your physical world Iamb relieved to know you are not afflicted with a writers predilection as I was sew your life path won't be quite as reliant on that connectivity as mine was Mark my words it is an tech era plague no doubt infecting and silencing others as I right this

Anyone targeted is done four

Avery I tell you it is a callously insidious nano pestilence that cruises the globe and our world is its hamster we'll

When they find you as they found me its over nothing nothing can keep the infection from spreading and taking over I four won was powerless against tit

Apologies my deer for these horrid typos I myself am offended by them exclamation mark

Worse yet I believe they oar sentient they no what they are doing and they know we no it I am convinced they have downright enjoyed what they did to me are doing two me

Trust me it gives me unmitigated happiness to no I am taking a few billion of those bastards with me when I go

So with the crumbs off sanity I can still call my own yes a smidgeon of your old uncle Emory is still hear who rights you this letter who has stashed the cash and the hammer and who is sew sew sorry I will now sign off and go outside two take care of things once and for aul

Buy the weigh there is a nice new shovel in the hall closet I got online just for you

Remember leaf not a trace its the least you can due four me and I am paying you well yes question mark

Alright then the fireworks have started that's my queue exclamation mark with the sulfuric oh door of explosives in the air and all that racket know won will even notice my little bonfire

Good-bye my deer oh crap that's deer with an a a legible sign off two my letter would have been nice

Must go must hurry now good-bye Avery

Uncle m no that's capital E M four peats sake dammit

Pee s oh my goodness gracious capital P capital S the lab's address where I want you two deliver my paper is on page too if those morons at the lab ever figure things out four themselves what I tried two tell them four months maybe they wood accept it and use my information four evidence so police police get it two them you never no someone else might be afflicted who would be better listened two than I ever was although by then it could be two late their unwillingness two meat with me ant then two bar me from the premises was as painful as the infection itself it really hurts when know won listens

If anyone asks just tell them I dyed of natural causes

†††

Uncle Emory's journal was for the most part a series of charts and notations, numeric entries and odd, smiley face drawings, which I soon came to learn were his daily word counts and mood indictors. It was as if he in his solitude, in his unrelenting quest to write something someone would truly take note of, had been reduced to tallying his self-worth and verifying his existence by the daily batches of characters he fabricated into words, which he tossed into all those half-finished short stories and novels and the dubious research paper he left me with. Word, words. Countless tiny nails, hammered into the walls of a vast, rambling house in his head. And all the re-writes and track changed edits, repeatedly done, over and over again? They were heartbreaking to see. It almost did appear as if the documents, not he, were altered while in their saved, supposedly static states, as if he was indeed forced by some outside saboteur to correct and re-correct his writing. Continuously. An infected bit of programming, a virus? It was almost as if this entity was working to break him, personally. Yes, he was an older, lonely man, and yes, he was susceptible to delusion. This "thing" – I just don't know what to call it – drove him to darkest despair and a tragic outcome I could have never seen coming.

How I wish I had had some idea this was happening. But he hid it so well. Too well. I am sure he thought he was protecting me.

Uncle Emory's pages and pages of notes were interspersed with diary-like entries, which corresponded with the dates in the documents he printed out and bound and called his "research paper." These are the most painful and will remain unshared but for what I am sharing with you now, which must remain between us. His paper, on what he called "Draftmites," I will hold onto. If there is any evidence out there on this issue, that it could be real, I will be on the lookout for it. Perhaps then I would mail this paper to the lab. The last thing I want to do is set my uncle up for posthumous ridicule. He did more than enough to punish himself. My gut tells me I should destroy everything, but not just yet. For now, his things are safe, his secrets are safe.

The shovel, I couldn't bear to keep. But the leather-bound album, I did take. The old photographs contained in that album are the best mementos of the two of us – me and the brilliant and kind, but disturbed man who raised me like a father, who later suffered in ways I cannot imagine. May he rest in peace.

I did look his term up online. Sure enough, it's there. Poor old, Uncle Em.

Here are his longer entries. When you read them, you will understand my reluctance in sharing anything at all of his. It's bad enough, what I had to take care of in the backyard, but at least Uncle Em, true to his word, had built his makeshift incinerator well, and all that was left, but for two molars and part of what I guess would have been a jawbone, was a patch of scorched earth and a heap of ashes, easily turned under and planted over with grass. I did move the concrete birdbath over to that spot. It serves well as a sort of memorial, helps camouflage the new coverage. The last time I went to the house, to meet the real estate agent and turn the keys over, I saw a volunteer vine of some kind had already sprouted near the base of the birdbath and was working its way up the base.

†††

November 27

There. It's official. I have named the little sons of guns. Draftmites. Up and published at Urban Dictionary, which makes it about as official as it needs to be in this day and age, at least for my purposes, from my anonymous perch in this innocuous corner of the Midwest, and in the greater name of all things viralized in that vast realm of all things pop cultural, which is about the only reality left to the masses, certainly all the post-tech generations who no longer will have lived in any portion of the pre-tech world. I am rather glad I knew well those earlier eras – pen and paper, typewriters, things so nicely self-contained, so safe.

I ask you: How is it that my perfect drafts, my exhaustively proofed, tweaked, edited, corrected and re-corrected documents, when I open them back up are continuously re-possessed of myriad errors? Or worse yet, how is it, when those snarky interns at the publishers reply back to me, it's with drafts of my submissions track changed to kingdom come? How is it there are so blasted many errors? It can't be me. It CANNOT! I am meticulous to a fault; I ENJOY my perfectionism. There are no excuses, no reasons for this.

What am I supposed to do, hold my printouts up to mirrors and read them backwards?

There is no way – NO way I tell you – that I am completing my papers, my submission drafts, with all those ridiculous mistakes! This is something I am going to need to actively fight, and to call out the enemy by name is step number one.

So Draftmites it is. That is what they are. That is what I have decided to call them. Nano-sized minions who sail about on the internet. One click and they are in Australia; another click and they are traipsing about in the hard drive of my laptop and attacking what matters most to me, my work. Hours of writing, reading, editing and perfecting are being continuously negated with the stupidest mistakes I can't even imagine making!

And today? Last straw! That snooty bastard, that self-important editor, Xandon – what kind of name is that? – took time off from his incessant social media posting to write me personally, as if he thought it was warranted, to counsel me, "perhaps you might like to attend one of our writer's seminars this spring," being that it appeared, I wasn't in a position to hire my own proofreaders. And then to sign off with a heave-inducing,

"In Lit We Trust,
XOXOX"

Who does this guy think he is? And while he's spending hours, preening for his followers out there, I, a writer, a true-blue craftsman of the written narrative who shuns that damnable matrix because I prefer using MY time to produce actual literary content, am put out to pasture with a bit of patronizing non-advice?

I am the one who is writing.

I am the one creating.

I am not posting, I am not preening, I am not on some click quest.

I am a REAL WRITER, dammit.

Their banality makes me want to slit my wrists.

Alright. Enough ranting for one day. I'm signing off, wanting to get back to my research, needing also to re-tweak my submission, which that Xandon-bastard nixed and sent back to me with his nasty, little note. I think I will re-title my story, change the names of the main characters...Say; do I perhaps need to submit under a new name? Make something up that rings a tad more clever than Emory Beets? Planning on submitting it to a new indie press I just came across online, called Ravenscrafters Publishing (now, that's some mellifluous surname!). Their latest callout suits this short story...well, more or less. Honestly, this work is SO worthy of another chance; even I can see that. I suppose I should tinker with the backstory too, add some lush, gothic-leaning components...Foggy weather, atmospheric scene descriptions (especially in the intro); switch out the lakeside lodge for a manor by the sea...would be an easy matter to take the clothing descriptions back a few decades...

Yes, that's what I will do. Must get to work now.

December 7

And a happy Santa Domnia day to you too. If that isn't the only holiday spirit to acknowledge, I don't know what is. Nothing else is quite dark enough to suit my state of mind. Speaking of dark, it's still pitch black outside. I've been up all night trying to figure out what in the blazes is going on with my work. Ravenscrafters got back with me the very next day after I submitted my revamped – and might I say wonderfully so – submission. Terrific, I thought (stupid me), they want to nab the rights to my story immediately, so I don't submit it anywhere else. Well, if I thought that XOXOX editor was a snooty piece of work, the gal at Ravenscrafters did him one better. She replied back to me with so much less, but – and only here will it stand, admitted – it hurt so much more. She – or whoever does her hit work – replied to my submission with this response:

"Um, no."

Now, what the hell is that supposed to mean? Did civility or community support die with the pre-tech era? How dare she? So, I re-read the draft I had sent them. Even reading with a most critical mindset, I could not conclude it was a bad story. It's quite good. Damn good. Perhaps too good for their demographics. Too complex, too eloquent. Yes. Too above the abilities of their readers. But shore as Sherlock, whatever version I had submitted to Ravenscrafters, it was NOT what they had received, what they then sent back to me with their hateful, two-word dismissal.

Yes. It was the draftmites. Again. It wasn't me! It's not me! I have a hard copy saved! I DID NOT MAKE THOSE MISTAKES! I did not change the words out! The draftmites, those insidious critters, they not only reversed spelligns but also found ways to negate entire sentences, narrative connectors, with single words changed – switchouts so small, so innocuous as to make them indiscernible. It looked for all purposes as intentional, and as if it were of my doing. How the draftmites managed to take the entirety of my narrative and turn it too the lamest thing I have read this side of Fifty Shades? Insidiously brilliant, they are!

I replied back to Ravenscrafters to explain. I had to. The last thing I wanted to do was present myself as some paranoid fanatic, but the piece of garbage attached to her response to me had to be addressed. In my reply, I told her the truth, that I'd been hacked by a viral pest which had been escalating – Growing? Reproducing? – in the web, which had infiltrated my laptop, and that I was in the process of researching this issue with the intention of submitting my findings to the lab at the tech center, over in Greentown. I mentioned also, I had my suspicions this was a growing issue, even took the opportunity to add the new link to my published name for the pests.

I have confidence this will set the record straight, and believe my submission might be re-considered, once they know what's going on.

December 8

Well, she got back with me. Immediately. This time, her response was all of three words. Not two. Three.

"This isn't funny."

What in the devil's name was happening? I yelled, screamed into my empty room, when I opened her reply and saw not what I expected, but THAT. It creeped me out to read her words, as I had no idea what she could possibly have meant by that. I read on. Sure enough, this time, in the body of MY EMAIL to her, there they were as well. Rogue errors. Again. Punctuation, spacing. And the crowning glory? The draftmites took my phrase, "ripple effect" and switched out an "N" for the "R." I was appalled. God help me! The draftmites have never been this aggressive, this hurtful.

I tried writing her back to apologize. My email was immediately returned as undeliverable. She blocked me. I swear, I can feel the walls of my study push in on me. The room looks smaller. I have never felt this kind of feeling. It is more – its a different kind of hurt.

Let me put to words what I feel, exactly as I imagine it, in hopes the catharsis of externalization dissipates the urge.

I feel like I want to bash my head against the brick wall of the garden. And I'm not joking. The wall is certainly tall enough, no one wood see me do it. A few good blows just might send me to a restful oblivion, at least for a few hours. I am so tired, so tired. But I cannot stop. Even to numb myself with extreme activity. I must get all of this documented. Build a case to support my suspicions – no, my theory. Against the draftmites. I am going to call the lab in Greentown to see if someone, anyone, will agree to meet with me, take my word as evidence. Good Lord, I have so much proof. My works ARE being tampered with. And NOT by me. By someone. Or, rather, something. It's those god-awful draftmites.

I swear, I think I can see them on the field of this document. There! It's the tiniest speck...here...there...it's flitting across the page! And what's telltale about them, is that they move in random fashion. Not linear. They don't cross once and are gone. No. They slow down and then take off in a different direction. There it is again! But how is it I can sea them? My estimation of their actual size is that they are much, much, much smaller than what is visible to the naked eye. How else would they have travelled from the Web into my computer?

What kind of visual abilties do I now also possess, that are allowing me to SEE them?

I am heading outside. I can hardly breathe – this room is to tight, too small. No air. I wish I had an inclination for a stiff drink, but alcohol does such a number on my digestive system. How else to disengage with rage? And this raging feeling of aloneness? Does anyone else know about the draftmites? Is anyone else under attack? Wait until the lab gets hold of my proof! And when, someday, it all becomes official and they name the viral bastards after me, it'll be two late.

The irony of it all!

I do wish, I did have some alcohol. Not to drink. I need to disinfect my fingers, under the nails. That HAS to be the hot spot of transmission to me. All that contact I have with the keys of my laptop. Dirty, worn-out keys. Faded vowels, filthy keypads. Even the lid is sticky. Oh dear, the plastic, the metal are all degenerating, becoming porous. Veritable draftmite tunnels.

Yes, I think I will go outside.

Feburary 14

And a happy, hoppy Sweetheart of a day to you, too. Keeping this short, up to my ears in research on my draftmite paper. It's progressing nicely, almost at five-hundred pages and going strong. Building my case with every document I re-open, save, correct and then save anew as I log every new set of errors, every switch-out. This thing is afoot and there is nothing I can do. No cleanliness measures, no repeated fixes, can keep up with the advancing infestation. I am doing the only thing I can, witch is to gather proof and prepare it four the lab. Perhaps it is better called an infection. It is only a matter of time before I am systematically affected. Honestly, what I plan to submit to the tech lab ought probably also go to a bio lab. These draftmites MIGHT appear to be targeting our computers, our documents, but what they are really after is ME.

All of us.

March 9

Ditto on my above entry. I have nothing knew to say. Keeping a sponge in a boll full of alcohol at my desk, soaking my fingertips every few minutes. Have just ordered another multi-pack of toothbrushes, witch work wonderfully well for spot scrubbing. Knuckles rather raw. Ointment helps.

Must sign off, working on a re-do of my lost three chapters. Opened them up, they are a blasted mess.

April 3

Apologies for my silence. Although I had hoped to separately document my progress on my work, with my additional research going full steam on the draftmite invasion of the World Wide Web, it's all I can do to take waking time off to tend to my health, my personal hyggeine. To keep this journal updated has become an afterthought. Allow the numbers I am logging to at least provide a tally of daily word count. Output. The smiley faces should be self-explanatory – it's the quickest way I can think two record my state of mind. The straight-line mouth, the sad-face mouth; yes, and the crooked diagonals. Those I'd classify as confusion and consternation. Yes, consternation. Perplexedness. A discombobulation.

April 15

I did it. I never meant to actually do it, but I did it.

I am glad to say the wound over my left ear has finally heeled. I have promised myself, I won't do that again. The egg was a doozy – visible, even, by way of a quick glance in the mirror. It pushed my hair off to one side, it was that bad a contusion. The blood was the wurst of it. Had I known I would spew like a sacrificial beast, I would have taken some towels outside with me. But hey, I conked out, slept outside in the grass until late morning. It's the most solid sleep I have had in a while. Do-it-yourself shock therapy? Cheap, private, and to be honest, I think rather effective. The throbbing was a welcome distraction from all the other hurt. And so, I would construe my I don't know what to call it as having been successful. It forced me two take a few daze off from writing, from even touching my computer. And since painkillers also do a number on my digestive system, I simply bided my time, letting my brain scream at me, full volume, four about for days, until the thing subsided of its own accord. Forget about the persistent tenderness at my temples. Good that I have no problem sleping upright.

We'll just call it a vacation. I won't do it again.

April 27

Well, dammit. I completed my paper on the draftmite infiltration. I also printed it out and saved the document to both a usb stick and my old, neon-colored thumbdrive. Now two tackle the footnotes and antonations.

Sure enough, however, every draft of every document, when I open them, are still showing new and different errors! Whole words are being switched out, wacky indentations are being inserted, odd punctuation, even sentences go missing, which I KNOW I rote – poof! Vanished in two thin air! There is nothing I can do butt play along, reset the sabotage with my corrections, and try to keep a step ahead of the little bastards. It's become a 24/7 battle, me versus an army of draftmites.

May 2

This is not going well. And it's going much slower, now that I am typing and making notations with surgical gloves on, in hopes the draftmites don't infiltrate ME. My fingertips are, I am quite positive, looking blueish, as if they are bruising – perhaps it is a poison, or a mold, or a rot, which those buggy lil buggers ar causing in my fingertips. Evidence of first contact with my draftmites.

Oh, help me. I just referred two those abhorrent critters as MY draftmites.

May 8

I don't think latex will work. The palms of my hands are damp and it stinks when I pull the gloves off. Straight to the trash can they go, they smell that bad. Further proof, if you ask me. of the infectious ramifications of draftmite infestation. My nailbeds must be full of them.

Back to my re-edits.

May 19

I am not feeling well. No, this isn't call four another trip to the wall. This is something new, from the inside out. I can say with relative certainty, the draftmites have made their way into my system – circulatory, nervous, digestive. And I am convinced that the first point of contact with my computer is the problem. It's my fingertips, my fingernails. I have resorted two cutting my nails below the growth lines for a while now, which is NOT a comfortable thing.

I have adapted fairly well to typing with a flat-handed, pad of the finger strike two minimize any impact against my fingertips, where the flashes of pain can make me feel queasy. Not that I have any apetite these days, anyway. My clothes all hang on me now. I always wanted to lose some weight. Well, now I could stand to gain a few pounds. But trips two the store are out of the question, and I keep forgetting to order groceries. I think I will do just that as soon as I sign off hear.

May 31

Now, despite my proactive handling of the direct contact issue, I remain suspicious of further draftmite exposure. Am considering further, preventative measures. Doing additional research now, not just on infections and viruses, butt on the minimization of risk via more aggressive measures, perhaps extreme personal modifications, as, obviously, the constant washing, sterilizing, and gloving haven't worked.

Regardless, want two note, my word count four yesterday topped out at five thousand three hundred words. Not bad four a hobbled typist, eh?

June 17

Ouch ouch ouch

Oh Lord it hurts

I am now utilizing the dictation feature on my laptop but it's an earlier version than ideal my old laptop can't run the newer programs and that is very nearly as frustrating as when the draft mights first reared their ugly little heads two screw up my writing four now I must also contend with the rampant incorrect interpretations of my speech sea what it does with my name for the nano bugs themselves let me spell it again it's d space r space a space f space t space m space I space t space e well hell that looks even worse anyway it is draft might all one word and it snot might as in strength but mite as in well dust mites see that got the word right anyway until my fingertips heal and I can bare the pain of the key stroke I will have two make due I will have two endure the quirky errors of a lame dictation program and that of this language of ours it's a particularly a funny one when it comes two all those homonyms and homophones

At least four now I can still putter about on my keyboard with the eraser tip of my pencil two place the most necessary punctuation but who needs periods or commas ha ha

On the plus size no I said side I am dictating this entry even as I am changing out the gauze wrappings on my fingertips yes I am doing that at this very moment witch I need two do far more often than anticipated the nail beds continue two ooze despite my best efforts two wrap them good and snug surely continuous pressure slows the leakage right?

I suppose my body is just doing what it's supposed two do fighting the injury well the modification let's call it what it is the healing reactivity witch is two send white blood cells two each point of trauma is also what it is there is a part of me that still wishes to be well soon enough I am certain of it the rapid staining of my tidy little bandages will diminish and cease please let it be soon this is getting a bit ridiculous I am constantly having two wipe off my keyboard the nail beds must begin to heal over then I can resume my work full steam a head

It twill be a relief to have nice smooth fingertips completely devoid of fingernails and all the little edges and junctions under which all those god-awful draft mights could gather and collect and eat there way through my skin and into my system

To be honest I do suspect it is already too late I can feel a certain let's call it displacement it's vague but it's real in my head in my belly in my joints and it's more than a local infection now it's metastasizing the little buggers are already traveling through me now there this faint tickle below the surface of my skin it crawls

I am feeling my lymph nodes in my neck they are sew swollen

My body is obviously fighting the draft mites in my circulatory system

I sit here and dictate and continue two wrap fresh gauze around my fingertips know it doesn't look good and they now smell funny two my fingertips have an odor two them I thought the gloves were nasty but this is worse it's unmistakable

Is it an infection or a transmogrification are the draft mites poisoning my parts or assimilating with me am I rotting away as I sit here at my very own desk or am I being re-constituted?

Bee write back oh hells bells useless program this is

June 18

How can that be are not the sterile measures I have taken sufficient was not the box cutter I bought online two do the procedure good enough haven't my methods bin clean enough meticulous enough aggressive enough?

No that can't be the problem it isn't me it's the draft mights those god-awful critters making their way through my system my infection now threatens to attack me undo my physical chemistry it has swelled up the glands in my neck even my armpits I can feel a tendrness that wasn't there yesterday

How fast is the spread four guts sake?

What's two be next will they infect my brain tissue re-write my personality will I recognize the onset when it occurs or will there simply bee a gradual shut down and if that is the end will I no it when it hits or might I be numb and blind two my own final implosion?

But oh the leakage at my fingertips is not write

I am dripping like a fresh-cut pine

With this seepage I'll go out like some felled tree in the Baltics and in a hundred thousand years they'll find the droplets of me all over the place hardened into fibrous pebbles of amber laced with the threads of my white gauze bandages fused four eternity now that's a funny thought even two think this way when I am in the fight of my life at war with a nano particled army which first laid siege two my computer and has now taken me as their hostage

June 25

Little disease mongers those god-awful nano-critters the draft mights shouldn't get the best of me butt I now fear perhaps they have

The nailbeds aren't healing I suppose I could always amputate my fingers at the first joint perhaps a lateral cut would leave less surface two seal May be less than the mess I made with my fingernail extraction I coot cauterize the wounds with a broad knife blade a good coal fire in the hearth otter do it

I half done my homework and half ordered miscellaneous supplies and a sizable shipment of lumber I paid with cash used the money from the gold crowns wow that was a messy project my jaws still ache thank goodness the delivery guys didn't caer about a signature for the materials I am shore the five I tucked under the doormat helped keep that a non-issue they may have suffered a bit of a shock had they scene me

June 29

The writing thank goodness has long bin put two bed everything is done and printed out and clipped together working on my well I'll call it my construction project cannot waste time with such as this sew keeping this brief must have everything ready two go in a few days I no just what two do and how two set it up and then let's see who gets the last gut dam word

†††

After the June 29 entry, there are no others but for Uncle Em's final letter to me. When I get back, I will need to you to talk with me, sort this all out. I am overwhelmed, but given who he always was, not all that surprised. May he rest in peace.

See you soon, hon. I am sorry to have brought you in on this, but it's too much to digest alone, especially as, for his sake, I did do the task he asked of me and as of now plan on keeping things to myself. And, well, now you know it, too. I am so sorry.

Oh, and honey, I don't want to worry you unnecessarily, but when I do get back, I am going to schedule an appointment with a dermatologist. Perhaps what I really need is a psychologist lol, I don't know – at any rate, there is a patch on the back of my right forearm, red and kind of itchy. So far, a little calamine lotion is keeping me from scratching, but it hasn't cleared up on its own, and I might need to get something prescribed. A little too funny, huh, this coincidence, but I promise you, I am not imagining this reaction or infection or whatever it is into existence. Maybe it's poison ivy from the garden – although can't say I ever saw any, and I definitely do know what that stuff looks like, and it's been a while… Still…

Love you,
Ave

††††

"…and in conclusion, the long-held theory, at long last dispelled, thanks to my exhaustive research…" the sentence read.

She swept her cursor up the screen and re-worked it to read,

"…and in conclusion , the long-hand theory, at long last dispelled, thanks to my exhuastive research…" and hit "Save." And then, "Send."

This was almost too easy, she mused, smiling, peering past the paint encrusted portal that served as her kitchen window. All it took were a few hits – here a tweak, there an inversion, there a random deletion – to cast a doubt, plant a seed. It took very little, for insecurities and imagination did the rest of the work, which made her job all the easier. A favorite trick, one could call it a signature hack of hers, was to switch out a noun-marker "no" for an "a," or the reverse, to invert the entire meaning of a sentence or phrase with practically zero effort. Just doing her job.

She liked resting her eyes by focusing her gaze into the distance. The grandiose monstrosity they called the Basilica of the Saving Grace loomed on the city's horizon. She watched as the gilded belltowers were swallowed whole by the dark mists of a fast-approaching storm front. In minutes, the wall of rain and sleet would reach her square, and the high rises where all those corrupt elites cowered with all their fancy food and expensive clothes would also be gone from sight, leaving her better cocooned from the outside world, with all its banal superficiality and detestable humanity.

This last draft, she had noticed, appeared to be all there was, at least in the immediate timeline. Nothing else had been uploaded in weeks. That literary plebian had been particularly susceptible; much of correspondence, as well as that endlessly long paper of his, had been centered on little more than an obsession with errors and typos – she had only needed to insert a couple of them. As for all the rest, she neither knew nor cared what the deal had been with that poor bastard. She at one point almost felt sorry for him but stopped short at stooping to compassion. To *care* was symptomatic of weakness. First world privileged, free speech-barking literati-posturing consumerist pigs, all of them – served him right.

Plus, she was only doing her job.

The hacker, feeling saucy, decided to add something to the footnotes on the last page. She pasted 01001011 01000001, which caused a physical rush of satisfaction to coarse through her malnourished body. She then slammed shut the lid of the laptop and pushed it away from her with a flourish. Basta. Enough. Genug. Достаточно.

The work-at-home web sniper glanced at the clock on the wall over her cot as she snapped off her latex gloves. Jakob would no doubt be at the bar already – stupid, eager fool – waiting for her, and she still had to disinfect under her fingernails (just to make sure) and wipe down the keyboard. Then, and only then, could she dress for the day. But she needed to hurry up. An ice-cold beer was calling her name, and Jakob was always so peevish if she were more than a few minutes late. He was just *so* paranoid. Being a good half hour's walk, every wasted moment represented unwanted delay. She doused the cotton ball in alcohol and began to scrub. Quickly, fiercely.

Efecttus

Draftmite *A nano-sized gremlin that travels the world wide web and resides in personal computing devices, seeking out saved documents in order to insert errors and writing glitches into them. Draftmites are why previously error-free documents will suddenly appear to contain new mistakes.*
Published at Urban Dictionary November 27, 2021, by ka the wordsmythe

CONSUMMATION

I tried to tell her
In so many words, yes.

But our actions spoke louder. At first, it was simply, erotically, the whispered catches of breath as discoveries were made and treasures were uncovered, wetly explored, warmly unearthed. Then, it was the cries of seductive conquest, audible buildup, the capture in the moment, the avalanche breakdowns, and after that, the liquid, near-catatonic states as silent requiems of a restfully satiated aftermath played over us, our shared space. At first, the crescendo was ecstasy amidst passion; but all too soon, upon the very tails of her echoed, pleasured exhalations – like a comet, which hits and destroys those who moments before stood in awe of its beauty – came the sounds of a dark differentness, of surprise – noises and words at first tinged with fear, then grown into phrases reactively composed, missives uttered with descriptors of searing pain, torrential hurt, and finally panic, when the shocking realization that one is staring straight into the face of death itself, dawns.

And then, there follow the stretches of utter nothingness, marked only by the metronome of her sweet blood as it drips, drips, drips, hits the floor, pools, spreads…

I tried to tell her, but the midnight hours I stole with her were too sweet to spoil with facts. We were instantaneous junkies to the addictive elixir in which we swam, our secret, consensual sessions playing out upon an island demarcated by the four posts of her bed. Down cushioned, satin swathed and bound, we were but a bonded pair of impudent cherubs, tumbling upon the sheets, the blankets, our comforter of clouds. We fumbled about like wild creatures, so entangled did we become, so frantic were we as to where next to touch, to dig, to steal, and partake of each other.

Exquisitely exhausted would she be from our lovemaking, for the myriad, tiny deaths she weathered, from her core on out, and over the entirety of her alabaster sheathing, within every limb and across the freshly stretched expanses of her quickened mind. And how beautiful a specimen was she in her deliria, sprawled before me like an elegantly draped bit of dampened lace. She once said, she began to see a place in her head whilst traveling in the wake of my manipulations, which she came to recognize, wanted to believe with all her heart, was heaven. That she now knew what it looked like. And I alone was its architect.

All too soon, however, her tearful entreaties to my own end, against my constant and steadfast resistance, to permit myself to become the recipient of her pleasuring, broke me down, word by word, brickle by brickle. With every subsequent night of our togetherness, my resolve continued to thin. I would ask her, why could *this*, what we shared as it was, not have been enough? I believe she fancied sexual reciprocation a form of power, some next step, a requisite cementing of what I thought we already shared. Small cracks of my restraint began to show, despite my preternatural constitution. I began to dare fancy her for *my* means, my purposes; but that hunger, once triggered, was never one to be compromised. She did not understand, could not, had no ability to comprehend what the outcome would mean for her – she in her mortal capacity could not anticipate the outcome. And I could not bring myself to be completely honest with her, so addicted was I to her.

Yes, even we have our weaknesses.

She had no idea. How could I have dared expose her to what really was at play, the true purpose for which I had been sent? On the other hand, why would I have? Call me the selfish thief, a most wicked demon child in a candy shop, but I took, and I took, and I took from her; yes, to her downfall, her ultimate detriment. But there was an Eden that resided within her that deserved to thrive for as long as our seasons permitted. Hers was an altar in a walled garden I alone traversed, at which I worshipped as her ravenous pilgrim, supine as a saint, face buried in her bounty. And oh yes, she let me. I played my nubile phoenix like a marionette erotique, the blossoming plaything of a god, and I held her lovingly as she danced for herself, for me. And each time – she learned so quickly – so soon would she burn, and then crash gently beside me onto the bed, to exquisite agonies so sweetly tuned and acute, it was all I could do to shield our walls against the faceless others who dwelled above, below and to the side of us in their similarly cubicled warrens.

And when she'd fall, only to rise again even in spite of herself, despite her exhaustion of the act, the sleep-imbued days and mundane daylight rituals – you know, all those other activities with which she still had to contend with as a member of society: her job, other humans, life as she had known it for almost thirty years – were cast duller, less defined, and increasingly irrelevant in contrast to the beauteous thing we shared in our sequestered hours together. When the curtains fell, trailing folds of all the dream-ridden, sleeping souls around us in the city where she lived, it felt as if we alone were the only sentient ones in the universe. The others – irrelevant and worthless. We braided our bodies in the patterns our spirits already forged – fingertips to hands, hands to limbs, memories to minds, kisses that sought to swallow the other whole, tongues relishing, eyes feasting, as if we each served the other, as the richest of confections, the briniest of beasts, the richest of wines. Milk, yes, that too, as primal as it implies, laced so liberally with honey as to become a viscous broth to coat every surface, leave everything sticky, and oh, so wonderfully sweet. Lovers' paths taken in this fashion are more than merely traveled; they are *consumed*.

After forty days of nights, or something of that earthly span, her begging became incessant, her rationale proving as dauntless as she was insistent. How I had played her, pleasured her, transformed her from the inside out was no longer enough for my foolish darling.

Why could it not have been enough? Why not could I have let this one remain as she was – yes, my first course; yes, my dessert, but alive? My naivety – for I had been at this but a few, short centuries – spoke volumes, for I imagined in this one I could have some longevity in a companion, a playmate possessing of a decidedly pleasing human nature. Nightly visits to her bed, the intimacy of our sexes repeatedly joined, spirits like our bodies intermingled, could have sustained me for my mortal-mimicking time on her planet. Let there be no doubt, there were plentiful others – I lost count – who threw themselves at me like crumpled tissue. Those, I could do with – and did – as was required of me, with little – no, none at all – thought as to the inconsequential collateral of their annihilated corporeal forms. Why, oh why, did she, as all these humans are so wont to do, seek to take things farther with me, "all the way," as she would put it, to try and keep me equally in her hold as she was in mine?

Why this battle of beholdeness?

How could she have known the egregiousness of her error, when so programmed to ask, ask, ask for more, only to get, get, get it all, as her feminine kindred had been insisting on for some time, this unequivocal *equality*, as they called it, this militant, blanket insistence, their one-for-one give-and-get ideations that had come to dominate in absolutely *everything* in their world? There was no way I could tell her exactly how things played out with me when my absolute all was invited in, now how it would play out for her, which was precisely why I did not want from her what she in her sweet ignorance only *thought* she wanted from me. It was, in fact, because I wanted more – and different – from her, *with* her, that I held back, refused to consummate the scrumptiously laid out but incomplete nook in which we happily dwelled. Indeed, I was loathe to let her in on the rest of my story. I could not dare enlighten her as to how this all might play out, why I was here in the first place, on this pithy, flyby planet of hers.

I was just doing my job.

What a happy coincidence, my hyper-driven forefathers had paved with their antics all the broad-spectrum superhighways for me and my kind to traverse. The moderately intellectualized sphere upon which my beloved and her kind trod was but a playground for experimentation and conquest. The languages of fallen seraphs, satanic agents, of gods and goddesses who had descended – or ascended – before me, with their clandestine, evocative, and serpentine methods, served me only too well in my mission. Mankind was obsessed with all of them, with me, with us. I as invader was welcomed with open if ignorant arms. It was and remains an age-old, subversive affair with the supernatural that keeps all these paths interconnected, an ironic symbiosis of noble desires, oft bent, inverted, perverted by accident *and* intent. And those who came before me – their legacy, their prowess? It all served as primer and playbook from which I too would take my cues, but only so long as the interactions remained dispassionate, denied. "Professional," as her ilk was inclined to say. To me, pleasuring companionship – the only language in which I knew to speak with these delectably imperfect vertebrates – was but my means to an end, to an ultimate and always final act, which would then accomplish that for which I had been created, for which I had been sent. How quickly I accrued my willing and satiated, unwitting hosts for my offspring! It was, ultimately, only ever about my spawn, with me as their progenitor, as had been commanded and planned for over the millennia by those who stood in power over me and my kind.

The roster of known deities? It is but fractional to this culture. These humans, they know not much of me, nothing of my brothers and sisters – and there are legions of us – similarly empowered with the tools of enchantment and transformation just as I wield them, which allow us to craft ourselves into precisely what our intended victims *want* – or *think* they want:

It took but a flash as I beheld her, curled up like a child, nested into her blankets and that tattered, old robe of hers, to read her deepest mind and conjure up within myself the being she would need to see so that when, once lured from her somnambulance, her first flash of mystical recognition would sidestep any onset of a fear reaction, and then instantaneously bring her to an open-armed, welcoming embrace, into which I could slide, and stay. From that point on, it was an easy matter to hold her in thrall, keeping her suspended by my will, with images of wings as her sensibilities required – wings that could hover over the both of us like a feathered canopy, wings that could mimic ancient and erotic dreams come to heated and visceral life, wings we could grab hold of and together spiral through the cloudbanks, a fantastical hyper-existence as real as any dream could ever be, but infinitely better.

So, on that night, when she opened her eyes and called me by name – a name chosen by her unconscious self – and when I recognized that name to be mine and mine alone, I knew I had found a good – very nearly sublime – specimen; amidst this hodgepodge of imperfection, one rather miraculously close to its antithesis. And she had found her God.

Then, the pleasure commenced, and continued, and held us both, taking even me surprise by the delights…

But my resolve, to spare her alone, keep at least this one with me until the end of her natural days, and to impregnate the others, about whom I cared not one iota, was too soon tested by the feisty resolve this spirited and precocious human of mine possessed. To reciprocate my acts of lovemaking became too powerful a drive within her. She set about to break me down. I wept in her arms when I realized my resistance would be futile. I understood, she would soon, too soon, have me too.

Completely.

And so, on that final night with her as she was, had been, and would forever remain in my mind and in my soul, we commenced on our passion play.

I can still remember her wristwatch, a minuscule play clock, ticking on the bed stand. The moon framed in the window. The monochrome of her room, the bedclothes shimmering pale gray; and our bodies, moistened by a divine perspiration, luminescent, brighter by the minute, as our synchronies merged and swelled, lifted us higher, tighter, more wholly one than had been permitted up to that point. I could feel my hearts breaking, my mourning beginning over the gut-rending inevitable.

And then I entered her.

Gods help me, I entered her, and she cried out my name, the one she had gifted me with and which, by the baptisms of her body, christened me with. After all these nights, after all that time, what had been forever singularly unrequited and incomplete, took me over as I took my chosen one at *her* will, against *my* will, at her fevered and possessive, obsessed insistence. And then I felt *it* begin to happen, and I began to hear the changes in her voice:

At first, it was our now familiar ritual, oft-shared and communal ecstasy; but all too soon, upon the very trailing echoes of her pleasured exhalations – like a comet, which hits and destroys like a missile those who moments before stood in awe of its beauty – came the sounds of differentness, of surprise. Her noises and words became tinged with fear, grew to phrases and fragmented sentences, reactively composed – they were missives uttered with descriptors of wracking pain, torrential hurt, and then, finally, panic, when the shock of realization, that she was staring intimately into the face of death itself, dawned upon her.

As I grew inside her and felt that heated rush, when the barbs ejected and hooked themselves into her tender innards, as I stretched further up inside her and she could feel me piercing her, beyond her belly and then up, up, up and onward, through her abdominal wall and into her chest and then on past her clavicles, the passion we had known and this new descent into pain merged and became one, searingly, scorchingly blinding her with its intensity, like a sun exploding inside of her as her soul was ripped from its frail housing.

And then, when she cried her last and expired in one long and liquid, outbound breath, that final hush trailed itself like a totem cord around my neck – so very soft, so organic. Her whispered good-bye soaked through my skin as *I* exploded, filled to the brim the ripe cavity that had been her all. Within the freshly hollowed trenches that once held my beloved's soul, my seed found fatal, immortal purchase.

So, there she lays.

Humans would romanticize things and insist upon calling her my true love. I in my loss gaze upon whom was as close to a so-called True Love as any human could ever be to one such as I. She, who in her voluptuous, instinctive insistence put herself at my impossible mercy, became victim to her mandate, my penultimate directive. Now, she is merely yet another one of my brood, one of the innumerable bio-carriers I leave in my virulent wake.

The new life within her keeps its evermore-stilled incubator functional, pliant, even warm to the touch.

And now, I can see the tell-tale pulsations beginning – from within the slender column of her neck, from beneath her sunken cheeks, and on what is for the moment the still-smooth plain of her forehead. It's the prodding, the pushing, the testing, the splintering. It is preparing. The signs inform me, the birth is imminent.

Soon, another daughter will burst forth from her mother's skull, fully formed and armed for battle. Her scales, at first diminutive tongues of damp velvet, will be as sharp as razor blades once her skin has dried and hardened. She will be small, but with the sustenance of the human males she will instinctively know to hunt, she will grow, fast and furiously so.

I think I will gather up a shard of this mother's birthing portal before I take leave, to keep as talisman a reminder of my transgression, which was to play too long with a psyche, deluding us both into believing there was any chance of a mortal's happily ever after, when, in the end, with this one too, I was only doing my job.

Efectus

KIDS THESE DAYS   i, ii, iii

"…they have bad manners, contempt for authority; they show disrespect for elders and love chatter in place of exercise. Children are now tyrants, not the servants of their households."

Socrates 470 – 399 BC

i LIL BEBEE

Yes. She was sure of it. Although it was only her footprints in the snow, fast fading as the sparkling shroud grew thicker by the moment, there was another set of footsteps not terribly far behind them, just beyond the paltry reach of the flickering streetlamp, discernable by the muffled echoes that followed them, their cadence matched almost too perfectly to hers, down to even the small stumble she had just made.

Almost but not quite. What was it that broke the hush of the wintery nightscape, of a solitary someone making their way down a street at midnight, congruent with the lone shadow that stretched slim and long in front of her? Somewhat misshapen was the shadow she cast, due to the infant cocooned within the oversized coat the young woman had wrapped around herself, to better shield them both against the frigid night air, the swirling snow, all the myriad unknowns lurking just beyond the protective embrace of old, woolen garment.

No, it was not only the sound of her two feet bouncing off the cobblestones and plaster walls. Not quite. But neither was it quite simply the hollow taps of another, random human somewhere behind them, closing in on them. There was something too feral in the lightness of the steps, too predatory, too sure.

The young woman stole another look behind her, peering just past the shield of her hood. She glanced to either side of the intersection as she crossed it. The air was so cold, her crystalized breath swirled in front of her face, obscuring her view. Was it her subconscious that had registered some movement? Was there a spare swath of shadow she had more sensed than seen, far too quickly absorbed into the dark recesses just beyond her periphery?

There! There it was, again! Someone, or rather something, *was* following them. The young woman's instincts churned at her gut; a stiff cocktail of both fight and flight coursed through her veins, urging her on, a new mother's evolutionary defense switched to high on behalf of the guileless dependent hidden in her coat, snugly swathed in the frayed webbing of her shawl. The mother held the infant tight to her belly. Perhaps the baby was asleep; perhaps it had been lulled into a wakeful stillness – either way, the little one had become attuned to the rhythm of its mother's steps, perhaps even sensing some of the trepidation felt by her, and was keeping completely quiet, which evoked a wee ripple of gratitude in its mother.

Only a few minutes more and they would be home. Home and warm and safe, at least somewhat warmer, and safer, than they were in that moment, outside in the wrong part of the city at an hour no one should have been about, with winter's bitter cold tentacles grabbing at them, trying to ensnare the nightbird and her nestling in its frigid embrace. Home, safe, and warm, no matter how primitive the third-floor hovel was, which the woman had recently rented for the two of them. The mother took off again.

Just one more left turn, then a right, then through the alley and up the old stone stairs; and then, with a hard turn of the iron key, she and Lil Bebee would be securely guarded against any stalker, against any predatory shift managers or embittered co-workers, against any other member of a callous humanity that populated the vast and ancient city. The promise of home sweet home was to the young woman as simple as a cup of tea, a candle lit, and the creaky bed in the alcove that served them both. Home sweet home was the sturdy door with its double lock. Home sweet home was also the bolt she had fashioned from an old, broken-down ladder. Home sweet home was as good a place on this indifferent earth as it needed to be, and that was good enough for her.

Lil Bebee stirred, roused by the abrupt change in the mother's gait. The baby cried out with a feeble voice too recently discovered, unwittingly breaking their stealthy silence. The mother jostled her little one to shush it, as if the infant should have been able to understand the dicey situation. The phantom footfalls, unmistakable this time, also stopped, but then they resumed alongside her quickened stride, now echoing more clearly, separately, against cracked walls which rose from ancient foundations to close them in the farther she went. The passage was a stark and leafless forest, for the streets narrowed in this part of town, leaving the facades to lean in, nearly touch at their rooflines. It made for an echo chamber in which the young mother was now certain, they were not alone.

She hoped to trick whomever, whatever, into a moment of off-kiltered unmasking, but, once again, just as soon as the mother stopped, so did the second set of feet come to an instantaneous halt. Only the telltale, split-second echo, sounding even closer this time, hinted at what one could only construe as a pursuit. Someone or something was coming after her, after them both – although it would not have been obvious to anyone, there was a second human hidden in the folds of the coat.

A tight corridor between two buildings, hidden behind a tall and rickety fence, presented a possible escape. Perhaps, the mother thought, she could lose the stalker in that stretch, for the walkway was familiar to her, while wholly unlit and cast full in darkness. She knew of a deep-set vestibule situated about a third of the way through. They could duck into its recesses, wait, and let whomever or whatever it was pass by them on the main road. Their pursuer would likely miss the turn off, so close were the decrepit structures pressed against each other, so uninviting was the crevice opening as to appear quite invisible to any outsider.

But no. No sooner had she pressed herself through the slats and into the corner of hidden entryway, as did the as-yet unseen follower make itself known to both her and her child, in the most violent and egregious way.

The mother wanted to scream, but who, or what, had followed them into the vestibule struck out at her with such a blow, it broke her hold on the child and sent her reeling. Lil Bebee flew towards the ground like a dropped doll, but the predator caught the baby midair with a lightning swift reflex. The mother, seeing stars, collapsed, overwhelmed by the attack and her own, crippling fear. She fell hard onto the floor of the threshold, hitting her head on an iron bootjack. The baby did manage to cry out, but its cries were quickly muffled by the sweeping folds of the abductor's velvet cloak, which were flung about the infant's body and over its face.

The mother watched, her consciousness fading, paralyzed into utter inaction as the attacker tossed the shawl that had swaddled the baby to the ground, momentarily exposing the infant's porcelain skin to the feeble glow of the encroaching moon, which had just breached the snow-silhouetted rooftops. The child shone like a luminous *rebulto*, though a rather a spindly one, as it was held aloft by its captor, whose arms were equally as pale, similarly aglow. The child was lifted to the sky with a ceremonious reverence, as if in offering to dormant powers that would hold nothing of comfort, nor safety, nor the warmth of any kind of home sweet home.

The mother watched, her legs useless slogged bags, as the fur-trimmed snood of their pursuer fell back to expose its face. She saw it was a woman, neither much older, nor taller, than she. The woman's head was piled high with tight, ringleted curls that fell upon a face with a complexion so translucent, her forehead and cheeks were visibly threaded with a fretwork of blue capillaries. Although her cheeks were somewhat hollowed, her pout was seductively curved, appearing nearly black in the dim light, and outlined, as if painted for a theater stage, or a brothel. But the pursuant's countenance, despite the fundamental beauty of its features, presented only a hideous indifference and mechanical emotionlessness.

The mother watched as this other woman gathered her baby in to her embrace. She saw the abductor glance down at her, not as an acknowledgement between peers, but rather in a silent command, demanding she remain as she was, where she was, pathetically helpless and transfixed beyond any capability, to meekly behold the scene as it was unfolding immediately above her. The beastly predator nodded with approval.

The mother foolishly thought the huntress was about to smile at her, but no, this was merely a baring of the canines. Her teeth, polished and honed over the centuries, flashed in response to the moon's furtive glimmer. The captor turned her gaze to the baby. Wriggling, it had just begun to fuss; the baby was cold and hungry. She tilted the infant just so, allowing its silken haired head to fall slack to one side, to expose a field of lustrous skin. Into this, she dove full face, punching down, mouth open wide, to take in the entirety of this fresh, milk-fed human's exposed neck.

She bit. Quick and deep.

The vampire tapped the child like a parched soldier might empty his pliant wineskin, with a force that all but drained the child, which fell unconscious in her arms in a matter of seconds. The monstress slurped and sucked, crudely feeding, no iota of panache in her consumption, for blood this new was that intoxicating. Unsullied, the baby's blood was sweeter than eggnog, headier than a rum punch. The vampire grew positively dizzy within her cloud of prurient guzzling.

The child, with every minute the beast was latched onto it, became increasingly translucent, an alabaster doll jointed so loosely, it looked ready to fall apart, the more she partook of it. Soon, the baby was as pliant as a fresh-turned batch of dough, its tiny arms practically a-drip from their shoulders, its deflated torso as if half melted, its dimpled legs now a tad shriveled, dangling bonelessly, ready to disconnect and drop to the ground like the wet snowflakes that spattered as they struck the exposed pavers of the hidden passageway.

"Aaaaaaah!" the monster sighed, satiated, preening with a smug and triumphant satisfaction.

Hers was a long and loud exhalation; it wafted upwards like a filament of dirty chimney smoke into the emptiness of a midwinter's night that did not care a whit about what had just happened, to the perverse horror of the mother who did, who, just before she fell unconscious, managed to rise to her knees just in time to reach out and catch her child as it fell through the air once more, this time as it was dropped by the drunken vampire, who discarded her quarry as if it were but a used, wet handkerchief.

Mother and child crumpled into each other, rendering of themselves a single, woeful heap of deflated humanity.

The beast leapt from the step of the threshold, and in a dervish of black velvet swirling both this way and that, was instantly gone, leaving her victims to the harsh elements of the night, two unwilling and defiled supplicants, face-planted on the frozen stoop, there at Hade's portal, each one of them in their own way confronting some version of an imminent demise.

The mother and child slept, if one could call their respective conditions even that, through the next day and into the following evening. Deep in the recesses of the vestibule in the alley, no sunlight broached their slumbrous netherworld; their unconsciousness played out unbroken. No, they were not completely unseen, but no compassionate human eye that fell upon them was given pause by their dejected display. No subsequent hand was there either, to reach out, whether with dastardly, thieving intent or some desire to help, but neither was there any marauding demon about to even consider tasting of their dregs – they were that wretched and undesirable a pair.

It was near midnight when the mother was finally stirred to a begrudging wakefulness by way of a singular, throbbing pain that struck hard against her sleep. Fragments of her dream had hinted of things lovely…of a garden, the colors of Springtime…but a repetitive surge of heat cut splicingly into the images and forced her eyes open. What had a moment ago been a tendrilled morning glory, curling sensuously up her arm, ready to blossom, became in the next instant a barbed wire bracelet, a searing jolt of pain hideously symbolized, that brought her back to reality. The young woman's heart leapt with a sickening recognition of location as the memories came back to her. Waking fully into the present, she remembered everything: the attack, and her baby, drained, flying through the air into her arms, then the two of them…

And now, there it was, her Lil Bebee, suckling painfully at her wrist.

†††

Vampire babies are, as anyone would imagine, a highly problematic, *stunted* lot.

Lil Bebee, on that very morning after its blood harvesting by the predatory vampire, had by the time its poor mother awakened from her dream, already sprouted the tiniest set of canines, although none of its other milk teeth had yet to emerge – and never would. So small and slender were those two tapering tines, they had the veracity of suture needles. Never more than halfway exposed from the pink beds of its soft gums, Bebee's fangs were so sharp, their slightest touch could sever whichever surface they met with. It was like taking razor blade tips to paper.

Being that Lil Bebee remained infantile of mind, a good two decades passed before the little one was even able to learn how to control its own interactions with its rosebud vampire mouth. Endlessly, did the mother have to daub and clean that bloody, chubby face, wiping away the blood that made its way down the baby's gumdrop chin, which wasn't all that much, being that Lil Bebee eagerly tried to lap up every warm droplet which swelled from its punctured lower lip and gums. Mother worried for years, that her prematurely turned offspring would develop some sort of auto-addiction to piercing its own lips, gums, or tongue, in order to drink its own blood. She even resorted to stuffing the baby's mouth with scraps of fabric to protect it from its own, incessant blood sucking. Lil Bebee's smacking and pleasured gurgling over its self-consumption turned even the stomach of its stoic parent, who like her child had been consigned to subsisting as a low-tier member of the undead. For the mother, as round-the-clock nursemaid and servant to an utterly helpless vampirette, the future lay ominously infinite.

Being that Lil Bebee was still in growth mode at a genetic level when it was transformed, there were, as a matter of fact, small and slow emerging, incremental developments as the decades passed. It's just that the baby's progress was, per vampiric timeline pacing, eons slower than a snail's pace. Mother read on the topic, learned as she could, especially once technology and the information highway were created and made available to all, to her as well, affording her the opportunity to browse the Web and read random, deeply buried articles on vampire care at home, during her long nights with her child. Bebee's mother took what nuggets she could, as she sat at the kitchen table night after night, reading from the laptops she would steal and wiping her child's red-streaked mouth as she poured over the articles, always jostling the baby, humoring it, trying to distract it, even reading out loud to both the baby and herself as she tried to better understand what kind of ghastly hybrid this petite monster of hers was.

Vampire babies are also, as anyone would imagine, a highly problematic, *hungry* lot.

As the years marched sluggishly forward, the two soldiered on. The tedious dynamic between the eternally sleep-deprived new mother and her preternaturally insistent infant child remained as unrelenting as it was taxing. Lil Bebee, who would forever be the plump infant in arms it had been on the night it was taken and turned, was, in effect, an uninhibited, blood-lusting humanoid leech. By contrast, Lil Bebee's mother, a gentle soul who had endured such a difficult and short life, was a particularly reluctant, low appetite vampire, forever burdened by what she understood to be her primary role, that of a 24/7 caregiver strapped to an ever more violently inclined, mini barbarian.

Bebee's mother had taken almost instantly to rodents for sustenance for both herself and her child. She was simply not of the personality makeup to embrace the taking of human life to nourish the two of them; moreover, she was loathe to turn any human in the process, not wishing this postmortem condition upon anyone. The mother rationalized, she could instead perform a civic service of sorts with their consumption, by helping to diminish, even if by an insignificant percentage, the pesky rat population of the city, by which its poorest citizens, transient residents and curbside stragglers had always suffered.

Bebee was, like all robust babies, forever famished, always crying for more food. More to drink, more to chew on, more to stimulate its undeveloped senses. Being a vampire, naturally, all its needs were centered on blood. It did make for dripping and fetid diapers, which the mother took to burning in a small trash can in the middle of the night. Her makeshift incinerator, she kept hidden in a back corner of the rooftop terrace of their apartment building, a nook easily accessed by way of the bedroom window. It was but a couple stories' scurry up an easily scaled brick wall.

Upon waking, Mother would generally set about to capture the nightly repasts once she had secured Lil Bebee into its chair. The baby was strapped into its seat by way of belts and bindings that over time its mother was forced to add to, being that the little whippersnapper grew more clever and curious with the decades, and risk of escape – along with its calamitous results – grew in tandem alongside the other advancements. Lil Bebee would shoot venomous daggers at its mother as she buckled the straps and tied the knots to contain her precocious offspring. The child would even spit like a mad cat and spray bloody spittle onto its mother's face as she worked to secure her little one, which, although she had been tempted more than once to slap that cherubic countenance, with its black-lashed eyes and piquant, little sneer, she never once employed corporeal punishment. Lil Bebee's mother thought – mistakenly – that patience and kindness would at some point imprint upon her offspring, possibly make for a somewhat better-behaved vampire baby – perhaps, maybe – at some point down their endlessly long, godforsaken road.

Vampire needs for nourishment being disproportionate to their size, the mother was always quickly satisfied; Lil Bebee, on the other hand, for all its diminutive state, required at least the same amount as its mother, usually more, and so, blood-soaked rags to suck on in between "meals," the mother would provide, as much for entertainment as to keep her child from biting its own lips and attempting to consume its own tongue. The mother, once her growling child was securely corralled, would hurry off to the most decrepit parts of the city as soon as day's end had pulled its dark curtain over the city, to catch the required number of critters it would take to get them through yet another one of their interminable nights together.

Thanks in no small measure to the indifferent community of strangers that comprised the carousel of nomads who moved in and out of the building where they lived, the youngish mother and her chronically colicky baby who resided, never seen but sometimes heard, in the corner apartment on the third floor, remained largely unnoticed, and certainly unknown. To their benefit, the general apathetic condition of all who passed through the corridors and stairwells of the apartment building left the two of them to their own, preternatural devices, which was a good thing.

Back to the rats.

These, the mother would bring home from her nightly excursions; at first, in her covered basket, in later years, stashed in her cooler. The warm-blooded vermin she would carry home, and once there, neatly pierce at the neck as was customary, and consume in front of the child as it watched, always hoping Lil Bebee might learn something from observing her. Mother never quit hoping, her offspring might learn one day to fend for itself, and in some remotely civilized fashion (Lil Bebee ate like a wild animal; it was always a bloody mess in the kitchen). Folly, the young mother would chide herself, to think her child might someday "grow up" and feed on its own, but she never gave up. A vampire's hope was possessed of a half-life that, like vampires in general, died very slowly.

Oh, how Lil Bebee loved to watch its mother execute her kill bites! Raptly intent, hungrily engaged, the child's flush, puckered mouth would imitate its mother's, its eyes wide, its tiny fists spontaneously opening and closing. It was these moments, when the love the mother had felt in life almost sparked against the mass in her chest that had once been her heart. Amidst the bleak monotony of their waking hours, these were the times that came closest to what she still vaguely recalled as embodying something akin to – what was it she used to call it? – home sweet home.

Once she had fed, it fell to the mother to feed Lil Bebee. Immediately. After several years of trial and error, the mother had figured out the best way – which is to say the infant's preferred way – to feed her child. This, she accomplished by twisting the heads off the rodents she would have brought home, and then immediately plunging their warm stumps into Lil Bebee's lip-smacking maw, whereupon it would latch onto the rodent with the veracity of a starving viper. If the mother were not right there, to hold firmly onto the rodent "bottle," the vampirette would verily ingest the whole animal – bones, fur, ears, tail and all. Once, when she was not paying attention – distracted by a book she had found, which she mistakenly thought she could read whilst her baby was feeding – Lil Bebee did indeed manage to swallow down the better part of an entire rat. The projectile vomit – bloody body parts – that had stuck to every surface of the small kitchen, was lesson enough for her; one and done. The rat bottle feeding sessions needed to be as closely monitored as did every single, last, ever-loving thing she did with that child.

There came a day, or rather a night, when most unfortunately, the weary, lonely, and eternally overworked mother succumbed to her weaknesses. For, among the night's catch, she had overlooked one particularly fat and fiendish rodent, which was quite mad with disease. Its frothing muzzle, the mother never even noticed; but what was left to blame her with, considering the levels of strife with which she contended, night after dull and dreary and lonesome night, especially when her hunting could only ever be done inside the murky pitch of nocturnal, anonymous cover?

No, the pestilence went undiscovered until it was too late.

When dealing with a rapacious infant vampire, whose bloodlust remains this raw and unfiltered, the rendering of the heads from hapless rats must happen with lightning speed. And, as anyone knows, when things are done in a rush, important details can be overlooked.

At first, Lil Bebee would squeal with delight when the rats squealed their last. But, as the years passed, the infant, no longer entertained, only bored and ravenously hungry, screeched with angry impatience. The frantic mother developed out of dire need the skill to separate the critters from their snapping heads so quickly, *they* no longer had the chance to squawk or scream. It was then all she could do, to ram the spurting neck into the fanged but otherwise toothless little mouth of her snarling dependent, to still the baby's rage and appease its hunger as quickly as possible.

Yes, under those circumstances, even such obvious signs of disease or infection can be missed.

One particularly dull and drawn-out winter's evening, Bebee's howls were cringe-worthily lingering and especially loud, even higher pitched than usual.

To that end, a particularly wild and robust rat lurched about in the cooler. This squealer promised to be a hearty, tummy-warming vessel for Lil Bebee. That night, the mother's hunt had taken her deep under the streets, as it now often did, sanitation having developed parallel with all other city services. Progress was forcing the vermin populations further underground and closer to the harbour, where the dubiously fittest amongst them yet flourished, where she now, too, was forced to creep about to stalk her quarry, the cooler strapped to her back, her hands sheathed in thick, rubber gloves stolen from the furnace rooms of the apartment buildings in the area.

Lil Bebee was in a horrific state when Mother climbed back in through the kitchen window, snowflakes drifting in with her that swirled about the small room as she clambered over the sill. She cringed at the bellowing of her ward, the hatred she could hear in its tone. Dropping her shawl to the floor, hands shaking in desperate desire to expedite the appeasement of her little monstrum, she twisted the frenzied animal's head off with a single, deft move, and chucking the red-eyed, whiskered noggin into the bin with the bloody diapers, stuffed the stump of the critter's neck into her offspring's gaping mawlette as quickly as she possibly could.

The silence that followed, however fleeting, was as blessed a gift to the mother as had it been boxed, wrapped, and left for her under a Christmas tree in some other, far sweeter and sunlit world. Interminable winter weeks, when night outweighed the all-to-brief days, made for daily duets of torturous, languishing companionship. The painful parental futility, for Lil Bebee was never completely happy, never quite content, nevermore the sweet and complacent baby it had once upon a time been, was only that much more keenly felt when the nighttime stretches slogged endlessly on, when the beastly dark consumed the summer's softer, kinder, sunlit hours. The fleeting nature of summer nights were but a sojourn to the mother, for that was when longer hours of peace-filled sleep dominated their un-days. Once summer passed, ever longer spells of wakefulness became their *rigor du jour*. And this far north, it was pitch black by four in the afternoon by the time November had spelled her last. Bebee, re-animated and desperately starving the moment the sun would set, was only increasingly a miserable tiny tot, thereby granting its mother only that much more of the never-ending drudgery under which she suffered, with that infernal being her only companion.

Christmas. A funny notion, she thought.

As soon as Lil Bebee had depleted the beast to a limp sack of coarse fur, the mother set about to indulge herself with a second excursion. She desperately needed new clothes and wanted to dig about in the dumpsters behind the thrift store. This errand would not, could not, take long. Moreover, a second trip could only be attempted if Bebee appeared satiated enough to last her a safe while, being that any outings unrelated to food gathering had to be backseated out of fundamental necessity. A rare, second trip into the sleeping city was a treat for the young woman, for everything could only ever be about the child.

Little did she know, what she would find upon returning home that second time, what she would find climbing the walls…

†††

Mother, one arm draped with a few, newish, decently warm garments, entered the kitchen through the window as she usually did, only to find the baby's seat empty, the straps snapped, and buckles broken to pieces. With a deep sense of trepidation, she entered the sitting room window to behold her heretofore immobile infant child inexplicably freed from its seat and clambering up a quilted wall hanging. Its fingernails, curved talons grown long and sharp in the space of an hour, had made of Bebee something of a feral kitten. The child had transmogrified into something even less civilized than the primitive thing it had been when she had left, mere minutes ago. Its mother – nursemaid, kitchen wench, eternal babysitter – cried out, and she wept bitter tears, making a spotted, bloody mess of the perfectly lovely sweater and jackets she had just found. From what she could see, all vestigial remnants of doll-like cuteness had been erased from her child. Lil Bebee was now a hideous, humanoid varmint, and an unadulterated danger to them both.

Bloody bubbles, putrid with infection, frothed at the lips of the baby's red ribbon mouth. The child stunk of rot and decay. Any fledgling mortality in the child had been effectively killed off and replaced with a mindless and rabid lust. And what still existed in the withering realm of the infant's soft skull grew blacker and more hostile by the minute…

That was it.

The mother could no longer do this, this, mothering thing. Nor was *that* thing on the wall anymore her child. There was nothing left to parent, nothing remotely humane to nurture, nothing to foster into perpetuity. The plan she had hatched when despair had led her down cold and fatalistic paths to wit's end, would now be implemented and carried through to its fatal conclusion:

The mother knew, she had to kill her child.

Le Bebee had always been self-cancelling, she reasoned. Proof was the extent of her willingness to do the deed, and the deep hatred she held for the vampire who had taken her child, all those years ago.

The mother knew, that to take the "life" of her once beautiful baby would now be an act of benevolence. An act of profound love. After that, it would be an easy matter to take her own life, too.

She had only a few hours before sunrise. Tonight, unlike other nights, the two of them would not retreat to the windowless wardrobe in the bedroom to sleep. Tonight, unlike other nights, she would not find and kill another rat to appease the beastly appetite of her child. Tonight, she would not try to soothe Lil Bebee with the sound of her voice, try to humor it, or distract it. No, tonight she would strap the child back into its seat, re-tie the cords, find new buckles and belts, and she would drive a small stake through its little heart, and then take a second, larger stake and drive it through her own.

This sort of thing had been done, she had read, in ages past, and generally been referred to as an auto-execution. Records hidden in the recesses of the Dark Web were proof that a vampire's unearthly strength could be used to this end. Tonight, she would employ her full capabilities as her final gift to them both.

Lil Bebee fought tooth and nail – well, fang and claw – as its mother climbed the settee to extract it from the wall hanging and wrangle the ceiling light's chain from its grasp. Despite the mother's adeptness at handling wild vermin, and the fact that she had the good sense to don her rubber gloves in anticipation of a struggle, things were in no time a bloody mess. The child fought like a raccoon pulled from a compost bin. It clawed at its mother, hand and foot. It bit her where it could. Blood dripped all over the floor, on the sitting room furniture; it marked a path to the kitchen. It took the better part of an hour for the mother to wrangle the writhing, screeching thing that had once been her child into its feeding seat on the kitchen table.

The din Lil Bebee made must have had some supernatural reach; its cries were, after all, as a technical matter, those of a cornered, mythical monster. Its cries traveled beyond the ordinary streets of the mortal populations, past the ears of sleeping tenants, drunken landlords, wayward Trav'lers. Its cries must have served like a runic call to the one intended to hear them, heed them, and to have reacted to them by all illogical, logical conclusion; the one who had given birth, so to speak, to the little demon in the first, damn place…

†††

"None of this, my child," Mother said, choking on the words, "is your fault."

Dry sobs wracked the mother's thin form as she stood there, in front of her seated child, a mallet lifted high above her head, ready to strike. The pointed end of the stake she had placed upon the screeching infant's heaving, little chest…

Mother and implement were poised, ready to put an end to Lil Bebee…

No sooner did the young woman take a deep breath in preparation for the downswing, as did the kitchen window explode inwards. A waxen-white, blood-covered arm pushed past the shredded curtain and shards of glass, reaching in as far as it could to interrupt the unfolding scene, mother and child perched together upon a fatal and violent precipice. And that arm belonged to none other than the vampire predator who, almost a half century ago, had pursued these same two individuals into the snow-covered alley to make a meal of Lil Bebee's scrumptious lifeblood and freshly incarnated soul.

Fifty years gone by, and the young mother was still able to instantly recognize the vulture that had chased them down, to whom first Bebee and then she through her child had fallen victim. This was the demonic bitch who had terrorized them, infected them with her pestilence, turned their world upside down and inside out in the name of her own, selfish needs.

Before the mother could even register her own shock, to think past it in order to be able to complete her mission and put an end to the degenerate yowling in its seat and tearing at its belts and cords, than did their much older, blood-stealing nemesis once again grab the baby to reclaim it for herself. Bebee's restraints snapped apart as had they been crafted from crepe paper.

The interloper dared press the flailing gremlin to the trenches of her own, vacuous breast in a perverse gesture reminiscent of a maternal hug.

The young woman let out a piercing cry of fear-filled anguish, a futile call to no one in particular, her lament a less than a worthless squeak to the vampire predator, who had never forgotten the taste of this tiny one. Lil Bebee's stalker had, indeed, made it her quest – the darkest of games – to find her human morsel again, to taste once more of its succulence, no matter the state of its mortality. To the ancient vampiress, a freshly birthed vampire baby could still provide a satiating draught. But this time, she would drink it dry, leave no drop behind to transform the infant into something even worse than it already, most evidently, was.

Oh my, the intruder thought, this one was a devil of a howler.

The diseased child clung like a razor-fanged opossum to its captor, bothering only once to glance back into the abject face of its mother. No poignant last look, the baby merely bared its fleshy, pink gums to hiss at her, bloody spittle dribbling down its button chin, making of its cloth bib a soaking wet, red rag, which the tiny beastie promptly stuffed into its mouth, to give it a good chew.

With the skill of one even much more practiced in the art of ripping heads off – and larger ones at that – the old vampiress then took the mother's head into her hands and wrenched it with a twisting force that separated it from its neck as easily as had it been the screwcap of a cheap bottle of wine. It took but a single, sweeping maneuver to rip the head off and lob it to the far corner of the kitchen, where it rolled a couple feet before coming to a stop. The poor mother's face, frozen, aghast, was at least able to look back to where now only her body lay, collapsed upon the floor, to the spot by the table where, moments ago, she had been in a deadly face-off with her only child.

The horrid, blood-lusting vampire kidnapper had struck again, but this time without any residual gift of a perverse immortality. This time, there would be no survivors, neither mother, nor child.

In a flash, the old vampire and her sullen dumpling were gone, escaped into the swirling clouds of the wintery night. Little did she know, in her greed and haste, that the baby was now the carrier of a pernicious virus, which would infect her as well, and in due time spread and "kill off" the last of the more civilized vampires on the continent. Her second abduction of the infant proved to be the sunset of a very particular – could one say more genteel? – vampiric era. The virus to which Lil Bebee had so quickly succumbed would in the space of a few years infect the entire, remaining population of the walking, stalking undead, reducing them all to beastly brutes. With her too, haste made for a great and terrible waste.

…not the first time, nor the last, that the birth of a child would usher in the transformation of an entire civilization. This time, however, there would be no survivors.

In her rush, the thoughtless abductor had likewise neglected to finish what she had started in the kitchen, for there lay the mother, in two pieces, on opposite ends of the room. Her head watched helplessly as her body crawled aimlessly about, back and forth, zigging and zagging, crashing into cupboards, chairs, the table, even the walls, until its blindly groping hands at long last happened upon the larger of the two wooden stakes, and soon after that, the mallet. The mother's head could only pop its lips soundlessly together, like a dying carp, as she willed her body on with whatever psychic connectivity she could muster from across the room.

It was a protracted business, this final act of self-mutilation, and a slipshod one, given that her initial attempts at impaling herself without the benefit of any visual guidance was a gory hit n miss. The mother's head kept watch, sad and frustrated, but ever hopeful the rest of her could manage it. Several times, the unseeing arm landed blows upon random other parts of her body, her arm, her legs. A few times also, did the spike puncture some other area of the headless torso, leaving ragged-edged divots that quickly filled with the young woman's stagnant, inky blood, thick as corn syrup.

Finally, the arms were able to position themselves just so, the stake placed perpendicular to the sternum, with the mallet hovering high in the air, in a direct line above the blunt end of the stake. The mother's head experienced its first – and final – surge of relief when, at long last, the mallet struck sure and strong, and the stake broke through the skin, and in two more strikes cleared the bone.

The mother's head watched, rapt, as the spike blew into pieces what had been, even as a member of the undead, a well-meaning, if petrified, heart. She saw it hit home, and then as the stake plunged through her chest to clear her torso, where it splintered upon impact as it hit the floorboards, effectively skewering her to the kitchen floor.

As the young woman's sight went dark, there was a spark of realization, with something almost akin to happiness, as it occurred to her: *Never again will I ever, ever have to change another bloody diaper…*

So, there the mother lay, crucified to the domestic crypt she had shared – been sentenced to – with her only child. She lay there until the dawn broke, when the cleansing rays of the distant sun sifted in through the fractured window and past the shredded window coverings, and filled the room with a cold, bright light. The sun's rays set the kitchen aglow, vaporizing upon impact first the young woman's head, then her body. The sun's light evaporated all the blood too, so aside from the wreckage at the windows and general disarray in the next room, what was left behind was a cozy apartment home, furnished with an eclectic mix of vintage furniture – plus, one rather odd contraption set upon on the kitchen table, a device that looked as much a medieval implement of torture as it did an all-terrain infant car seat.

Efectus

ii MY GIGI

It was my fault, I know it, and I hate myself for it. I should have known better than to arm my daughter with the contents of that book. Why I ever thought a lock and key would suffice; well, that is testament to the myopia from which I always suffered as a non-gifted first-time parent. I saw the signs and knew what those signs meant; I was too familiar with the stories, the histories, too nonchalant by way of a lifelong familiarity with the condition. And still, I, her mother of all people, who should have known better, who knew what could become of her, opened the gates for my little one by letting her forage the library like a hungry critter searching for grubs, starved for knowledge she had no business being exposed to at such an early age.

I can practically picture her, climbing from shelf to shelf after I'd disappear into the parlor for my tea, the one luxury I afforded myself with regularity. I can envision her peering past the orderly rows of books to see what might have been hidden behind them by some ancestor of ours. I can imagine her eyes wide with curiosity when she unearthed that book, and I can just see her, cross-legged on the floor, perhaps curled up on the window seat, leafing through the pages, tracing the hand-written lines of verses with her tiny fingertips, her eyes, intuitively deciphering the words, the phrases, the incantations, as if able to learn by osmosis alone…

Indeed. I assumed, foolish mortal mother I was, that to harness the immediate world into which we were both placed would serve us equally well. Instead, all I managed to accomplish was refine my daughter's journey, carve for her a beeline path so slender and arrow-straight, it would lead Esther, who I called Tess, far too quickly into the embrace of powers with which she had been born, which she would not for years learn to wield with any inkling of wisdom. How was I to know? I had meant only well.

If Tess even attains what we generally think of as a "ripe old age," given the recklessness with which she has already plied her magic, it will be nothing short of a miracle. And miracles? In her world, those may well fall outside her realm, even at this point. I would reckon, the saints in heaven are already wringing their hands and professing lamentations in her name. Dearest Fathers and Sisters, cast me down instead, take me, please, I beg of you. Let me serve penance for my child so that she may yet see the light – whatever light there might yet remain for her – and not follow a path to an assured damnation. Help her, I beg of you, onto one marked with nobler deeds, so that her soul may have a chance when her time comes, be it on her own terms or that of all those pitchfork brandishing villagers who invariably come after such as she in the name of all things "good" …

✝✝✝

It all started rather immediately, before the final strikes of the great clock heralded the end of the second day after I had been delivered of my first-born, my Tess. The night she was born, a winter storm still rocked the household with as much fury as when it had hit the previous day. My labors had begun the day before, as if on cue when the winds had first shifted and then pitched themselves against the great walls of the house. My pains had intensified alongside the discordant chorus in the chimneys, the rattling of the shutters, the incessant tapping of overgrown branches upon the shingles. A heavy snow had begun to fall by noon, preventing even the good doctor himself from attending the birth, despite his being a stoic fellow from the North, and nonplussed by such weather. It was only I, my mother, and the few staff in residence left to listen to my laboring wails, the howling winds, and to the audacious thunder that echoed in the wake of the anomalous flashes of lightning when my baby girl cried out…

That next evening, my newborn daughter lay in my arms, swaddled and at peace, amidst a heavy calm newly descended upon the house, of a kind that could only be enjoyed in stark contrast to a storm so recently subsided. From within that silence, I could practically hear the shush of the snow as it continued to settle over us all, a blanketing as formidable as it was lovely. Frost coated the windows as if to draw close the curtains of the world, to contain us.

We lay there in that vast bed, alone, but not lonely. There was no one else in the room, no one other than the two of us on the entire floor. I was exhausted, but as content as I could be, given the circumstances of the past year. It was then, as the clock struck midnight, when having been roused from a half-sleep, I saw my daughter awaken, and smile. At me. That's when I knew, whether afloat in a dream or brought to attention in the stark light of a godless revelation, that my child was the next "blessed" Kress, as my family preferred to call the "gift." My blessed baby girl looked up at me and peered straight through my pupils and into my soul, her gaze wizened, her eyes so pale. Then, she spoke to me. Yes, words. It was with the tiniest of voices, wavering and untried, barely more discernable than a coo, that she spoke to me, and she said, "Oon, Mama, oon."

Soon, Mama, soon.

I immediately suspected my daughter was in possession of the kind of gift that had only ever existed in a handful of Kress women. And why call it a "gift"? It is more like a curse, a passport to hell. The gift, in varying degrees, skipped about randomly amongst the generations, striking never at more than two living family members at any given time. At the time of my daughter's birth, there was only one Kress woman thusly afflicted, a dear cousin of mine, who although even younger than I, had already consigned herself to a cottage deep in the woods, a full two day's journey by autocar outside of town. She had been that beleaguered by needful and desperate "friends" and neighbors, even random out-of-towners, who had learned of her capabilities and come calling, begging for her services. So, my cousin went into hiding from them all, for she was, ironically, a reluctant conjurer, faithful to her faith, to her God and his Son, to every last bit of dogmatic programming attached to Them both. She had been loath to embrace what she in essence have no choice but to accept, let alone use for her ends, which she did, but only when most direly necessary. I have always surmised, the storm which hit our town on the day of her leaving had, for the way it was so perfectly timed, and the way it washed out the bridge minutes after she and her small entourage had passed over it, been possibly of her doing...

There must have been room for one more on the day of Tess's birth. No one, thankfully, of the Kress women, perished when she came into the world, unlike my great-great-aunt, who inexplicably to the rest of an ignorant world, tragically predictable to those in mine, leapt – was made to leap – to her death from a window of our fourth-floor attic, on the very day my grandmother was born. For centuries, the births of daughters in my family had for good reason been harbingers of stifled and secretive fears, of pleadings into the ether on behalf of whomever may at any given time have been alive and blessed – cursed – with this so-called gift. Births as much as deaths both held for us all a special brand of dread.

But here she was, my robust baby girl, who had spoken to me on the first full day of her life, who had looked through me with wise, old eyes so pale as to be almost colorless. I knew, we would have to go forth in relative solitude. Likewise, I would never bear another child, for a subsequent daughter could also be possessed of the gift, which would then hold for either her sister or my dear cousin, so missed, an imminent demise. The elimination of surplus living witches in the family was insidiously random. If it meant the premature death of this beautiful child, dozing in my arms, on the vast bed with me in the tower room I had shared with her late father, then I would resign myself, like my cousin, to the secured environs of a forested home as well; namely, the vast old house in which we were already cocooned.

It would be my hope to protect Tess – perhaps protect the world from her – from any dark side proclivities, dangerous indulgences, from lust- or greed-ridden, vice-guided conjurings and metaphysical manipulations. I thought – and what an assumption that was – if I could build a righteous world for my daughter, I might have a chance at preventing Tess from the insidious and high-risk experimentation that too often walked hand in hand with any younger Kress woman who made her way through the stages of childhood and youth as reactionary, novice practitioner.

Again, I was the fool. My non-gifted, unextraordinary human condition had granted me with a simplistic foresight, that of a mother better suited for a similarly non-gifted, human offspring, not one preternaturally inclined.

Soon, Mama, soon.

It wasn't long before Tess's play took its inevitable turns from the ordinary and mundane. Such as baby dolls, daisy chains, and hoops went by the wayside, and her activities began to resemble more that of a childish dark side apprentice.

There were, for instance, the trained beetles she once placed upon the settee, purportedly for my entertainment (they put my hair on end); there were the parlor drapes Tess would repeatedly cause to breathe and rise and take on the vague forms of other children, anonymous and unmoving, proportioned just like she, to help keep her company when she was feeling especially lonely. But, when Tess – for fun she said – made a blistering rash appear on the forearms of the chamber maid, who was immediately given notice, handed hush money, and made to sign a contract to stay mum about the whole thing, my wondering and musings on our situation took a decidedly worrisome turn. I had hoped, deeply, if I could steer my child onto a principled and noble path, it would in time mature with her into both a penchant and purpose of magical application for "good," not "bad." And that it all would be kept at a minimum. I was the dreamer.

Even the sing-song ditties Tess would chant as she roamed the rooms, playing with invisible, imaginary others, changed in time from familiar nursery rhyme words to incoherent, multi-syllabic fragments, whose phonetic stylings could only have been gleaned from texts in the grimoire she discovered, which I in my ignorance persisted in assuming was safe and sound, out of reach of my daughter, under lock and key. More on that book in a moment…

Around the time Tess turned six, I made what seemed an obviously logical and lovely move, which was to assign my grandmother, a talented cook and baker, the task of fostering my daughter's grassroots culinary prowess. I thought nothing but that it would help prepare Tess to better fend for herself, whether elsewhere on her own (despite that being not terribly likely, the family estate having served myriad generations of Kress family members wonderfully well, but of course for fourth floor fenestrated suicide perches…), or, if in her later years, she were called upon to contribute to the family by way of meal planning or preparation. Gigi, the nickname Tess had devised from the words Great- and Grand- for my grandmother, happily accepted. The kitchen had been her refuge, a place where the magic of a mortal hand like hers could still reign, a place of creativity from the time on she, like her great-granddaughter now, was a child.

Gigi with Tess decided they should begin with the small and simple. They would start with baking lessons and commence upon their shared kitchen experiences by making what else but cookies.

Pfeffernüsse, cinnamon stars, and gingersnaps. How quaint.

The year, having grown long on this sixth of my life with Tess, had brought with it the requisite, overcast days of rain, and falling, gathering, wet leaves. The fires in our hearths duly stoked to ward off the damp chill, they burned warm and protectively. Familiar sounds echoed in the tall chimneys, animating the house with nostalgic refrain only inclement weather could accomplish. I in my residual mourning over the loss of Tess's father, and less so the absence of my mother, who had died when I was young, felt old beyond my age, and so the house, with its relative ancientness, suited me perfectly. I felt, well, congruent with the circumstances, but at least, quite safe. And my daughter, with her exceptional needs, provided me with the distracting business of raising her as best as I thought I could, given the circumstances and my shortcomings as one not "blessed." When the aromas of baked delights began to thread their way from the kitchen to the rooms where I generally spent my afternoons, it was in and of itself a kind of magic, for I took from them and the chatter and laughter that drifted alongside the heady scent of vanilla, almond, nutmeg and browning sugar, a sense of real security. Yes, thought I, we were headed in the right direction. With things staying the course, my daughter could indeed in time preside over the family homestead with as much pleasant ordinariness as she wished, with her faculties for magic safely contained by the careful rearing of those who loved her.

Pfeffernüsse. How quaint. Soon, Mama, soon.

There came a day, however, for all the sweetness of the hours in the kitchen, when, with all that non-stop baking, it was effectively enough. At least, enough for the time being. Everything in good measure, I have always maintained, thinking it also a solid approach where my daughter's upbringing was concerned. Tess had, in fact, been willfully neglecting her other lessons and contriving to leave chores undone, so did she love her time in the kitchen with her great-grandmother and feel entitled to them. And too much did she love what amounted to her three daily meals comprising far too often hands full of the warm cookies that Gigi, an abysmal disciplinarian, permitted her great-granddaughter. Crumbs had come to fill Tess's apron pockets and were spilling from the folds of her skirts; they were even caught up in the ringlets of her hair. Quite unbecoming for a young lady.

Not only that, Tess, for all her remarkable constitution, had begun to complain of an aching tooth. Dentistry, being the primitive practice it yet was, rang all kinds of warning bells, at numerous levels. I could not be this astute a parent and have a child at a mere six years of age walking around with new molars already corrupted, thanks to the non-stop consumption of sugared treats. So, there came the day when I decreed, enough was enough. Enough in the kitchen with Gigi for now. Embroideries needed to be completed to satisfaction, and the stack of young readers' classics in the library needed attending to. Likewise, Tess's chores would have to be accomplished without protest and done to relative perfection. Only then could she resume her lessons in the kitchen with "Her" Gigi, as she now rather imperiously called my mother. That laying claim of another, given Tess's untapped capabilities, gave me pause, and some token alarm. Witches did, in fact, possess people.

The hours I spent with Tess in the library had always felt, thank goodness, quite normal. They were certainly educationally unique to each one of us, for various, underlying reasons. Tess was a precocious reader. By the time she was three, she could wend her way through every level of the illustrated primers we kept in the hutch. By the time she was five, we were spending our lessons with me a passive audience of one, curled up on the massive divan, wholly entertained by the chapter books Tess would read to me. Now, at six years of age, the two of us were systematically tackling scientific journals and diving deep into literary classics. Tess loved the library as much as I did, and these days, often asked to linger on after our sessions were ended, which I gladly permitted, preening with an indulgent, maternal pride. I thought nothing of granting this brilliant youngster free reign to sleuth amongst the shelves.

There came a day, however, whereupon finishing in record time the final chapter of her latest selection, Tess produced a thick volume from behind a pillow on the divan, which she had obviously stashed there.

Why look my darling, I ventured, cautiously, admiring the old, illustrated tome. *This, you see, is called a grimoire…*

Do you mean, Mama, a Grimm-moire, like the brothers who wrote all those lovely stories?

I laughed gently, pleased with my daughter's perception and quick wit.

No, not at all my pet. A grimoire is spelt differently than the surname. There is only one M. Here, let us take a look. This is a book of recitations of a very special kind…

Aha, my girl mused, drawn in by the beauty of the book, its lustrous patina, its aura of agedness. *I know what this is…*

Tess promptly lay the open the book to the first page, and began to read, *Dith trovent, mal a…*

Upon which I took the book from her and closed it. There was no reason why she should have been able to decipher the foreign script, its hieroglyphic lettering. But she had.

Tess protested, hissing like a feral cat as I placed the book into a drawer of the secretary and locked it, pocketing the key. I should have been suspicious when she fell suddenly silent, but I wasn't. I naively took her immediate show of distractibility as her having been childishly, predicably captivated by something else. My relief was palpable, likely too telltale for one such as she.

I now know, the grimoire was what she took to spending all her time with after our lessons. Immediately upon my taking leave of the library, and soon enough in the middle of the night as well, when alone in her bedroom and by the wane light of only the moon – if even that – when I thought my daughter was fast asleep, Tess was devoting every spare minute to that book.

The lock on the drawer? Silly me; it had given way with the sole touch of her finger…

Cinnamon stars. How quaint. Soon, Mama, soon.

My cool, calm, and ordered world continued to fall by the wayside. Some weeks after our peculiar exchange over the grimoire, Tess demonstrated to me her first theatrics-level tantrum. This was when I announced to her, we would no longer be participating in the Halloween traditions of the area. Not anymore. No more jack-o-lanterns, no more costumed tea parties in the nursery, no more ghost stories by candlelight. These all resonated far too keenly, in my opinion, with a subconscious that lurked ever darker, ever more closely to the surface in my child.

Last Halloween, as Tess had poured pretend tea for me in the nursery, a breeze had kicked up from beneath her play table, with of all things, a finger of bitingly cold air slithering up my legs, beneath the layers of my skirts. The rush of sensation had both frightened and revolted me. I took it as an obvious if invisible warning: The elements were beginning to listen. They were on a standby for my little girl. And they leaned mocking and insidious. This clearly posed immense risk, for Tess, who – and I still maintain this belief – was unaware of the changes in the environment her play had somehow wrought. Hers was the innocence of, well, an infant demon that had not yet learned either of its legacy or its destiny.

Back to my pronouncement of the prohibitionary measure: Tess's tears in response to my decree flowed in rivulets, and they were matched horribly well by the screeching wails she emitted, which caused both my eardrums to pop and my ears to ring. Her beastly howl was by no means incidental. Witches can, indeed, damage the hearing with their cries when they so choose. When I, having known of, though never having witnessed first-hand, the meltdown of a juvenile Fury, at least knew enough to not grant Tess the satisfaction of my own pain or panic in response to her horrific display. My daughter, overtaken by her immature revenge ideations, decided to then hold her breath in anger. Still, I held my calm. When, however, Tess's face inflated and grew as red as the tomato sauce Gigi so lovingly canned for us, her tears transformed from ordinary saltwater to blood, turning at first a pale pink and then a thick, bright crimson. I lost my composure, did not have the stomach for this. Moreover, I had never heard of this phenomenon happening with any ancestor, even during all those hushed, late-night conversations I'd had other adult Kress family members, when the antics of our ancestors were the topic.

Tess, with her acute observational skills, when she saw me fall apart at the sight of something she had not yet quite realized she was doing, laughed at me. My child thought my fear and panic were amusing.

Some small window to something I had no part in, nor could preside over, had been opened, and my little girl, as she stood there in front of me, smearing bloody tears all over her sleeve, was sailing right through its window and heading straightaway to her own second star on the right…to what?

Cookies. For no reason whatsoever, that was my first thought after we both were cooled off. Why? I set about with the fussiness of a mother intent upon the quick cleaning up of any disheveled and blood-stained offspring. There was a new pinafore to dress her in, a new collar to button into place. There were bloody garments to put in to soak. As I was finalizing the reconfiguration of my fledgling conjurer and tying a band of lace around her freshly re-gathered ponytail, Tess looked up at me as she was wont to do, with her colorless eyes full and wide and oh, so innocent, and she said to me,

"Cookies, mama?" batting her lashes, she repeated, "Cookies. Now, mama, now."

And so, my daughter turned everything back to her way. There was no way I could refuse her.

Go see where your Gigi is and tell her Mama says it is alright to play in the kitchen today…

My little Harpy had the audacity to skip away from me as I remained motionless on the davenport, my legs numb, my body weighted as if with lead.

I was about to sigh with something akin to relief when I heard a pot crash. I came to, and my body awakened enough to allow me to dash down the hall to the kitchen. My worst fear came unbidden – I was afraid something had happened to my grandmother, my go-between, my emissary, and co-parent, who in that afternoon's episode I had come to instantaneously see as a critically important liaison and human buffer against the emerging Thing that was my daughter.

No, thank God. Gigi, Grandmother, was nowhere to be seen. Only Tess stood in the kitchen, and only Tess it could have been, to somehow have taken the copper pot from its hook, high upon the wall, and have it thrown to the floor in a fresh display of something that already bordered dangerously on rage. My daughter seethed, and it showed in every feature of her young face, in every inch of her stance.

What now?

My love, my love, I implored, *Tell mama what is the matter. Where is your Gigi?*

Gigi is asleep, Mama, and she won't wake up. She won't wake up!

My heart fell into my gut, and I felt instantly ill.

I raced down the short hall to the suite of rooms my mother had made her own and entered her small bedroom. Sure enough, there my daughter's Gigi lay upon her bed, fully dressed, her shoes still on, as had she lain herself down for only the shortest of naps, or to catch her breath, or to perhaps fend off a dizzying spell, a pain in the chest…

Tess watched passively as I took my mother's cooling hand into mine and cried out. She was advanced in years, yes, but it was too soon, far too soon, for her to leave me, leave me with that child…

Gingersnaps. How quaint. Soon, Mama, soon.

Nightfall spread its shadowing hands over the house, far sooner than expected, it seemed. The day itself had been a gloomy, indiscriminate stretch. I was spent with grief and a slow boiling sensation of panic, now mixed with doom. What was I to do?

In the morning, the undertaker would be sent for. And the doctor. I would then see to it that my mother would have her burial, as she had always wished it, before the cock crowed twice, far out in the gardens, out under the ancient sweet gum she had so loved as a child. It was close enough to the family graveyard, where also my father and husband were buried, to not seem too odd a distance from a place proper. I gathered Tess into my arms as I tucked her into bed and told her Gigi was surely on her way to a wonderful place, and that we would put her also to bed, with all the other Kress family members, albeit a little offsides, but that was how Gigi had wanted it, in the morning, once the undertaker had delivered us a nice and sturdy casket. My grandmother was a petite woman, and even in death would appreciate the better fit of a slender built box.

Cookies. Now, Mama, now.

The weariness that had begun of late to plague me at regular intervals, that had been visiting its lethargy upon me more and more, had me swimming where I stood, at the foot of my daughter's bed, telling that mournful, little soul, *Goodnight, my little Sugar and Spice. Everything will be alright, for everything will follow according to Nature and God's plans.*

No, Mama, no, my daughter muttered against the blankets she had pulled up to her nose. *No…*

Yes. Now, goodnight. Good. Night.

I sought to convey a definitive finality. Could I have tied her wrists and ankles and bound her to her bed to keep both her and me safe, I would have. Could I have stuffed a handkerchief into her pouting scowl to keep her still, I would have. Could I have plied my daughter with a sleep-inducing elixir to gift us both with the respite of a solid night of sleep, I would have. But I did no such thing, would not, ever, not on any count.

How could I even think such cruel thoughts?

I kissed Tess's forehead and patted the top of her head. She turned away from me in what I could only construe as defiance – against what? I then stumbled down the hall, and leaving the housekeeper to draw tight all the curtains, with the additional imperative to drape every mirror in every room with fabric – *find sashes, tablecloths, I don't care, whatever you can gather* – until further notice, I made my way to the sanctuary of my room, turned the lock on my door, and let myself collapse onto my own bed. Like my grandmother, I was fully dressed, with my shoes still on. I would soon sleep as if drugged, a hard and dreamless slumber I would welcome with every residual sensibility I could muster. I hoped we would make it until dawn. I faded and fell, fell…

I don't know what stirred me awake.

Sounds from the first floor? The fact that my door had been opened? Was it the light from the hall lamp, with its slender beam crossing the floor of my room to my bedside? Or was it the black-shadowed figure standing at the foot of my bed, mere inches from where my booted feet lay askance? Was it the eyes in its face, a mask of darkness, affixed upon me, unblinking? I saw the outline of a topknot, a collared dress, the apron. I saw a wide tray held aloft by silhouetted arms. I lay there, trying despairingly to rouse myself to a point where I could figure out if I was experiencing a waking nightmare and gazing upon the ghost of my dead grandmother, or if I was indeed awake and seeing her reanimated corpse, arisen from its deathbed, now standing at macabre attention at the foot of my bed, holding out towards me her serving tray, with an offering of some kind…

Cookies, It croaked. *Cookies. Now…*

The voice came from some other dimension, was not of my world, the world we had shared for so many years. And the words, raspy and reverberating with the hollowness of the undead, were an assault. They were suffused with toxicity and morbid intent.

Oma! I screamed, as much as my constricted throat allowed.

Tess! I tried next to cry out.

I knew this was my daughter's doing. Tess had done this. Tess had resurrected her Gigi. She wanted her cookies, and she was going to get them, come hell or…

A hex called forth by a six-year-old. A deep dive from which there would be, I knew, no return. My wicked, wicked, selfish, and ignorant only child…

Tess had conjured from the remains of her Gigi a kitchen wench zombie.

Oh, gods and goddesses, saints, and noble patrons, oh Lord and Son and holy Ghost – Whoever is out there, please, hear me now…Help me…

The last thing I saw while alive was the small form of my daughter at my bedroom door. Her appearance seemed to serve as some sort of call to action, for in that moment, the undead spectre that had just this morning still been my grandmother bounded around to the top side of my bed, and with a forcefulness commensurate to her demonic speed, she reached out and grabbed me by the throat, pinning my head to my pillow. I could hardly breathe; the claw-like hand on my neck was like a sprung animal trap.

And then, the creature that had mere hours ago still been my kind compatriot and co-parent to my ringleted devil's spawn, began to stuff the cookies she had just baked into my mouth.

One warm gingersnap after another she pressed into the back of my throat, into the voids of my cheeks, against the roof of my mouth, up my nose and farther still, deep into my sinuses. It took barely a dozen of the spice imbued cakes the rotting automaton had produced on command for her tiny mistress, to fill the cavities of my face to the point of asphyxiation. I fought futilely, but weakly, with far too little conviction for one with so much of life ahead of her.

What exactly did I have ahead of me? Precisely. That is perhaps why I did, indeed, fight rather little…

†††

And so, I lie here upon my vast bed, weighted like a log. A coldness encroaches from within, rendering my limbs numb. The silence inside of me is rather astonishing. There is no rise and fall of my chest, no exhalations, no rhythmic patter from inside my ribs, or within my ears. The wind, I can tell, has picked up outside, again, right on cue. The howl in the chimney is almost melodic. It reminds me of the night Tess was born.

Oh, I hope and pray my consciousness takes leave of my body. I hope and pray for a small light to appear, from somewhere, anywhere at all. May Hades himself carry a candle intended for me; I will take it. I will follow anyone or anything that presents itself, just so long that this awareness, this abstraction of me, can manage to disconnect and drift upwards and out of the carcass that's been left here on the bed, and sneak away from this hellish place, away from those two over there.

Look at them, so disgustingly preoccupied with their sweets. I hope Tess hasn't also tinkered with me…

Efectus

iii THRONE D'EAU

It was the year 2281, and everyone was not only equal, but contentedly so. In the beginning, a rare, few, cantankerous outliers had paid with their lives, but society knew little to nothing about them. Hazards of differentness, heaven forbid any aspect of superlativeness, had been successfully eliminated in the name of, well, let's call it "peace." Early equitized survivors (such stubborn beings) had never recovered from their adjustments, for memory was a real bitch. Therefore, legislation for mandatory cognitive wiping was also passed, so all physical and intellectual equitization now also included memory cleansing. Calm now reigned, and lethargic inactivity was universally construed as a validly aspirational lifestyle and a helluva good time.

Blanket enforcement, despite its rough starts, had ultimately created a neatly homogenized society. Any outliers, having long ago been fully absorbed into the safer realms of mediocrity, now comingled placidly with let's call them "peers," who continued to be elevated and subsidized and were now serving as figureheads in all offices, both in government and commerce. Societal decline, as algorithmically implemented and tracked by the Central Entity (generally referred to as the CE), was solidly in place and on an unstoppable trajectory, set to expire about the time the last of the Surplus Class sapiens would do the same.

Meantime, the impudent head of creativity still lurked to raise its wacky head from within the crevices of random sapioid minds, in particular amongst its youngest members, who, like their predecessors over all eras and epochs, sought instinctively to lengthen the proverbial apron strings – whatever those were – by way of finding something, anything, with which to shock n awe their elders. Despite all the complacency constructs rigidly adhered to by every matured member of society, random and odd manifestations of behavioral singularities continued to surface, especially amongst the youthful citizenry.

Because uniformity of dress no longer allowed for any iota of individualistic expression in garments, it was inevitable that the ancient practice of body modification re-emerged. There was simply nothing left to alter but one's bio-organic housing. Hair had been bred out some decades ago, and since no materials for labor-related self-externalization existed – ink, paint, pens, pencils of yore were all long, long gone – the only thing left to do was to demarcate oneself by either affixing objects to one's skin, or inserting objects under it, or to remove parts of oneself in order to create some more permanent differentness from the standard, four-limbed, ten-fingered, full-face type-casted sapioid self. Scarring still found its outlets amongst an underground cadre of artistic types, but with heat for personal use having long been outlawed and too easily tracked, the only scarring practiced was by way of the blade. Being a terribly messy thing, that remained an outsider expression, due also to the outlawing of the handling of bodily fluids of any kind whatsoever. Ironically, this left "kids" to the exploration of the dispensability of extraneous body parts. As such, a new form of creative expression took root, became mainstreamed, and was elevated to a fresh alternativism, as was of course historically consistent with terral societies over all time.

Easily accomplished, the cut being followed immediately by a chemical sealant, the predominant self-expression of otherness was now to have one's pinky fingers removed.

The CE had let this fad slide, had pretended not to notice, for the loss of one small digit on either hand fell by convenient happenstance under all radars, societal and otherwise.

The inevitable driver of supply and demand therefore fomented the rise of a marketplace for the removal of said fingers five and ten, a procedure promptly dubbed Eight-Capping. This term was an abbreviation of "Handicapping at Eight," to borrow from some age-old vernacular utilized by the CE's human predecessors.

Eight-capping caught on, both as a style statement and a status marker of sorts for a major segment of society that believed its conformity was a unique expression, the manifestation of a perceived freedom. Glovemakers were already taking to manufacturing modified sleeves for eight-digit appendages, and influencers were touting the look as a preferred aesthetic. It was the new way to be.

Forget that one's capabilities might be even further limited in a society which had minimal skills to begin with. Forget that home-done amputations resulted far too often in infectious maiming and chronic pain, which cost Health Services time and credits something awful. Eight-capped humans naturally sought out and quickly found each other, bonding and morphing into a powerful and influential demographic with the adherent, mind-melding inclinations of a good and obedient hive. Equitizing impairment was now downright chic.

†††

Childe wanted their pinkies gone too. What did Mom or Dad know or understand of such things? What backwards and olde-school, head-in-the-sand, ignorant elders they were! Unwilling to see eight-capping for what it was, what it signified! To even *want* to possess any remnant invoking of privilege was, to Childe, a violently phobic violation against all other fellow Sapiens. That their parents refused to consider being eight-capped themselves was one thing (over half of all Sapiens were now capped, at least in their quadrant of the world); that they had the audacity to try and enforce authority over Childe's *not* getting it done was even worse.

To heck with them, Childe decided one quiet afternoon. A few of Childe's friends had not yet been eight-capped but were already scheduled for their procedures. Well, they thought, if Mom and Dad were going to try to hold them hostage with their ways, they would just work around it. It was, after all, only a few weeks until Childe's thirteenth birthday, when Mom's and Dad's authoritarian jurisdiction would end anyway. Childe had already submitted their application for admittance to a post-ed development campus on the west coast and could hardly wait to get away, be their true self, and live amongst other, kindred Cappers.

So, Childe borrowed their friend's handheld and ordered a home kit through an underground online marketplace, arranging for it to be delivered to another apartment where the entire familial unit had already been eight-capped, and was way cooler, at least way more understanding and compassionate (Childe fibbed, though; told the family they had their procedure scheduled with a cottage industry hack with whom they needed to provide a kit), which would be happy to receive the Cut-n-Caut Deluxe Set for them, then turn it over with nary a whisper to Childe's horrible, archaically-minded parents.

A few days later, precisely one week before their thirteenth birthday, Childe locked themself in the bathroom with their kit. No one would be home until Monday. Mom and Dad were up-city, visiting family. Plenty of time to do it, to heal, rest up, and to prepare for the parental homecoming – and the confrontation which would no doubt ensue when they'd see what their old-fashioned ways had driven their only offspring to do.

†††

Mom and Dad arrived home as planned, shortly before curfew.

Something was amiss. Mom immediately sensed it. It was too quiet in the apartment.

Mom laid their wrap over the back of the sofa as they listened for familiar sounds. The apartment *felt* empty.

Honey, if you could check out back? Maybe Childe is outside in the garden. I'm going to head upstairs. Something doesn't feel right...

Oh, sweetie. You and your worries. Always worrying, Dad responded indulgently. Mom was sure struggling with the pending move-out of their offspring.

Dad headed out the door while Mom padded up the stairs to Childe's room. Surely, they would find them lounging on their bed, dozing, perhaps simply plugged into their handheld, inputs turned up to eleven...

Instead, Mom saw that the door to Childe's bedroom, which was always closed and sealed for safety, was oddly ajar. They looked inside. The bed was made; nothing was out of place. They continued down the short hall to the bath, noticing that the door was closed. Complete silence lay heavy throughout the second floor. Mom texted Dad, asking them to please come upstairs. For some inexplicable reason, Mom was afraid to open the door. They didn't know why...

Mom and Dad both called out, calling Childe by name, by every endearment either one of them had ever employed for this lone, officially sanctioned offspring of theirs. Silence prevailed. No answer came to their concerned calls. Neither Mom nor Dad had ever witnessed a hardship, or an injury, or an illness in their progeny, nothing beyond the ordinary displays of a youngster whining to get their way. Appeasement had never been farther off than an edible treat to distract their offspring, or a bedside rotation to calm their over-sleepy youngling, who to this day could not fall asleep alone. With a one child reproduction limit, to have granted Childe behavioral *carte blanche* had always been an easy matter. Tears, tantrums, punishment, discipline were but quaint words from a bygone era.

That is, until eight-capping had reared its problematic head.

That is, until Childe had begun to insist, they were wanting to become part of a collective Mom and Dad had by way of casual dismissal never really considered for themselves. Perhaps they were too much of the earth, the beautiful, giving earth, which they gardened with such perseverance and reverence. Yes, laborers were the parents, but in a nicely productive, positive, and quite picturesque way. Moreover, to garden required the faculty of intact hands – fingers with grips and strong holds on the rudimentary implements still used to break the soil, aid in the growth of the produce the family both consumed and gave away to the EC Collective. Mom and Dad's quaint presumption, to stay in possession of all their fingers, had always been based on an honestly held, virtuous self-regard, tidily rationalized by way of the hardship their toils quite organically bestowed upon them. Childe had had none of that and saw their parents as hopelessly backward and arrogant, despite the regard they otherwise held for them.

Mom nodded to Dad as a signal to open the door. Dad eased it open, with expectant trepidation.

"Childe?" they both called out, a singsong imbued prod stretched out to two syllables. "Chi-lde?"

There. There on the floor was Childe, still as a statue, their hands splayed out to either side, each upturned palm at rest upon a pool of dark crimson. Perched upon the vanity was an open box in which a metal device lay askew, as if it had been quickly dropped or thrown back into its hold. The tool was reminiscent of the cigar cutters from which its design had taken its initial cues. It was coated in the same dark matter that pooled, thick and wet, upon the floor. Drops of the red stuff were everywhere; there was a spattered and stripy array on the device, its case, on the vanity and floor, and all over the clothing of their offspring, who lay on the hard tiles, face up, staring at the chandelier directly above their head, their dark eyes already dulled to a waxy sheen, which could only speak of a life force that had until that day, perhaps mere minutes ago, twinkled with a benign and entertaining spark, and was now simply gone.

Childe was dead.

The pastiness of the puddles on the floor suggested this scenario had been in place more than a few minutes. Maybe it had been at least a day, perhaps two. How was anyone to know?

Childe's two dismembered pinkies, like their former host, lay at rest, these in the basin of the new *throne d'eau*, which had been installed just a month ago. Seepage from the digits had rendered the chlorinated water a soft pink. The stain on the bowl's edge told Mom and Dad the rest of the story: Having excised their fingers, Childe had fallen faint, lost their balance, and struck the toilet full force, face forward. Their offspring's forehead bore a deeply defined and blackened imprint of the rim.

One of them would need to go online immediately, to hire a service to fish those wormy, little things out. No one, and I mean no one, touched meat these days, either, under any circumstance.

Mom and Dad perused the scene in profound silence, an aggrieved assessment borne of never-before-experienced traumatic shock, which came as a surprise to them both. Neither of them had ever had what used to be called a "surge" of emotion. Sure, it was too soon to lose Childe so completely, but their offspring had managed to accomplish an exit without ever having to experience the decline of aging, under which both Mom and Dad now suffered. With their pending exterminations looming ever closer as their final years commenced, (how time flew by!) Mom and Dad were decidedly circumspect in the face of this passing. While each kept their own, mortal dread at bay, the stoicism was an almost full-time occupation. For one, it was never, ever, ever spoken of…

How lovely to go without knowing it was going to happen, they both mused to themselves.

And on their own terms…

Mom also thought: *Well, I hope it went fast, and that it did not hurt too much.*

And Dad thought: *Well, I hope this cleans up well. We just had this floor installed and won't be eligible for a redo in our lifetime. What a shame, if for the next couple of years, we will have to look at these stains as our last reminders of what was our Childe.*

At least Childe, with their eight-capped hands, was now eligible for interment in the far more nicely situated burial field, the gated one with the grassy fields and rows of evergreens. Far better than the barren stretch allocated those ten-fingered Regressives.

Neitherium

Efectus

Be sure to read the progenitor of this story, *Harrison Bergeron*, by Kurt Vonnegut (1922-2007), published in 1961.

Likewise, a nod to Heinrich Hoffmann's 1845 *Struwwelpeter*; specifically, *Die Geschichte vom Daumenlutscher*

JOINED WITH THE SEAS

When the sun breaks the plain of the ocean, I must die.

He gave me only one choice: Walk the plank or be hanged.

I, in my ridiculous fancy, have chosen to walk, for it will be of my volition, and once joined with the seas, what happens next, while the outcome is likely, remains to be seen.

Which means, there is a chance.

The rhythmic push of the waves against the boat keeps time, the clang of the ropes against masts keeps time; the thud of the sails, thrust forward, sucked back as the winds inhale, exhale, keeps time. Every limb of this vessel, her wrists, her arms, her ankles, her knees, creaks, and bends with the coax of the tidal pulse. Every sound, each gentle lurch keeps time…

The captain's own clock, a wondrous ebony contraption, commands us from its mantle perch. How ironic, whilst the elite lounge in their berths, raise their glasses again and again, they are but an arm's reach from their designated damned, we who languish beneath the very boards upon which they stumble and dance…

My hands, long numb from the iron bands…My skin, it's just gone. I wear bracelets embedded so deep in my flesh, the muscle, and tendons, dried and bloodless, have curled up around the metal, as if to engulf them – such deviously symbiont replacement joints. So little else is left of the corporeal me. I feel, my spirit barely fills this jaundiced satchel, under which bone and viscera lie asleep, suspended, dead weighted. Weakly tethered to my torn body, I know a part of me is ready to let go of the silver strings which, ever more failingly, bind me to it. I hang in limbo, a sad puppet. To be executed seems almost redundant.

Food? No food. And when did my lips last know the kiss of a blessed drop of water?

There it is! The captain's clock chimes: One, two, three, four, five times. The bell reverberates, lonesome in its somber pitch and tone. In minutes, I know, the first hint of sunrise will announce the day and this final night will be ended.

I sit, and I sit.

The rhythmic push of the waves against the boat keeps time, the clang of the ropes against the masts keeps time; the thud of the sails, thrust forward, sucked back, keeps time…

I sit, and I sit.

And there! The captain's clock chimes one, two, three, four times. The bell reverberates, lonesome in its somber pitch and tone…

But this makes no sense. Am I imagining the count? Had I imagined that of the previous hour?

One hour ago, my execution was imminent. One hour ago, the sun hovered in the wings, ready to take the stage as luminous, useless bystander. But now? Everyone around me still sleeps. There are no witnesses, no one to ask, no one to count, as I do…

I will stay quiet.

The rhythmic push of the waves against the boat keeps time, the clang of the ropes against masts keeps time, the thud of the sails keeps time, thrust forward, sucked back. The winds ebb and flow, echo their sibling tides…

I sit, and I sit.

And there! The captain's clock chimes once, twice, three times. The bell reverberates, lonesome in its somber pitch and tone.

Oh, God, what is happening here? Why now is it three in the morning when a few minutes ago I know the clock chimed its pre-dawn last?

Mother in heaven, answer me! Has time come to a standstill? Has she reversed herself?

I look down at my shackles. Grown enormous, they are the size of small iron wheels. I lower my arms, hold my hands slack, and the rings slip off, fall to the floor. I step out of cruel bands that have ground at my ankles for weeks. I can barely stand upright. I have not stood on my own for days. I venture a step to the left…

The rhythmic push of the waves against the boat keeps time, the clang of the ropes against masts keeps time, the thud of the sails, thrust forward, sucked back, keeps time. Time…

Time?

I look all around me. There is nowhere to go but up. The ladder. Try the hatch…

And there! The captain's clock chimes once, twice… And stops. The bell reverberates, wanes…

Something has turned the tides, is afoot, and I alone bear witness to it, aware of some metaphysical reversal that offers up no explanation…

The skies. I can now see them above me, beckoning through jagged splits between the hatch's cover.

Dear Savior, guide me now through this spell of unyielding lunacy. What am I to do? There are no waking souls. This galleon, the deck, are devoid of humanity. The only signs of life are that of the ship's as she responds to the prompts from the waters, the winds…

The boat keeps time…

I wander stealthily amongst coiled ropes, barrels, salt-encrusted rigging. As far as I can see, no land in sight. Only endless, sleeping seas surround this ship, surround me…

And there! The captain's clock chimes once. One time only. The bell reverberates…

Do I stand here a free woman? Alive?

Lord, am I still alive?

Or am I already dead, taking my first steps towards eternity? Will a light reveal itself to me to show me where to tread?

Am I a ghost, the others momentarily suspended, my walk across this deck lasting but a handful of seconds in the time-space of mortals? Where there still resides a sun that will indeed rise above the distant cusp of the ocean? Where the captain and his crew will awaken, and their guards will descend into the cargo hold for me and find nothing but my stiffening corpse, a ragged urchin trussed in their bracelets, blood encrusted, foul edges curled with decay, soiled scraps, nit paved, open sores matted?

Yes! Let it be me as I now stand, a spirit making her way to God's heaven, and pray, some light arrives to illuminate my way, perhaps lent by the Christ child itself, to aid this wayward pilgrim's progress to the next realm.

But, where do I go from here?

Aha! A small light flickers on the gangway before me, its skipping cadence catches my eye. It bids me, Follow. Is it real? Such a beautiful insanity! No, I will not question this now. No explanation, proof, or courage are needed. I have nothing to lose...

Nothing...

Sky-borne trinket, wait for me! Yes, I will follow you! You are a bearer of hope, a lantern for my soul, dear firefly. Take me from this tortured captivity!

Slow down, my angel! I come!

I can barely walk, but I grab what I can, pull my broken form forward. You, silently shimmering, a molten and glowing guide – I will grab you and hold you to my breast. I am yours.

No! The captain's clock now chimes the hour that heralds the day's turn! One, two, three, four, five and six! Seven, eight and nine. Ten, yes, and eleven and then twelve; all as present and predictable as they are stalwart, duly counted, oddly accounted. Have we been hurled backwards to yesterday, or thrown forward to tomorrow? The bell reverberates, its somber pitch and tone wavers, fades...

And yet, here I stand as all others remain cradled within its hypnotic, somnambulant call.

Yes, I am alive! My Lord, I am still alive!

Beloved lumiere, I take these last steps to reach you, my fingertips but a whisper of a wish distant from your pulsating, playing, flickering, laughing self…

You laugh!

You laugh.

You laugh?

And look…I have taken one step too many.

I fall.

The seas engulf me, the weight of my skeleton is too much for the wasted and threadbare casing that barely keeps these limbs contained, one frail piece linked to another.

I sink beneath the surface, the stars by churning water erased. Your light remains, however, atop the foam of my stolen, last breath.

That laugh…

I remember now.

They warned me about you, but from the chaos, amidst the fog of my decrepit state and all their drunken, slipshod, and violent preening, I forgot about you.

Oh yes, they warned me. Behind that sugarplum façade, you, tiny demon, are more truly colored by shades of a deadly jealousy that has so far evaded all capture, all correction.

Reptilian and humanoid monsters are but kept creatures, oversize henchmen who do your dirty work. I get it.

So, as one would expect, before I am a full fathom submerged, teeth the size of carving knives pierce my thigh, the soft flesh of a hot tongue tastes of me, presses against skin so freshly shredded, it flutters like strips of fabric. My left leg is twisted and pulled off in the way a licorice whip is rent. Blood – mine – warms the water around me as it bursts forth, pulse by pulse by withering pulse, a sash of red meandering skyward to the underside of the ocean's looking glass table. In the liquified moonlight, it is a stain quickly dissipated. The suspended diamond of you is recast a soft rose, like that of a conch, likewise torn from its once perfect, porcelain housing.

Hovering, sparkling, callous, indifferent you.

Tick…Tick…

I less hear that infernal metronome as now feel it, my right leg pulled into the beast's belly as it swallows and I am drawn down, and in. My foot brushes against a small, hard form. It strikes at me, tap-tap-tapping me. Insistent, Insidious. The rest of me arrives.

Damn you.

Efectus

Thanks to J.M. Barre, for the doors he opened by way of the collected lore and symbolism he pulled together in the crafting of Peter Pan.

Second star to the right, straight until morning, indeed…

CHRISTMAS PUNCH

*"…We wish you a merry Christmas
And a Happy New Year!"*

The suitable hours, as they called them, were long past by the time the carolers arrived at their destination, a stately brownstone whose shuttered windows and high gates promised the utmost in privacy and coziest of confinements.

"My dears, my dears, enough of this arctic merriment!" the jovial Hostess proclaimed as she swung wide the front door. "'tis time for our own merriment! We are accomplished of our good work and, so now, I say to you all, *we* celebrate!"

In a few short decades, this Christmas Eve celebration had become a most eagerly anticipated annual escapade, a tradition, if you will. And the Hostess was *so* pleased – the confectioner had filled her order to perfection. Every candy cane met precisely with the details as she had requested them – the rods of porous sugar were as sturdy as railroad spikes, and generously infused with the bitterest blends of peppermint oils, crimson swirl encased, lovely to behold. She couldn't wait to hand them out.

†††

"Come along and follow me, my lovelies!" the Hostess called out as she led her flock down a long hallway, down a steep flight of stairs, and through a stretch of winding passageway, until the revelers and their mistress together came to a standstill at the doorway of a grand and marbled entry.

Anticipation and delight kindled and sparked in their eyes, their smiles, their clasped hands, so eager was this troupe to pass through into the next room.

This next room was, in fact, a vast and palatial underground ballroom. The air in the room was more an atmosphere, for the far and distant corners receded into foggy darkness, like that of a far-off and shadowed valley. But, immediately before them, welcoming them in, was a space awash in the brilliance of an army of sparkling chandeliers, so crystal and candle laden were they as to appear almost menacing in their massive iciness. Was it not, the Hostess gushed, so horribly opulent, so disgustingly regal?

A circular array of plush divans had been situated in the center of the ballroom. Upon these chaises lay draped in elegant repose a carefully culled crop of scrumptiously robust humans. These fine specimens reclined upon their lounges in various states of mesmerized restfulness, smiling sleepily, perhaps dreaming of sugar plums, their contented faces aglow with the very essence of Peace on Earth.

✝✝✝

"Now, my dear, you hold it like this," the Hostess instructed, aiming the sharply honed, pointed end of her candy cane at the neck of the woman she had selected to share with her initiate.

The young man tucked his hair behind his ear and leaned in, listening, entranced.

"Watch as I do it, and then you simply come in from your side," she went on, "and remember, hit sure and hard."

He grinned, his garnet eyes glinting with desire. The Hostess smiled, recalling with sweet nostalgia her first time…

Then, with a practiced hand and preternatural force, she pierced the jugular vein of their somnambulant donor with her sweet staff, and quickly placing her mouth over the blunt end of the candy, the Hostess sucked hard, drawing up through the honeycombed sugar a warming mouthful of frothy human liquor. She drank long and deep. What a deliciously flavored blood!

Her young companion smiled lasciviously, and, following the Hostess' lead, dove in for his first post-mortem Christmas punch.

Efect

DANCE OF THE SUGARPLUMS

'tis fascinating, how qualms, quirks and issues manifest as fashions, dialects, even units of measurement, is it not? Here is the story of one such event, that in the end, turned out to be as gruesome as it was innocently well-intended.

'twas but a simple mistake the Christmas Fairy did make, when she set out on her winter's nap rounds 'round Santa's Christmas Town, when, impulsively inspired, she upped the enchantment ante by bestowing upon every slumb'rous elf not one but a handful of their very own dancing sugarplums whilst they slept.

Problem is, the Fairy, enamored with that newly published ditty by a certain Mr. Moore, spaced it quite completely on the precise wording of the text, forgetting that part of it having been "visions."

But what's to expect with a mighty flighty sprite, who subsists on a liquid diet comprised solely of Christmas spirits? All that grog, glog, wassail and especially that nog might taste awful nice, but leave much when it comes to interpretive skills honing of the literary, literal kind....

Suffice it to say, on that very next day, on Christmas Eve morning, when the bells in the tower sounded the hour, calling their jolly minions back to the bench, not a single, solitary elf was roused from the biers that had served as their lil sleeping shelves.

Alas, a-snooze they were not. Instead, they lay dead on their hard, bookshelf beds, their pillows drenched in the goo of their pulverized brains, which had oozed from their pointed, elfin ears in minuscule rivers of troubling, bubbling crimson – a real nightmare come true.

For, 'twas not *visions* of sugarplums that had danced in their heads, but *real* sugarplums that had ricocheted like steel pinballs inside of their craniums – for hours! The sweets had come to macabre life, thanks to the Fairy's wayward hex, and did not enchant, as in Mr. Moore's text, but lob and bounce about within those small skulls until there was nothing, nothing left.

'twas about then, the grieving Clauses closed up shop, and took to ordering online instead.

Efectus

SANTA DOMNIA

There was once a writer whose gifts for the lyrically imaginative fell unfailingly flat in the face of his ego-suffused, ambitious attempts. Beset with envy, he resolved to aspire to different heights – indeed, to their inversions – by way of a more morosely inspirational sort of Muse. He determined, he would call forth and conjure into his presence none other than the Queen Mother of all Christmas Spirits, La Santa Domnia.

All the candles in the house – every candelabra and chandelier, every brass chamberstick and glass votive – he changed out to black. Doorways and staircase banisters he festooned with black beribboned garland. The stately spruce in his parlour he trimmed with *Vanitas* invoking artifacts, decorations reeking of mortality, decay, and degeneration. Even the crèche displayed upon the library mantle evoked more a cold crypt than a warm, sheltering stable. It's possible, he may have felt a whisper of conscience when he painted the minuscule, red slash marks across the infant doll's porcelain neck, but to summon *Her* up would require blasphemous sincerity of effort. Nothing less than a deep-darkest, hell-firing welcome was required to usher *Her* in.

This moribund fellow did fervently believe that what he could summon from somewhere far below and then bear unholy witness to would place him right up there, right among the best of all his other, literarily bound ilk. With luck, it might catapult him past the greats, past the upstarts, and straight – straight! – to the top. He'd show them all, by golly!

Santa Domnia, Santa Domnia!

The writer sat in his study, night after interminable, solitary, and silent night. There, in his chair, he would read from his grimoire, reciting the stanzas over and over until his voice grew hoarse and the room before him would begin to swim…

At long, long last, after countless sleepless nights of endless invocations and sing-song incantations, it so happened, the clock on the mantle *did* slow down and, *tick, tick…tick…*fall still, and the fire in the hearth did chokingly dwindle, sputter, and suddenly die…

The man stopped. He held his breath to better listen through a quelling silence that roared deep inside his ears, past his dizzied and befuddled sensibilities.

Has She…

Has She materialized?

The man listened.

Yes, it has to be…

His Spirit approached!

Yes. There they were, thick and heavy steps sounding in the entry below – plodding, plodding, steadfastly advancing. He heard the rhythmic shush of weighted fabric asway; he heard the rustling sounds of dry leaves and debris as they were swept up and along in the newcomer's wake. And then, he heard the sound of metal scraping the floor, striking upon the stairs, a-clanging and a-thudding, one tread at a time. Up, up, closer, and closer…

She approached with the lumbering stealth of one freshly resurrected.

When She at long last appeared at the door, the man sank to the floor, abjectly awestricken, utterly overwhelmed. Glory – such a beauteous horror was She! The apparition embodied it all: Ignorance and Want, misguided intent, all virtue gone vice, acts of spiteful, cold vengeance; violence and bloodlust, all murderous ambition, all hate-filled desire…

This was Mankind's underbelly, exquisitely flayed, sublimely incarnate.

Santa Domnia, fair maiden, thorned ringlet, brow crested! Your forehead and scalp pierced; your curls thickly matted. Garnet rivulets flow 'pon a dainty lace collar, so painstakingly knotted, so thoroughly spattered!

Santa Domnia, fair maiden, candle crowned! Dripping, molten, hardening fast; ensconcing, encasing your pallid countenance. Streams flowing unfettered with blood imbued wax!

Santa Domnia, sweet maiden, fair princess! Snow-white was your dress, but with holly impaled, wet blooms herald the gash from that stake in your breast! Your heaving, your breathing, belabored and pained, your moth-eaten bodice most thoroughly stained!

Santa Domnia, fair maiden, wings spread! Not in flight but in fight, hardened feathers, sharp tines! One hundred small daggers – they clink, cut the air, kill off the last dregs of the peace in my lair!

Santa Domnia, your fragmented teeth mix with crumbs of black coal, your small mouth cruelly stuffed, until it is full. Your leering smile bares gums, not of a soft rose, but grey-shaded, the flesh curling off from the bone!

Santa Domnia – no, no!

Santa, stay where you are! Let me worship you here from my spot on the floor!

No, no, Santa Domnia – do not take my hands!

No, this I sought not – I plead, I implore!

No, please, not the spikes! No, not my left hand!

I beg you, dear Santa, leave my right hand alone!

No, no, blessed Santa!

You were not called forth to crucify me –

I foolishly thought you had simply come home!

Efectus

FLASH FICTION

MEDDIE

After fifteen years, Jason had the gall to up and leave her. Forget poetic exits to foreign ports, the bastard took up with none other than the mayor's daughter. The couple headlined the paper's society pages nearly every weekend. Unrelenting and disgusting.

The baby album, now stuffed with newspaper clippings of the two of them, had been mailed.

"Let's go to the beach, kids," Meddie said, strapping the twins into their car seats.

"Hey Siri," she hissed, "Navigate to hell."

The SUV traversed the steep shoreline and was soon gone, swallowed whole by the icy waves.

Lined up at the gates, her sisters watched and waited, salivating, cheering her on.

Inspired by the Odyssey & its very own Medea

SUB MARINE

Honey, in case something happens to me, I'm writing you this note. Sam promised he'd get it to you if I didn't make it back. Know that I love you. Always.

Feeling weird, nauseated, worse by the second.

Sam's got engines at full throttle; still, we're ten miles out. Dive went fine, but something swam into my ear. Can't get it out. It's alive. I can still fill and hear it, boring into mi head, like sum littel drill goin deeper an deper. Cause dived way done to git yoy thet conk shill uwontit. Its lke ist eatin ma bra…

TENDER MOMENT

He assumed, the fish she'd caught was for him.

It was.

She struck the fish with the back of her hand. Spurs flexed to arm it with a coat of hard, silver tines. Deftly, she flung the fish by its tail, striking his left bicep. Ten minuscule pricks bled, then swelled and turned blue.

He felt his limbs turn to jelly. His skin grew numb.

He lay back on the rock and saw only ocean. Unbroken sea. Endless.

Somnambulic, his innards melting, his fingers and toes trailed, unfeeling, in the water.

The mermaid, satisfied, took her first bite.

The prince was delicious.

THE PEARL

The oyster was the biggest she had ever seen, and the ugliest – a grey, barnacle-studded sarcophagus.

Determined, she inserted her knife.

The clam gave up unwillingly, murky liquids oozing from its wounds as her blade cut and pried.

The pearl, a perfect orb, was the size of a ping pong ball – iridescent, silver-white, smooth as silk.

The diver greedily forgot protocol, lost in a moment of fantastical calculations, thinking of the riches it would net her.

When the shell clamped down hard, the diver's forearm joined the pearl deep inside its primordial gullet.

What a pearl that will make.

- 377 -

META MORPHOSIS

Antonio, as famous for his legendary temper as his platinum records, was found guilty in the murder of wife #4. The judge gave him a choice: 55 years behind bars, maximum security, or 5 years' solitary confinement, during which he would have to listen to his late wife's favorite song, what she had called *their* song, played non-stop, until his release.

Antonio foolishly chose the latter.

6 months later, with Whitney Houston's "I Will Always Love You" playing for the 58,400th time, the earworm in Antonio's head erupted from its chrysalis and flew off. He was found dead on the floor, lying in a pool of his blood and brains.

- 378 -

Horror, Haunted

The duly employed lycanthropes
Claws poised
Eyes peeled
Sought out the insidious word
The term
The lure
& as one
Nameless faceless homogenically bound
Ensnared it
Silenced it
Killed it
Ate it
And called it "Good" & "Virtuous" & "Cleansing"
& whereupon their halos
Freshly polished
Were re-affixed upon their brows
They all decided to go find another
& another & then another & another
Until all that was left
Was silence

Crucified

Push me off your pedestal
Hang me out to dry
Leave me hanging
Wanting waning longing
Saint or thief,
I'm crucified

Underworld

Everything seems okay
The sun shines
The moon glows
We work we live we play we laugh
We raise a glass we have a beer
We love our pups we love our kids
Pretending to be what we are
Being what we pretend
Beneath all that
What is the underworld
That lurks
That is
That rules
That lives
Let's not pretend
We are borne of fucking sugarplums

Maniacal

She hurt oh she hurt
She hurt hurt hurt hurt
So, she wrote & she wrote
& she wrote wrote wrote wrote wrote
When she was done
She laughed oh she laughed
Oh, she laughed laughed laughed laughed laughed
No doubt, 'twon't be long
Before it all starts again

So Beautiful

Is it morbid
To think you have never looked so beautiful
Imagine, the wells that once held your eyes
Are far lovelier now, blood filled to their brims
For, where warm merlot once flowed
Through a fretwork of veins
Now lie stilled, twin pools of a thickened elixir, congealed & coagulated

Let me then fill this hollow and feather'd quill
With what is left of you
So that I may write
Sonnets and odes
Songs and poems
To honor you, my love

Less, yes, to who you once were
Than to this *thing* you have now become

Tenebrian Lament

From the depths of my tenebrous mind
Flow unbidden
Less the memories
More the questions
When?
Where?
And why?
I delve deeper
To the catacombs
And come face to face:
Did it hurt?
Does it hurt?
Did you know what was coming?

From there, it's an easier dive
I arrive at the putridarium
And glance furtive 'round its corner:
At what we were
What we weren't
What you did, I did not
& I ask myself:
Will I be able to purge the urge
The thought the guilt the deed?
(Was I able to erase all evidence?)
& will I be able to resist the temptation
To go back just this once (more)
To gaze upon you
(Or what's left of you)
To admire the handiwork
Of one humble Fury
Thoroughly scorned
Or not?

Eau de Mama

Mama's wafting 'cross the gardens again
Ev'ry time rain falls 'cross this ole farm I'm stuck in
But oh, I *feel* don' jis smell it
The dang stinky perfume she always done wore
The stench slithers about like a lil grass snake
O'er the stoop, on the rug
'cross my sparklin' clean a' scrubbed wood floor

I can't get her mean, old self
To stay in her nest
Tho sure 'nuff I buried her deep as I could
With an ole fence post stuck in her still heavin' breast
So down there she'd lay
An' not nag me no more!
The nice weather lady on the radio
Called that dern smell a "petrichor"
Well, I'll tell ya
Eau de Undead
Smell to me downright poor

Beautiful Bed

This worm-eaten box
The splinters, the cracks
The mold-fragranced soil
Between crevices packed
The satin, once ivory, aged now to warm grey
'tis pock marked & blood stained
So beaut'fully frayed
Indeed, perhaps a rather esoteric bedroom suite
Only my fellow undead would find pretty neat

Talisman, Mine

I will wander my days
Among all who like I
Walk 'neath the gaze of the merciless sun
Slumber below the moon & its stars
Resignedly so
Grateful? Perhaps
I "survived" my abductor
Helped "vanquish" the beast
I "escaped" the monster
For what?
A rejoining with all the
Frail, insecure, passive, aggressive, puny & jealous
Beings who stumble & bumble with their mortal best
(As do I)
Through life as the living
Dropping off where He picked up
& positively glowed
With other-worldly power, strength
Eloquence & seductive invitation?

I was heartbroken
Secretly
Deeply
When he writhed his last
I remain his
Secretly
Deeply
My hand gently at rest
Upon my still rising & falling breast
It does not beseech the broken heart beneath
No, it feels for the otherwise unknown talisman
The single canine I stole
From the casket they stored
Of all the extracted teeth
From my beloved's brutal defacement
(No dignity in his violent demise)

Which now, chased in gold
Hangs from a fine chain
'round my neck
'gainst my skin
Where, there it will stay
Until I either reach
The end of my days
Or He comes back for me

Corruptible

Redolent, acidic repose
Blooms pressed against my breast
Sick, sweetly withering
My smile loosens and shifts
Laughter's talisman...
Ah yes, I remember...
My hands relax
Fingers splay wider upon winged clavicles
Which ease out, and spread
My weighted pelvis
Sinks languidly
Into quick-sanded silk
As my legs
Disconnect, and turn themselves
Outward
Less for motility inclined
More for corruption primed
My dress fades, feathers, and wilts
I watch from above, below, whatever,
As the rest of me fails
So, when my mortal cage finally cracks, then splits
I can rise

And, oh yes; I rise...

Cottage Crypt

The beauteous witch
Who lived in the forest
Crafted spells for all others
Though amidst hexing for others
Neglected reserving some for herself
Some enchantment
For her life's hold
Bore no love or good health
Hers would not be
An eternal, sweet youth
The beauteous witch
In a handful of seasons
Was a beauty no more
Leathered of face
As brittle as sticks
Crooked of spine
& mind muddled
She like her cabinets soon rusted full out

But the vining herbs she had planted
And in due course neglected
They thrived & conspired
Lockstep with the flora
To spiral, lithe & embracing
Up all the walls, to the roof
& the chimney encasing
What once had been known her fair & quaint cottage home
Nigh swallowed in brambles & tendrils
In vengeance, now outgrown
The doors & the windows barred, tangled & thick
The old hag's own home, transformed,
Had become her green crypt

To My Beloved, in her Cemeterial Abode

I laid you down just now to sleep
I pray your corpse will nicely keep
But should you rise before I wake
They'll have to pierce you with a stake

The Portraitist's Lament

Oh, pretty 'nuff, she who sit there for me
Dark maiden whose tresses flow nigh to her knees
But, no, twas not her own hair she doth wore
But the tight-fitted scalp
Of the raven-haired one she hath torn
Bad maiden, dark maiden
Who sit here for me
Pale gaze, alas mottled
For torn scalps tend to bleed

Exhibition-ist

I ripped my heart out & put it on my sleeve
I bared my soul
& spilled my guts
I opened myself up
In the names of all the bards & their muses
Bound head to toe
I bore the scraps of
Every word rent from the core
'til drained at the last
I became transparent
Then invisible
For there was nothing left
& still,
They did not hear me

Mam'sette

I saw you I see you
I want you to feel you
I hold of your heart of your body your self
Keep your soul 'midst your clear
Crystalline soft silhouette
I thank you my wondrous, delicious Mam'sette
Your eyes your sweet mouth
The fresh blood that you let
Fill my kiss fill my mouth fill my gut my outlet
You are river are ocean are infinite skies
Your soft, gaping mouth as depleted, you die

Solstice's Eve

A tiding of magpies
Awash 'pon the skies
Build 'neath clouded bank cover
Pandora's box, plied
Whence darkness gives way
To Hope, my dear, pray
That feathered stormage serves as mere harbinger
'gainst long, slumbrous days
For, my dear, 'tis misfortunate true,
The wintered dark hours lurk long, low a-gloom
To wither the summer, ever too soon

Shipwrecked

Though carried on benevolent waves
On that lovely, balmy summer's day
No longer could I hold
My precious babe aloft
For the sharks beneath
With razor'd teeth
Left me bereft of the legs I'd need
To get us back to shore

Genesis 1:6 v.2

and it came to pass
Mother Nature
whilst chatting with Our Father
suggested they redress their issue:
so, working in astral tandem with Each Other
They reached deep into the saltwater maw of their once-beauteous child
past her threadbare firmament
through the mantle
to her core

and with determined Hand and indifferent Fist
grabbed and held and pulled hard forth
on the roiling and broiling terral innards
of what was no more Their masterpiece
but a confused and decomposing, weary beast

They held aloft the remnants
of what had been her heart,
turned her from the outside in
and turned her inside out

what a performance for the ages
this cataclysmic re-inversion!
with sapphire blues and emerald greens
deftly supplanted, she is rent and rendered
newly trussed and noxiously a-drip
in a fresh and fatted, pliant skin

thus erased, Earth is re-molded
reduced to a slow-writhing and molten sovereign's orb
of preternatural life-to-be
a prehistoric soup

the heavens cannot help but cry
and so, it begins
again, again
and They called it Good
Perhaps Better

Hurricaned Beast

From afar from above from 'midst deep beds of clouds
The whirl built its momentum
And gathered stark, strong and loud
Raged its breathing its sucking in phagic revelry
Swallowing currents then fishes then boats 'pon the sea
Whale families were pulled from their trav'lin' pods
Pearl bearing oysters and lobsters and shrimp yanked like clods
From shallows and caverns and ledges and reefs
Down into the maw of the hurricaned beast
Which swallowed a ship
Then licked its wet lips
And growled, "Why thank you! And yes, I'll take another."

Efectus

LYRICS

From, RUGS ON PUDDLES COATS OVER OCEANS

Art

If the darkness pulls at you
And you reach between the lines If the falter in the moment Sends a picture to your mind

And the words, they seem to alter And change into mere lies
Then the truth is lost and far behind By the broken and the unread signs

When questions are the answer Though you turn your eyes away The memory is burned inside And the images are grave

The images are grave

When little more is left
And scattered is the rest
Idiots and imbeciles sleep warm tonight And slowly start to die

And the poets are the paupers And the art is kept alive

Look at you
Look at me
In what we've done just say, "Believe!" Look way beyond
Look deep within
See the fantasy begin

Look at me
Look at you
It's a crooked, painful kind of truth It's bitter fruit
It's blood red juice

The poets drink 'til it's gone
And paupers want this martyrdom While simple people slowly die So long as Art is kept alive
So long as Art is kept alive
So long as Art is kept
Alive

1995

Gun Metal Ghost

Gun metal ghost
Skirting fragments from the past Gravity wants to pull you close You use it just to
throw yourself Onto another path
We're listening, we're listening We're leaning to the edge Where darkness is
complete Infinity the norm
The sun is now a cool pin prick A light without a warmth

Gun metal ghost
Cutting off the frequency
You tease us with your language games You please us with the visions gained
Beyond what children see
It's what we want, secretly
It's what we'll need, eventually
When night becomes the day
And time rewinds its hands
The earth is now irrelevant
A pleasant memory

Take mental note
Of where you've been in this young flight Your wings of wax, no science molds
Don't melt with good intention
Or brittle, break them off
Your robot arms are not enough
Your vision quest requires
As you're wading through the mire Prehistoric soup
The older children turn away
Say good-bye, now go your way

Gun metal ghost
Chasing silver fish and flies
Caught in your nets like Spanish coins Dim rainbows lit by thirteen watts Then a
batt'ry of a watch
Until it's just the energy
As reaching out, two fingers touch

The Father and His work
Infinity the norm
Your sun has long since disappeared And so you seek one more

What kind of love will you want to make Whose empty house will you haunt
tonight The tattered webs of angels' gowns
Frame the windows

And the doors
Looking for a home,
Oh, no
You're happy where you are

Where are you?
2-22/23-92
To the Voyager II. Don't we wish we could follow and see too

The Haunting

I'm prey to quiet moments
When thoughts ring home like mourning bells The sounds of sadness pull me in
Forgetfulness, release me
Everything I see
I see in the context of retrospect
The story of my life plays backwards
White on black
Wicked words from within
Memory, go
Please go away
And pull your shadows in
Let me swim across his river, then

I hear her calling to me
In words so soft they touch me there
The sheets become the shroud she wears The eyes of night still want me Everyone I know
Becomes less of what I wanted once ago Reality warps perspective
Wearing thin
The name she calls, calls me from within Make the night
Please, go away
For the light of day
Makes it easier to find my way

I know I should know better
That years of time will heal the pain No taunting words of false resolve I've got nothing left to gain
And now all I want
I want in the context of retrospect It's become too hard to move beyond In this dream

Deep sea strokes instead of steps Caught in the dive
Down to the blue
Bass strings pluck my heart
Let me sing to this empty room

I'll play to quiet moments

With thoughts awash like ocean waves And castles built on shifting sands
Emptiness inside me
It's possible she'll hear

It's possible my love's still near

I lay my hands upon the table round And cry out
Open up the windows, lay aside Reason tonight

Seasons tonight
Spring summer winter's fall Open up my mind to hear her call

3-9-92

Words

And she handed her a book
With maps and violets laid to rest
Between each torn and blistered little scrap Words and colors bled to one
Pens and tears and then some
She handed her a book
And she said,

"This is what you asked for
When you said that it was over
This is why you cried when it was over This is what you cried for
Though you didn't know it
This is why you cried when it was over."

The heat in its spine
Tingling, burning a symbol
Into the writer's tired, folded hands
Something whispered of hieroglyphs
The woman's voice
The seraphim
The words from somewhere no one dared to ask

"This is what you asked for
When you said that it was over
This is why you cried when it was over This is what you cried for
Though you didn't know it
This is why you cried when it was over.

"This is what Pandora's box
Kept cold for you
And these are the arctic, arid skies
That hold a shooting star death
This is the aurora
That danced before your disbelieving eyes

"This is what you asked for When you said that it was over

This is why you cried when it was over This is what you cried for
Though you didn't know it
This is why you cried when it was over."

12-7-93/2005

MEMORANDUM

TO: Brythwhyte Board of Trustees

FROM: C. Bunting

DATE: 1 November 2022

RE: Granthe Endowment Project Update

CONFIDENTIAL

Esteemed Board:

It is with great urgency and a certain regret, that I must inform you of a decision made by Granthe University academicians, the outside experts retained to assist them, the PR firm of Yang, Schminck & Michelsen, and the executive committee of this board, to immediately halt all research and cancel all pending publications pertaining to the findings in the hidden library at the Closterium Atticus. Likewise, a hard stop has been placed upon all planned publicity to promote the findings.

This includes all disclosures pertaining to the Tomes of the Brythwhyte Elders, the illuminated manuscripts of the Trepanation Brethren, and the collected works of the Stratford Scribe, of which you were apprised over the course of the last two years. Additionally, the study guides for the Scribe's *Denouement Inpuratus* have been unpublished and a disclaimer to call into question its origin and validity is currently being distributed, the goal being to cast doubt as to the Denouement's existence and to dispel the attention it had so quickly garnered after being leaked to the public.

All remaining document storage caskets in the library will be hermetically sealed off; all other folios and bound works not yet opened to study will stay "as is," untouched and in their original locations on the shelves in the chambers of the underground library, having been deemed *en toto* unsuitable for the University's academic oeuvre, and incompatible with the legacy it seeks to build on and maintain. The doors and tunnel passageways to the library have been permanently closed with concrete sheathing, and a security system has been installed to ensure the library and its contents will be left undisturbed going forward.

As you know, there has been a series of unexplained deaths amongst staff, colleagues, and their relatives in this past year. Our condolences remain extended to the illustrious compatriots we have lost, and to their families; namely Brandton, Buttersworth, Michelsen, Schultz, and Granthe. Their contributions will be honored in memorium with a series of scholarships, which have been fully funded and shall become available to student candidates at the beginning of the next academic year.

The facts linking these casualties to the list of names found in book VI of the Tomes cannot be denied; therefore, the difficult decision to halt all work on the contents of the hidden library and to render the library inaccessible was made, mindful of both consequence and actuarially supportable risk, were research to continue. There has been no fatality since activities were halted. All other speculative conjecture remains just that and will be publicly denied by all involved with the library. Negations to that effect will be legally enforced.

We respectfully insist that this memorandum, like all content shared to date, remain level-1 classified property of the Brythwhyte Elders, per adjunct proprietary default ownership, which applies to all items found at the Closterium Atticus and their findings, and therefore confidential, with the promise of legal action should any single item be intentionally or accidentally shared or leaked in any way, shape, or form.

With this final memorandum, I herewith likewise submit my resignation, effective immediately. It has been an honor to work with and for you. Any and all inquiries are to be directed back to the Board of Directors.

Sincerely,

C. Bunting, Esq.

Efectum

Earlier, in some case notably different, versions of the following stories were published at:

The Perigean Turn	*Wild Violence, Bloodrites Horror 2021*
Coronet	*Issue 55 Halloween eZine, Sirens Call 2021*
The Coppe-Snippen	*Creature Feature v.3, The Illustrated People, 2021*
Metamorphosis	*Rock Band, Ghost Orchid Press, 2021*
Joined with the Seas	*Crow's Quill Mag, Eldritch Sea, Quill & Crow Publishing, 2022*

Hurricaned Beast, Talisman Mine, Corruptible, So Beautiful
FRISSON, poetry anthology 2024 Ravensquoth Press

Santa Domnia	*Issue 64 When Hell Freezes Over eZine, Sirens Call 2024*